Other Titles from Post Mortem Press

These Trespasses by Kenneth W Cain
Dellwood by Ginny Gilroy
The Beer Chronicles by Scott Lange
Rabbits in the Garden by Jessica McHugh
Perpetual Night by Georgina Morales

Anthologies of Short Fiction

Uncanny Allegories
Isolation
A Means to an End
Shadowplay
The Road to Hell

Available at postmortem-press.com

THE LORD SAID UNTO SATAN

By Hugh Fox

Post Mortem Press
Cincinnati, OH USA

Copyright © 2011 by Hugh Fox

Cover Image copyright © 2011 by Conde | Dreamstime.com

All rights reserved.

Post Mortem Press is a subsidiary of
 Bee Squared Publishing - Cincinnati, OH

www.postmortem-press.com

No part of this book may be reproduced in any form or by any electronic or mechanical means including information storage and retrieval systems, without permission in writing from the author. The only exception is by a reviewer, who may quote short excerpts in a review.

Printed in the United States of America

ISBN: 978-0615465173

FOREWARD

What I really set out to write here was a detective story; what I eventually produced was an hallucinogenic horror-story that is more like the *Nightmare on Elm Street* films than anything like Sherlock Holmes. The book, in a larger context, became a meditation on the presence of Evil in the world. Still, Conan Doyle was my model. Where the departure from my model begins to take place is in the mind of the detective -- through whom the whole action is seen.

Detective Gugel has spent years in the South American jungle and actually is an initiated shaman. He is especially devoted to peyote and peyote, along with his shamanistic-yogic training, has given him certain "powers." He sees the everyday world as merely the foyer that leads into a gigantic spiritual arena where "real" reality exists.

A woman has been napalmed to death in her driveway in Grimore Park, a wealthy suburb north of Chicago and Gugel is called in on the case.

But the plot isn't anything, in the same way that the "plot" as such isn't anything in the *Nightmare on Elm Street* films. The whole excitement of the story is in Detective Gugel's "visions." Like he's on the elevator in the Kellogg Center at Michigan State and the murdered woman appears to him. The hallucinations continue. These hallucinations represent (to throw a little of my old friend Bill Blatty's *Exorcist* in here) the incarnation of Evil in the world.

For me, ***The Lord Said Unto Satan*** is "reality" framed in "hallucination."

Hugh Fox, East Lansing, MI
March 2011

CHAPTER 1

Myrtle pulled into the driveway feeling that she was driving into some sort of measureless, pleasure-less, underwater black cave. Pleasure dome of Kublai Khan; cavern on the edge of the bottomless trench at the bottom of the sea, the giant seaweed-clumped- together, oaks towering above her in the darkness. Oversized cul-de-sac, black silk shadow-bag sacks; the kind of sacks that cat-catchers stick cats in...feeling very cattish...and afraid...all the houses around them so new and the trees as ancient as Cain...it didn't make any sense.

And the streetlights on their street were so teeny and far and few between that they hardly made a dent in the all-engulfing night that cupped its hands around them, getting ready to blow them out.

No one around, 3AM and all their suburban buttschmuck neighbors were out on their asses by ten, their perfect little cosmo-control boxes in their effete little white paws.

Still chizzy-freezy earliest spring, but when she stepped out of the car into the condensing shadows, she still almost expected the sound of leaves instead of just wind and emptiness.

"Come on, move ass!" she snarled at Mabel, who had fallen asleep on the way home.

Startling her awake.

"OK. OK!"

Slowly getting out of the car like an old lady.

Myrtle's sense of foreboding still ballooning up, feeling as if the whole sky was going to crash in on her. Slimy sea-weedy hands around her throat, quartz fists descending on her skull, bleating out at the night a horrified "Who's there?"

"Me!" Mabel, a petulantly fragile old teapot.

Myrtle stopping, wide-eyed and overawed.

"It's as if there were..."

"What...?"

THE LORD SAID UNTO SATAN

Mable facing the massive oak tree trunks all around her, the next house fifty yards away, asleep in its soundless dead brick yuppy complacency.

"Let's get into the house..." Myrtle's terror dripping all over Mabel, soaking into her soul.

"I told you I wanted to build a brick garage connected to the house -- with an automatic door opener!" Myrtle shrill. The other tech-god there for a moment in the midst of all her primal terror.

The wind shrill. A cold front moving in. More like mid-January than mid-March. No snow. Nothing white or light just the light-sucking textures of the leaf-littered driveway, the dead ground, the dead tree-trunks, sky...dead, dead, dead...morto, muerto, mort, mortality...a landscape designed to suck up light...life...

Moving toward the front of the house, when They made their first move. Shapes. She could see them now. Fine-tuning black against black, so fine she wasn't really sure they were there at all, what with her fuzzy eyes and mind from all the shit she'd shot, drunk, sniffed, always feeling that she was the Power and (invincible) Glory. The Word made flesh still more Word, wavelength, spirit than flesh, until she had to confront the hard-edged, cutting Out There.

Then the first "something" was thrown, breaking against her leg.

Fucking kerosene, or...

"Who the fuck are..."

Emerging through the skeleton bushes now, wrapped in, what was it, black velvet robes and masks, their faces blacked out.

And how many were there?

Some sort of fire-dart fired into her leg, flames flashing up in slicing pain. And then they all came raining down. The crockery. Bulbs. What the fuck was the stuff in? And then the spray, ejaculating all over her, sticking to her skin, not kerosene, but...

"You can't kill me!" she screamed as the fire whooshed up across her. Fire snakes twisting across her neck and legs, "I am immortal. I don't need this body!"

Rushing toward one of the shapes, wondering what decaying dimension they were from...the forces of Darkness against the forces of Darkness, what sense did that make? What splinter rebellion now?

But the shape sidestepped, and Myrtle ran headlong into the side of the house, the rough, old bricks grating the flesh off her left cheek, breaking her nose, the pain-switch suddenly turning on now, every inch of her screaming...catching a glimpse of Mabel scurrying inside the front door with the boy.

What hadn't he witnessed, the little shit!

Then blind as the flames bubbles across her eyes, gagging, like someone stuffing a rolled-up newspaper down her throat, feeling herself go down.

"But this can't be!" her mind spoke, and then the echo came bouncing back, augmented a thousand fold, BUT IT IS, IT IS, IT IS...

Crumbling from inside out, sizzling, melting, smelling herself burn, like a good Mexican churrasco, tempted to chomp off a piece of her own arm. What was she, more pork than beef, more llama than dog? The fire eating up into her nose, searing into her ears, her hair all gone, a horrible image flowering in her mind for a moment as she saw herself as she really looked, all her body-building, diets, aerobics, Nordic Track turned into bald, char-broiled churrasco, the fate that man was born for, the reason flesh is torn for...

Gibberish, babble, her brilliant, eternal, gifted, trained mind nothing more than a babbling ping pong cavern of pure gibberish now, little skittering voices skating across the surface of the pain as she felt herself fall the first, then the second, then the third time, Christ, Christ, Christ, whispering to herself against the gagging and strangling, "I always hated flesh anyhow, this planet, system. I am my own resurrection and my own life, beyond this... I shall return" Counting down: three, two, one ... zero. Down on her back, her charred, pterodactyl claw hands reaching up, giving the finger to the sky in one last mindless, wordless, gesture of defiance. And the rest was silence as Mabel looked out at the driveway through the window and began to scream, scream, scream.

THE LORD SAID UNTO SATAN

CHAPTER 2

Detective Gugel, eyes, closed, meditating on the four thousandth toe of the million and second foot of God, contemplating its mother-of-pearl toenail and its quartz skin. The fingers of his mind softly touching across its exquisitely polished surface, somewhere on the edge of creation, the cosmological-meditative system of the Zakut Indians in the Colombian jungle, where Gugel had spent five years becoming a Class A (Anal Eye) Shaman. Feeling his soul ooze out into the God-Reality like toothpaste out of a tube. Oozing with evacuated-out-of-himself splicing-with-the-godhead joy, when Pain-in-the-Ass Ackerman pulled to the curb very carefully and still managed to scuff the tires. Gugel suddenly back in his body, in the here and now, like a reverse play of a genie emerging from the bottle act.

"Damned high curbs, you'd think I'd be used to them by now! I'm such an idiot!" bitched Chief Ackermann.

Larry was supposed to counter him with "Don't be too hard on yourself, Chief," but didn't say a word, very unhappy at being back in Grimore Park, on Earth (much less an uppity-yuppity northern Chicago suburb) at all.

A very ordinary, ordinary red brick house. A little touch of a peaked cottage look in front, but it wasn't where Snow White lived, that was for sure. Even Grimore Park had its iffy rental areas.

Monaghan, at the curb waiting for them in a dark blue suit, a face like a bowl of soggy cornflakes. You'd think it was 3PM Monday afternoon instead of 3AM Sunday morning. A makeshift Monaghan production floodlight in the driveway...

"Hi ya, baldy!" Larry needled him, "You got the pictures?"

"Listen, Lar!!"

Oughta be pissed, but as much as he tried, he couldn't get mad at The Gugel. Nobody could.

Ackermann hopped out of the car like a cricket, but Larry could have used a winch and pulley. What was he doing here anyhow, when he oughta be home cushy and cozy in bed asleep...not for money, not for fame

What a mess -- an inordinately tall female corpse stretched out uncovered on the ground, some shreds and fragments of clothing left around the groin and waist where the fat had broiled, expanded, and protected the fibers. Looked like the remnants of jogging shorts and shirt, the jogging shoes surface-burned but pretty much intact, the whole body itself charred, like a piece of burnt steak. Full breasts. Epidermis gone, the upper layers of flat cells sizzled and popped, like the ballpark franks that 'grew' after they'd been cooked.

Hard to say about the hair. All gone.

Larry remembering a dig back in England, uncovering a mass Peat-Bog People burial. Thousands of years of peat-"tanning", almost perfectly preserved. First image. And then roast rabbit or cat or rat, or one of those string-tied rump-roasts like his Mom used to cook when he was a kid. Powerful-looking woman. Must have been quite an athlete. Powerful runner's legs.

"She must have been doused with gasoline and set on fire," Monaghan went on unfettered.

No trace of gas-smell, just the acrid, retching stench of charred fat.

"Or maybe lighter fluid, barbecue starter, you know that..."

"Clam up, will ya, for Zakut's sake!!" snapped Larry.

"Zakut? Come on, Larry!" Monaghan always feeling culturally deprived next to Larry's hands-on mysticism/shamanism. Larry was independently wealthy (since his marriage). He and his wife, even after they'd started having kids, spending decades in the South American jungles. Which, Larry was convinced, was, as he put it, "the last place on earth where authentic Paleolithic spirituality has survived."

Larry raising his hands, closing his eyes. Shushing Monaghan as Ackerman looked skeptically (Ivy League'ishly) on.

This was sacred ground now too. A life had been taken. The ancient rite of murder. Civilization hung in the balance. All of history groaned. The curse of Crazny (the Zagut Indian anti-god, the Lord of Darkness and Chaos) was on them all until it was solved.

THE LORD SAID UNTO SATAN

"Well...so I was here, now I'm gonna leave it with you lovebirds," said Ackermann, "Happy honeymooning."

"The fun's just beginning," said Larry contemptuously.

This was the kind of thing that just didn't happen in the walled-off Grimore Park Eden. All kinds of Powers (money) out there that would want scalps if this sacrilege wasn't solved and revenged pronto. All these miles and miles of already historic pseudo-chalets and Bavarian castles, actual English cottage thatched roofs and tons of Mayan Prairie School wood-glass monastic monstrosities. All the money involved, all the fear that the Out There (Chicago) was finally invaded even Paradise Garden.

"Whatever I take, I've earned," Ackermann defensively hard-edged (his specialty), then (PR) softening, "And come in when you want tomorrow, don't play supermen, you two." And he was gone.

"I don't know, why irritate the poor...," Monaghan forever bitching Larry out for his edge toward Monaghan.

"Yeah, real poor," said Larry, never quite able to forgive Ackermann the fact that he had been born with a silver spoon in his mouth, didn't have to marry to get one, like himself, both of them cops solely for fun/mental health, not salary. Sure that Ackermann. like himself, donated most of his salary to worthy causes like the new Chicago Museum of Modern Art, the Art Institute, the Chicago Civic Opera, Loyola, de Paul, the University of Chicago, American Cancer Foundation, the usual " he's a fucking Nazi!"

A little too consciously ostentatious with his six hundred dollar Czech suede coat and clipped haircut and little moustache, careful little gold cigarette holder, careful little gold-rimmed glasses. And his father's father had begun life as a chicken-butcher on Maxwell Street, slowly evolving into Ackermann's Chicken Bits, Chicken Fingers....eyeballs, assholes...

Class-war anger peppering across Larry soul now like a soft, noxious rain, as he began to try to re-center. Phase One.

Ommmmm. Calmmm, Save me, oh Zakut, It-He-She of a million faces, facets, glories, powers, God-Goddess of light-years and crocodiles, the calender round and the black holes in the asses of the universe that is also your flesh and breath.

Dipping into the baggy, cluttered right side pocket of his shaggy brown tweed jacket and pulling out a little brass vial, popping a pill into his mouth; a little contemplative chemical help from a blend of datura, ayahuasca, teonanacatl, peyote (Larry's own recipe) never hurt...
"Kearney been here yet?" asked Larry.
"We just got the call an hour ago, you know how he is."
The coroner. How could anyone fifty have such terrible acne?
"And witnesses?"
"Lar, I don't really know, there's..."
"If you don't know, why expand it into variations?"
Walked back out of the floodlit area, reached into his pocket for his flashlight, which he always carried with him except..."Got a flashlight?"
"In the car." And Monaghan went and brought it back, handed it to him almost reverentially.
Had Monaghan faked out. All of um faked out, the Nagual-Shaman of their Nightmares...
The hard-earned aura always there, after his years with the Zackuts, sampling the rest of the Paleo-/Neolithic buffet with the Huichols in Chihuahua, the Cashinahua in Eastern Peru, the Kogi in Colombia, the years in Tibet, Anatolia, reaching into the ruins at Çatal Hüyük and Haçilar, getting inside the Dimini and Prodromo cultures, trying to get the too-long dead to talk-- and they sometimes did...in faint trace-whispers...*moloch, melech, great sea goddess-god...don't let us vanish,drown, silt down to the bottom of timeless- , spacelessness.* At least always with cosmic background hum of THE BIG MONEY around, even if it wasn't really "his," but poor, broken Maxine's."They," his soul-mates, could feel it in him when he appeared and they looked into his bright, prescient Jaguar Shaman x-ray eyes.
"Turn off the floodlight," he told Monaghan.
And then once they were off, Larry moved back to the back of the driveway slicing it all up with his flashlight beam.

THE LORD SAID UNTO SATAN

They hadn't raked their leaves the Fall before and the driveway was a mess of leaves devolving into slick black slime.

Larry went back to the garage, checked the driveway with surgical concentration, on and off the concrete, then out into the street, along the curbs, the front lawn, back and forth, forth and back, waiting for his Nagual Nature to switch on, checking and rechecking, everything registering and getting catalogued, tagged and evaluated...and it was already beginning to grow and snuffle and nudge against him, on the edge of revelation and epiphany. Monaghan just an overcooked slice of eggplant. Pure, passive spectator.

"Waddaya got on the murdered woman?" asked Larry.

"I've got a name -- Myrtle Bannister..."

"Myrtle?!?!" Joke name. Until you sucked on it, massaged it, and its sacred significance began to come back -- sacred to Venus. Venereal.

"Anybody else in the house?"

"There's another woman, three kids and some oriental..."

"Yeah."

Larry contemptuous. Monaghan made everything sound like a grocery list. Went up and rang the front doorbell.

No answer. All the lights on like a goddamned showboat, though.

Rang and rang again, was just about to either heave through the door or forget it until morning, when the door opened and a tall, heavy, edematous woman in her mid-forties appeared. Sickish, flatulent, worn-out, drained, mushroomy, overcooked, hen-flesh. Touch it and it disintegrates in your hand.

She stood there like a blind newt. Cavefish.

"Gugel, Grimore Park PD, I'd like to ask you some questions..."

Nothing. Flat-waves. Zero.

"Can you understand what I'm saying? Der Mond ist blau/The moon is blue...."

Nothing.

"All I wanna do is help. Formigas-barigas/ants-bellies..."

Nothing.

Began to zoom in inside of her, dive through clouds of collapsing smoke. Nothing. Blank. No fizz. No fuzz. The morning after Apocalypse.

"You oughta really read her her rights, Lar" Monaghan whined. Her brain an empty ballpark on Christmas Eve.

"Let's go!"

"But Larry..."

Larry didn't answer.

DON'T TALK TO FOOLS. (Talmud.)

JUST LEAVE, his voices screaming inside him. Kali dances, Ganesa snorts! BE MERCIFUL. Tyreinian, Balbeckian, Ollantay-Tamboan, Sacsahuamanian ruined walls. Andresite. Granite. You couldn't even put a hair between the blocks.

6.

"Can't you understand grief?" asked Larry. "I'm Radon Klaus," answered Larry with Agammemnon-like solemnity, "I come in through the cracks in the basement wall. I'm breeze, light, THOUGHT. Come on, let's go!"

"Ackermann's gonna have our asses," Monaghan insisted, insisted, insisted.

"Ikh zol handlen mit likht, volt di zun nit untergegang'n/If I sold candles, the sun would never set.

Turning to leave, pulling the door shut, when there was a noise down at the end of the hallway, and Larry, with forbearance, watched Monaghan jerk instinctively, hand toward his gun. Smiled. As a dog came running down the hall, the ugliest little warthog dog that Larry had ever seen, big hyperthyroid bulging eyes, hairless, kind of white and pink and piglet-ish, barking, barking, barking at him and Monaghan, followed by a porcelain-skinned boy who looked like...Larry's first thought was The Infant of Prague, The Messiah/Moshe/Moses finally come back, carrying the weary world in his redemptive hands...

"Mommy, Mommy, I had this horrible dream that Myrtle was dead and turned into a zombie and....."

The kid's room was on the driveway side. For a horrible, sinking moment Larry thought that...at the same time noticing a faint, distant, animalish, zoo-like stench that he filed for later reference...

"I'll be right back," he told Monaghan and rushed outside, almost expecting Myrtle to be somehow (the Essenes on the first Easter) GONE,

THE LORD SAID UNTO SATAN

spirited, snatched away, anguished at the possible snatching away of all the little incriminating mouths in her very own.

Expecting her to be gone...

But she wasn't.

Monaghan following him back down, stepping out from behind a bush.

"Larry, you're spooking me out...Lar..."

"It's/they're still here," Larry wide-eyed, tensed, whispering, as he looked around at the surrounding envelope of night, little inexplicable dead-spaces in Amazonas/the Madre de Dios, "presences..."

Time sunk into the deepest well of night, beyond redemption or remedy. And then, as he was standing there, he looked up and saw the sky begin to lighten up almost perceptibly, from black to the darkest navy blue, the first notching up toward dawn.

His heart lifting up as he lifted up his arms toward the East, and sang.

"HA! TIRA SAKA RIKI!"

"That's beautiful, Larry, what is it, Latin?"

"Pawnee," said Larry, "the Pawnee Hako Ceremony: 'Behold sun, Now!' The daily rebirth of the sun-god."

"That's amazing!" said Monaghan, all moist-eyed, not a bad Jake, really, him and his mashed potato ("Hold the gravy!") face, Larry smiling, going back up to the front door, back inside, the dog still barking, the little boy gone.

"Where's the kid?" he asked Ms. Catatonia."How about a little help, huh?"

Looking at him, erased, faded jeans, spilled salt, a little mound of dog pooh, an abandoned farmhouse in the middle of Kansas in the middle of May, stiff, dead curtains and mazes of faded wallpaper halls. Then the radiant, glowing, luminous, ten foot tall messianic boy coming back into his mind again, Orpheus returned, bringing the New Year with him, the gods returned in human form. Larry gave Monaghan the LET'S VAMOOSE sign as Monny started back up the stairs.

"We're wasting our time here..."

And out they went, Monaghan starting to say goodbye to the Lady of the House, still standing there, Bone China, quartz, pillar of salt, staring out at them Larry, pulling him by the arm, "Come on, willya," at the same time feeling deep twists and turns of compassion for her, her sister/lover/friend, whatever-she-was, roasted in her driveway...and she probably...

Larry went into the garage. An old orange Suburu. Felt the hood. Nothing. Opened the hood up. Engine block still a tad warm. Then closed it and walked outside again and faced East. Tirawa, Tawa, Intiwanna...after the sub-arctic Spring night, the dawn coming in now like a rush of pink-purple pigeon-cloud archangels.

"I will go unto the altar of God, to God who giveth joy to my youth," he murmured under his breath.

"What's that now?" asked Monaghan.

"Something they took out of the Mass, the idiots," answered Larry, walking out to the curb again to Monaghan's cold, dead asparagus- green Cavalier.

"What are you looking for?" asked Monaghan.

"A decent question," sneered Larry, "You got a pencil and a piece of paper?"

Monaghan handed him a purple Flair and a spiral (on the top) mini-pad. Coisas das Tias, thought Larry, "Maiden Aunt crap." O jeito d'eli/Monaghan's style.

There was a FOR RENT sign on the front lawn. Shore Reality. G. Spryszoki, 7242 N. Sheridan Rd., Rogers Park, 372-6942...

"My car's over at the station, don't ask me why," said Larry, "come on!"

"Come on yourself, Lar," Monaghan, getting all prissily piqued, like someone has disrupted one of his favorite doilies on a key coffee table in the middle of his perfect parlor, "I mean..w..w..what the fuck did we find out?"

"Plenty my poorly feathered friend," a wry, indulgent grin spreading across Larry's Moby Dick of a face, "we found out there isn't one but a crowd of murderers, and the chief-murderer, the gang-leader, so to speak,

is a Caucasian male outdoorsman type, maybe a duck hunter...and the relationship between the two women, I'd guess that..."
 Larry stopped, interiorizing, listening to his angels....
 "Guess what?" Monaghan all frazzled with impatience, "You're a fucking mind-swamp, Lar...we've got directives and procedures, pal..."
 Larry raising his hand.
 Ex-cathedra.
 "Just a sec..."
 Something "humming" in the driveway, chanting at him, pulling him back, half-melted, decayed voices, the ruins at Cluny suddenly trying to reconstruct/reconstitute themselves, wait, wait ,linger a little longer, it's all here waiting for you...
 There was enough ripe persimmon light now for him to see everything. Only what he needed to see wasn't seeable, the whole driveway now awash with chips of ancient stone voices, HERE, HERE, HERE, HERE...racing down and exploring for a moment inside a small mound of leaves, and then, yes, he touched it, pulled it out and looked at it --a small, woven grass bracelet.
 Monaghan, suddenly tumbling through the leaves like a fat collie.
 "So wadidya find, pal?"
 "An African marriage bracelet...maybe a hundred years old...Kenyan, probably. Brides give (gave!) them to grooms.....now everyone uses regular wedding rings...why, oh why, did the Spaniards have to destroy all the statues of Viracocha in the Andes?"
 "Vira...?"
 Larry sidestepping Monaghan's encyclopedic ignorance.
 "The question is who's the bride and who's the GROOM? And who's throwing what at WHOM? And why?"
 Monaghan standing there looking like he'd just stumbled on the Empty Tomb on the First Easter.
 "OK, so it's time for beddie-bye for you, pal. First take me back to my car. I couldn't stop now if my life depended on it...and maybe in some kabalistic-shamanistic way it DOES...," taking Monaghan by the arm and steering him back toward his car again, "I'll be back this afternoon to make some latex moulds..."

CHAPTER 3

Spryszok's, of course, was closed when Larry got there. But peering inside the windows, both hands cupped around his eyes like he was peering down into the bottom of the sea, he saw a light under the door in back, went around the side through a broken-bottled empty lot with the new weeds of Spring just beginning to poke their pale thin green fingers through the rebirthing ground, around to a back door with an ugly old iron outer gate protecting it (locked from the inside), and knocked, hard, loud, insistently. Of course there wasn't a bell -- you weren't supposed to know anyone lived in the back.

"Who is it?" a heavily-accented voice muffled through the door.

"Gang Busters," answered Larry, his own accent the incarnation of Old Chicago.

There was a doughnut place on the other side of the empty lot and the soft, sweet odors of frying doughnuts drifted over and bathed Larry like warm rain. He would have given his immortal soul for half a dozen chocolate cream-filled doughnuts right now.

"I haf no vay of knowing dot is true! a muffled voice corkscrewed through the door.

"Come on, Myrtle Bannister's just been murdered. I need some information..."

The inside door opened and the old man didn't even look up as he unlocked the barred gate. Waved him in and THEN looked up.

He was maybe 75, 80, bald, bright blue eyes, wearing a green plastic eyeshade the likes of which Larry hadn't seen for decades.

It was a comfy little place, an old armchair, an old frame bed, an old stove next to a dirty old sink.

The TV was on CNN. A reporter's fat, florid, exuberant face in front of a tumbled-down landscape of half-demolished buildings. Spryszok pushed it off before Larry could catch the theme.

"It's never going to be solved over there...the Amorites and the Philistines, Ottoman Turks, Jesus...I love everybody...how about solving Chicago, New York, Kansas City, Memphis, how many homeless here? How many millions," then taking a closer look at Larry, smiling a big

THE LORD SAID UNTO SATAN

tuna-fish smile, "You ARE an obese sonofabitch gangbuster, aren't you?!? You wanna cup of coffee already?"

"If you let me go and buy you some doughnuts," answered Larry and suddenly there were tears in the old man's eyes. The Doughnut Messiah had finally come to his gutted-out, pogromed old stetel.

"Vhy not?" he said.

"What kind do you like?"

"Vat don't I like?"

And Larry walked through the empty lot, the kind of empty lot he had spent half his life on the Chicago South Side playing in when he was a kid. Come back in fourth months and it would be Amazonas. But would Amazonas be Amazonas?

Anastasius' Greek Pastries...ahhh...even heavier...

"Gimme a dozen of mixed," he said and started to salivate as he watched the doughnut hole round Korean behind the counter pop them into a big crisp waxed bag. Paid, came back, the old man had already relocked the gate, had to open it again.

"A little hyper-cautious aren't we?"

"Dere's so many animals out there. It's like when I went to Florida once before my wife died. We were going to retire down there. Went into the water. There was a ripple in the surface maybe fifty yards avay from me. Not even a 'ripple,' a 'wrinkle' already, and I had this vision of WHAT WAS OUT THERE IN THE FUCKING VATER. It was an aquatic jungle. That vas it for me, out of the water and I never vent back in. Who needs random violence. God made the vorld and then took a vacation. That's the Chicago streets today," said the old man, big, big coffee cups on an old table over in the corner covered with a slightly crumpled red and white checked tablecloth.

"Very comfy here," said Larry, gingerly sitting down on what looked like an antique maple chair, all splayed out in back like a peacock's tail in full display.

"It's good enough for me. I couldn't stay in the same house after my wife died. My life is full of ghosts as it is..."

"And mine isn't?" countered Larry.

"Cream and sugar. I suppose you take lots of cream and sugar," said Spryszok, his sad, foreign face full of sad, foreign ghosts. What (vat) was Larry picking up, Prague spires and tales of the Wienervald Vienna Woods in earliest Spring, like now... screams (resistance) in Baroque Warsaw....Jude name-tags, blue tattoos...Aber warum Ich?/Why me?

"How could you guess?" said Larry, sitting down, and Spryszok produced a half pint carton of Half-and-Half out of the fridge, a blue flower-print sugar bowl out of the cupboard over the sink.

"So who's the other woman who lived in the house with Myrtle?" asked Larry, feverishly fishing into the bag, trying to look laid-back and casual, making sure he got THE chocolate cream doughnut. The rest he could have cared less about.

"Mabel Fudge," he answered, getting up and getting a plate that matched the sugar-bowl, carefully piling all the doughnuts up in a stolidly square, tapering off Maya style pyramid.

"Mabel FUDGE?!?" Larry laughed, eating his doughnut slowly, savoring the chocolate cream, wondering what made these doughnuts Greek. They tasted pretty fucking "naturalized" to him...

"They were both deadbeats, owe me three months rent. I was going to evict them. Which I hate, of course, but...Myrtle was from..."

Larry put his hand up. First in Sunday school, first in Life. Trinity, triplets, three...

"Let me guess...KENYA!"

"Right! I guess you checked the records."

"Just a guess," said Larry, a silent prayer of thanks to Tati Wari Fire-Grandfather Sun, thinking so Myrtle was the Bride who gave the wedding bracelet to a mystery Bridegroom, and so Mabel got jealous and...,"What kind of a relationships did the women have?"

"Vat should I know about such things?" asked Spryszok.

"I think you see right into the hearts of matters," sneered Larry.

"Like you, you sum of a bitch. Not that I want to," answered Sporyszok, "it's an unvanted gift, more of a curse. Fudge is from Michigan. East Lansing. Recently divorced," the old man letting it all run through his head like an old movie, "something about child-abuse...Fudge obsessed by about it, Bannister always shushing her up, like I vasn't supposed to hear anything, it vas a big secret. Fudge's husband works at Michigan State...."

"And Fudge herself?"

"They both vork/vorked at Babbit Labs in Skokie. I had a brother-in-law who worked there too. Died of cancer, which I think was vork-related. When I was a kid growing up in Prague you never heard of cancer the way you do now..."

"This is just the beginning, pal," said Larry, looking through a peeled-off spot on the painted-white windows, big drums of 'something' out in the lot, a rusting-out car surrounded by sprouting grass and flowers, Larry amazed at the persistence of genetic forms, like going through Gary on a train and all along the tracks the same old weeds and wild flowers, "What did they do at Babbitt?"

"Research something. I'm a simple man. Anal retentive at dat," Spryszok shrugging his shoulders.

And how delicately he ate his blueberry doughnut! Meissen at the court of Franz Joseph.

"Well...," Larry got up, like a whale breaching. Spryszok suddenly disturbed, remembering old Pham, the Golden Triangle, 1968, the whole family dead, every time anyone would leave he'd start to cry.

"And the rest of these doughnuts?"

"You'll eat um," said Larry, "anything else you can tell me?"

Spryszok righted himself psychologically, the Danube flowing, flowing, flowing through him, back on even keel.

"I shouldn't presume to say vat I'm going to say," he started to say, accompanying Larry to the door, unlocking the barred gate yet again, Larry hadn't even noticed him re-locking it, Spryszok lowering his voice, looking around at the sad empty room, "if I were you, I'd start in Michigan..."

"Why?" asked Larry. If Spryszok was depressed by his leaving, Larry was just as depressed leaving the old man alone again, Spryszok calling up inside him long, lost splinter-memories of his dead father, slices of images of his own father in the midst of a massive coronary, falling down on the bathroom floor, head against the corner of the marble washbowl, dying, screaming at Larry's Mom, "Get the boy out of here, don't let him see this. It'll be a nightmare for him forever..."

And it had been.

Nightmare. Daymare.

"I don't know," said Spryszok, his eyes half-closed like he was trying to peer into a crystal ball in the middle of his stomach, "When they talked about the man in Michigan; that was real anger, even when they tried to tone it down. They didn't want I should know a ting. You know what I mean. Involuntary revelations. I talked to them a couple of times ven I went to collect late rents. Everything was Michigan, Chicago meant nothing real to them. Horrible things had happened in Michigan. Just an old man's hunch. I'd start in Michigan."

He stood there, his shoulders in a fixed shrug, his face screwed up into a mask of elfin quizzicalness -- vat do I know? The best I can do in the middle of Mystery, is listen to my Voices.....

"OK," said Larry, just about out the door when he popped (as well as he could for his size) back into the room, grabbed the other chocolate-creme doughnut that he just had spotted. So it was a zoo with two Pandas!Wunderbar!

"If you don't mind...?"

"It's been such a pleasure. If you ever need a house...anything..." Standing there almost in tears. It was a long time since Larry had since anyone so alone...shamelessly transparent.

And Larry was gone, back through the empty lot, remembering when he was five, six and he'd fallen down on broken milk bottles in an empty lot like this, cut his knee, tendon, down to the bone. It still hurt him on cloudy days.

The empty lot full of hisses and snarls for a moment as Larry reached the sidewalk and got into his battered old Volvo, chomped down on the doughnut and pulled away from the curb.

THE LORD SAID UNTO SATAN

CHAPTER 4

Back home. 9:48 on the car clock. Mrs. Barker not there yet. Was she coming just a little bit later every day? Maybe not. Stop counting, Let it all flow into the immense NOW.

Up the almost pink, thickly carpeted stairs. Maxine's frou-frou taste -- while she still had any taste at all.

All his goddamned dreams. Even after she'd had her first brain cancer surgery, he'd still imagined driving all over the country with her, South in the winter, North in the summer, junkets to Spain, the Midi, him and his fragile, failing Ophelia bride and all their millions, her millions, her father's millions -- the big surprise bonus after her father's (The Count's) death.

The only reason Larry detectived at all was mental health. And, he'd reasoned, it would have been just as mentally healthy to travel the world with his dying Beauty -- if the beauty hadn't disappeared too, along with everything else. But then came the strokes and the stuttering and slurring and drooling and twitching and incontinence. And then, after the second stroke, everything shut down, so that she was just a pair of eyes in a head that didn't know who it was.

He opened the bedroom door and Thunder bounded off the bed, came over and started licking his hand. Larry really wanting to kick him in the balls, wanted him dead too, this universal wehrmacht loathing for everyone and everything...

"Asshole!"

But then he nudged him away gently and knelt down and took him in his arms and hugged him as hard as he could. He didn't seem to mind.

"You poor son-of-a-bitch; it's not your fault."

Then upstairs, into Maxine's room, Maxine tiny, white, shriveled and inert, like a leaf of withered cabbage, her eyes open but FIXED. The world could come tumbling down around her and she'd never know -- or give a damn. Although you had to leave the lights on in her room twenty-four hours a day. Turn them off and, well, she couldn't exactly scream but it came close. Like a scream under water, inside a vat of lemon Jell-O.

"I've gotta go out for a while," he told her softly, tears in his eyes as he dropped his robe on the floor and started putting on the first things that came to hand, ending up in an old white cotton suit that made him look like an ante-bellum Mississippi riverboat gambler. Not that he gave a shit about how he looked, no matter what he had on still always hating his body, his fat...zu sein oder nicht zu sein/to be or not to be...existence itself.

Yeah, blame his daughter Sarah for being a fat pig -- he'd willed her his genes, hadn't he? Just like he'd willed Lissie her madness. His own mother had spent her last 30 years inside the Illinois State Mental Hospital in Dixon!!! And one of the psychiatrists had put it on the line to him just before she'd died: "It's passed through the male to the females."

Looked at his massive ursine bulk in the three-paneled mirror on the closet door and felt like kicking the glass in...

"Shit!"

Over to Maxine.

"Mrs. Barker'll be here any time. I've gotta go on a little business trip..."

Totally expressionless. No, come on, that wasn't true. There was plenty of expression, wild, raw, primitive, cornered frozen TERROR! Something out of the caves or before the caves, when the human beast just roamed and shuddered, squatted, whimpered and ate his neighbor's brains...

"Poor pet."

He bent down and kissed her mottled, raw, wrinkled cheeks, then around her desperate eyes, as if his lips could chase the desperation away.

Thunder nuzzled against his legs, and gave Larry a couple of affectionate nips and Larry reached down and petted him.

"Take it easy. You've been out already, you'll last until Mrs. Barker gets here."

He checked the bed. Everything dry.

"You want to do potty?"

THE LORD SAID UNTO SATAN

The eyes seemed to say no, but he couldn't be sure. The eyes didn't know what the bowels and bladder wanted. No brain left to connect anything TO. At least he liked to think there wasn't. What if...if...the whole time she was lucidly thinking, thinking, thinking, Einstein, Zweistein in a fly's body inside a hot, dry, sealed room...

"Why don't we just get up and go potty, save the trouble of having to clean up later?"

No, said the eyes savagely, leave me alone.

He went into the bathroom and got the white enamel bedpan and slid it under her. And the bladder took over. This heavy, thick flow of urine that smelled like kidney beans and corn bread.

"See," he said with genuine gentleness, "another few minutes and that would have been all over the bed."

He emptied out the bedpan, rinsed it and put it back on the hamper next to the bathtub, walked back into the room, bent down and kissed her on the lips, little spit-bubbles around the corners of her mouth and all. **My love, my dove, my beautiful one**...remembering the old Zakut saying Nuta(The Great Goddess)nem-glog (may be ugly), zabalinski (but) Nuta Nuta (The Great Godess is the Great Goddess).

"So I'll see you in a couple days, pal..."

Doesn't wanna go,

Doesn't wanna stay,

Can't manage to cut it either which way...

Threw a couple shirts, a razor, Peartree and Marianne Sandlewood Shaving Cream and Lime Cologne into a little black Brazilian leather bag..as the front door downstairs, was opened oh, so quietly and carefully.

"I love you," he said. One last kiss. Millions and the most palatial mansion on the North Shore, a flying wing of a house poised as if for flight out across the lake; and all the king's horses and al the king's men couldn't put Maxine back together again.

"I'm up here," Larry called out to Mrs. Barker.

One last after-the-last-kiss kiss and for one brief moment she was even beautiful, perfect, whole. One last whispered "I love you..., kranki dash" in Zakut, which just didn't cut it when it came to love-language, nuzzling into her neck and hair. And then he was off, rumbling down the stairs.

"I'm going to have to go up to Michigan for a few days," he told Mrs. Barker, giving her a little hug, "it's a big murder case. It'll probably be all over the papers tomorrow morning."

'I can just stay on fulltime," she said, kids still in Jamaica with her mother, being raised far away from what she considered Yankee Dog Corruption, the money the only thing that wasn't corrupted, a "boyfriend" she was moving toward marriage with. But that was a loose, cool, easily modified tie...

"That'd be great," said Larry, "Let me give you some extra money...," going into his wallet, handing her four hundred dollar bills, "Think that'll be enough...?"

"More than enough," she said, big, bounteoux, buxom, a natural hormonally-tuned Buddha.

And, of course, he'd pad her check. He always took care of her. He loved her in a childlike, dependent, beholden way.

"OK, pal..."

Another little abrazo. His style.

"Don't worry about a thing," smiling a wide Burmese-Jamaican Buddha smile, "keep your mind clear for detectiving..."

"See you in a couple days, then, pal," and, leather bag in hand, he hustled out to the car, nervous, hating long drives, hating the creepy-crawly Unknown. If he just gave in to the real him, he would have crawled into bed next to Maxine and spent the rest of his life in a fetal position sucking on his thumb.

Opened the car door and the whole car flamed up and he was covered with a sticky flaming ooze that he couldn't snatch, pull, claw off...

"Christ!"

Blinked...and it was gone. And it was just an old warrior of a Volvo in the middle of a blooming white Dogwood-canopied driveway.

Mrs. Barker in the doorway.

"You OK, Mr. Kopf?"

THE LORD SAID UNTO SATAN

All she'd seen, of course, was an old blubber-butt potential cardiac arrest case standing a short and agonized moment staring at an empty car, his mind shifting back and forth between vision and reality -- uncertain for a moment as to which was which. Then...

"I'm fine," he called back, threw his bag in the back, got in the car, and off he went in a hurley-burley cloud of blossoms and tree-seeds and remnants of last autumn's leaves.

Hi, ho, Silver, Sliver, Slobber away!

One last wave to Mrs. Barker and then out into traffic.

CHAPTER 5

Once Larry had gotten past the Chicago traffic-knots and the Gary-Hammond industrial stench, the trip up to Michigan became a kind of sentimental journey for him. It was a trip he and his parents used to make all the time when he was a kid. Mid-summer into fall. Up to Holland, up along the lake. Tomatoes, apples, peaches. And the dunes, Indian Dunes State Park, the Michigan dunes, all the dune-hills covered with an epidermal layer of grass and trees. But you knew it was just a few cells away from being an ancient sea-bed.

Everything greening, the bright op-art Gatorade freshness of early spring. If he'd looked out and seen a Mastodon out there in a clearing, eating up a tree, he wouldn't have been surprised.

When he got to where he had to turn inland toward Detroit, he did it reluctantly. It was like his father was in the car, this benevolent, poor sap banker's presence, wearing his rimless glasses, the windows open, the wind blowing his weak Woodrow Wilsonish pale hair.

And then Crazy Mom, always neurotic about drafts and colds -- her specialty. Never aware that it wasn't drafts at all that made her sneeze; and she didn't have constant colds but was a tangled ball of pernicious allergies.

How to turn a perfectly glorious mid-summer afternoon into venereal Hell.

His father's death replaying through his mind again, "Get the boy out of here...get the doctor...I don't want him to see this," as if he wasn't seeing it. Remembering being taken out of the room and put in his own room, told to read *The Wizard of Oz*. That was that. He never saw his father again. And he would have given anything now to have stayed with him until he died, bleeding, suffering, agonizing, dying, every moment he could have had with him, no matter the circumstances. Because once he was gone there would be fifty, sixty years without him. Maybe more. Maybe less. How long was he himself likely to live? When his father had died, Larry was only four but a four was still yesterday.

THE LORD SAID UNTO SATAN

"How can anyone remember things from the time they're four?" Stanley Belson had challenged him one time, and Larry had answered him, "If that's all you've got..."

Remembering, the hardest part of surviving.

He reached forward and defensively turned on the radio, dialed around for something serious. Found one station, a little crackly and distant. Rachmaninoff's Symphonic Dances, the last one, the one that Rachmaninoff had been going to call Midnight. Rachmaninoff on the shores of Long Island Sound, Gugel on the shores of Lake Michigan...

One of his favorite composers, the unabashed entrega/surrender to the Romantic impulse, the gift for hummable melody.

"That was Simon Rattle conducting Rachmaninoff's Symphonic Dances, with the City of Birmingham Symphony orchestra. This is Dan Bared on WKAR FM, East Lansing; broadcasting from the campus of Michigan State University."

A big green sign on the side of the road -- KALAMAZOO, 10 MILES.

And for a moment, anyhow, Larry zoomed in ecstatically on the present, the air filled with a flurry of snowy seeds from the cottonwood trees alongside the road. Driving into an endless impressionistic forest. Hemingway's Michigan, Michigan before the lumber-spoilers, timbered, saurian, ancient.

Hindemith's Mathnias der Mahler on the radio now. The perfect musical accompaniment for his mood -- dark, romantic, and soaked in a terrible sauce of foreboding...

Although he always launched off into The Unknown like this, following hunches, guesses, hints, intuitions, The Voices like willow wands inside him (almost) always leading him to where the water, gold, the demons were.

As he drove into East Lansing, OK, he said to the other (bureaucratic) voices inside him telling him to make it official, keep within the rules, OK, be zany, be The Prophet, but check in, smooth down irregularities that he'd already indulged in by just taking off the way he had, not talking to anyone. OKAAAAY!! And he'd told Monaghan he'd be back in the afternoon to make some latex molds on

the scene of the crime. Sure, the afternoon after
Apocalypse...sliding...always sliding toward the edge of Reality into the Abyss...Mescalito...Ayahuasca..Flesh of the Gods...the Gods Giveth and the Gods Taketh Away, Blessed/Cursed Forever Be The Gods...on the other (inside) side of the Doors of Perception...

Quality Dairy.

Stopped. Phone outside in an aluminum and glass booth. Called the Grimore Park PD.

"Gugel here, lemme talk to the Big Ack Ack. How ya doin'?"

"Where are you, Larry?"

Sheryl. What a pale name for a second generation Palestinian. He loved her. Desert-bleached bone skin, black tourmaline eyes forever full of erectile midnight promises. She was the musk of violet mandrakes. Like Maxine in her flowering.

"East Lansing, Michigan, pal."

"Jesus, Larry...here's Ackermann."

And Ackermann was on the line.

"East Lansing, Michigan? Football season's over, pal, what the fuck's going on?"

"I'm following a lead. The Bannister woman and her girlfriend lived up here before they moved to Chicago. The voices are talking to me, Ack Ack..."

"Ack Ack, my ass!"

"Not a bad idea," Larry's whole soul a smear of contemptuous irony.

"I mean it. And as far as voices talking to you are concerned, here's another voice -- get your ass back here immediately or you're out on your ass."

"Waddaya got, some got of ass fixation?" Larry laughed. It was like trying to fire Jesus Christ-- YOU'RE FIRED AS MESSIAH, PACK UP YOUR CROSS AND NAILS AND CLEAN OUT YOUR TABERNACLE.

"OK. So long."

"Wait..."Ackermann's pain, confusion, frustration coming through all his official officiousness. He needed this one solved more than any other case in his career. When demonic Chi-town invades King

THE LORD SAID UNTO SATAN

Burb...."you really on to something, Lar? This is one of those cases we've gotta wrap up, man or we're gonna look like shit in the papers. Think about it! The elegance of the Near South Side in the year 1900!"

"Detectiving is magic, my friend, not the golden fleece" answered Larry, sounding very BBC Overseas Service for a moment, "Remember the Case of the Tattered Penis, the Titless Phlebotomist? Not thy gods, but mine, shall speak. Or I could always just go on with the case on my own, andthen after it's solved go to the papers and TV. Can't you just see the headlines -- FIRED GRIMORE PARK COP SOLVES CASE ANYHOW!"

"You smug, fat son-of-a-bitch! Without Maxine...and her money..."

"And you without Yale..."

Invertebrate protozoan excretory pore. He didn't even make it to asshole.

"Larry...,"Ack Ack forcing the Fuhrer in him to make itself small, foam over fire, " OK. Your record shouts for itself. But schnell, Liebschen, we've gotta get this fucking thing wrapped up FAST. We're talking regal real estate here. Remember what The Shadow knows. Project out a little bit. Remember South Shore?"

And HE hung up. OK. Larry feeling his old messianic, nagualish Chosen One self again. Scrunched out of the booth, the paws of a giant spirit jaguar starting to close around him, only when he turned to face it, poofty poof!, it was gone.

He went into the Quality Dairy next to where the phone was and bought a triple Deathwish Chocolate cone. Offhandedly, he asked where the East Lansing PD was. Then back outside into his car, laughing about language, *motherfucker*. The baddest of the bad. He who fucks a mother, or cunt, "You fucking cunt!" "Vagina that fucks!" Excretory-reproductive Manichee dualism. Whatever the Body does is foul, the Spirit, only the Spirit, is divine...

Found the PD rather easily. Impressive big beige brick shithouse. Maybe a little too much building for such a dinky town, but....explained to the very youngish good-guy, mustached academic type on the police desk "Listen, I'm Officer Gugel, Grimore Park PD, just north of

Chicago," flashing his badge and I.D., "murder last night, possible links to East Lansing. I'd like to talk to...you'd know better than me..."

"No problem."

He got on the phone, three rings.

"Listen, you've got a visitor from Chicago. You free? He'll tell you all about it...," then back to Larry, "OK, down the hall here, room 4, you're looking for Detective Woods."

"OK. Thanks."

Down the hall, opened the door, a chunky, cynical-looking guy sitting there, bald on top, a fringe of red hair around the sides, big ears, deep-set eyes. He wasn't going to win any beauty contests.

"Hi, I'm Detective Gugel, Grimore Park PD. It's a small suburb north of Chicago. There was a rather gruesome napalm murder last night." A little *vague* for a moment.

An unexpected energy-dip; the long drive; the barbed guilt at leaving Maxine alone in the house even with Mrs. Barker there. At some level deep inside him feeling that he ought to be chained to her, papoose her around on his back, never be separated from her, even for a moment. Come on, Deathwish, kick in! He screamed at his villi and brain, kick in! I need you!, "I've got a couple of leads that point back to East Lansing..."

"You'd be surprised how much shit goes on here. We just had a major marijuana bust last week, a couple of murders last year, suicides, mainly Orientals... Sit down. You look bushed..."

"I could use a good night's sleep," said Larry feeling jaguar shapes vaguely threatening, pawing around in the air behind him. But he was beyond caring, just pure Aztec crystal skull clairvoyance. Getting inside Woods, in spite of the Frankensteinish surface, layers and layers of good guy, not an ounce of guile in the man. Feeling Woods feeling at home with him, like he'd known him forever, pouring Larry a cup of coffee, handing him a packet of Cremora, four little brown packets of sugar.

"So what's the East Lansing connection all about?"

"The murdered woman's 'roommate' is a woman named Mabel Fudge. Her ex-husband is a professor here, and..."

THE LORD SAID UNTO SATAN

Wood involuntarily tensing up, a couple of four alarms going off inside him, then forcing himself to realign, ommmm himself down.

"Yeah, I know all about that son-of-a-bitch. I'm the one who fingered him. I'm Chief Detective now but that's very recent. I was a foot soldier for years. And, yeah, we pulled that Fudge guy in a couple of years back..."

"For what?" asked Larry.

"It's sad to talk about. Child molestation. His little boy (the perfect porcelain child Larry had seen?) It seems that a couple of years ago, when Fudge brought the boy back to his mother in Chicago, the boy had said something about..." Woods reddening, getting up and closing the door to his office, lowering his voice. "It seems that the boy said something about his father putting his -- that is, the boy's - penis in his - that is, the father's- mouth. The two women made a tape. I've got a transcription of it somewhere if you'd like to see it."

"Yeah, yeah, I'm trying to, you know, get a global picture. Background, gestalt, ambience, context..."

Woods lifted his eyebrows in a little disbelieving, unimpressed scowl, got up, went over to the file cabinet, happy to be able to move, obviously feeling simultaneously over-comfortable and uncomfortable in Larry's presence. Red Alert, Alien Presence, then the red softening into orange, pink-violet, baby blue...

"Let me just ask you, the two women, Bannister and..."

"The two Monster Dykes, you mean," said Woods viciously, pulling a file folder out of the cabinet, lifting out a stapled-together sheaf of papers.

Of course Larry already knew, didn't he, Myrtle was the driver, Mabel the car, Myrtle the plowman, Mabel the willing plow. He could have recounted the whole thing before he read a word.

"I've got an extra copy of this if you want to hang on to it..."

Woods handing him a copy of the transcript and Larry giving it a careful glance, his eyes wolf-spiders greedily stalking up the green parchment trunk of a banana tree.

FEMALE VOICE: So did your father put something in your mouth?
CHILD'S VOICE: Gum. He put gum in my mouth.

FEMALE VOICE (with Kenya accent?): Gunk? He put gunk in your mouth?
CHILD'S VOICE: Yeah, he put gunk in your mouth.
Genug ist genug. Just what he'd expected. Glancing at the introduction, typed in very fancy italics:
The child suffers from allergies. The women apply allergy cream to the child's genitals during the interrogation...

In order to get him aroused? And was that something that the "Female Voice" had read into the recorder?
"OK...that's enough...."
Enough and then some. Something profoundly stupid and psychopathic about the whole thing. All Larry really wanted to do was sit and close his eyes and Buddha into the reality of the transcription and feed on its jellied, decaying flesh, maggot into the textures of Myrtle's and Mabel's collective mind. Text conterminous with mind. Beginning to go off into a mantra of MIND, TEXT, TEXT, MIND, forcing himself back into the room, Woods radiating quiet impatience.
"So, what was your final feeling about Professor Fudge?"
Woods took a package of Dr. Bonner's real root beer root flavored sugar free gum out of the middle drawer of his desk, offered Larry a stick.
"Healthy stuff, thanks," said Larry sarcastically, the sarcasm lost on Woods.
"Well, I don't know how far you've gotten into the case, but do you know about his, how shall I put it, 'sexual schizophrenia'?"
"I don't know for shit," said Larry, "I'm on Square One," obsessive, guilt-ridden preoccupations about Maxine still buzzing around inside him like a ravenous mosquito. Why didn't he just say I'm an old grub-bug with a bad back and millions in el banco, and just have just stayed home and fucking babysat fulltime for the rest of his life...
"Well," Woods continuing, totally unaware of the maelstroms roaring around in Larry's head under his Buddha-calm mask, "he kind of always presented himself as one of the old Catholic boys, daily Mass and Communion most of his life, President of the Saint Vincent de Paul

THE LORD SAID UNTO SATAN

Society when he was in grad school at Harvard. Ascetic, fanatic, otherworldly. But Mable showed us certain pictures of him in drag...."

"Well, we all have a Carnivales persona, don't we...?" Larry smiled, surprised at Woods' monochromatic naiveté.

"As a matter of fact there is a Brazilian connection," Woods warming up as Larry sat there smiling. Old Grandfather Fire blowing softly on the embers of his mind. "Fudge and his wife had lived in (Woods tentative and skittish again, as if the word about to emerge were a hot toasted marshmallow in his mouth) concubinage with a Brazilian for almost eight years."

The two Fudges and a Brazil nut in a love triangle. The cloyingly gooey Riemannian geometry of inevitable, fatal intersections.

"How long has Mable Fudge been living with Myrtle Bannister?" asked Larry.

"I don't remember all the details," said Woods, "but from what I understood, Mabel left the threesome because the Brazilian nudged her out."

Mable forced out -- THESIS. The sick, trumped-up molestation charge/tape -- ANTITHESIS. And the new SYNTHESIS?

"But if Professor Fudge was going to kill anyone, wouldn't it be his wife?"

"Who says he didn't try?!? In the dark. A pail of gasoline gets thrown. Or what if he saw Mabel as a passive stooge and Myrtle as the active, corrupting agent. Of course, there's a lot more to it. It's a complicated, multi-valent case," said Woods.

"OK," said Larry, pulling a little Cuban cigar obsessively out of his pocket, lighting up, sitting back and closing his eyes and starting to descend to the Macumba world-center of shamanic death, resurrection and total clarity, "Lemme just see if I can get this into some kind of coherent whole. You've got the Angry Fairy Dad, Angry Dyke Mom, two other women on the sidelines, the murdered woman on one side, the Brazilian conspirator on the other. What does it add up to in terms of motivation?" Larry asking himself out loud, seeing it all triangles and rectangles, isosceles, equilateral, obtuse, acute, scalene, scaly, scaled up, down....tensions, stresses, resolutions...

"I hate to be petty," Woods interrupting, "but this is a smoke-free facility..."

"Oh, I'm sorry," said Larry, squishing the cigar out in a pouch-shaped little brass ashtray that he always had waiting, like a hungry mouth, in the pocket of his jacket.

"I think the key is in the whole Futurotech Scam -- the Royal Jelly Project," answered Woods cracking his knuckles like punching down on a bowlful of Graham Crackers, then back into his file cabinet again, a kind of microbiological, tennis pro quickness about him, handing Larry another manila envelope, Larry opening it to the first page, a nicely laser-printed title: FUTUROTECH – CASENOTES.

Then inside, page after page of carefully typed-up notes. Interviews, a list of interviewees:

Dr. Mascher
Priscilla Pringle
Jenifer Grump...

"There's not anyone really called Jennifer Grump!?!?" laughed Larry, a thin thread of smoke emerging from his pocket, giving his cigarillo one last definitive squish, Woods dying to know how he did it, Larry's white suit staying immaculately white. "Another victim of Myrtle Bannister's? So what did she do, go around collecting victims?"

"Kind of...she was kind of a Praying Mantis-Vampire type," said Woods. "Myrtle Bannister had been trying to get a handle on a million bucks most of her life. She was brilliant, erratic, anti-erotically over-mental, remorselessly angry and sadistic, relentlessly evil. I don't know how you see evil, Gugel, but I see it as (Woods' voice deepening, darkening, pulling monsters out of the bland grey casein walls) as equal to, if not superior to, GOOD. Evil advances through the world horned and monstrous, tramping The Faithful underfoot with great glee. It glories in the death-screams of The Martyrs..."

"Nicely done," said Larry ironically, making with a little patty-cake applause, thinking about an unbearably histrionic performance of King Lear that he'd seen at De Paul some 45 years back, "You should have gone into drama."

THE LORD SAID UNTO SATAN

"As a matter of fact, I did, the first three years. Then switched into Criminal Justice. Drama on the streets, off the stage. You're inside it, not just mouthing someone else's words. We've got the most educated cops in the world in this town, my friend," he crowed with a fiery red smile. He really did look like a Tlinglit beaver totem dipped in ketchup.

"How did Myrtle fuck over Grump?" asked Larry, wanting an Enemy List. Polarization wasn't enough, he wanted fine tuning.

"Got her in the gut, got her fired, got a whole slew of people fired. Juggernaut destructiveness. Like I said, relentless..."

"Tie the juggernaut destructiveness and the Royal Jelly business together for me," asked Larry. He wanted the cloud called Myrtle Bannister to become a face and start talking. He wanted to hold Myrtle's voice in his hand, bounce it up and down in his palm, savor its weight, texture and poisonousness, like a scrofulous toad.

"Well...," Woods sitting back, getting Einsteinian again, the fingertips of both hands touching, forming an arch, like a church, "it's a question of simple biological mathematics. Royal Jelly doubles, triples the life of the Queen Bee. My father died at 72. Theoretically he could have made it to 144...216...," Woods repeating 216 with Armageddonish finality, "TWO HUNDRED AND SIXTEEN!"

"But invertebrate and vertebrate biology intermeshing...?" scoffed Larry.

"What I've seen with these eyes...," said Woods, popping his eyes wide open, "I've been in the labs and looked in the cages, seen the charts. But I guess that was the problem. Like inserting a silkworm disease-resistant gene into soybeans by means of some sort of Oak-Gall technique. You've got to bridge the plant-animal gap and I'm still very vague about the whole thing, even though Griller tried to explain the whole thing to me one afternoon when I was investigating the big heist."

Larry's hand going automatically into his pocket for another cigarillo, slipping one out of the package, fingering its sacredness, the Quiché Indians never using anything more (boiled down, concentrated, turned into thick black Power) to open the doors of enlightenment.

"Griller? Heist? It keeps growing, like overnight mushrooms..."

"Oh, it's somewhere in the packet I gave you. Lemme take a look," Woods reaching over and grabbing the case notes he'd given Larry, finding what he was looking for, handing it back to Larry, finger on the name.

Griller, Larry -- Former (original) head of Project Queen Bee. Now at Rabun Gulch Labs in Featherquilt, Tennessee.

"And the relationship between Griller and Myrtle Bannister?" asked Larry.

Woods sat down again, started cat-cradling around a big industrial rubber band in his fingers.

"Well, the way I see it, Myrtle bumped Griller out of his job too. He was just another obstacle on her way to absolute suzerainty. Of course he was a drunk, faked results, Clairol'd some grey rats back to black again -- at least that's what Myrtle claimed...," Woods sitting back and laughing a deep Santa Klaus laugh, "he was an asshole, I'll tell you that. I can't believe some of the asshole things he did. On the surface pure unadulterated Michigander Dutch Reformer Latter Day Saint. And then all this fudging on results. Of course Mascher was always pushing for practical on-the-line results." Larry looking down his list -- Mascher, Dr. Adam R., Executive Head of Futurotech -- 109 Boland Hall, Professor Emeritus, Microbiology, "and Vest was always after Mascher." Larry re-consulting his list: Vest, J.D., the money behind Futurotech, semi-retired head of Recycling International, Futurotech offices, corner of M.A.C. and Albert in University Mall building) to take it out of theory into practice, the hard and fast buck. Not that I can blame him, huh?!"

"And Myrtle Bannister was trying to take over the company?"

"The whole research end of it. That's what it looked like to me. Divide and conquer, pulverize the opposition. And to her everyone was opposition. And she did manage to get rid of everyone but Mascher -- and then quit. Tried to take the whole process with her to Chicago. Take it all away from Best. I'm not surprised she ended up the way she did. I don't think she turned into Mother Teresa after she left here."

Woods re-opened the middle drawer of his desk and took out a small, gold-papered gauntlet-shaped box, opened it up and the room filled with the luxuriant smell of dark savage chocolate, LANCELOT embossed in flowery Baroque gold all over the cover. He passed the box across the desk and Larry discreetly took one small gauntlet-shaped piece, thinking crusades, the crusaders bringing back the radical luxuriousness of knives, forks and the art of shaving to Europe from the Levant...

"It was crazy. When she quit she was making a hundred grand a year and her girlfriend twenty. And together they could have lived on thirty thousand, banked the rest. But Myrtle quit in a huff and then within two weeks, when Mascher went to look for some certain cell-groups they'd been working on, they were gone. Never did find them. There was a little pre-trial inquest in which Fudge's present wife, Chichi -- the Brazilian they'd been living in concubinage for eight years -- testified simply that Myrtle and Mable had left the cells in her keeping before they'd gone off to London to visit Myrtle's parents. Those cells were the cells that were missing and, had, in fact, been mislabeled so that nobody could have tracked them down to begin with," Woods stopping, flushed, trying to keep centered, "It's all so fucking folded in on itself, like Origami. I'm so used to cases like the math tutor who killed and dismembered one of his students, put the pieces in garbage bags and put the bags in the trash outside his apartment block in Spartan Village. Fingerprints all over everything, blood all over a shirt he'd put in his goddamned dirty laundry hamper. But missing cells? What the fuck were they going to do with them anyhow, without Vest's marketing savvy. They didn't have a lab, didn't have shit, didn't really have the capability of keeping the cells in liquid hydrogen for safe storage. Which, I think, is ultimately why, just at about the same time, Myrtle married Ali..."

"I thought Myrtle was supposed to be a dyke," objected Larry.

"Well...as far as that goes, who stays defined...but, anyhow, it wasn't a real marriage. Ali had his own problems too. Senegalese, a condensed little ebony statue of confused sexuality, forever -- unsuccessfully -- trying to find justification for his confusion in The Koran. But he did have access to liquid hydrogen. OK? Not to mention the fact that Myrtle and Mabel were always trying to lay a smokescreen down over their own homosexuality. Another paradox. Gay shame. When they moved down to Chicago I think they took the cells with them -- and then I lost track of the whole case. Thank God!!!" Woods popped another chocolate into his mouth, offered one to Larry, who took one and then the box went beddie-bye back into Woods' desk drawer. "Where are you staying, Gugel?"

"Any recommendations?"

"Well, there's a Marriott just two blocks over, but I'd recommend the Kellogg Center," and he drew a little map on a memo-pad, tore it off and handed it to Larry with a handshake and "I'll be in touch. I'm curious as to what you come up with. OK?," walking with him half way down the hall, shaking hands again, whispering "You wouldn't be willing to part with one of those little cigarillos, would you?," Larry taking out the package, handing him one.

"In the old days, before tobacco get bewitched, I used to smoke one of those big old Havanas after brunch every Sunday. We've got this little place out in Okemos, back deck just on the river. I'd sit out there five, six months of the year and smoke my weekly cigar like it was some sort of sacramental ritual..."

"It's like the ban on chemical weapons," smiled Larry, "a bullet in the brain's fine..." Woods, looking a little puzzled, then a smile. A little pat on Larry's arm and he turned and walked back to his office. Larry walked down the corridor toward an exit sign; filled with a draining, depressing sense of death, as if he wasn't alone. But the Anjo da Morte/Angel of Death was there with him, hovering just on the nether edge of visibility, feeling very old and fragile, depressed by the idea of just how wiped out you were when you died...obliterated....as if your whole life were just one mosquito-brief spring-summer, and then the scythe was being raised, and...

Through the doors at the end of the boring beige corridor, and out in front of the station again in the bright, unyielding Spring sun, canopied over by the surreal yellow-green buds of newly-budded trees, the green whispering to him for a moment YOU ARE OURS, YOU WILL ALWAYS BE OURS, and he was back in the Madre de Dios jungle again, drinking down a foul boiled-down concoction of condensed tobacco, first the nausea and vomiting and then THE VISION...expanding out into the Sacred Now for a long, humming moment, putting on his polarized sunglasses that made everything look bloodlessly blue, standing and letting his spirit slide into the blue-

THE LORD SAID UNTO SATAN

greenness of the leaves and grass, inside the blue-red-purple of the tulips, the blue-pink of the crabapples, the exotic blue-white perfume of the Anise Magnolias, closed his eyes and became giant blue-white perfumed wings humming-birding it into the flower-cup intensity of a very special, private NOW. When he heard a voice.

"You OK?"

Opened his eyes. A young cop genuinely concerned.

"Fine," answered Larry, "Just fine. Agronomical Buddhism. Just on my way over to the Kellogg Center," condensing back into ordinariness, going over to his car parked by the curb across the street, getting in, starting up, trying to figure out the map Woods had handed him. Case! Ha! This wasn't a case but Leibnitz, the Periodic Table, a ball of lint, a dark wood in the middle of his life. Laughed to himself. If 50's supposed to be middle age and your father dies a week after his fiftieth birthday, how long do you think you really have left?

"Fuckit!" pulled out into the street toward the Kellogg Center.

CHAPTER 6

The Kellogg Center, Larry was informed by a plaque in the recently redone (in kitsch Art Deco) lobby was the "laboratory" of MSU's restaurant-hotel school.

When he approached the check-in counter, the obviously Malaysian, cadavorously bulging cheek-boned clerk asked him right off "Are you Detective Gugel?"

"I might be," he smiled, both complemented and terrified.

"Detective Woods called a made a reservation for you, described you..."

"Ah...," the terror puffing out like a match as Larry signed in, feeling unexpectedly good about himself, a beautiful Malay-Chinese (?) bellhop (bellhop-ess?) appearing and escorting him up to his room, Larry feeling that the whole dynamics of the place reeked of academic showmanship. The whole game of using future hotel managers as coolies sucked...although...on the other hand, it wouldn't hurt to give managers a more global sense of the whole hotel business in terms of basic class-struggle economics. And it all a sign, wasn't it, of a hitherto unimagined degree of cultural globality ...when he was growing up in Chicago, the only oriental you ever saw was at the local Chinese restaurant, period!

He took his bag from the (Ibo? Nigeria?) bellhop's hand, reached in his pocket and found a large blue topaz and handed it to him.

"Thank you, sir!"

For a moment not quite sure what he had in his hand, and then it sank it.

"Thank you very much."

Entered the room, closed the door behind him...and instantly smelled the verboten, acrid, stale, stable stench of an unfiltered Camel. There in front of him, over by the window, sitting in a delicate Dansk armchair that looked like it shouldn't be able to sustain his enormous weight, sat a black-eyed, black-haired fatty in a Hong Kong tweed jacket, a black and red wrinkled stripped tie loose around the neck of his frayedat-the-collar white shirt. He had a bottle of Jim Beam in one hand, a half-empty glass in the other.

Larry reached for his hip holster, his Out Walking the Dog gun...but he hadn't strapped it on, his Jiminy Cricket conscience chiding him Gettin' ole, Larry, me boy, you're not that far from the Shady Knoll rest home, are you, my boy?!?!

"You wanna drink?"

"No thanks, Bryan," Larry giving it a shot, usually a great guesser. The guy with the bottle laughing wildly.

"No, no, pal, I'm not Fudge, I'm Griller..."

Larry sang froid chill for one horrible fluttery, off center moment. Then, refocusing, calm. In and out of Nothingness to Everythingness. Zen Buddhism, Zen Judaism, the heartbeat of the cosmos. A sudden lightning bolt zinging down into the space at the center of his soul. Going into the john and unwrapping a cellophane-wrapped water glass and holding it out to Griller; jerking the glass away when it got up to the one-third mark...

"I thought you were down in Tennessee," said Larry, curious as to how Griller had zeroed in on him so quickly and so precisely. Woods or a leak in Woods' office? Underneath all the superficial railing against him, Woods had seemed sympathetic to Griller the Victim. What sort of internetting psycho-plasmic info-web was being woven around his (Larry's) little visit to Football Town?

"Yeah, yeah, seeing I was in Chicago for this AMS meeting, I got to talking to Mascher and he give me reason to believe I might have a chance to get back in here. I don't like Tennessee much. Regional mindsets, accents, you know...."

"They're already on the wane, don't worry," said Larry, "regional linguistic-weltanshaaung variations are postulated on the kind of phonemic isolation that is totally eliminated by the media-glut...what's AMS?"

"American Microbiological Society. It really should be Association, but then it comes out AMA, and..."

Griller had a skid-rowish overnight growth of beard fungusing all over his face.

"Who else was down there?" asked Larry hollowly, his own voice echoing around in his head inside some sort of crystal skull echo-chamber, poised to hit the deck, implode, vanish, all kinds of shapes moving around inside him, shadowy groupings and re-groupings. What was Old Grandfather Fire trying to tell him?

"The whole gang, everyone from the Royal Jelly Project..."

Didn't the asshole realize what he was saying, or was he the compulsive Judas in this whole sad Way of the Incineration?!?

"What about Fudge?"

"He's an anthropologist."

"Chichi?"

Griller stopped.

"As a matter of fact I DID see them in the Palmer House bar. She looked like a Spanish dancer, black lace, white face, just a delectable touch of decay around the eyes,"

Larry took a sip of the whiskey, closed his eyes and his mind tumbled full of images of ancient forges, anvils, hammers...

"The sacredness of CRAFT!" he thought out loud for a moment, the images of the Perfect Salami, the Perfect Bar of Patchouli Soap, the Perfect Shang Bronze Pot spinning inside him. "Whatever you say here gets immediately dropped into the deepest sacrificial cenote of total anonymity!"

"It wasn't murder," said Griller in a sudden compulsive panic-confession reflex, hulking over toward the door, Larry stepping back and letting him go, "just primal, cellular JUSTICE!"

Out the door like a big fat rat, Larry gulping down the rest of his whiskey and as it slithered down burning into his gut wondering *if the whiskey itself was yet another instrument of cellular justice...some almost subliminal undertaste of....*

Over to the door, Griller already gone, the corridor empty, rushed over to the EXIT door, opened it. Listened, nothing. Maxine had always bitched him out for his spilling his guts at cocktail parties, but he moved toward death with the weightlessness of the Truly Innocent. Feeling the wings of the Angel of Death starting to beat all around him. Wanting to go the way the great poet-mystic, Menke Katz, had gone; lying down.

THE LORD SAID UNTO SATAN

"A little pain in my chest," three, two, one... The kiss of God. Gone...
Over to the elevator, one light descending down to the lobby – five, four, three, two... the other elevator up on eight. Larry pressed the down button. Doubting that the button, the hotel, East Lansing itself, were really there. As the elevator stopped and he got in; doubting that it had stopped, that there was any elevator at all, to stop, doubting he was there to stop it. A tall black woman with a bushy Afro-ish head of brown hair already inside. Running shoes and a red and white stripped jersey under a cottony kind of "raincoat." Big bug eye sunglasses.

"What's yours?" she asked, poised over the button-panel.

"Lobby."

And she pushed "L" with acerbic finality.

No other buttons lit up. So where was she going? And how did she get it to move without any destination?

"Thanks."

"My enemies insist on casting me as a killer witch" she said. The accent? Auckland? Christchurch? Dunedin?

"Yeah, well...you know..."

She could easily have a nice long thin stainless steel filleting knife hanging on a loop inside her raincoat.

"Do you want to see my scars?" she asked.

Larry's divine jaguar-shaman voices starting up inside him, *Here, not, here, not here, hear, hair, not here in your "Hair's to ya..."*

"Do you want to see my scars?" she repeated again.

"No...," he answered, blocked, silted up, frozen, a frozen icepick stuck in the center of his dead aphasic brain.

It won't work, mind-screaming at Griller and the gang through the elevator walls, *It won't work on me, I'm not hair, filtering out into the elevator shaft, blago bung, blago bung, bosso fataka, schampa wulla wussa olobo....*

"Yes, you do!" she screamed and opened her coat, pulled up her jersey, her whole belly held together with a long, lateral just-stapled black-red clotted suture...reached up and pulling off her hair...wig...the whole skull just reassembled, serum still oozing out of the edges of the

40

stapled-together pieces. And then he realized that she wasn't "black" at all, not "black" black, but burned, charred...

"Would you like to put your hand in my wounds now, OH YE OF LITTLE FAITH. You KNOW who I am!!!"

She took off her glasses. The eyes Auschwitz, Nacht Und Nebel killing fields of none but the pin-cushion frozen pinwheel moon-rock despair heart.

Myrtle Bannister!

The whole time hovering just out of sight in Death's Dream Kingdom and now it was time for his autopsy. Her hand reaching under her raincoat, whisper-winged bat-voices fluttering around the corners of the elevator, "Blasphemer, blasphemer, blasphemer..." Paralyzed, trying to move, like trying to swim up from The Deep toward the shining underbelly of the surface and not moving at all...

BOING! A little bell rang. Lobby. The door opened...*and he was alone in the elevator.*

Larry waiting just a little too long...as the door began to slide shut again and in the corner Myrtle began to re-materialize as Larry lunged at the doors and they snapped open again and he kerplunked out into the beatific green pasture fields of the Lord lobby.

Everything so blessedly normal, the pace of hallucination/possession versus the pace of the everyday.

Larry ran out the front door of the hotel, no sign of Griller. Another fat man like himself who moved at the speed of light. Came back in, started to walk over to the desk, then spotted a stairway and uncertainly began to walk up the six mushily unreal dream-flights back to his room, expecting a reincarnation of Myrtle at any moment,once inside his room, feeling the walls, expecting his hand to go through them, but it didn't, remembering the months he'd spent among the Jivao hardly knowing who (or IF) he was...at the same time his jaguar shaman past tight around his shoulders like a bulletproof raincoat...

Called back home to Chicago, almost expecting it not to be there either, images of the whole earth bare, dead, frozen, floating through his head like a fleet of frosted glass Christmas tree ornaments.

Mrs. Barker answered after ten rings.

THE LORD SAID UNTO SATAN

"I was down in the basement doing laundry," she explained.
OH, YE OF LITTLE FAITH, WOULD YOU LIKE TO PUT YOUR FINGERS INTO MY WOUNDS!?!
"How's...how's Maxine...doing?"
"Are you OK, Mr. Gugel?"
"Yeah, yeah, yeah," he answered, re-centering, ommmming in again on the real earth in real time, the little toe on the four thousandth leg of The Great God Krazny -- pure black tourmaline. "How's Maxine doing?"
"Unchanged, Mr. Gugel. She did everything in the bed again this morning. And I tried to coax her into doing something beforehand. I'm going to put a ham sandwich in the blender for her for lunch, let her drink that. And what's happening with you?"
"You really are there, aren't you?" asked Larry, the question not whether he would ever die, but if he had ever lived, reality itself the Great God Krazny's dream, and he awakes and it all disappears.
"Too much so," laughed Mrs. Barker, her ample black Bodhisattva face there in front of him for one soft, stroking, comforting moment
"OK, listen, I'll call back tonight," he answered, his mind filling up with images of graveyards for a moment, graveyards on
hills overlooking immense rivers, graveyards in little out of the way forests, behind old farmhouses sadly unguarded for a moment, when you cease to be, what's the difference that you've ever been?
"George is coming over tonight, if that's OK with you."
"Sounds good to me. Talk to you later."
And he hung up, for a moment still feeling transparent, porous, more like gas, a cloud, then flesh, the voices of The Dead whispering out of their graves "When you're here, what's the difference who you fathered or mothered, kissed or killed...,'" then thinking about George, the father of her three children. She hadn't seen him for twelve years, twelve years he'd been in Jamaica without her. And then suddenly he'd reappeared -- and it looked like a plain, ordinary, bourgeois marriage this time around...
"Bless you, Mrs. Barker," he said to himself, went to the closet, opened the door...

"You can come out now," his voice as spongily soft as an orchid, as sinus-cleansing as Bay Rum, as kinesthetic as a shower of stove bolts...

And out she came, snuggled inside rows of minks and silver foxes, landy, languorous, long-haired, cow-faced...at least that's what her enemies said. To which he always retorted, "When Homer wanted to stress the ultimate in beauty, he'd always refer to Hera as ox-eyed!"

She was wearing a long, black silk kimono printed with red and purple poppies....

"Very nice," he said as she came into his arms and, reaching up under the kimono, he savored her black mesh-lace- leotarded body, "So you've been doing your aerobics....," loving a face-lifted, tummy tucked skeleton with huge saline-implant tits, anorexic, bulimic, surgical, all erotic-ecstatic Will.

"Just for you," she said and they floated over to the bed like Chagall dream-lovers.

"How's the case coming along?" she asked as they fluttered down on top of the puffy quilted cotton bedspread, a touch of the rustic and homey in contrast to her high-tech sexuality. Queen, King, Galactic size bed.

"Let's just worry about our case," he said as he took her long, lean Lady of the Unicorn right hand and put it down where it counted, the whole room slowly medievalizing now, the windows peaking into gothic stone, a distant sound of Gregorian chant filtering through the walls -- the Easter Rite. Why did The Church ever exchange Gregory for guitars?

"I am your love and you are my lady, the mystical rose mandala at the center of my soul..."

"As you are mine, my love," she said and they lie there immobile, the stone statues on the tombs of Los Reyes Católicos in the cathedral in Granada.

This is
what I was made for,
for this I came.....

His face wet with tears.

As tired as the earth itself, wrung ragged and exhausted through all its successive eons of battered, flowing change.

THE LORD SAID UNTO SATAN

And then he was asleep and the screen went dreamlessly white.

It was late (but still bright) afternoon when the phone rang and jolted Larry back into the Now.

"What's next?" he said, not entirely sure the phone in his hand was the phone in his hand, not entirely sure that the sunlight wasn't moonlight and that he wasn't just embarking on some sort of blurred shamanic vision-quest.

"That's a marvelous way to answer the phone," said the voice on the other end. East Coast, a touch of Boston Brahmin.

"So, Bryan, we meet at last," said Larry, totally and unswervingly on target, whatever it was that had been in the whiskey somehow reactivating his shamanic powers so strenuously acquired in the Wirakutaland of his beloved Huichols...

"I just thought that you'd get to me eventually, I hate feeling stalked; and I must be a prime suspect. I certainly had reason enough to do in Myrtle Bannister...," fake Cambridgian slipping into real Chicagoese, "I thought maybe we could have dinner tonight..."

"So the lambs come voluntarily to the slaughter. OK. I'm as passive as an empty blackboard."

"I'm over on Acorn Avenue, 652, you can get directions at the reception desk. Come at your convenience. It's a nice walk..."

"For me a nice float," said Larry, impressed by this interconnected ganglionic gang octopus one-for-all-all-for-one-Volvox-brain, the minute you touched the web the whole COLONY panicked, Larry's mind suddenly filled with dark, emerging shapes that never quite emerged, "A bientot!."

Hung up feeling panicky, The Great Fear flowing around, in and out of him, dissolution, anonymity, becoming pictures in a trunk in someone's attic and then another generation turns and the attic and the trunk are gone, great-grandpa becomes Troy I, II, III, not one name from Haçilar/Çatal Hüyük...

"Do you think I'm doing the right thing?" he asked the closet.

"Follow your chilam-shiman-shaman voices, stay on the other side of the existential wall," answered Windy from inside, her voice full of silver foxes and minks, a giant curled tail of a purr...

"Why did you ever drop me?" he asked, as if he didn't know already. Him and all his rat's ass possessive jealousies. She could never BE his as long as Maxine was alive, and it looked like Maxine would outlast him and everyone else, and you can't fence in The Wind...but...

No answer.

He got up up and slid open the closet door, wanting so much to have her there nestled among her dream-furs. But this time it was empty except for a check-out notice pasted greedily on the wall. Empty hangers on an empty steel pole.

"Hypocrite lecteur! Mon semble! Mon frere!," he hissed at the empty closet, then pulled the door shut and took off his clothes, walked into the bathroom, turned on the shower, testing it carefully until it was just a few degrees short of scalding, and then got in, convinced that the minute he got in he'd dissolve, but getting in anyhow, pleased to discover that he was just fine.

CHAPTER 7

Acorn Street was nineteenth centuryish. All Amerikanski neo-classical farmhouse. Christopher Wrenish, Adamsish style, porticos and columns and all kinds of carefully lathed porch railings, the Acropolis midwesternized and democratized. Where the gods became people and the people gods. They'd all begun white, although later Hippy-Yippy tastes had added some blues and purples. Huge oak trees and, oddly, two different kinds of squirrels, black and grey, and no in-betweens.

Fudge's place had a big flower box on the front porch, filled with multicolored Petunias. Larry could see an overturned toy truck in the side yard, overgrown with grass. Children fled. Snatched away!

A nineteenth centuryish park bench on the front porch. Larry turned around and looked at the vista you'd see sitting on the bench -- the fin de siècle street, huge old houses dwarfed by the overwhelming presence of the ancient trees. Rachmaninoff at the Villa Senar. Coleridge in his lime-tree bower.

A twenty year old in tight black lycra pants and floppy grey sweatshirt ran by. Very nice, very Windyish. The every-day as non-stop dance recital.

Reached up and rang the bell and a pert little sexually-charged Edith Piaf in a black lace blouse and skirt, lace legs and Spanish dancer black suede shoes wrapped around the legs, answered the door. A little (Les Dames du Bois de Bologne) anachronistic, perhaps, which made her even more effective.

"Bryan's expecting you..." Into the living room and a little fuzzball dog sidled up to him, did an obscene little ass-wag dance, and licked his shoe. He heard another dog stir in the kitchen. Le Chien Andalou... "I'm Chichi...I'll tell Brian you're here."

Larry smiled a silent smile and sat down on a plush brown sofa next to a window overlooking the flowering side yard. Chichi slipped up the stairs like a shadow and Larry closed his eyes and listened to the wailing of the walls. Oh, what mortal agonies had been endured within these sad walls, walls that wept for retribution...

Then opened his eyes again. One full wall lined with books, Amerindian artifacts in little custom-made cases on the other walls, spearpoints, potshards, some wood-carvings from Amazonia. Then into the dining room, a whole collection of bronze Hindu-Tibetan-Nepalese gods, bi-sexual Siva, with a breast on one side, no breast on the other, Yama, the bull-faced monster Lord of the Underworld, with a woman "plastered" on to him in an inexplicably intense tantric act of love.

He walked over to one of the bookcases. Eça de Quiero! Nobody (but himself) read Eça de Quieroz. And Oswaldo de Andrade. Nobody read Oswaldo de Andrade; always describing himself as a major writer in a minor language. A copy of Os Sertoes. Euclides de Cunha. But nobody, nobody but himself, read Euclides de Cunha!

More bookcases on the other side of the window next to the TV, VCR, camcorder on a tripod, a whole shelf of books by Fudge himself. Novels, poetry. Bryan and Bunny Fudge. Bunny Fudge?! He opened up one of the Bunny Fudge volumes, picture on the back cover of a very Slavic-looking overweight Bryan in drag who looked more like a buffalo than a bunny. The Dream of the Engulfed Cathedral:

I repeat the mantras of the waves,
seek deeper into the nothingness of
Self,
other selves from the other side of
selflessness
rising to meet me from the
bottom of the ocean
pond...

What was it, an ocean or a pond? And the "mantras of the waves" was re-re-refried 1960's Kerouacian Mexican City Blues beans. But otherwise...

Larry had the uncanny *déjà vu* feeling that he'd walked through some sort of Star Trek time-warp door into a negative, alternative

THE LORD SAID UNTO SATAN

doppelganger version of his own psyche. It was a raw, savage, expressionistic Amerindian-Hindu time-warp version of his own soul. If Maxine had walked out of the back room just beyond the dining room miraculously healed and whole again, he wouldn't have been surprised...

He reached into his shirt pocket and started smoking one of his little cigarillo pacifiers.

Stirrings at the top of the stairs.

And a shaggy-haired, amiable but angst-ridden Pudge came clomping down, all scratchy tweed pants and tartan plaid tie.

"Howyadoin'?," pure Chicagoese, "Chichi's such a rotten cook, I thought we might as well just go over to The Club!"

THE Club! There couldn't be two?!?!

"Tudo bem!" chanced Larry, "Fine with me."

"Não posso acreditar, voce fala Portugués!/I can't believe it, you speak Portuguese!"

"Pasé un tempo comprido no Brazil durante la guerra segreda en Pará, e entón fique estudando shamanismo con os indios...quería aprender/I spent a long time in Brazil during the Secret War in Pará and stayed on studying Shamanism with the Indians. I wanted to learn..."

Larry stopped. What exactly had he wanted to learn living in the jungle? Going from tribe to tribe. Taking the sacred drugs; stripping off the outer envelope of Reality, one layer down and then another. Living inside the sacred landscape of Viracuta, looking for the five-pointed star, the sacred blue deer Peyote. Listening to the voice of Fire Grandfather inside him, going back to the beginnings of the beginnings, as if there were a whole other world folded inside "normal," everyday reality...

He felt like he was a stuttering, stammering twelve again and couldn't ask for a quart of milk at the local grocery store.

Fudge, with unexpected sensitivity, stepped in, took Larry lightly by the arm...

"Let's sit out on the porch. It's the best time of year."

"Good idea," answered Larry, relaxing back into his massively self-confident, grazing buffalo self again.

"I hate to be inside this time of year."

"So do I, so do I..."

The sun already dipping into the trees on the horizon. It was all sparkles and sparks. A cool breeze. There was an old wood-slatted aluminum chair that Buckley sat on, gave Larry the bench, pulled the chair opposite him so there was a sense of direct, intimate confrontation.

Chichi came out with two glasses of apple cider.

"A little aperitif?" smiled Fudge.

He was about Larry's height, a little thinner, but not much, a big round casserole of a head, pale blue eyes, a tousle of obviously dyed (blond) hair. On the surface he was easy and affable, but Larry picked up all sorts of subterranean currents coursing through him...anxieties...DREAD...the face didn't stay affable but was crisscrossed with momentary spurts of knobby, rheumatoid horror.

"I don't know much about the secret war in Para," he said, "I was in Minas...Bela Horizonte...that's where I met Chichi..."

Chichi sat down next to Bryan in an aluminum tube chair with a webbed plastic seat and back that looked like it needed changing. In fact everything about the house looked a little neglected and worn.

"Figueiredo was in charge of the whole thing," said Larry, "That's how he got into the presidency. There were scores of Che Quevaras throughout South America but only a very few of them got any big PR like Che himself."

"What were you, a military 'advisor?" asked Fudge.

"Something like that," answered Larry laconically, tense, the door closed tight on his whole 'military advisors' past now, very purposefully making an abrupt change in topics, the matador at the moment of kill, neatly sliding his sword through the cervical vertebrae of the bull, right into the heart, "So you were in Chicago on the night of the murder?!?"

"What murder's that?" smiled Buckley maleficently. "You mean the execution?"

Griller's words.

"Do you hear what you're saying?" asked Larry, working at getting pissed at Fudge's haughtiness, much too attracted to Chichi's perfect black lace spider legs, imagining her crawling all over Fudge...or himself. The way he always wanted Maxine to look, but she, of course, she never had, even before the cancer. Super-rich bitch beyond-fashion/surface disdain for what the plebs/the Out There lived by...

"Pequeña aldea, grande inferno," answered Fudge, "small village, big hell."

"But you were down in Chicago! With the others..." Larry insisting.

"There was a big convention," said Chichi. Black lace spider alibi!

"I miss Chicago. The Art Institute. I'm still a Life Member, had lunch in the Member's Lounge, felt like people for a moment, the Neolithic Chinese, you know..." said Fudge.

"If that's what does it for you," Larry answered scornfully, the 'other' REAL, off-the-lake. endless slums and abandoned warehouses, ominous alleyways, empty lots, sad, sullen dispossessed faces from all the nooks and crannies on the face of the Earth Chicago, fast-forewarding through his head, "it seems like Myrtle Bannister's whole enemy list was in Chicago this week."

"You're driving down a country road at three AM, don't see another car for an hour, come to a stop sign, are tempted not to stop, and suddenly a car comes over a hill on the other road at eighty miles an hour, and if you hadn't stopped...The Law of Synchronicity," said Fudge, a sudden frantic freeze-over in his tone, "she had lots of enemies before she ever came to Chicago, and I don't imagine she stopped collecting them after she got to Chicago."

"We never could get anything out of her about her past," added Chichi.

"She'd drop a reference once in a while, a previous marriage, eight years in Baton Rouge, a child named Hannah in London with her mother. Just enough to give you the impression that she'd had all these endless previous lives and that each compartment of her life was totally separate from the others, like she hadn't gone through a series of interrelated experiences, but really had had an immense series of separate, compartmentalized lives. Like she'd been married, heterosexual, and then, when she was here, she was intensely homosexual, although even then she'd have outbursts like 'I'd like to get married and have long hair and a long dress and have children and be perfectly, perfectly, perfectly normal.' And then, in the midst of all that, she ran off with my wife..."

Chichi getting up. Feeling embarassed?

"I'd better call and make reservations."

As she went into the house, Larry getting in a subtle little glance at her aerodynamically perfect legs...

"Fill me in a little," said Larry.

Fudge put his half-empty glass of cider down on a squat, very Spanish-looking wood table with a cast-iron ashtray in its center.

"For me the center of the tragedy was using trumped-up charges of child sexual abuse as a legal device in order to take little Bryan away from Chichi because Chichi had testified against Myrtle in this little pre-trial inquest revolving around Myrtle's having stolen some key cells that were the center of the whole Royal Jelly project, and then using the same device again to alienate me from my daughters. And I think Myrtle was the brains and the energy behind everything, Mabel never has been anything but pure passivity..."

Fudge moving through irateness to rage, to a kind of Chekhovian melancholy weepiness, tears in his eyes, on the edge of total breakdown.

"But you 'edged' Mabel out, didn't you? You paired up with Chichi and wanted her out, didn't you?" asked Larry.

Larry wanting to get totally inside the termite colony of Fudge's soul, hungry for Aztec crystal skull clarity in the midst of all this old Frankenstein in the Lime-Pit/Swamp dry-ice fog-machine opacity.

"You wanna know what kind of guy I am?" asked Fudge, up on his feet, Larry wondering if was really flustered by the suggestion that he'd edged his sainted wife out of his marriage for a little wisp of black lace aerobic fluff, or just doing a final exam routine for Drama 101 "twenty years of daily Communion. I'd walk around with gravel in my shoes to tame my passions. Every afternoon I'd pray, read spiritual classics in the evening -- Thomas A Kemps, St. Francis de Sales, Tertullian, St. Augustine. And the little boy...I love him more than anyone else in my life. You think I'd go around sucking on the kid's DICK?! And everyone, even the cops, knew I was clean. It was all this big game. But that's how you destroy kids. It wasn't just me and the cops and the lie-detector asshole and the shame, but THE KID. The fucking kid has the right to a clean, decent non-distorted story of his childhood. You know

THE LORD SAID UNTO SATAN

how kids are who have been abused; the fact of the abuse hangs over them for their entire lives. And for him to have lived through a childhood filled with lies and distortions...you know what I mean, what I am/did is what he is/will do..."

Fudge stopped, shaken, his eyes filled with tears.

Hard for Larry to doubt his sincerity.

"What about all the androgynous Bunny crap?" asked Larry quietly, the quiet privacy of the confessional, "Is there a Saint Bunny in the hagiology of your private theology?"

Fudge sat back down, his face a swirl of mixed emotions. Mainly surprise, though, wasn't it, surprise that Larry had done so much homework...

"I don't know, my own mother, she was a hundred feet tall and my father was a smudge on the deck floor....it's like there's two sexes inside me, but....."

"But?"

"It's totally unrelated to the kid. I've never had a homosexual anything with anyone. It's mainly just Me and Me..."

"I don't know, the only happy homosexuals I've known have been dead," said Larry tauntingly, playing out a little line, hoping for a bite..., "Let's even say you never had any errant impulses toward your kid. Never did a thing. Still there was the fact that all that private double-life that you'd been carrying on all your life, Bryan by day, Bunny by night, was exposed and held up to ridicule...punished. There's your motive right there. And you didn't blame poor little victim Mabel for anything. Your whole wrath was directed against Ms. Flaming Dyke Myrtle Bannister. You (let's not even say it was "you," but Bunny, the woman scorned/ridiculed) went down to Chicago under cover of the microbiology convention, drove out to Grimore Park, waited for the two women to come home. It's all very clear. Consistent, logical, obvious..."

Fudge just sitting there with his head bowed, the Lamb of God waiting for the slaughterer's mallet, then slowly looking up, his whole face soaked in tragedy, "Wanting's one thing, but...as a matter of fact, when I started getting interested in guns instead of black lace unitards and wicked, wobbly heels, I got out my old copy of Suzuki's Zen Mind, Beginner's Mind and turned back into fog again..."

"OK, so who had fog lights?"

Larry pulling his list of Myrtle Bannister's enemies out of the inner pocket of his suitcase and showing it to Fudge.

"Come on, how about a little help."

"She sucked people dry, it wasn't like she was human at all, but some kind of animal...."

"I want candidates..."

"Or you could view her as pure zealot, purifier -- IF YOUR EYE OFFENDS YOU, PLUCK IT OUT. All her 'victims' were seriously flawed. Only who isn't; the flaming reformer always ends up dead in his/her own private bunker..."

The sun was down below the houses across the street now. A delicate breeze slow-motioning from the North filled with a delicious, edge-of-cold freshness. *My heart aches, and a drowsy numbness pains my sense, as though of hemlock I had drunk* .Larry out of the mood for any more of this shit, longing to simply give himself up cellularly to the evening, existentially meld, melt, merge with sky, birds, breeze. But...

"Some nobody comes in from the outside, and suddenly...."

"No one ever knows what to do. Most lives are spent in perplexed ambiguity...and then along comes..." said Fudge lazily, falling under the spell of the evening, a girl in a tight lycra fuchsia jumpsuit running by with an immense ponytail trailing behind her like a blonde cometail. If a dragonfly with a six-foot wingspread had buzzed by, Larry wouldn't have really been surprised....

"IN THE BEGINNING WAS AMBIGUITY AND AMBIGUITY WAS GOD AND AMBIGUITY WAS WITH GOD," said Larry in soft, breezy mockery."There were times that even I felt she had the right to take the cells she'd been working on, when I was convinced that she'd been fucked over by Futurotech, that you couldn't copyright an idea, that she was a woman under siege and that justice lay in her taking the initiative and exercising her rights," answered Fudge as Chichi came out even silkier than before, a little darker shade of lipstick, another slash of mascara...

THE LORD SAID UNTO SATAN

"Well..." Standing there in the doorway, a black and white Death's Head moth poised for flight.

"OK, OK, vamanos" said Fudge, reluctantly getting up. Squirrels in the trees, a distant dog's barking twisted in the wind, the pert, sprightly new leaves, the squeaking and squawking of the birds, a monumental tree tall lilac bush off his to right, exhaling its sugary perfume out of the darkest amethyst blossoms he'd ever seen, Larry closing his eyes for a moment and blanking out entirely. The long drive, the bad night the night before, Maxine's life/their lives as the Via Dolorosa all mapped out for a long countdown into nothingness..."Are you alright?"

Balloon-man Larry, the human blimp, that's who he was, floating up into the stressless sunset, the higher he went the longer he saw the sun, if he went up high enough the earth would never rise/sun never set, it would just be eternal up, up, up, lacey, languorous, liquid, lazy...

"Do you want me to call...?"

Chichi's unexpectedly brassy, almost-Russian-accented voice twisting like a corkscrew into Larry's right ear, as he opened his eyes...,"I'm fine, really, just a little tired," laboring to his feet, walking down to their Chevy Cavalier with them. Into the back seat...and off they went into the lilac-laden dusk.

Windy inside his head quite deliciously gushy, "Wonderful, you're wonderful, you really are" all Isadora Duncanish, with the long boysenberry-colored scarf wrapped around her neck blowing back like liquid kites in the wind, "Lush, crushed, cushy," reaching over to kiss him and, as he puckered up his lips and ever so imperceptibly raised his head to meet her lips, whoosh, she vanished into the infinity of the setting sun...

"Ahhhh, the Doctors Fudge," said the receptionist/switchboard-operator as they walked into the University Club, "you all look so nice!" A fat, ruined blonde, an overblown about to de-petal rose, gone-to-seed gorgeousness, giving Larry a well-worn, low-toned buddy-buddy smile as if they'd been beer buddies for centuries.

The Maitre d' in the dining room more polished, the lazy, smug, sluggishness of a well-oiled...Larry guessed, hmmmm... Cypriote...conducting them over to their table with a flourish of menus and bows, "The special tonight is filet mignon with caviar sauce...and the stuffed pork chops are very nice too...," a slow graceful turn, "enjoy your meal."

Larry wanting to hit him with a little Greek, sick games, letting it go, flow, snow, blow away...settling back, wondering how far he was from the final thoughts, breaths, fears of the final moments of his final day....

They'd hardly started studying the (mostly French) menus when along came a turkey-breasted, blooming, beaming wind-stewardess.

"So how are you? How about a nice Bordeaux Cabernet Sauvignon? The usual."

"What do you think?" Fudge asked Larry.

"Sailing to Antarctica," he smiled, nodding a contented yes.

"You're not Professor Fudge's brother, are you?" she asked Larry.

"I'm the Finger of Doom, the Angel of Death, the wrinkles around the eyes of God."

"Well, you're certainly here at the right time of the year," she smiled, giving him a little pat on the cheek and waddled off after the wine.

"She's, it's, everything's very low pressure, really," Larry rather begrudgingly, against his will, feeling comfier and comfier, asking himself why didn't he just retire and revisit his sacred places, down the Urubamba River, all the dead ruins in Antisuyo, the clarity of the Atacama Desert, travelling with Neruda, over the mountains from Chile to Argentina, the mudflat northern coast of Colombia where the earliest pilgrims from the Neolithic

Mediterranean landed, the sacred Kogi in the sacred Santa Marta mountains...taking mummy-bundle Maxine with him, what was the difference what she understood or didn't understand, she was his love, his dove, his beautiful one, even if all she was was ashes in an urn....looking around at the raw concrete walls, heavy brick columns, massive windows, very Frank Lloyd Wright prarie-ish, the cloistered Palenque-Uxmal Maya sense of closed-in sacralness, a pool in back, still covered over with a dark blue pool-cover, another month and he could just see it filled with the bouncing kineticism of raw-nerve kids, and decaying old people dutifully doing their laps....looking out on forests beyond, a little dot of super-civilization in the midst of raw, burgeoning wilderness. He opened up a little package of garlic rye crisp, heavy on the butter and then a little extra salt, "It must be nice for the kids in the summer..."

"It WAS!" Chichi unexpectedly raw, jagged edged.

"What's the situation now?" asked Larry, popping a long, limp tingling lime green pepperoncini into his mouth and chewing it together with the rye crisp into a tingling, garlicky paste.

"Well," she answered, putting on a little brake, "everything was OK until December. Not OK-OK, but 'better.' We had little Bryan much of the time and Mabel, in the mixed heat of passion and research, was glad to get him out of the way. And from what he said, it appears that rats and tanks and centrifuges were appearing in the basement in Grimore Park which to me, anyhow, meant that Myrtle had set up a lab in their house and had brought the stolen tanks and cells down there and was trying to cash in on the whole thing. We didn't know where they lived or worked, would always pick up the boy at the Art Institute. And then idiot here started to write his hate-letters..."

"OK, OK," said Fudge looking around edgily, feeling protective and defensive in this, his soft underbelly workplace-playplace territory, waving at some little darkish hairy guy and his wife over in the corner, explaining "Le Blanc, French department...," then lowering his voice conspiratorially, "I've got this cousin in Chicago who guessed that Myrtle must have been working at Babbitt Labs. So I gave it a chance, called and asked to talk to her and when she got on the line I just hung up and the next day wrote her a letter about keeping her hands in her own lab-coat this time around, and another saying that Chichi has been testing some of the cells from the same batch that she stole and they were totally worthless, ha, ha...and another calling her a total fake and saying I was glad she took herself so seriously because no one else did...or could..."

"I don't know," said Chichi as tense as a snare-drum, "they were trying to hide out and do their thing. So they were crooks. So leave them alone. But then the letters, the fact we knew where they were, got Myrtle really crazy. The taunting, bear-baiting, barbecuing..."

On the word "barbecue," Myrtle's barbecued corpse suddenly there on the table in front of Larry for a moment....reaching for a sesame-seed stick and it just as suddenly disappeared...

"We don't know what effect, if any, the letters had as long as nothing else went wrong. But then in the middle of December something else DID go wrong..." said Fudge taking a deep, tortured breath as a waiter with a raw, scrubbed potato face and short blond facial hair, suddenly appeared, "Are you ready to order?," Larry hearing him in German, "Fertig? Sind Sie fertig?"

"How about the Sirloin Tips in Bordelaise sauce for everyone? It's the special specialty of the club," suggested Fudge.

"Warum nicht," said vegetarian Larry...except when he wasn't.

Only for Chichi the menu had become a chessboard and she couldn't just improvise a move.

"The prawns...?"

"What can I say," the waiter smiling a nervous little Heinrich Himmler smile, Larry hearing "Was kann Ich sagen...?"

"OK," Fudge all full of little in-takes and out-bursts of breath, "let's try two Sirloin Tips, one Prawns...," looking at Larry, "baked potato or wild rice? Salad dressing?"

"Baked potato, blue cheese," Larry quick and habitual, as if he'd been there a thousand years, scanning around the dining room, everyone old, solid, stolid, beatifically routine-bound, as if it really were a dining room on an intergalactic voyage.

Fudge dittoing Larry's order, Chichi going for garlic and oil dressing and wild rice, the wine steward bringing in the wine and Larry ceremoniously giving it the taste-test.

"Very nice, oakish, almost herbal, blunted serrated edge...."

The stewardess giving him a little seal-flipper muted applause.

"I love the way you tossed-salad up the words!"

And the wine got ceremoniously served, the minute the stewardess had left, Larry impatiently getting back to brass tacks.

"And what else went wrong?"

"Well, my daughter, Millie, was up here for a visit over Thanksgiving and she went to a party and got to talking with the son of one of the professors in the microbiology department who she didn't know was one of the sons of someone in the microbiology department and told him all about the centrifuge and the rats in the basement at home. That was it -- rats and centrifuge, no sterile hood, incubators, the expensive stuff. So the kid told his father, and his father independently came to the same conclusion that we'd come to-- that Myrtle must be using the basement for the cheapo part of the research and the equipment at Babbitt for the big stuff..."

"The point, the point?," Larry all pincushiony, tachycardyish, stiflingly overheated, "there was some sort of major CHANGE..."

Too much needle pointing and quilting, Larry urgently wanting to get to Intihuatana, Where the Sun was Tied.

"I wrote and told them about our speculations...taunting, mocking, ridiculing... and whatever communications we had, however poor, were cut off. I'd picked up Bryan Junior in Chicago early in December. You know, I get the whole month of December off. And I used to call a couple of times a week and talk to the boy and my daughters and Mabel would talk a little to me..."

"And then?"

"Silence. A foreboding kind of silence...what I'm getting at is that whole story about little Bryan saying something about me sexually molesting him...there was war in the air before I ever brought him back. When I took the boy to Chicago for Christmas on December 21st, Mabel wouldn't even look at me or talk to me, got the boy in the car and was going to drive off without a word when I asked her 'What the hell's wrong?,' and she looked at me vague and twisted, shook her head and drove off..."

"Well, you can't really blame them, all your constant prying and blabbing things around, like you were preparing a case against them" Larry surprised that Mabel had ever consented to any visitation privileges at all.

"But we didn't know where they live. There was still that sense of privacy, and then I just happened to find out -- one of those little twists that happen...the best laid plans of mice and men, and all that. All mail had been going through Mabel's mother in Nebraska. I'd send things to her, she'd readdress them and forward them to Mabel. Mabel and Myrtle were off the map...and then one day the mother made a mistake and misaddressed one envelope and it came back to me -- with just one number wrong. So when I was with little Bryan one time in Chicago right around Thanksgiving, I drove up to the approximate address and he pointed out the house. Vest, the head of Futurotech, had been saying he wanted to track them down to the ends of the earth, so, idealistic dummy that I was, I called him up and gave him the address about an hour after I got it. Although later, when the shit hit the fan about the child molestation charges, he said he'd never used the address I'd given him; although if he had already started to build up a case against them for stealing the cells. There was already all that business about Chichi testifying that the missing cells up here had been intentionally mislabeled so no one would even know which cells were really missing. And my other daughter, Tillie, Millie's sister, had been living with me for about six months after the divorce and had been nasty to her mother and refused to talk to her on the phone. So...maybe Mabel thought I was behind her nastiness --although I wasn't. And there was the immigration service's investigations of marriages with aliens and I've thought that maybe they started investigating Myrtle's fake marriage and she blamed me for putting them on to her...," Fudge's face getting all muddled, flushed, confused, like a slow-motion movie of a breaking plate, "I don't really know, it might have been something else that I've never thought of. But the fact is that all of a sudden Myrtle and Mabel decided to annihilate me; and in a way I can even say they were justified...all the little pieces coming together, and I just couldn't shut up...."

Fudge's cool completely gone now. Even Chichi embarrassed, starting to pat his arm to calm him down a little.

"Não precisa agitarse /Don't get all worked up."

"Maybe I should have become Bunny full time," Bryan starting to cry, wipe his eyes with the big green napkin "pass over the line, get rid of the professor-me once and for all, live, go crazy...instead, what the hell, I had six kids, played it straight for them until Chichi took the lid off and said 'Why don't you express yourself, be what you really are,' all that Sixties liberated, anything-goes bullshit, and then it was professor by day, showgirl at night, sex with the two women, everyone all dressed up like a psychedelic whorehouse...."

"I don't know, I've been around the track a couple of times myself and..."

"To take all our shared, private, secret stuff and turn it into a revenge tactic...."

"All you're doing," said Larry empathetically sotto voce, "is convincing me that you were straining to kill Myrtle Bannister...she'd gone into the dark room of your secret shame, thrown on all the lights and started filming...it happens a lot, people wanting to get punished for their crimes...wash away that guilt, the raccoon fishing-washing instinct..."

Bryan totally ignoring Larry, totally, self-indulgently solipsistic.

"That's what she specialized in-- getting into people's secret shames. Like Mascher, for crissake. There's a guy I never thought anyone could get to, but Mabel managed."

Another link in the growing chain...

"What about Mascher?"

"His weak point was/is his professional pride. I see him as a kind of superannuated fake, but on the surface he's all an elder statesman-prophet grey-haired eminence type. Well...Myrtle had gotten rid of all the lower echelon duds in the company and she decided that her next target in line was Mascher himself. Get rid of him and establish absolute suzerainty? Well, she met this guy down at Wayne State who had it in for Mascher because he'd given him a 'tainted' recommendation letter years before. He told Myrtle one day that the whole Royal Jelly Project was a pig's ass and that Mascher was an amateur poseur who ought to go back into music and leave the sciences up to the big boys. So Myrtle came back up to East Lansing and at the next staff meeting got up and repeated, word for word, what the other guy had said, you know, the old JE T'ACCUSE technique, pointed at him, face to face. She hadn't really said anything substantive, but everyone thought he was going to have a heart attack. He could have just ignored her, make her look like a fool, instead got up and staggered out, 'You've smeared shit all over my entire career...'"

Larry feeling oddly on comfortably familiar ground now. Myrtle just like his mother and grandmother, just like home...as the waiter came their way carrying a huge aluminum platter with three stainless steel-capped dishes on it, carefully placing it down on a stand next to them, uncovering the dishes with a wizardish flourish -- VOILA! Everything visually exquisite, the green beans almost fluorescent, the sirloin tips bathed in a rich shallot-speckled wine sauce, the baked potatoes bulging in wrinkled aluminum foil jackets, Chichi's prawns piggishly pink and spread out like wings.

The wine stewardess came proprietarily sauntering back over very interested in the lay and lilt of the table.

"Parfait! And the wine?"

"Very nice," Fudge and her touching hands. Just a touch, but...

"You know, my fiancé and I would like to invite you to the wedding. You've been a kind of 'witness' to the whole thing over the years, and..."

"I'd like to come..."

Larry struck by Fudge's total 'ease'/'easiness' in this, his world; finding it hard to imagine him a fraction as at ease in any other place, any other role...and by the same token unable to see either Mabel or Myrtle really part of this latter day courtliness of it all.

"Anything else?" asked the waiter.

"I guess not," said Fudge, the wine stewardess disappearing with a soft kiss on Fudge's head...and they dug in...the light fading on the forest and the pool and golf course, Larry thinking that it must be gorgeous here in the Fall with all these oaks and sugar maples...oaks and maples and Death. Whispering to Windy inside him, as he stuck a piece of bordelaised sirloin into his mouth, *I can't believe it's coming to an end, that fifty years have gone by and all I've got left is another decade, maybe a little more, a little less*...tears of infinite longing in his eyes, *ewig, ewig*, eternity, eternity, Windy as always throatily compassionate, *You've got lots of time, mon cheri, lots and lots of time left, and you've always got me...I don't age...*

"You know that little Bryan slept in the same bed with Nina and me for the first five years after he was born," Chichi said, breaking into Larry's private little reverie, "I've had a couple of abortions and I'm Rh

Negative and I couldn't get pregnant...all this biological saudade...what's the word..."

Larry had to think a moment, but it was there.

"Longing."

"This primitive, instinctive biological 'longing,'...and then the three of us got 'married' down in Brazil with candles and rituals and everything and in a sense, when Bryan was born, he was our baby, belonged to all three of us. And that's the way he was raised to see it too. We even talked about my taking hormones and nursing him too. But then, when Myrtle came into the picture, Mabel totally changed and she dumped all three kids. Just dumped them. And little Bryan used to cling to me like a little chimp. Especially after she left on December 7th two years ago. Like he was all just 'shattered' and couldn't figure out why Mom wasn't around anymore. The same day we went out and bought a Christmas tree to cheer him up, distract him a little and she said she was coming over, but she never came. Decorating the tree, being with the boy and everything was a big thing for me and Bryan, but for her, she was like crazy, totally changed...."

"Why did she ever leave in the first place? Why did she feel she had to leave?" asked Larry, dispassionately clinical, the kind of distanced stance that always got doors to open slowly.

"She changed. She was having trouble with her job in the art department. They kept her on as permanent temporary, no tenure, no insurance, no retirement...hung by a thread and the thread was unraveling. She started hanging on to me. 'I got Bryan away from his first wife and now I'll get you away from him,' she told me one night. What kind of dominatrix crap was that? I hate to be anyone's blood- and air-source....you know what I mean?"

"Sure," said Larry, looking out the window, finishing the last dregs of his wine, his clinical distancing very easy for him, there but not there, the last touches of light in the sky, the night-presences coming alive again. Wasn't that a bat zinging by he maple trees? Myrtle's bat-soul. Hardly had touched his food, a little meat, a few green beans a nibble of potato and that was it.

"Can one smoke in here?" he asked.

"No problem," said Fudge and Larry lit up a charute. His first and last love after meals, even if the meal itself was only fragmentary. There was a time when he was at Northwestern when he smoked during all his waking hours, until his tongue was almost raw every night.

"Let me see if I get the sequences right, OK?" said Larry, taking a little spiral notebook out of his jacket pocket. He loved little notes, had whole shelves in his 'office' at home, filled with rows of little notebooks, pretend-intending that some day he was going to put them all together into a book, knowing that that day would never come, "Bryan, you go down to Brazil and meet Chichi and she moves in with you and Mabel. Ménage a trois."

"Actually Mabel brought Chichi home with her. Chichi was studying English. Her brother was going to Canada, she was in her early thirties, unmarried, no prospects, in Brazil, three-three and unmarried, you're an antique..."

"Come on!" Chichi objecting.

And rightly so, thought Larry. His kind of antique. Perfect life-size inflatable doll-machine.

"So, OK...from the beginning, Chichi belonged to Mabel."

"I didn't/don't 'belong' to anyone."

"Of course not, of course not," Larry all apologetic, humble, humbled, "but she wanted to make you exclusively hers..."

"And I played along a little. Mainly out of curiosity, just to see what I was capable of. We always had three-way sex, everything three-way, even the bank-accounts.But then, when we got back to the States, Mabel kept wanting to get rid of Bryan; and, to be honest, I started wanting to get rid of her..."

"Chichi!" Bryan objecting, "não e o momento de confessar tudo..."

"Maybe it is the time to confess everything!" Larry doing a little objecting on his own, then getting intensely back to his notes, "So you closed down on Mabel, and Mabel went out and got Myrtle..."

"It was so crazy. We actually started going out to Lesbian things together. Like shopping. And that's when Myrtle got a job at the lab where I was working. Myrtle convinced Mabel to get a job in the same lab and I guess we were supposed to be like three sisters or something.

THE LORD SAID UNTO SATAN

Only I was in love with Bryan and, besides, I wasn't very conspiratorial. Myrtle, I think, got the job in the lab with the specific purpose of stealing all the secrets. I was kind of half-in, half-out of the whole theft, and when I testified against Myrtle and Mabel, for them, anyhow, it was some sort of betrayal of a sacred trust. Only that's the way Myrtle was about everything. She was sacred, secret, clandestine, private...and everyone else 'out there' was just merde...what I think you'll find out is that the suspect list stretches all the way to Singapore," said Chichi, "and that's just here...there's probably a whole other list she'd developed down in Chicago."

"OK," said Larry, fumbling around in his coat jacket, taking out Woods' tentative list of suspects, "what about going down this list of suspects, giving me some idea what Myrtle did to each person on the list?"

"Well, I never was really that far 'inside' all the details," Fudge started to say, Larry all set to put the list back in his pocket, Fudge reversing himself, "well....let me take a look," curious as hell, glancing over the names, "OK, let's take Priscilla Pringle. By the time Myrtle zeroed in on Pris, she'd more or less taken over the whole shebang..."

"Which I really can't understand in the first place," said Larry, sucking on the last few drops in his wineglass, the way he used to make love to Windy, linger on, fight finishing, climaxing, "anyone that abrasive, nasty, negative, paranoid, how did she ever get a foothold in the power structure...?"

"Too bad you didn't have a chance to meet her," said Fudge almost sentimentally, "at her best she generated a sense of high urgency and excitement. She'd absolutely convinced Vest, the head of Futurotech, that she was some sort of Edison or Steinmetz or Pasteur and that production of The Pill was just around the corner if he'd throw in entirely with her. She was almost a kind of Gnostic Christ...tremendous charismatic voltage. Sometimes I was almost even convinced that, OK, she was personally an idiot, but professionally messianic. She certainly took Mabel in. Almost like demonic 'possession.' Demonic. Were there/are there angels and demons in this world or is it all just archaic myth?"

The waiter came over, meticulously checking and then removing the plates.

"And for dessert?"

"How about Snowballs all around?" suggested Fudge with fatherly overbearing.

"Snowballs in Hell," smiled Larry, "I'll try um, whatever they are."

"Me too. And a cup of decaf," said Chichi.

"And regular coffee for you gentlemen?"

"Why not," said Fudge.

"Fine for me too," agreed Larry.

Big deal, a cup of regular coffee. They should have taken what he had taken over the years...

Breaking off a part of his soul and sending it on a search inside his interior caves, looking for Windy, "Baby, where are you?," no answer in the immense hollow emptiness inside him, as if Myrtle had swallowed her up, smothered and drowned her...filled with a monumental sense of sadness, edge-of-suicideness, then her voice as small as a kitten when the Snowballs and the coffee came, *"Don't worry about me, my dearest dearest dear, plus tarde, mon cher, cher cheri...."*

Her voice as calming as a Peyote wafer. Relaxing now, everything balanced, static. Just as long as he knew she was there...waiting...

The Snowballs literally were snowballs of ice cream rolled in coconut and floating in a puddle of hot fudge.

"The best thing on the menu," said Fudge, "I'm not called Fudge for nothing. I'm a lot like my father. The older he got the more he subscribed to the philosophy that the greatest of all pleasures was FOOD. He was enormous when he died -- and enormously happy -- at age 75!"

"My father died at 50," answered Larry flatly, "which is a bit disconcerting as I move toward fifty-three. You're about forty-five, I'd guess, right?"

"Fifty-five actually," answered Fudge, "but Chichi did a facelift on me in Brazil while she was still surgerying. Plus hair-transplants, lots of tender loving care, megavitamins...."

THE LORD SAID UNTO SATAN

"Nothing wrong with a little honest vanity and survival instincts," said Larry digging into his Snowball. Almond-flavored ice cream sprinkled with an acrid, almond Viennese marzipanish topping.

In the single bitter-sweet marzipanish taste were hidden whole crumpled pages of Christmas memories for him. One of his mother's sisters who'd never left Saltzburg would always send them Marzipan. And they visited her, what was it, twice... Saltzburg...Vienna...snow and the Wienerwald and the faery Ringstresse that had so overwhelmed the young Adolph Hitler.

The Hapsburgs had tried.

"OK, " said Larry steering his mind back into the Now with difficulty, enjoying the swirl of memories gyrating around inside him like leaves after a heavy rain, being swirled down into sewers, "OK, so Bannister is messianically IN, in charge, Mein Furher, what does she do to Pringle?"

"Pringle's just had a baby and she's all tender breasts and maternity," answered Fudge, "she's a brilliant biochemist, her husband's in med school and she's torn between maternity and career, has this 'thing' about nursing her kid, but she's tied to the job, so...she starts to milk herself on the job..."

Chichi's face going all grapefruity.

"That always sounds so gross."

"But it really isn't," Fudge defensive, "maybe it was half an hour a day. Or less. She'd go into the women's John and milk herself into little bottles, I don't know, a couple of times a day. Then bring the bottles home and that's what the babysitter would feed him with the next day. Great immunization for the kid. And great for Pris too. Did you know that women who nurse have a much lower rate of breast cancer?"

"Out of my area!" said Larry, "Of course I'm in another phase of life now, much more interested in burial plots, headstones and wills than in the prophylactic problems of motherhood..."

"At any rate, Myrtle found out about the nursing and went crazy. She really did find it disgusting. 'Abomination,' was the word she used. And what the hell did it have to do with her? 'It's like public masturbation,' she'd say, "milking herself into a bloody bottle.' She went to Vest and complained about the time- loss, expanded it into a general picture of 'unprofessional behavior' -- and asshole Vest fired her. And not long afterwards she broke up with her husband. I don't think she's had a job since..."

"OK," said Larry, "what about Griller?," thinking that Fudge had to know about Griller's visit to his hotel room; he must have been on the Gnostic internet somewhere, mustn't he?

"Without going into details, whatever Griller had been doing, he'd been doing it for fucking twenty plus years... and six months after Myrtle appeared he was edged out of the department...kaput!"

"But, of course, he did fake results..."

"So?!?" Fudge not in the least surprised that Larry knew about the faked results bit and Larry not in the least surprised that he wasn't surprised, "Like I said, whatever he'd been doing he'd been doing with impunity for decades, and he'd still be doing it now, *if it hadn't been for Myrtle!!!*"

"But he should have been found out, shouldn't he?" asked Larry sipping on his coffee -- just a little touch of almond-flavoring in it too. Remembering Viennese sugar-covered almonds for a moment, a cold, snowy Viennese imperial Baroque corner for a moment, his grandmother's hand in his...then the word "Ewig/Eternity," Mahler's something or other, Ewig, ewig, ewig, for a moment as if he had been dead for a hundred years and was watching this whole scene on an old video tape...

"Not to mention the fact that Griller had been married for twenty years, and six months after Myrtle appeared on the scene, the marriage was over, and his wife and three kids had left town..."

"You're starting to make Myrtle sound like some sort of very unsubtle African virus," smiled Larry , looking back at his list, "What about Grump? And where do you get these names? Is there some kind of ugly name contest going on?, " wovon kommen diese Namen/where do these names come from, echoing obsessively through him for a moment.

"Just typical Michiganders, your average cross-section," said Fudge. "Although Grump kind of fits Grump, a little horse-toothed blonde with a lot of colic."

THE LORD SAID UNTO SATAN

"No, she's really a cutie," objected Chichi.

"If you've got a thing about overbite," insisted Fudge, "Well, Myrtle started this rumor circulating that Grump was Griller's girlfriend and that she'd helped him fake his results. Myrtle started checking and re-checking all of Grump's lab results and if nothing else proved that Grump was monumentally sloppy. She got bounced, no decent recommendation from the company, cracked up and had a breakdown and ironically ended up working for Myrtle's previous employer, an Englishman named Garrison over at Bio-Dynamics. Myrtle had had lots of problems over there."

"What kinds of problems?"

Fudge looked puzzled.

"No specifics. Myrtle's whole 'past' for all of us was always kind of all shadowy and vague...camouflaged..."

"There was something about her stealing notebooks," said Chichi, "data that she had accumulated on the job. She brought in the police and they served as peace officers when she went in and got her stuff. They were working on trans-species transplants...with the ultimate aim of using dog and monkey organs in humans..."

"One little thing sticks in my mind," said Fudge, "when Myrtle first came on the job at Futurotech, Griller knew Garrison over at Bio-Dynamids and Garrison had told him that Myrtle was bad news from beginning to end and by the time she had begun work Griller had spread the word 'Don't trust her. Work with her, but keep an eye on her.' Very prophetic."

"And also provocative," purred Larry, against his better judgment starting to see a lot of the case from Myrtle's perspective, "Myrtle's anger didn't just take shape in a vacuum."

"In a way it did," said Fudge sophistically, "she was always just excuses looking for causes...on the kill..."

"Galileo working for Geotech, so who owns the heliocentric theory?," asked Larry, lowering his voice to a sacred basso profondo, echo-chamber whisper, "An awful lot of macho-centro manipulative counterpoint seems to have been going on full time..."

Chichi and Fudge exchanging glances as the whole psycho-drama began to get wobbily shifted, as if Myrtle's giant, gaseous, spidery, tentacular Presence were there in the room again, something mushroomy and gaseous that you wanted to flush away, shoo away, smack with a fly swatter, turn on the air conditioner and drown out its all-pervasive, noxious little buzz.

Larry more aware of its (her) Presence than Chichi and Fudge could ever be; but almost welcoming it (her), her giant ugly face plastered ectoplasmically across the wall in front of him. The good guys may have been (somewhat) good, but were so overwhelmingly humdrum, righteous...

Larry sat back, suddenly immensely tired. It was dark outside now. Birds, bats, 'presences,' whatever was there, or whatever was emanating out from them, all erased by the blackness...and he was suddenly filled with an immense fatalistic indifference, as if it didn't make the slightest difference to him whether he and the whole world with him either were or weren't...looking for a raison d'etre for ever having been or not been. And not finding it.

"Well, I suppose I'd better get a little sleep. It's been..."

Laboriously getting up. Pains in his lower back. Tomorrow it would be his neck or shoulder or... travelling, vagabond pains that refused to settle down and stay in one place...

"We've enjoyed it," said Chichi, Fudge not saying anything, not exactly giving her a dirty look, but....

On the way back into town Larry riding in the back seat, much of the ride through dark fields, outlines of barns and clumps of trees on distant hills, newly sown fields, the farms and forests on which the university was originally based, Larry's mind begin to churn out questions again...

"Another little thing that's especially hazy, Mabel's leaving...after the three of you lived together for eight years very much in love, everything three-way...."

"Solomon had a thousand wives, why begrudge me two," said Fudge lamely.

"But what went wrong?"

"I didn't want to be uma viada any more," said Chichi bluntly.

THE LORD SAID UNTO SATAN

"But you didn't mind be 'queer' for eight years?!?"

"Mabel began to change, lose interest in Bryan, wanted to run away somewhere, just the two of us -- and the kids..."

"I don't know," Larry unconvinced, yawning a gigantic yawn, his jaws and chest hurting, esophagitis, or...hating the idea of coronary bypasses, never going to a doctor, let it just happen, as the leaves fall, so fall I, "Chichi comes into the marriage to get out of Brazil, emigrates to the U.S., gets totally involved with the Holy Trinity, tries to have a child, only that doesn't work, Mabel shares her child with her...what happened, from Holy Trinity to Holy Twosome, I mean, what the fuck..."

Larry stopped. No answer from the front seat, sat back, closed his eyes, died a short death....and when he opened them again they were back in town, in the middle of the vast institutional architecture of Michigan State, agricultural college beginnings, so be it, an imitation of the Ivy League, too much crassily modernistic claptrap, but here and there you'd see an old rough stone tower, a nicely antique slice of red brick wall covered with newly sprouting ivy, pretensions that slowly "worked," took on their own patina, the same way Harvard had copied Oxford-Cambridge, and it had worked too...

"Back among the living?" Fudge asked, looking at him through the rear-view mirror.

"Not quite!," yawned Larry, thinking that maybe it was time to just retire and be old, something he'd never imagined he'd become -- until now.

"You're a bit of an over-simplifier, aren't you?" Fudge asked nastily, a little bit of "Bunny" (with claws) in his tone.

"I don't think so, if I'm going to have to take sides, I guess I can see it more easily from Mabel's point of view. And if Myrtle Bannister were half the heart of darkness character you paint her to be, you're lucky you're both still alive....," said Larry, toying, probing, playing...as they moved into the ritzier-snitzier latest-thing neighborhoods, and then slowly back, toward their place, through the 30's, 20's, 10's...the fin de siecle...

Their street the most picturesque (oldest?) of all. It really was like walking into a scene from Our Town...Amerikanski Neo-classical, crickets cricketing, a bunch of preppy students walking down the middle of the street in the direction of...what? the bars?

"If I were going to kill Myrtle," said Fudge as they got out of the car, "I would have done it around the time of the divorce trial, or...I'll tell you when...when the cops picked me up and I was 'investigated' for sexually molesting my little boy, based on some asshole tape that Mabel and Myrtle made up, Myrtle asking him 'Did your father ever put anything into your mouth?,' and the kid answering 'Yeah, gum,' and Myrtle said 'Gunk? He put gunk in your mouth?' It would have been easy to kill her off when I saw the transcript of that tape supplied to me by some police agency in Chicago, I forget the name...but I wouldn't have done it with a bucket of fucking gasoline, " Fudge turning to Chichi, "remember that antique show we went to in the Meridian Mall, that nineteenth century gun with the broken firing pin? It was like the perfect way to get an unregistered gun and, I'll be honest, I almost got it, got it fixed and made a surprise visit to Chicago. I've never been so fucking mad in my life...never felt that murder was so justified...that's when I started doing Zen every night, and began to write Haiku..."

"But the kids are still all down in Chicago. Mabel and Myrtle won! Why should the anger have gone away?" asked Larry wearily, an old Samurai who just wanted to find a bank opposite a waterfall in a scroll painting and lie down and fall asleep.

"The anger didn't go away, but I've been just waiting, Mabel's been sick, heart and lung problems, always thinking 'eventually, eventually'...what if she just died/dies...?" said Bryan fatalistically.

"Kids just all go off to the four winds anyhow. Like birds," said Larry fatalistically , "Mine are gone. The empty nest...and the mother peahen, my wife, is almost dead....did you ever see Ugetzu? You get replaced..."

Another Samurai moment.

Zen-Tibetan dissolving, then Bryan occidentalizing back into the Now.

"Yeah, I almost forgot," getting up and going into the house, coming back with a little French string shopping bag full of cassettes, "I've got

THE LORD SAID UNTO SATAN

these tapes, random thoughts about Mabel and the case...I made a set of copies for you."

"OK, OK," said Larry, Mr. Pre-Media primitive, ashamed to even admit that he didn't own a cassette player, would pick up one tomorrow, "Listen, it's been..."

Been what?

Shaking hands, walking down the front steps that could use a little paint, across the street to his car, loving the ambience, jeito, essence, house, trees, the decaying almost historical quaintness of a past a faint hundred years old, a living Spoon River Anthology...like a dimly lit up river boat, a carriage on the celestial railroad, nineteenth century normality that had been invaded by exactly what...?

Only then, as he opened his car door and looked back again and waved goodbye, he saw the white porch, columns, windows, like a giant skull. He didn't have to wait 30, 20, 10 years to die, he was already dead...remembering his father for a moment, after he'd had his massive heart attack and a paper-thin ventricular aneurysm had developed that could rupture at any moment...not wanting to really "interact" with anyhow...somehow hollow, drained, ghostly...just waiting for "it" to happen....

Maudit, maudit, maudit...damned, damned, damned...

He got into his car, and they stood on the front porch and waved and he waved back, almost as if it had all been family, a visit to his kids, brother, sister...at least best friends...and then he pulled away from the curb and dissolved into the sulfuric acid darkness...

CHAPTER 8

Larry drove back to the Kellogg Center and parked in the parking structure. There was this "patch of civilization," buildings all bunched together, parking structure, hotel, dorm across the street. But then beyond, between parking structure and hotel, a walkway that led into primal blackness, the smell of a river, the ominous, amorphous shapes of giant, ancient trees hulking in the waiting blackness. He already heard the tissue paper voice folded inside the soft Spring air, "Blasphemer...blasphemer...blasphemer..."

Wind through the willows.

A sense of the darkness pulling on him, spirit-winds blowing him toward the river. But instead of going riverward he forced his way up to the snazzy new Art Deco entrance to the hotel.

"Fuck this shit, man!"

Stopping at the door itself as if there were some sort of invisible force-field blocking his entrance that didn't seem at all to touch other guests walking around him unaffected, "Excuse me," "Excuse me," feeling, somehow, that he ought to follow the pull into the invisible world surrounding and engulfing the visible, a jaguar-shaman sacred-drug initiated Traveler Between Worlds, Hermes-Massau eater of the thorn-apples of immortality, the heavy mist-voices from the world tree at the world center calling to him to come home to die, be shredded and then reassembled....

Weri rawha hitkasharu

The visions are coming...

Uruhurihi!

Let it be so!

And he gave in totally to the pull of the voices-forces, *for this I was born, for this I came...was trained...*

Walking between the parking structure and the hotel now into the moaning whirlpool darkness, out of the fringes of light into the ever-deepending darkness, totally alone, each step a step back a thousand years into the territory of the most ancient gods...

THE LORD SAID UNTO SATAN

The trees here from earlier, dawn ages, the university a recent transplant on to this sacred soil. Walking into whorls of shadows, the trees getting denser and denser as he lost himself among their ancient arches. It was all an untouched preserve here and the trees were left as they fell; what grew grew, what perished perished, the gods were in charge, not man. Following the pull of the river until he finally found himself down on its banks, feeling that other hims in other lives had been here a thousand thousand times before.

He sat down on a grassy bank overlooking the river and waited...waited until the rest of the world went to sleep and night thickened and clotted and began to swirl around him in strands of living tentacular fog...until he began to feel her presence again, knew what was coming next and sat cross-legged and hunched-over like a dead man. Let her come in and possess him, let her win, that's how she would lose...until the fog-ropes wrapped oppressively around him and he was totally 'contained' and bound and she thought she had him. Evil from the four quarters of Night and Eternity. In the beginning was the Word, instantly matched by the Anti-Word, Light, Anti-Light, life, decay...

GOOD!

The whole area was boxed-in now and self-contained, cut off from the rest of the universe. He was totally alone in the heart of dead, limp Negativity, forcing himself to stay as passive as he could, allowing the fog to circle around and around him, beginning to hear her short sniffs and rumbling growls, like distant, accelerating thunder, carefully shielding his thoughts from her probes. "Come on! Come on!" Totally drained, a pair of lobster claws hidden under a rock-ledge at the bottom of the darkest seas.

NOW!

He almost wanted her to know how much he longed for The Encounter as the growls and sniffing intensified and suddenly she was there, incarnate in front of him, flesh like rancid mould, spotted and splotched lard, cheese-flesh, bloated white inner-tube flesh, decaying rubber stitched splitting on to the surface of Night, anti-worlds of eyes and howling mouths condensing in the blackness above the river, her body limitless and only spottily defined, rasping, grating tentacles, nightmarish epiphanies of the other side of the divine coin.

As he reached out to grab her, her mushy, toilet-plunger mouth folded in around his face, and she inflicted the first rasping sucker-foot slashes on his arm ("Blasphemer!"), the drooling saliva burning hot and acid on his skin ("You will pay for your blasphemies!!"), as he rose up up, hollow now ("How dare you question I WHO AM?!?!"), his eyes and mouth starting to glow, moving in slow motion, every pore exuding light, beginning to expand so that his body became glowing dough clouds of light, funnel-circling around into a radiant noose that even she, Tiamat-Gorgon, could never guess would...

TIRAWA
TIRA-WA ATIUS,
FATHER OF US ALL,
OLD FIRE GRANDFATHER HEART OF TIME...
Aaurgh!

The fire-noose crisp bacon crackling now, circling around her slimy throat, her amorphousness slowly getting defined by frying, searing fire...

Trying to counter-encircle him with her barbed tentacles but with every suck, bite, touch, every lash out to suck the fire out of him, the air thickened with the fishy stench of charred slime.

He pulled tighter and tighter.

TIRAWA
TIRI

Circling above her now, *Oh, Fire Grandfather, center of the forge, cross, crucible, NOW, NOW!!!*

And he pulled his fire-rope body so tight around her thick throat that she began to spasm and gag, her eyes becoming silent-screaming saucers of terror, Larry enjoying the sweet irony of how her second death was becoming a replay of her first death, understanding what the witnesses who had been there must have felt to see her writhe burning into Hell, Grandfather Fire against Grandmother Sea. It was either strangle him, break loose or...feeling himself starting to slip and melt, liquefying, fighting to re-stabilize, -solidify...WILL, WILL, WILL...

THE LORD SAID UNTO SATAN

And then suddenly she was gone and the night was holy again, his fire-rope body circling around a dead center of total emptiness.

And the Vision rushed in -- in the middle of elaborate Shang-Chavín circles of Baroque oriental fire, he saw an office, a woman at a Xerox machine, a hippo-hips in blue acetate pants, wearing a yoke-necked pink acetate blouse, a face as round and brown as a barrel-lid, the skin leather, 'tanned,' a beer-drinker's tan, sitting drinking coffee now, looking up, directly at him, startled, aware that there was a window on her world...then the vision closing down like a stone door and he was back as simply "him" sitting on the bank of the river, a young couple walking by, kissing, screwing around. As he struggled to his feet, startling them without meaning to, the girl squeaking and whining, the guy all macho mortal combat raw, "Hey, man, what the fuck..."

"Sorry, I'm sorry. Sumimasen. Gomen nasái."

Walking up from the riverbank and making his way back to the Kellogg Center, high and flying in the midst of simple hallelujahs of lights and automatic sliding doors. How many hours had it been? The dining room closed, lobby empty, lights low, messianic hushed lauds of sacral medieval stone calm starting to whisper through the cloisters and vaults inside the center of his down-boy(!), calmate (!) soul.

Half way through the door he looked up and saw the whole facade lurching top-heavy toward him, the building itself growling deep circus-drum earthquake growls, "Blasphemer. How do you DARE?"

Ancient tophets of blasphemous skull-temple profanations...alive but still stenching of moldy, flayed flesh stretched across the surface of the building. He could hardly move/breathe, while she was ready for Round Two.

Gave up. Simply gave up, seemed to give up, let only the giving-up surface of his soul stay visible, careful to hide whatever other plans, thoughts, hatreds he had bubbling inside him, turned and went back to the parking structure ignoring the stench that hovered over him in the sky, waiting for her to descend, knowing he had secret, deep-well Old Grandfather Fire reservoirs of strength that he could draw on if need be. But she was all show, wasn't it.

Getting into his car and driving over to Buckley's, feeling the tension decrease as he neared the house, the graduated progressions out of Horror into Neutral, then Peace, Venus bright in the East, waiting for the sun. He made the sign of the Venus-Cross in his mind as he got out in front of Buckley's house:

Sacred Morgenstern/Morning Star, Lord of the four (dots) quarters, New Sun, Ahau, Apu, Little Lord.

And how, now to target in on Ms. Lard-Ass Acetate?!?

WHO was she? And how now to follow the thread of Old Grandfather Fire's vision into Realtime? How many times during his long, corroded, eroded, rusting out, patched and repatched career, had The Vision come, hovered, vanished, and the Case never been solved?!?!? As if Old Grandfather Fire himself could never again totally reincarnate into Real time again....

There was one light in the Fudge house -- downstairs, living room.

Larry rang the doorbell, wondering, wondering, wondering about Ms. Acetate Lard ass. Could she have been the woman who had been milking herself? What was her name, Grunch, Bunch, Crunch...? Is this what it meant to be an aging shaman, rib-pains, shoulder-pains, twisted ankles and a rusting memory?

Fudge came to the door and turned on the front-porch light, didn't seem the least bit surprised to see Larry.

"Come on in, I'm just watching Pagnol's Caesar. Do you know Pagnol's work?"

"I'm not much into films," said Larry coming in, "I was wondering if..."

"Myrtle always said that that area around there, the Beal Gardens, that stretch of river, were her private reserve."

"Everything seems so sacred, calm, 'protected' here."

Six o'clock Mass every morning for twenty years, Our Lady of Peace, him, the priest, the organist and the cold, dark gods.

"Let's see, we've got this great back room. The old man who died in the house, had it built for himself so he wouldn't have to

walk up stairs...," Fudge leading Larry back through the living and dining rooms, the TV and VCR on but blank blue, feeling even a little more guilty about having interrupted Fudge's viewing-time...curious as to what he had been watching...Panyol?

"Twenty five years after having bought the house, I'm beginning to understand all that stairs-bit. In the summer I come down here to escape the heat, when Fall comes, I reluctantly leave and start hiking up the stairs again..."

"Nice room...very nice..."

Wood ceiling. Spacey punk-face drawings all over the white plaster walls, very eightyish replays of sixties originals.

"My daughters and their friends did those -- BEFORE MY DAUGHTERS WERE TAKEN AWAY..."

The air ionized momentarily with wailing ghost-octopus presences...and then, WHOOSH, Kyrie eleison, Christi eleison, they were all squeegeed off the windshield again.

Bed on the floor. Wood rack, futon, red-shaded lamp hanging over the orange and yellow lotus-patterned bedspread, an old rustic oak-cabineted stereo next to the bed. The room had its own bathroom and there was an antique oak dresser over by the bathroom door, psychedelic people-floating 60's posters all over the walls, a big oak rack of CD's on top of the dresser, next to a rack of cassette tapes.

"If you want to listen to some of my meditation-tapes, the originals are all up here," said Fudge, going into the bathroom, coming back with a white terrycloth robe, going into the dresser and pulling out an enormous pair of pajamas.

"These ought to do the job. I bought them down in Buenos Aires one time, after one particularly well-fed year. Talk about sausages!! That was the year, man."

"Right on," Larry smiled, patting his belly, "'diet' always sounds just a little too much like 'die' to me..."

"You wanna to watch Pagnol with me?"

"Nah, I'll be lucky to even manage a shower, wash off the sins of the world and all that," said Larry, qui tollis peccato mundo, feeling like a cross between a rotting chicken thigh and a chunk of moldy acorn squash.

"OK, pal, dorme bem, sleep well, the door locks from the inside."

"Yeah, I'm really worried," Larry feeling totally at home, feeling guiltily compromised and sold-out for a moment then "Screw that!," moving over toward the bed, stopping, turning, in mid-step, "One last thing,among the suspects is there any very fat woman who likes dark blue acetate pants-suits, drinks a lot, is red -, leather-faced, bangs across the forehead, works in a (Larry calling up the vision again, details he hadn't noticed before) totally glass-'cage' office, coffee machine over to one side, xerox machine on the other, all the vertical supports grey..."

Fudge stopping, something inside him stopping, the Earth itself stoppint and all the buildings and mountains beginning to tumble down in beautiful clouds of pure chaos, a look of angry defensiveness involuntarily spreading across Fudge's face for a moment, defensiveness, terror and then rage.

"Amanha!/Tomorrow! OK?"

"Copping in, copping out...OK."

Fudge making a very visible and happily successful yogic tug toward re-disintegrating/-centering...

"So have a good sleep!"

"And the fat-ass in blue?" the Gila-monster in Larry's brain refusing to let go, grinding its poison-jaws back and forth in Fudge's flesh.

"Amanha!/Tomorrow!," Fudge very aware of Larry's mind-probes trying to get inside him, closing doors, putting up screens.

Larry pissed, unsuccessfully pushing and pushing at the screens inside Fudge's mind, feeling so close and yet light-years away, Windy inside him purring *Calm down, cutie, scissors never cut stone, play the game!!!*

Calming down, the archer becoming the arrow, the calligrapher the brush, the swordsman the sword, the detective the murderer and the crime, the name of the woman on the tip of his/their (collective) tongue...I...I....

Then gone entirely.

"Thanks for nothing!" said Larry.

"Come on, come on, you don't want me to kill your bulls for you," smiled Fudge sardonically, gently closing the door, Larry standing there listening to Fudge's footsteps receding, creaking across the old floor-

THE LORD SAID UNTO SATAN

boards under the padded rug, locking the door-knob lock, checking the locks on the windows, looking in the full closet (all full of Bunny's [?] feather boas and El Cheapo black draped acetate dresses), then went over to the dresser and took out one of Fudge's "Think Tapes" (Meditations, XIV, November, 1989) and stuck it in the stereo, plugged in a pair of earphones he found on the floor next to the set, put them on, opened the stiflingly tight top button of his shirt, pushed Play, lay down on the futon fully clothed.

He should brush his teeth, shower...but not tonight, telling himself "Deixa, deixa, let it be, let it be," as Fudge's deep, anguished (stereoed) voice flooded into his ears:

This whole breakup is so tragic because it's such a common ("Common!") end to an uncommon relation-ship. WE WERE THE GREAT LOVERS! And now our love becomes the metaphor for universal change and dissolution. Volney's Ruins. Going through ruined Ur or Mohenjo Daro and realizing that the dead streets and houses and temples all once teemed with very ordinary, very daily LIFE...

How can Mabel taking Snarling Dog Myrtle seriously? It's her true nature to snarl at strangers, and seeing that everyone always ultimately remains strangers....

Myrtle is the fire, Mabel the coal, Myrtle the finger, Mabel the trigger, Myrtle the chalk, Mabel the blackboard...

I can't really blame Mabel for the child-molesting bullshit. I can see the whole scene replaying in my mind. Myrtle sees something on the TV or reads something in the newspaper about using child-molestation charges against the father in order to get custody, Mabel nods assent, out comes the tape recorder. Myrtle simply does, no resistence, unimpeded kinetic wartime mentality energy.

And Mabel's pure moudability...Aristotelian potentiality/Material Cause, Myrtle the lead-soldier mould and Mabel the liquid lead. Which hurts me infinitely more than if it were the other way around, because for more than 20 years I worshipped Mabel as Morning Star and Evening Star, lighting me to bed, there to begin the day with at every dawn. And all she really was was a sucker-headed tapeworm sucking shit in my bowels, the same way she's living in Myrtle's bowels sucking Myrtle's shit....

Larry reached over and turned off the tape. Genug! Genug!

A little music. Should call home, check things out again...and yet again, and again. Too late. Amanha/Mañana. Uneasy about "presences" out beyond the windows in the crawling darkness.

Myrtle out there still waiting for him.

"Take it easy!," Windy's voice uncoiling like an ermine boa inside him, "Mama Windy's here to take care of you, just stretch out, kick off your shoes, feel your toes and your legs..." He kicked off his shoes, *"Head back and forth, squished into the pillow, skin under soft blankets, focus in on untensing/softening your neck muscles and shoulder joints, become a mindless skinball, skin-tube...let go...I'm waiting for you just on the other side of consciousness..."*

He let go and there she was on the terrace at The Club, Maxine just had had her brain cancer surgery and he'd left her down at Passavant, couldn't stand the idea of going home to lunch alone, and so he went over to The Club.

Windy all by herself wearing a wide-brimmed airfoil chiffon hat that looked like Brasilia, a chiffon dress, all sorts of bushy, luxuriant, maid-with-the-the-flaxen-hair hair pulled back into a loosely-tied pony tail, tied with an enormous orange chiffon bow.

Bacchus, Bacchanal, Gaia, Pound's first Canto, The Birth of Dionysius...

"I wonder if... may I join you?"

And when she turned full-face toward him, he was amazed at how young she was and, close-up, not really pretty. The first word that came to mind was 'grainy.'

"I'd loved to be joined," she said and he sat down, on another level, in a simultaneous other dream, crying in his sleep now, feeling the years of remorse and separation. Fudge and his lost love/children, what about his own lost love (s)?!?! And if his children weren't lost, they certainly were in absentia.

"Do you come here often alone?" he asked as he sat down.

THE LORD SAID UNTO SATAN

"Not often!" she said, like a Renoir cow, a smile of great primaveral power, *""C'est le premior fois/The first time!"*

"Le premier fois? Pour moi aussi....it's the first time alone here for me too...like this," and she extended her flower-chiffon-gloved hand, which he gently kissed, lingering on its carefully calibrated softness.

"I'm Windy...."

"And so," he almost said, but didn't, merely gave his name, *"is the day, the world, my soul..."*

The tears kept coming, but on the terrance in the wind and the wash of sunlight and shadow, other levels of lamentation and loss hardly seemed to matter.

CHAPTER 9

The next morning Larry woke up to the smell (and noise) of Fudge toasting English muffins and making coffee, the strong smell of amaretto stamped on the air. Even stronger than what was becoming his own fetid, garbage dump stench.

Larry came out of the downstairs bedroom, waved at Fudge, "Smells good..if I may use the phone...my calling card...."

"Whatever."

"Chichi?"

"She's already been working for an hour."

9:05 on the kitchen clock, just over the stove. Dialled home. An hour earlier in Chicago.

A male voice answered.

"Tarzan!"

"Tarzan who?" Larry played along.

"Tarzan Stripes Forever, yak, yak, yak, yak, is that you Larry?"

Mrs. Barker's almost-husband. After years of seesawing around it looked pretty close now.

"How ya doin'? What's new?"

Sudden seriousness on the other end of the line.

"Things have been getting pretty crazy around here. We tried to call you at your hotel, but...Sylvia's upstairs with the doctor. Let me bring the phone up to her..."

"OK, I.....," not wanting to even think what he was thinking. Windy, in their brief few heydays/hay days, always urging him to put Maxine into some nursing facility fulltime, like putting a dog in a kennel, *"Put her away somewhere, for her good as much as ours, you know she's going to outlast us all!,"* and he always had always expected her to outlast him with his diabetes and high blood pressure and all his fat, had always been sure that he'd go like his father, 49, 50...and he was already 52.

THE LORD SAID UNTO SATAN

"Hello, Mr. Gugel...," Mrs. Barker on the line, "It's been pretty bad. She's had some convulsions, started vomiting. I called Dr. Renikoff and he109.
wants to put her in the hospital, wants to talk to you...."
Resnikoff on the phone, techy, tough, oceans of compassion, the best brain-man in the world.
"It looks bad, Larry, it looks like another stroke. First the cancer, then the surgery, the radiation, the stroke, now number two. I'm afraid the time's come to put her somewhere where she can get the around-the-clock care she's going to need..."
"I'll be back in...I don't know...a couple of days...a week, can it wait until then?" Larry feeling like he was talking to his dead father or God the Father or some elder star-man space-ambassador from Galaxy Z.
"Well, she's in a coma right now. She's got to go into the hospital immediately..."
"I should wrap things up here in a couple of days...," repeated Larry, for a moment wondering what he was doing there at all, this particular murder seeming less and less a murder every minute, more and more like some sort of inevitable, natural event, like a flood, earthquake, meterorite shower..."
"Larry, I'll be blunt -- stay away a year. It doesn't make any difference. You can't do anything here anyhow. You want to talk to Mrs. Barker again? I don't know if she'll ever know the difference again...you get to the end of the line, pal, you get to the end of the line..."
"Yeah, sure..."
Mrs. Barker back on the phone.
"I'm sorry Larry..."
"Yeah, me too, listen...,' stopping, choked up, trying to refocus, took a deep breath, forced the words out, " there's no sense your staying around full time once Maxine's in the hospital, maybe you can just come in, take care of the dog a little or put him in a kennel. No change in salary. Do what you think is best..."
Total trust in the woman.
"I'm so sorry, Larry..."

"Me too," he said, added a labored, clotted "I love you," Mrs. Barker a kind of substitute for his dead sister who had died of leukemia at twelve, the only reason Larry's parents had had him at all, to substitute for her.

"Me too, Larry, you know that."

Hanging up, filled with a tremendous urge to simply break, break down, everything always vanishing, vanishing away, his father's heart-attack that he wished he'd never seen, falling down in the bathroom, blood out of his nose, then his mother's slow, devouring cancer, until there was nothing left of her but a small, numb, mute, curled-up-on-itself shell...his dead sister...his absentee kids...

"Bad news?" asked Fudge, Larry standing in the doorway, afraid to get any closer to Fudge, what which his stench and all.

"My wife's had a second stroke. I suppose I should be here at all...e sou bem cheiroso," lifting up his arm, sniffing at his armpit.

"Shower after breakfast," said Fudge, "and I'll give you some fresh clothes...I've got too much of everything anyhow," and Larry walked in and sat down at the kitchen table, allowed himself to be passively served. A little goiabada/guava jelly on a well-buttered English muffin, a heavy sugar-dosed cup of amaretto-laced coffee.

He practically snorted the muffins down. Snort, snort, snort snort, downed the coffee non-stop...

"Who needs heavier drugs than these?" he laughed, "caffeine for me is everyone else's cocaine."

"Too bad about your wife!" Fudge reaching over and patting Larry on the shoulder. None of the usual gringo taboos about men not touching men.

"Yeah, she was/is a great woman, the only person I ever knew he was above, beyond fashion. She'd had it all since she was born. Her father had one of the great fortunes of Europe. Czech. Jewish. Got all the money out before the Anschluss..."

"There weren't many who did," Fudge lowering his head for a moment in a kind of momento mori silent prayer/meditation.

Larry joining him.

Then reaching over and getting a second muffin.

THE LORD SAID UNTO SATAN

A jar of Nutella. Just opened. Chocolate, hazelnut, one of his favorite things in the world. Spread it on thick, then added a little guave past, closed his eyes, chewed, enjoyed.

"Yeah, you never know how long you've got!" Fudge said, "the Angel of Death's always out there just waiting. And ten years later you're a bunch of old pictures in a trunk -- if you're lucky."

The two of them sitting there in silence for a few minutes, then Fudge getting up, going upstairs and coming down with a pair of white pants and a white shirt, some jockey shorts and a white tank top.

"Here, these ought to do the trick."

"Great, great," said Larry, taking a clean spoon and dipping it in the Nutella. Sucking on the spoon. Slow. No hurry. Feeling even more than usual that everything was porous, melting, vanishing. He if'd looked down and seen his leg begin to dissolve, he wouldn't have been surprised.

Then the spoon was sucked clean, he was tempted to try one more scoop but resisted the temptation, got up.

"Great breakfast."

Evoking Belém, João de Pesso, the Brazilian coast south of Rio...

"We try to get down to Brazil at least once a year," said Fudge, "keep in touch with paradise."

Larry smiling, giving a little wave, into the bathroom, all filled with fancy soaps and back-washers and shampoos.

"OK."

Turning on the shower and dousing himself liberally with patchouli shower gel, washing his hair with papaya shampoo, feeling it was OK, just to have lived, just to have BEEN, once, once in the rainforests, the Santa Marta mountains, the Urubamba valley. He'd be joining Maxine in Never-Never Land soon enough, spending lots of time wondering how he'd go too -- a stroke, heart attack, cancer. Always wanting just a kiss-of-God death. A sudden pain and auf wiedersehen....

Getting out of the shower and rubbing himself dry with a luxuriantly large white towel.

They knew how to live, these two!

Put on the clothes that Fudge had given him. Perfect fit. Took his own fetid clothes and carefully folded them into a little bundle, fished an empty plastic bag out of the wastepaper basket in the bathroom and stuff his stuff in it, said a silent goodbye to the charming French-windowed room he'd slept in, the big old elaborately-carved cherry wood bed he'd slept on top of.

Heavy, big trees outside. All just beginning to come back to life.

Fudge in the kitchen doing the dishes, when Larry came out, turning off the water, drying his hands.

"OK, pal, not such a bad fit."

Fudge walking him to the front door, Larry filled with curiosity about all the artifacts covering the walls, on built-in shelves covered over, museum-style, with low-glare glass, feeling it was a house you could spend years in, just studying pots and spear-points, pieces of Neo-Inca weaving, carvings of Morning Star gods from Amazonas....

"Thanks for everything," said Larry and the two men embraced for a moment, very Brazilianized, "primitive," primal, basic...

"Good luck!"

Fudge standing there and waving what seemed a perfectly sincere and good-humored wave as Larry drove away thinking sadly "My luck, your DOOM!"

THE LORD SAID UNTO SATAN

CHAPTER 10

Pym Hall. Room 005, a hideaway stuck at the end of a subterranean tunnel at the bottom of a massive Norman style brick pile of a building that looked more like a medieval fortress than a lab.

Door open, Mascher sitting behind a massive oak desk studying graphs, a TX-400- stereo over in the corner, an old Glen Gould CD on, The Goldberg Variations, Gould ,as always, humming away recklessly to himself as he played.

Mascher looked like an aging Semitic Apollo with just a curl of a Dionysian sneer about his full, sensuous lips. Full head of stormy, graying hair. Lots of aerobics and cottage cheese. Lots of pool, saunas and soft sofas. Lots of nooky.

Larry knocked on the door frame. No reaction. You'd have thought Mascher could have smelled him...Mr. Patchouli...

"Hell-o-o!"

Still no reaction, Larry finally marching into the office like Alexander the Great, and slouched bulkily in front of the desk like a big bag of dirty clothes.

"I'll be right with you," said Mascher out of a deep resonating well of concentrated intellectuality, still not looking up.

There was an old oak wingback chair right next to where Larry was standing. He decompressed, sat down and waited.

Of course Mascher knew who he was and why he was there. This whole super-meditation gig was pure charade.

Larry closed his eyes, The Goldberg Variations disappeared and he was inside the low, guttural roar-rumble of Tibetan Buddhistic lion-chanting. Himalayas and Andes merged and Yama charged roaring across the cracker dry landscape, as Larry slid into his own private internal (OMMMMMMMMMMMMM) void.

It could have been a minute or a thousand years, when Mascher's voice finally condoned down through the dead air into the frozen sanctuary at the center of Larry's soul, "What can I do for you?" Larry slowly digging up through crystallized Lagoa Santa mammoths to the thawing surface of a very feeble, hardly-worth-the-trouble now.

"Detective Gugel, Grimore Park PD," slowly reconstituting himself in the present, again filled with an unshakeable feeling that he ought to be somewhere else, some pass in the Himalayas, his final last steps to his final last shrine, walking into the spider heart center of the Great God Krazny's million and one alabaster-lapis lazuli arms, "and you know why I'm here, although I have to advise you that you don't have to answer anything before consulting with an attorney, and anything you do say can be used against you."

Mascher staring at him with fixed, cold, black marble, bottom-of-the-Atlantic-trough fish-eyes.

"Something about Myrtle Bannister's tripping on a roller skate and falling into the Grand Canyon?." starting to laugh, like a lion roaring, his chest as resonant as the Carlsbad Caverns, Lascaux, "What a pity. I was such a fan of hers. Brilliant woman. Since she's left the whole Royal Jelly Project's turned into Royal merde...."

"What about Myrtle's repeating Finkelstein's allegations about your being a rank amateur, a kind of slick professional fraud -- in front of the assembled notables of Futuro Tech?!?"

"I'm afraid you've been misinformed," Mascher suddenly reptilianly cold, cerebral, "Myrtle and I were the best of pals. In fact, I adored those massive legs and breasts of hers. If she hadn't been queer.... All sorts of juicy Dionysian depths under that intellectualoid Apollonarian surface. I used to imagine her and Mabel making love, the shear technical wizardly...."

"Such a freaky coincidence that you were at the Microbiology Convention in Chicago on the day of her murder..."

"Along with every other microbiologist worth his salt, at the annual Microbiology Association convention."

For a moment Larry troubled with the idea that Mascher was a spirit of some sort, that this whole Myrtle Bannister business was some sort of demonic war that he had no business touching at all. Then daring: "Still, there's all that business about Myrtle attacking you last year and your standing up and saying 'You've ruined my life.' Something to that effect.

THE LORD SAID UNTO SATAN

Although," Larry looking around at the stereo, the tweed jacket hanging in the corner, the rows of notebooks in bookcases along the walls, the electronic microscope and all the other highest tech equipment, "you don't look too ruined to me."

Mascher closing his eyes in an act of self-containment and control, as if he were about to turn into someone-something else if he didn't put on the brakes hard, his voice turning into a swaying hooded cobra, about to strike, "Prove something, asshole. Get real, already...do you have any hint of what you're dealing with here? Open your eyes, get out of the nightmare."

Opening his eyes, reptilian now, the irises elongated, yellow, dead...

"As if I'd never before been where you are," said Larry, taking off, an eighteen foot wingspan, gliding toward the world-tree at the world-center, embracing inevitable death...rebirth...feeling his hands begin to turn into jaguar paws, his canines begin to lengthen and taper.., "What about , what's her name, the fatso in the blue acetate pants-suit?"

This time taking a massive effort on Mascher's part to keep it all tied down and under control, massive green-black coils beginning to uncoil inside him, his jaws starting to unhinge...his voice a thin carbonated hiss now...

"Why don't you just get the fuck out of here..."

Larry feeling his claws begin to unlock and bend open, finding himself hungry for a fight in the Spirit-World, holding himself in, thinking of the four millionth and first hand of The Great God Krazny, all rubies and emeralds, with black tourmaline fingernails that he started to bend down to kiss....

So the acetate bitch was the Keeper of the Keys.

The Great God Krazny lifting his four millionth and first hand, his burning-sun comet-tail voice filling the limitless caverns of Larry's shaman-soul, pushing Larry away, lifting him to his feet, "Now!!! The whole room filling with the smell of burning flesh, the Jaguar Nagual Chilam Balam Shaman in Larry rising to his full height, the serpent and the rainbow, the serpent in the tree in the center of the world whose teeth had to be sown for the year to begin again, standing larger than a hundred lives, flaming-prophet-eyed in front of Mascher's demon deathhead, roaring "You rotten son-of-a-bitch," as he psychoplasmically-instinctively, reached down for the top left drawer of Mascher's desk, Mascher trying to stop him, but Larry pushing him away, pulling the drawer slowly open...where there was...

An old picture of a very youngish Myrtle at the bottom of the otherwise empty drawer, a javelin in one hand, about to launch off into victory with long, lean legs and enormous breasts,

Herakles among the ant-people, the glass on the picture broken and lines radiating out from the heart, like it had been stabbed with a screwdriver. And glued to the head a chunk/lock/wad of half-charred hair, and for the first time Larry saw a flesh-colored bandage around Mascher's wrist, and suddenly he was there watching Mascher rushing forward toward Myrtle's burning body, a blunt child's little paper scissors in his hand, snipping off a lock of the burning hair as if he needed a trophy, relic, proof of the fact that she had really been finally consumed...

Mascher not alone in the vision, other forms and faces flickering on the sidelines, it was a Kali yuga Fifth Sun sacrificial Sabbath sacrifice, only to WHOM, WHAT, WHY...? Tiamat versus...?

Larry suddenly humbled and confused by his ignorance about the complexity of the politics of the Netherworld...but grabbing the picture and the hair, some sort of vodoo-pilgrim impulse inside him especially anxious to get a real-life sample of Myrtle's hair...

"Get out of this one, you bastard!" said Larry in a deep, resolating Tibetan dream snow-leopard chant-whisper-growl. Mascher grabbing the picture back out of Larry's hands.

"What does it prove, asshole, that we were disillusioned lovers?" Mascher's voice full of calm savannahs and plateaus. Mascher standing there in imperial Roman triumph, lifting the picture up in his hands, an anti-Moses with anti-world tablets on an anti-world Sinai...

And all of a suddenly Larry simply didn't care any more, all the wanting in is world suddenly cut loose and sliding down its greased runway into an indifferent sea.

"You lose by winning," he said with a contemptuous Japanese temple guardian demon-snarl, then, as an afterthought, crumbs to the

THE LORD SAID UNTO SATAN

demon sparrows, mumbling inarticulately to himself/to 'them,' "Ikutsu ari-másu ka?/How many are there?," slowly becoming aware of the phantom "group"" off in the shadows inside him, trying to call it front stage center in his mind, magnify and penetrate it. But no go.

Then, to Masher's greatest frustration, he simply turned and left, Mascher snapping after him, "Jesus, you really are a psychotic, aren't you? You're not going to be on the street for very long."

Larry, reactionless, out the door.

Which is how you did it in the spirit-world, cloud, cloud, never scissors, not a sharp edge in the whole wide sky, just the assassin sun.

CHAPTER 11

1035 Spartan St. Priscilla Pringle.

Grass uncut. Neighborhood a little seedy. Small poor, frame, white shingled houses. Something out of Second World War building codes? The house itself embalmed. No lights, noise...a low budget House of Usher.

Larry rang the bell. No answer. Another ring, and then another...and finally a woman came to the door with a baby in her arms, wearing a faded blue shirt-waist dress that had been hastily buttoned up. One small fresh baby, a healthy-looking chunk.

"Yes?"

Ugly cow-nose and lips, slow-burn metabolism, long, lazy afternoons of pure suck...

"I'm Larry Gugel, Grimore Park P.D., northern Chicago suburb. I'm investigating the death of Myrtle Bannister..."

"Come on in!"

A sudden energy-jump, anguish, Delft blue plates dropped from church towers on to grey mosaics of ancient flagstones, the sky ripping open in ripped poppy-petals of searing flame.... and he followed her into the living room, toys and blankets and baby-clothes all over, the room vaguely reeking of a yogurty sour-milk stench, "Don't mind the place. I could care less. Could I offer you a coke?"

"Great!" said Larry and she went into the kitchen with the kid hanging on to her like a chimp, and he sat down on a sofa that close up vaguely emanated the sweet Attar of Roses smell of stale urine. She handed him a glass with a can of Coke. The glass had a little milky film on it so he just drank out of the can, as she unbuttoned the top two buttons of her dress, opened her nursing bra and started suckling the boy again.

She was a little uncomfortable because she expected him to be uncomfortable -- but he wasn't at all. To him it was all just

THE LORD SAID UNTO SATAN

Mediterranean sanity, in the spinning gyroscopic realm of the Great Goddess.

"I guess I know about Beryl's death," she said with the sluggish, stunned visionary clarity of an opium eater, "car accident, wasn't it?"

Larry half-closed his eyes, The Vision-Cloud suddenly there hanging between them, Larry trying to scan across the choirs of hooded monks and detail in the blanks. Was that her pig face, over to the left of Mascher? Tried to "close in" on the image, but it sizzled into zero, like spitting on a pot-bellied stove.

"So you haven't been able to get a job since Myrtle got you tossed out of Futurotech?" asked Larry matter-of-factly.

"Beryl was a woman under siege. More than anyone else I've ever known, she lived for war. Of course Griller had smeared her before she even came on the job. And I always admired her guts...," she rambled, as Larry's eyes strayed around the room, playpen in the corner; from where he was sitting he could see dirty dishes and pans all over the sink.

"I hear your husband walked out on you after you got fired from Futurotech," he said, psycho-scanning the house for something tangible, something humming just out of spirit-sight, his jaguar projection self sniffing all over the place, ears cocked, trying to focus in on whatever she was trying to hide, wondering if she'd gotten her 'relic' too and somewhere in the bedroom there was another drawer with another picture in it, another lock of charred hair...

"In a way Myrtle was the most misunderstood woman I've ever met. I don't even think I really understood her. Was her motivation greed, sheer anger/revenge, or was she ultimately after quality control, real science, professionalism. And myself aside, if they'd given her what she wanted, gotten rid of the dead wood, all the macho games and players...if, if, if...?"

The monster boy kept sucking and sucking and sucking, Larry trying to imagine her younger and thinner, get rid of the clunky low-heeled boats of shoes and put her in sandals and a wide swirling skirt with a leather belt and a silver and turquoise buckle, let the hair grow out and get rid of the rimless glasses...Was she ever young? Was there ever a spinning young Hippy Moment in her life, or was she born a rancid, stodgy, evasive middle-aged, evasive slob?

"What I'm really having problems with, " Larry tenaciously ignoring what was so obviously prepared material, a smiling, soft, gooey, blond oatmeal script, "is believing in the possibility of conspiracy, given such a cast of academicoid nerds. Conspirators are usually made of sterner stuff, aren't they, clipped hair, lots of mirrors and soap and super-egos..."

She stopped nursing, pulled the boy off her breast, snapped the bra shut and rebuttoned her dress. A moment of fumbling, all-thumbs hesitation...and then...

"Anyone's capable of anything if they're pushed hard and far enough."

Larry suppressing a carefully generated, sleepy toad yawn."OK."

"I'm as radical a feminist as anyone else. I saw us as The Sisterhood. Only in her Sisterhood there weren't any nursing mothers. No next generation, it was all just a big stainless steel tit-less wonder jackbooted now. And I eventually come to the conclusion...you know how most people are mostly OK, just a little flawed, a little blur here, a little crack there, with her it was all reversed...like she was the incarnation of..."

Stopped.

"Trust me," said Larry, more Padre Confessor, Friendly Hindu Psychiatrist, Black Hole, than cop.

She reddened. Surrounded by forty thousand students and all the infra-structure that went with them, and she had become a trilobite in a piece of fossil shale right in the middle of Atacama desert nowhereness...

"I...I wanted her to love me too," her tongue snaking around her already wet lips, "not physically , venereally, but, I don't know, 'sororally,' is there a word like that?"

"Why not? Soror -- sister..."

"OK, like a sister," starting to cry now, chewing on her lips, the boy limply asleep in her arms, heavy as a bag of gravel, but she refused to put him down, hung on to him as if their lives depended on it "only a sister accepts uteruses and breasts and lactation, it's not all just mind-chess...like she was an avenging mind from outer space that had floated down and possessed a human body. What was the point of getting me

THE LORD SAID UNTO SATAN

fired because I was breast-feeding my baby and still holding down an eight hour a day job? How else could I have done it but by milking myself? And no...I've just never been able to find anything else since then. My husband was in medical school and our whole existence was postulated on the fact of my working, and then, all of a sudden, BANG, I got fired and we started to have all these horrible quarrels about money. So I started burrowing further and further into myself ; and, no, I wasn't going to go work at Subway...which was one of his many suggestions for me to get other jobs. Finally he just took off and left..."

"And dropped out of Medicine?"

"Not at all. He went out and got a bunch of loans and he's got some kind of part-time job at the Health Center. Doing fine. Plenty of lean white legs to follow down shiny white corridors. That's one problem he's never had. So my life got trashed and what did Myrtle get out of it? So she got rid of everybody and had it all her way. So, so what?!?! Evil isn't just the absence of Good. That's Thomistic nonsense. It has its own 'presence' and essence and creates its own agendas and realities. It's as real as salt. God isn't talking to himself in Job, Satan lives and thrives..." She stopped. "Maybe you should go."Afraid she'd said too much, drying her eyes on the sleeve of her dress. "Really, maybe you should go."

"Of course you were at the convention in Chicago too, I suppose..."

"Unsuccessfully job-hunting."

"Yeah, sure," he answered, finishing off his coke when what he'd really have like was some heavy, sleepy, soporific, smoked tea, heavy sleepy sandalwood incense in a heavy sleepy Siva temple, a thousand heavy sleepy women massaging melting butter on a heavy, sleepy, five hundred foot tall gold-leafed Siva lingam,...,"Do you really think the pact will hold up watertight? No defectors?"

"Defectors?"

No flesh-colored bandages on her hands, but the whole room screaming out for revelation, grinning gargoyles dancing on the stage in the center of her psyche, traces of "something" there hurtling toward him/them..."Everything always comes out. Napoleon's murder. All it takes is a single hair and the right tests. There's always a portshard, slip of paper, loose tongue, guilt that becomes unbearable," Larry starting to think about her breasts inside her bra, enormous, still-wet nipples, her swollen labia, vulva, Our Lady of Laussel, Magna Mater, Great Goddess sanity, the only time in world religion when any of it made any sense, the Earth itself a giant womb waiting to receive the seminal homage of the New Sun after the winter solstice, bringing it all back to life again...

Then suddenly, swiftly, recklessly getting up, opening the closet door, which he suddenly realized was the center of all her screaming guilt.

"If you don't mind, Nature....."

Nothing special. A whole bunch of coats her husband had obviously left behind. Her own coats. Nothing special there either, except...one dull pink raincoat whispering to her "Me, me, me, me," Larry sticking his right hand into the deep, full, silky acetate left pocket of the coat and palming a matchbook he found there, turning ("Oops! Wrong door!), deftly shoving it into his suit coat pocket as he turned...

"It's right down at the end of the hall on the left," she said.

"That's OK," he answered, "Maybe it's better if I just go...getting old. And I didn't sleep last night, what with the visitations and all..."

"Visitations?"

As if she didn't know. Even after he'd finally gotten to sleep, his dreams filled with vague bat-fluttering, and when he'd open his eyes, it was as it they had been there at the window, frightened off by his waking up...

"Let's call them dreams," he said, faking a yawn, moseying over to the front door.

"Why don't you just give it back," she said, getting up and coming toward him.

But he didn't stop, opened the door, stepped out, down the iron-railinged front stairs, deft, quick, a balletic, tap-dancing bear.

"It's like when you're trying to prove a Phoenician presence in the ancient Americas and the Mochica Indian adobe brick-makers would sign their bricks and you check out the signs against old Sinai-Punic alphabets and...."

"Give it fucking BACK!"

THE LORD SAID UNTO SATAN

Trying to be menacing large now, from Bird to Bear-Mother, Eve to Medea...but she didn't quite have the claws...edge...

"Or southeast Asian elephant-fish-crocodile Makaras all over the grounds of Maya ruins...," answered Larry, pouring himself down the front steps, out into the driveway, irresistible lava coming down the mountain slopes and sizzling into the sea, stopping a moment, solidifying, just as he opened his car door, "Of course we can always simply TALK. I make very cozy, comfy deals..."

"If I...COULD...DARED," she said looking around at the trees surrounding the house, the air itself, 'presences,' eavesdropping, waiting...the boy in her arms stirring, opening his eyes and looking around, once reassured that she was still there, closing his eyes again...back to sleep, hanging in the hammock of her arms.

"He'll grow up very sane," said Larry as he got in his car, smiled, waved, started to close the door.

"If he has a chance to grow up!" she practically screamed at him, still this universal awareness of 'presences' around her in what seemed to Larry, with all his prescient gifts, a perfectly flat, warmish, lovely Spring day. Her face all twisted and pained. Her skin like raw spaghetti.

"Everything's fine!" Larry reassured her, traced the life-giving spiral of The Great God Krazny in the air, blessing and protecting her and her house and child forever, closed the door, opened the window, waved a last wave, "finer than fine..."

And he got into his old Volvo-Vulva, Up, up and away!

"How do you like her?" he asked Windy, who was curled up on the back seat, as he drove past a monstrously gnarled old willow next to a white shack of a house, thinking that the willow itself turned the house into a palace, that, in fact, the whole town was all palaces of trees, with little houses stuck in here and there, as if they'd been reluctant to disturb the ancient, natural beauty of the place, feeling Spirits everywhere, "presences," it was Heaven on Earth, he had been transported into Dimension Beatitude, was more at home here than he had ever been anywhere since he'd left the Santa Marta Mountains in Colombia.

"How do I like her?" Windy unexpectedly shark skinnish, sharp and rasping, "I don't! She is just a cow...and a dangerous one..."

HUGH FOX

"*A once and future beauty,*"
"'*Nur einmal, einmal und nichts mehr, gewesen zu sein*/Only once, once and no more, TO BE,' you mean; that's what you always told me," she said and curled back up, one stretch black satin little finger emerging from a curl of Silver Fox, after he had kissed the finger, the hand disappearing back down into a cloud of fur....
    Larry pulled the car to the curb next to a strangely isolated, exotic little park, benches all over the place, Petunias already in place, reminding him a little of Kensington Gardens, finding a bench, sitting back and pulling the matchbook out of his pocket:

Prasad's Indo-Chinese -- The Best of
Gourmet Cuisine, from India and China
And All Points in Between. 1045 W. Dunstable,
Grimore Park, Illinois...

He'd been there a couple of times, his whole being flooding with associations, the smell of sandalwood everywhere, the giant bronze Kali-Ma statue in the entrance, as you walked in, Kali perched on a victim's body, eating his bowels, hardly the most appetizing sculpture to have in the entranceway of a restaurant, but...
    Gongs banging in his head, tasting the sultry, rich taste of his favorite Oolong Tea, suddenly filled with the Clarity of Old Fire Grandfather, who always wanted to reveal all, but never did, little nudges and insights as to where to put the pieces in the giant bloody puzzle, but never more than that...
    "When you become a god..."
    If any one of them had paid with a credit card, getting them all closer and closer...
    Feeling five thousand years old, at least, Çatal Hüyük, Hacilar...pains in his ankles and chest, no energy left...all he wanted, really, was to retire and just be old, sit around waiting for death, dipping down into death's dream kingdom gracefully alone...closed his eyes for a moment...back in Prasad's...shadow shapes, very un-conspiratorial...a commando sense of joy and uplift...crusaders on the way to the Holy Land....

THE LORD SAID UNTO SATAN

Opening his eyes. A touch of rain in the air.
No one around. Depressing. He was such an easy target.
Walking back to his car, never feeling more alone in his life...

He drove back downtown, past a big dark brick department store, Jacobson's. More like it. More like the real thing. A huge parking ramp, pulling in, a record store right next to Jacobson's. Went in and bought a Walkman and batteries...wanted to listen to the Fudge Tapes.

Browsing around in the CD's -- Lily Boulanger, dead in her twenties, but she'd left a considerable pile of work behind. Some artists such bright, brief lights, and then other poor souls like himself, looking back on their almost century-long lives and seeing nothing more than wasteland, stubble, dead, sea-weed clotted beaches...

Taking the CD *In Memoriam Lili Boulanger* in his hand and hearing the music:

Dans l'immense tristesse
et dans le lourd silence...

In the immense sadness
and heavy silence...

A woman coming to a cemetery, to the grave of her dead child, imagining it alive again, singing to it to put it back to sleep...thinking about Maxine...what was he doing here anyhow when she was slowly penetrating (coach and horses) further and further into the Forest of Death...

Starting to cry, a young girl, skinny, big eyes, long face, coming over to him.

"Are you alright? Anything I can do?"

"No, no, I'm fine," he said, imagining her in fifty years, in her seventies. Very easy to imagine. Just add in a little sag and a few wrinkles, "Thanks, though..."

Out on to the street.

Such a bustle of young people. All the legs and roller blades, energy, past a restaurant called Castellani's Italian Market.

OK. More like it. An old world touch.

Went in and found a place. Marble topped tables and heavy wire chairs, Italian groceries all over the walls. It was a place where you when up to the counter and got your own stuff. Self-serve. A little middle-aged Italian behind the counter.

"Nice place!"

"A replica of my grandfather's place in downtown Lansing -- that's been out of business for years. Opening up here was like bringing him back to life."

"So you must be Castellani!"

"That's the one. How about a hard salami sandwich on a sourdough roll? That sounds like you!"

"Okay. It does...it doesn't sound like me. Even looks like me."

"New in town, huh?" asked Castellani as he deftly sliced open a sourdough roll, and sliced nice thick slices off a big old, white-mould-splotched Italian Salama, cut the moldy outer skin off before he put it in the bread.

"Hopefully just passing through. And I love Chicago, but this town..."

"It's got a certain charm, huh?!?" said Castellani.

"I like the trees. I'm a mystic."

"Christian?"

"Zakut!"

"Oh....."Castellani obviously not wanting to admit he didn't know what Zakut was, Larry said it so forcefully and matter-of-factly, "Business trip?"

"Murder business, I'm a cop."

"A murder here...? That Pakistani guy who killed and dismembered his wife and tried to put the pieces in garbage bags, like no one was going to notice a leg or a head...."

"No, it didn't take place here. But the murderer/murderers may be here...I'm just starting out..."

"It wasn't that, what's her name, Myrtle Ban-something..."

"Bannister...that's the one."

"It got a lot of press around town. She wasn't exactly popular, if you know what I mean. She used to come in here once in a while.

Cappuccino. And she liked Italian cookies. A big woman, a kind of a funny aura about her. I'm pretty good about auras. And she had a funny one."

"What do you mean 'funny.'"

Castellani, thin, incisely-cut features, the blackest possible hair, white skinned, very naturally "bright"-looking, stopped, focused, "The dark side..."

"She had a 'dark side' aura?"

"That's the best I can do," he answered, getting back to the business of the sandwich, "you don't want lettuce and tomato, mayonnaise, anything to interfere with the flavor of the salami, right?"

"You know me!" said Larry, a fanatic for pure, hard, penetrating tastes, no dilutants.

"And how about a real root root-beer, no synthetics?"

"OK, sounds good."

"Let me just put a few pepperoncinis here on the side," said Castellani, putting a few pickled Italian sweet peppers on the place, adding it up an old turn-of-the-century cash register.

$6.23.

"Thanks a lot," said Larry and went over and found a seat by the window, bit into the salami and roll and chewed ever so slowly, letting the taste roll around on his tongue, taste, smell, texture...it was perfect..a little sour bite of pepper...enjoying the students walking by outside. They seemed so fresh and serious. Reading the labels on the cans of groceries. How can Olive Oil be double-virgin? Cans of dried tomatoes. He loved dried tomatoes. You never tasted a tomato until you tasted it dried.

A guy with a face like a Blake angel sitting at the table next to him was talking (in a very nice, brittle, Oxonian accent) about having been in Zermatt, Switzerland the summer before, "And I seemed to have a trifle too much to drink, or perhaps it was the altitude, seeing that I am totally a sea-level creature, but I went for a little walk after dinner and was strolling along when suddenly I realized that the ground just in front of me dropped off and the next level down was three thousand feet lower. So I kind of fell backward and came to an abrupt halt just, just, just on the edge..."

Laughing. All of his listeners, two Chinese, what looked like a Dravidian from South India, and an English woman with immensely fluffy hair and a horsey overbite, all joining in with his laughter.

A very serious-looking Lesbian couple next to him, playing footsy, drinking their cappuccino's and eating their pieces of pecan pie in great solemnity. Not a word passing between them.

An old tweedy-looking professor with bristly porcupinish white hair talking to a beautiful, thin, intensely white young woman all in black: "What I've noticed in the last few years is the tremendous change in young black women, their intensity, their career goals, their focusing, even their appearances...."

In the background, just right, nothing intrusive, Resphigi's "Pines of Rome," the section (Larry forgot the exact title) where the nightingale sings at the end.

Larry kept chewing, sipping at the very pungent, penetrating root-beer, sat back, began to feel very nostalgic about Europe, after he'd finished Northwestern and married Maxine, and her father had died and willed her twelve million and they could do whatever they wanted, so they'd spend six months in Paris, and then, it got too cold, they'd moved down to Rome, and when it got too cold in Rome, then down to Cadiz, summers in Vienna, Prague, Budapest, always feeling himself, somehow, part of the ex-Hapsburg empire. Rilke was a kind of Zakut Indian shaman, wasn't he? His Paris diaries -- how to maximize the moment.

Larry closed his eyes for a moment and he was transported instantly to someplace in Brazil, up on a hillside, the sea below, a little village...so the favelas/slums looked shabby and sad like everywhere else in Brazil (most of the world), but there was a certain romantic lilt and fall of the hill and a special beauty to the curve of sea meeting land...standing there in a mystic uplift, when suddenly a pipe broke and viscous black sewer-stuff, shit, yes, but a thousand times condensed and more vicious, started pouring all around him, trying to find a hillock to stand on, but there was no place to escape to, getting swept away in the stream of putrid, excretory mud, when he opened his eyes and...

Castellani was standing there, a piece of pecan pie and a cup of coffee in hand:

THE LORD SAID UNTO SATAN

"A little dreaming there! Looks like someone has been keeping the midnight light burning a little too much..."

"Getting old! And it's true, Chicago isn't quite around the corner..."

"Compliments of the house!" he said, putting the coffee and pie down, "and I put a little hazelnut flavoring in the coffee. Just a little extra touch. Enjoy!"

"Well, thanks...."

Larry truly touched.

The place was Old Europe at its best...times that most people had forgotten about, when the Great Goddess ruled and Romania/The Danube Basin was the cultural center, and the center of worship was tits, life, milk, wombs, birth, sex, the goddess everywhere from mouse to hedgehog, owl, moon....

Fucking delicious pie. A thick layer of pecans on top, floating on a lake of rich puddingish 'sauce.' The crust sweet and crispy, not just 'container,' but something you could have rolled into little balls and served separately, that's how powerfully they smacked of themselves. And the coffee just what he would have expected, primal, powerful, carefully brewed -- like a hand carved door on an ancient Etruscan cottage.

He toasted the boss. The boss toasted him back.

Salut!

He'd been born in the wrong fucking century. Internet my ass. Instant annihilation. No lost inscriptions to decipher. Just press a button and instant annihilation...

After he'd finished, he took a personal card out of his wallet, not Larry Gugel -- Cop, but Larry Gugel -- Private Citizen, and handed it to Castellani.

"If you're ever in the Chicago area, give me a call. We've got this place on the lake. North shore. Plenty of room...take care..."

Another handshake, and out on the street, half a block down spotted a street phone and he reluctantly called Jennifer Grump down at Bio-Dynamics, wondering what kind of name Grump was anyhow, weren't there any Reillys and O'Hares, Segals, Webbs, around, names that appeared more than once in the universe?

"Hi, this is Larry Gugel..."

"Yeah, I know all aboutcha, Larry. Listen, I'm about to go to lunch, but I always brown-bag it, come on over and join me. Down Grand River, past the Convention Center, you'll see a sign for Impression Five museum, follow it, turn left, then look for the Bio-Dynamics sign, you can't miss it..."

"Impression Five?"

"As in five fingers. It's a kid's museum."

"Ahhh, so..."

"No, no connection, turn off the deduction machine, there's nothing to deduce. The kid's museum's in an old factory. This used to be the old factory-warehouse district. My boss got a deal on an old building, that's all...be waitin' for ya..."

And she simply hung up, making Larry feel like his face had been slapped. Good. Good. Just what he needed. Get him out of the time-to-retire, old nostalgia mood; get him into his back-in-the-saddle, old sumi wrestler, Larry the Lion-Hearted mood again.

On his way out of the parking lot, he asked the woman in the cashier's coop the way down to the Convention Center.

"Out of here, make a right, then another right, couldn't be simpler!"

"Thanks..."

Following the traffic flow west.

What a busy beehive of a town. Cambridge was more affluent, Berkeley affluent-nerdie, Northwestern pure snob, Kansas pure ivory tower, Austin old stuff, UCLA pure brass and porcelain (and lots of Bon Ami), Iowa rarified, almost scary isolation...here it was Nice Guy-Nice Gal territory, kind of soft and tempered, you didn't see anger in the faces, but what you saw was a lot of ambition, beauty. He'd drive by someone twenty wearing short shorts and a flowered, long-sleeved sixtyish blouse, carrying her books in a plaid backpack, lust after the long, sleek, perfect legs, then the fine-featured little white face with its backswept hair....then suddenly see the face turn forty, fifty, eighty...the same intense, hungry, pioneering, exploratory fervor in the eyes. It was as if whoever they were, their very essential 'selves,' were constantly sliding back and forth in time...

THE LORD SAID UNTO SATAN

He could see the unimpressive capital building way up ahead. Not like Minnesota. St. Paul. Now there was a classic, Greek stark, starched beauty! But here is was clumpy, not a sacred temple on top of a sacred acropolis of a hill, but a profane nineteenth century wrought-iron industrial penis-head mushroom stuck right in the middle of downtown...

Posh East Lansing flowing into bare-ribs Lansing. A close copy of the Tenderloin in San Francisco.

Rescue missions. Big signs...JESUS SAVES. May-be...only hardly here....

But there was an attempt at downtown decadent reversal, a new Raddison Hotel attached to the Convention Center. Which looked impressive in its own Pompidou-like way -- iron pipes and bright red paint. Why did they always have to copy something French?

He saw the Impression Five Museum sign, turned left, went down a road to an area next to the Grand River, power station over on the left, the river itself to his right, Impression Five, true enough, in an old brick warehouse next to a car museum, then one more building down, there was the big Bio Dynamics sign and next to *it*, sitting on the front steps, a taffy-colored cat woman in a lab coat, who reminded him a little of Windy -- a small, blonde Windy playing not mad, but super-sane scientist.

"I got you this," she said, handing him a can of Pepsi, "we can share my lunch."

"I've just eaten, but I can watch you," he smiled, really quite careful in his eating habits, all appearances to the contrary -- and he followed her down to the river.

Picturesque. Downtown Lansing on the other side of the river, a miniaturized version of a real city. Like an eagle that early on had just stopped growing and never got bigger than a sparrow. But it was green and lush, a boardwalk that ran along the river, a bald, droopy-mustached coronary candidate jogger, giving them a nod as he passed them by.

She went directly to a bench that she obviously saw as her private throne, and he sat down, sat back, his soul swelling and expanding out at the simple green, watery invitation of the day.

"Not bad, not bad...you see a lot of civic 'intentions' in motion..."

"That's one advantage of nothing-towns," she said, "they're always trying, but they never get there. Not like Vienna, say, where they 'got there' ten times, ten layers of, so much so that you feel overwhelmed, squashed... all the old voices still in the woodwork: Mahler, Wittgenstein, Freud, Egon Schiele..."

She talked 'funny.' No accent, inflection, like one of those robo-synthesized voices on voice-synthesizers for the mute.

"So you spent some time in Vienna?" Larry reaching out for something to have in common with her.

"Not much, just at a convention with Dr. Griller."

"Ah, so the rumors..."

"No!" the flat robo-voice protested, "nothing like that...just business...I almost said busyness. We were certainly very busy. You know, the Viennese are always trying to keep up, get ahead of the rest of the world in everything. It's like an imperial habit they've never broken. I listen to Radio Vienna in English every night. I always feel it gives me a little 'edge,'" she said, digging into her brown bag lunch, handing him his can of Pepsi, trying to hand him half a fatty meatloaf sandwich, which he gently waved away.

"No, I really couldn't. I just had the queen of all salami sandwiches over at Castellani's..."

"Yeah, it's fun there. I love it too. Ambience...ambience is all, don't you think?"

"I do!," answered Larry, feeling distressed as he felt himself begin to re-soften again. All this baggy Spring weather, and now this innocent shepherdess of a girl with a robo-voice who he couldn't even remotely imagine being involved with a witch-burning, "What bothers me is that you all seem so consummately..," reaching for the word as he reached into his pocket for his cigarillos, then reached in again, starting to play a dirty little game, now, as if there were another Trickster Self inside him that wouldn't let Old Good Guy Larry just sag away like an old potato pancake on a bench on a balmy Spring day, "You don't happen to have a match, do you?"

She had a little purse in the side pocket of her lab-coat...

THE LORD SAID UNTO SATAN

"I don't smoke, although sometimes I'll have a stray...," opening the purse up. Black Chinese silk. He reached forward in a clumsy well-intentioned fat-man lurch...

"It's such a stinking little habit, but...," she was saying as he knocked the purse out of her hand, spilling the contents all over the ground.

"I'm sorry, I'm such an oaf, elf, nightmare" he said, as always playing little etymological games inside his head, how else do you ever find out what things really mean, kneeling down, all part of the usual little shaman-games, like extracting stones and bloody clots of mucous out of the bellies of the sick, climbing like monkeys or squirrels to the tops of tepees, tents, house-post poles, flying to the Walpurigisnacht belly-button Center of the World for ritual dismemberment and rebirth...beyond-the-speed-of- light sleight-of-handing the matchbook he'd filched out of the pocket of Priscilla Pringle's raincoat into the piles of pennies and quarters and reading glasses, keys, credit cards, bank and sales receipts all over the ground...and then slowly rediscovering it..."Ah, here some matches after all..."

"Good, I thought I might just have some somewhere" she said, bending down and helping him refill the purse with its contents, when they'd finished, sitting back down on the bench, offering her a cigarillo, which she took, lighting up hers, then his, both of them sitting back and expanding out into the now like banana trees in a hot house, as he casually read the contents of the matchbook cover:

PRASAD'S INDO-CHINEE -- THE BEST OF....

Stressing Grimore Park, Illinois...Gri-more Park, Ill-i-nois...then just lolling back, closing his eyes for a moment, and when he opened them studying the swollen spring clouds and the swollen spring river. He never liked summer and winter. Not really. Just the seasons in movement. Like to feel the flow of universal time, hated stasis, stagnation...

A busload of kids drove into the parking lot of the Impression Five Museum and the kids began to noisily unload...

"It's a great little museum for kids," she said as they trooped inside and everything got quiet again, "all kinds of exhibits about magnetism and electricity, sound...the only problem is that, being hands-on and everything, it's more like a playground than science. I don't know if they ever can make the link between the kind of stuff they have here and pure science..."

"So you're not going to bite?" he asked.

And she reached into her lunch bag and pulled out an apple and handed it to him.

"I imagine you can just crack it in half."

Which he easily did, started chomping on his half. An excellent combo of tastes -- the cigarillo smoke and the apple-taste.

After she'd finished half the sandwich, she broke it up into little pieces and threw them at two squirrels who were hanging around just wanting for a handout.

"Good combination of tastes," she said, biting into the apple and then taking a deep drag on her cigarillo.

"So you're inside my little game?" he asked cynically.

"It doesn't take a lot..."

"OK," he said, disappointed, feeling that he'd lost his edge, was becoming a plate glass window instead of an elaborately painted Japanese screen, "why don't you tell me a little about your leaving Futurotech. Did you get fired?"

"You're not losing your edge, you're just dealing with a group of people with the same edges... Having lunch in Grimore Park doesn't make anyone a murderer. I already got a call from Priscilla the Earth-Mother, Mrs. Milk Factory...didn't you find the whole milk-thing just a little overdone? A lot of the things Myrtle did I felt were one hundred percent justified. You get too much weirdness into any operation and it gets freaky...."

Larry feeling cancelled out entirely now, down to normal size and still shrinking.

"And don't feel cancelled out, either, I'm really a nice guy, empathetic, compassionate. Everything's 'normal' for all of us, we're cruising through life...and then all of a sudden we're not on board any more...that's kind of what you're afraid of, isn't it. I mean the situation with you and your wife?"

THE LORD SAID UNTO SATAN

On target. One hundred percent on target. His old health, the kind of vague lethargy he felt most of the time, back problems, prostate problems, he never really slept well, all kinds of unexplained cold and hot sweats at night, and now with Maxine definitely on the River of Death, it was almost as if the Angel of Death/O Anjo da Morte had begun to hover around him as well, it was just a question of time...when..."How the fuck did you find out about that?"

She shrugged her shoulders, smiled.

"Internet. Maybe it was internet. Everything's on internet, isn't it?," she said evasively, getting up, "you want to walk a little?"

"Sure."

Starting to walk along the river, South, wasn't it, toward tall, wild, stretches of woods, mixed right into the middle of the city, like they'd been afraid to cut, touch anything wild, when they'd first settled here.

"And about my getting fired...OK...Griller was taken off the project until he dried out -- permanently. Which was fair enough. Only I don't think he'd capable of drying out. He's one of those subliminal, permanent, built-in drunks. And he never came back, went back to teaching again -- and Myrtle took over. She had all the answers, that was her whole aura. And there was a billion dollars just around the corner if only Sax would give her The Power. Which he -- quite logically -- did. The only other real 'power person' still left was Mascher, and she tried to mash him, if you'd pardon the pun, but he was quite unmashable. So she turned to me, the last 'memory,' 'link,' 'trace' of Griller still left in the lab. She started riding me, checking and re-, re-, re-checking all my experimental results until she'd invariably find some little slipup. And there's always little slipups, aren't there. If God's so perfect how come the prostate, which invariably enlarges in older men, is right in the path of the urethra? And all this little picky-picky stuff is my particular weakness too...my father and mother and my father's mother, who lived with us when I was growing up. I was the built-in gremlin-in-the-works. If it rained, it was my fault. And so the more Myrtle probed, the less there was to find. She was turning me into a super-perfectionist. But she had to annihilate me, didn't she. That's what they're here for, isn't it?"

"They?"

Talk about little slip-ups.

Her mind filled for a moment with a gigantic scene of celestial magnitude, vast galactic spaces filled with winged 'troops,' vague, cloudy, biblical, pre-, pre-, pre-, pre-biblical...IN THE BEGINNING WAS THE...what beginning, and how could it have ever begun, and if it hadn't begun how could it have always been...

Suddenly turning off entirely.

"I mean she would have annihilated Mabel too if Mabel hadn't annihilated herself! She's the most chameleon-like person I've ever met. When she was with Bryan and Chichi, she started working for a B.S. in Bio-Chemistry because Chichi had/has a special interest in Bio-Chemistry. When it had been just Bryan, she was the poet because he was the poet. If she'd fallen in love with a leopard, she would have grown spots...only, so what if I was loosely tied to Griller? What was the point of getting rid of me, especially as I got sharper and sharper, more and more efficient...? Of course Griller did fudge results. He wanted MONEY, so he magically created results. Let's put that on the table right now. And Mascher was always going to the newspapers and making declarations and pushing Griller to get results. And Priscilla did waste tons of time 'milking herself,' which I too saw as a kind of public masturbation. Believe me, she loved doing it. It was a big auto-erotic show. And Gillespie was a kind of Creole-Cajun fuckoff who dodged work like it was a silver bullet..."

"Gillespie...?"Larry slithering his hand inside his inside coat pocket and getting out his suspect list, checking it out, "I don't even know if he's on my suspect list...ah, yes, here he is..."

Getting further and further into forest now, not too spooky now in the Spring with the leaves just coming out, but in the middle of Summer, or in the middle of Fall, on a cold, cloudy day...

A lot of people like them, just walking, or jogging, Larry definitely not feeling up to too much more of a hike.

"Even Juice was a kind of fuckoff....."

"Juice?"

Larry checked down his list again. No juices.

THE LORD SAID UNTO SATAN

"Juice for short because he's an OJ Fiend. Raymond Jewell. From the wilds of Iowa. Our computer expert, always a bunch of CD game-disks in his lab coat. Total nerd. Great when he worked, and he always got done what he had to do, but the slightest chance to screw around, and there he'd be...very creative...he'd even creative his own games...Immortal Combat...Angels versus Devils...set in heaven...you know, the revolt of Lucifer, the Morning Star..."

Larry ignoring her, still fastened on to his list.

"What about this guy, Sax...?"

Stopping, tossing his down-to-a-small stub cigarillo into the river (which she seemed shocked at), lighting up another with the matches from Prasad's restaurant in Grimore Park, then holding the matches up in front of her as if they were a crucifix and she was Bela Lugosi, just getting out of his coffin for a late snack.

She shoved her own cigarillo into her Pepsi can and put the can into her sandwich bag, making a little ecological morality play out of the whole thing, started walking again, stopped....

"Maybe we should go back..."

"If you'd like," Larry answered, putting the matches back in his pocket, very low pressure, passive, simply waiting. And not aggressively either but humbly, solicitous, "are you OK?"

"I'm....."

And she started to cry, kept walking, crying, quietly, like the softest, minimalist Spring rain, as they passed by a bench, wordlessly sitting down, a few crows overhead, a railroad rumbling and hooting in the distance...

"It's better to just get it all out. I can get a special deal for you," said Larry, sitting down next to her, "it'll all come out eventually, someone will 'break.'"

Larry expecting her to unload the whole story, feeling like he was fishing off a pier and there was a big pike out there playing with the bait on his hook, nudging it, nibbling at it, if he just sat back and waited....letting her cry it through, waiting for the crying to subside, it was coming, you could hear it on the other side of the horizon, the crying subsiding, wiping her eyes, all tremulous and shy, like a very young girl who had let a very sheltered, isolated life...and then she began, hesitant at first, "Do you think..."

"'Do I think'...OK...what else?"

"The Book of Job...God gives Satan a nudge and points him toward Job...or Satan in the Garden of Eden, tempting Eve...the war in heaven between the good and bad angels...is there a Satan in this world or not? Is there some Force/Forces alive and well, and is it here all around us?," stopping, looking around her, Larry starting to feel his skin crawl. Out there in the forest, the sudden materialization of 'forces,' Larry noticing the power line towers just over to their left, for the first time hearing the hum of the power surging through the wires..."Are there invisible, malignant 'things' out there, superior to us, invisible, immortal... Do you think God ever, ever, ever talked to Man? That it makes any more difference if we kill than a person than swat a fly? I mean you can't even imagine how great it was to work in that lab before Myrtle came along. I'd babysit Griller's kids and be over there for dinner all the time. All of us were. Friday night pizza parties. And he'd always pick up the tab. Of course later, during his 'disgrace,' it turned out that he was charging it all to Futurotech. But Sax never seemed to notice -- or even care. We were more extended FAMILY than just some JOB...and then Myrtle came along and..."

"And..." Larry making himself small, a partial vacuum, whatever she had inside her to tell needing a vacuum to expand out into, "And...?"

"Do you believe that Satan really said to Christ on the cross that if He (Christ) would bow down and worship him, he would save him? That that Satan was the same Satan who tortured Job and gotten Eve to eat the apple in the Garden or Eden..."

Larry hesitating, feeling IT out there in the forest, coming toward them, a swirl of power around them...no one else around now, no more joggers or roller blade freaks, just them, and a growing swirl of negative power...

"YES, I BELIEVE SATAN EXISTS!" screamed Larry, up on his feet, grabbing her by the arm and starting back toward downtown, feeling the anger in the power-swirls around them, the IT, whatever that IT was in the forest, roaring now, the roar of a thousand lions, train

THE LORD SAID UNTO SATAN

brakes screeching, buildings collapsing, thousands of panes of plate glass crashing on sidewalks, Larry beginning to run now, totally out of shape but still managing it, someone running toward them now, Larry not sure what/who it was, at first thinking that he/it had a lion's head, but then, as he got closer seeing it was just some middle-aged guy out for a little noon run, feeling ITS power decrease as they rounded a bend and the city was there in front of them again, feeling his own Forces begin to activate, Old Grandfather Fire, The Great God Krazny beginning to descend...IT retreating now, singed by the Other Fires that lay sleeping in the air, by the time they got back to Impression Five and their bench, the air cleansed, all "presences" but Old Grandfather Fire gone, Larry thanking him, the huge face there in front of them, hanging over the water:

"I can't thank you enough..."

"If it wasn't for you, I wouldn't even BE...in myself, yes, in the world, no..."

And he was gone, Jennifer suddenly in his arms, Larry loving being needed, Jenny such a small package of a woman, like straw, maple leaves, the wind itself.

"Hold on to me for a minute, Larry...I want it all to be over with. We all thought..."

"Yes? 'We all thought...'"

Suddenly angry, pulling away from him.

"I've got to get back to work now."

"OK. I wish that..." Larry started to say, I wished that you'd spilled the beans, gotten it all out, slit the goddamned case open like a calf on a butcher's table...

Her hand across his mouth.

"No you don't." Glancing down at her legs. Too thin. She was going to have old lady thin legs before she was forty, old lady legs and old lady face. Chici, on the other hand, under all that stretch lace and silk and taffeta, was all pure bounce, resilience, Jacuzzi and trampoline flesh..., "I love you, Larry...I really do..."

And she was gone, Larry standing there watching her go, wanting to follow her, but standing his ground, feeling a touch of evil in the air, like a pinprick through the fabric of universal Good, a voice hissing through, full of claws and fangs, 'You'll never find out anything, you asshole dilettante, as if anything matters anyhow, dissolved in all-time, melting wax flesh!!," Larry closing his eyes and praying "Old Grandfather Fire, Keeper of Time, Lord of The Zodiac..."

And Tata Wari came back, healed the pinpricked wound in the fabric of Time and Larry was left standing there totally, totally, alone, depressed, space, feeling like he was standing on a chunk of astroid somewhere beyond Pluto instead of on the back of the Grand River in Lansing, Michigan in the middle of a sweaty Spring afternoon.

An old, old lady, all made up, with bright lipstick and adroitly bleached terrier-cut hair, wearing a classic black suit, black pantyhose and low-heeled pumps, walked by with her wise-man-faced fluffed-out Pomeranian...

"Are you OK, young man?"

"Fine, just fine," he said, "just meditating."

"Oh, I'm so sorry...," the old lady apologized.

"No problem, no problem," Larry answered, digging her upswept, cat-woman sun glasses, black plastic, filled with rhinestones, as the old lady resumed her walk, calling after her, "Hey, I like the sun glasses..."

"Just some old things out of an old drawer," she answered, "a relic...like me...."

"Come on, you look great!"

"Thanks, young man!"

And he walked back to his car and went into the trunk, randomly picked out one of Fudge's talk-tapes and stuck it in his Walkman, got in and drove down to Futurotech to talk to...Sax...yeah, he was the one, Mister Biga Boss, as he drove away from the capitol, for no reason at all starting to think about his uncle, Lou, his mother's brother, his principal male model, the man and the horn, big, bright bass sax, playing his heart out against the backdrop of old Killer Chicago, feeling like driving back to Grimore Park and handing in his badge -- permanently.

He felt like he was on the wrong side in the Battle in Heaven, teamed up with the dragon and against Saint George....

THE LORD SAID UNTO SATAN

But then the old Gnostic worm in the center of his brain, began to stir...and he reached into his brain and turned the (burning) page, sat back and turned up the volume on Fudge's tape...

CHAPTER 12

Everything in stereo. Very nice. Larry depressed for a moment thinking about how much he was missing in Century Twenty, outside of everything in his own a-technical void:

There's the Reality of my Head, dream-reality, and then there's the Reality of Reality, the way things really are...

My head-reality still sees me and Mabel in Romeo and Juliet terms. We meet, love swells like a bitch-in-heat's vulva. There never was such a love on the face of the earth before. We were the first, primordial couple and everywhere we walked became Eden. We were passion, madness, an unbreakable bond.

And then she leaves/is kicked out by Chichi, and she re-bonds with Myrtle, becomes my mortal enemy, falsely accuses me of sucking on my little boy's penis, runs away, hides, keeps the children away from me...all the boringly predictable Queen Mean tricks. Maybe that's the saddest part of it, that every year thousands of women falsely accuse thousands of fathers of child sexual abuse, just to get custody.

I keep replaying in my mind the whole film of her back up here secretly initiating the divorce behind my back, in order to take advantage of the legal dynamics that give the attacker the edge over the attacked. I see her driving down Grand River, follow the car back to Myrtle's place out in Okemos, approach the car, they run me down, having already filed the divorce papers that day. They thought the

papers had been served on me and that I was out to get them. When all it was was seeing Mabel driving down Grand River with the boy in the back seat when I was being told she was still in Kansas. My arm is broken, I'm down on the ground...and they drive off. I've got a compound fracture. My little boy in the back of the car has seen it all, seen his mother run down his father. Later on he tells me that when they left me there on the ground, they drove to the police station and tried to get a cop to come out and arrest me, because there was a restraining order in place to keep me away from Myrtle's place.

THE LORD SAID UNTO SATAN

Restraining order?!?!? Preemptive legal strikes?!? Mabel, who in her entire life always avoided The State/The Law/any kind of legal proceedings, ending up paying almost twenty thousand in legal fees to fuck me over, all our personal sins made public...

Only was it HER? Nothing to do with the Mabel I knew for twenty years. But cast her as Myrtle's Mabel, Evil for the sake of Evil, Mabel as Myrtle's pet demonic monkey...and then it all rings true.

I want my shamanic Dream-Reality back. Real- Reality is a nightmare, only we're all inside the nightmare of Myrtle's head now, all of us Myrtle's dream-puppets, and the only way to stop the dream is to STOP THE DREAMER...

Larry pushed OFF, pulled off his earphones...

"Asshole!" he screamed at the Walkman/Fudge, "you talk too fucking MUCH!"

Spotted a street phone booth up ahead in front of, what was it, Sparrow Hospital. Pulled over to the curb, the guy behind him honking.

Larry gave him the finger.

"Fuck you!"

Larry had had his turn-signal on, what are you supposed to do, never turn?

Dialed information, asked for Brian Buckley's phone. Two numbers, one home, the other office. Took down both on the envelope of an old electric bill he found in his inside coat pocket. He wasn't gonna be in no office, man, he had to be home, was a goddamned bedbug, pillow-commando, office wasn't his style...

Tried the home phone.

Three rings and there he was, spacily grouchy like the Universe better not cut into his world.

"Hello...."

"I'm following an impulse," explained Larry, "I was on my way to see Sax, but...are you free?"

"Cafe Espresso, fifteen minutes..."

"Which is...?"

"M.A.C. and Albert."

"I'll find it."
"Fifteen minutes."
"I've been listening to your tapes," said Larry, "just a few minutes, but..."
"I figured you would," said Fudge, "Seeya over there, pal!"
And he hung up, got back in his car.
Funny, as he moved into East Lansing again, how he felt he was coming home, students appearing, almost all in uniform, backward baseball caps, T-shirts, shorts, sandals. Lots of women in long Indian skirts. Lots of hair. Earrings. A sense of intense sensuousness. Under the surface they were all sybarites, night fell and a thousand thousand legs opened up. So many Orientals. He could sit for a year at some cafe just watching them and after the year had passed, come up with a thousand page meditation on THE FUTURE IN THE NOW....
Found Cafe Espresso.
Another stage-set place like Castellani's.
Lots of dyed hair here, Living Dead T-shirts, skull earrings, leather pants, the guy on the Espresso Machine speaking French, the piped-in music French...just a little too precious for poor old proletarian Michigan.
Fudge not there yet so he ordered a cappuccino with a little touch of almond flavor, an almond-filled croissant, more memories of Marzipan Vienna, as always feeling haunted by the past, the Great Clarity always there, as if the Past and its passengers, never left him but was standing there just a little in the shadows -- Mom, Dad, even his dead sister who he'd never met, but was forever being shown pictures of. Endless stories about her. Tall, blonde, spacey...had she really died from meningitis, or as a teen-aged, spaced-out whore?

Gemütlichkeit, is it right,
for one sad head to be filled
with so much Night?

"Bury her already!" one said chorus inside him shouted, "Bury your dead!!" But they wouldn't be buried, and his mother started coming

THE LORD SAID UNTO SATAN

toward him out of the shadows, carrying a platter with tea and cookies on it...just as Brian came in the front door, looking very, very freaky.

All in black. Black velvet pants. Je-sus! Black leather jacket. Black suede cap that might have been kosher if it had just been regular black leather...

"Howya doin'?"

Went up to the counter. The guy behind the counter knew him. Of course. Big exchange of bullshit.

Got a cappuccino and a bran muffin.

"I didn't see those!" Larry said, pointing to the muffin.

"Contrabando," Fudge smiled sadistically, "And it's the last one!"

Sat down.

"So how are you doing?" asked Larry, suddenly relaxed and full of fellow-feeling...

He hated the term "male-bonding," but...

"OK," said Fudge, shifting into High Seriousness, "I'm working on..." He reached over to a sideboard filled with spoons, sugar and napkins, grabbed a napkin, "this!"

Drew:

"That's the Maya Lamat. At least it's Lamat in Yucatan. In Highland Maya it's a Kan Cross...and, of course, the Brahmi letter for Ka is , you put a dot on it and it becomes KAM. "

"So you're trying to establish a prehistoric link between the Indus Valley civilization and Meso-America?" asked Larry.

"Exactly," said Fudge, thrown a little off balance, "exactly, exactly." No one else was supposed to have the slightest hint about such things.

"I've been listening to the tapes," said Larry, guttural and grinding, "Why don't you just turn yourself in, you're almost as confessional as I am. Only I haven't barbecued anyone...yet," finishing off his croissant in three bites, getting up and getting three more. Another nine bites worth.

When he came back to the table, Fudge's face was soberly depressed. Jesus Complex. Good Friday, "good" because The Year God has to die for Spring to begin...

"I don't know if you know about my letters to the Grimore Park Police Department. I've been assuming all along that they're what got you up here in the first place..."

"News to me," answered Larry, "They probably threw the fucking things out, filed them under, you know...."

"After Myrtle and Mabel left here with the cells...they'd been so fucking wild up here, these Lesbian bars, drugs...a lab in their basement. And I knew they weren't going to stop. Why had they gone to Babbitt Brothers in the first place, all of Babbbitt's experimental work on thymus and rejuvenation..."

"So what did you write to the Grimore Park PD?"

Fudge wincing a little, then moving into fatalistic resignation.

"Well, I wrote to everyone, phoned everyone, told everyone everything I knew..."

Larry stiffened. A spoor hung in the air, fetid, dank, rotten, the coffee shop suddenly filled with kamikaze lightning and a flight of huge blue butterflies.

"Who did you contact at Babbitt Brothers?" he asked, tingling, erect, exalted, San Juan de la Cruz in the middle of a 'visitation,' knowing what came next -- Mrs. Fat-Ass Acetate Tan.

"Well, I wrote to Security first, just simply told them about Myrtle's track record. I thought if they just knew who/what she was...the psychopathic serial killer with the shy smile that the family picks up hitchhiking, and at the first rest-stop slaughters them all, throws their mutilated bodies into a ditch, and drives off with the car..."

"And their response?"

"One unexpected response. First a guy named Kalakofsky wrote back and said they knew all about Myrtle's 'past,' she was under surveillance."

"I wonder what they really knew -- and how," said Larry, as a skinny, grey-haired woman came in with the deadpan red-headed guy who looked like a carved prow-post on a Viking ship.

"Hey, cutie!" said the woman, came over and gave Fudge a hug and the wooden-man shook hands, "Howyadoin' pal?" The woman couldn't have cared less about Larry.

THE LORD SAID UNTO SATAN

They went over to a far corner. Obviously a lot was going on/had gone on, between Fudge and her.

"Just local writers," Fudge explained.

"She must look pretty good in the buff, even now," said Larry, flat, brutal, crude.

"I wouldn't know. I'm this big Puritan, you know, all bark, no bite..."

"Is Bunny a transsexual Puritan too?" asked Larry, still as raw as possible, "or is 'she' the exception to the rule. There always seem to be exceptions to all rules..."

"Mass and Communion every morning for more than twenty years," Brian getting all squirmy now, as sugary-sweet and glazed as a cinnamon roll just out of the oven, "No sexual experience as a kid. Never masturbated. A virgin on my wedding night. My first marriage to the Bolivian Indian...," sitting back, shaking his head, rubbing his eyes, "I don't know if anyone is around any more like the way I used to be. Church in the mornings, church in the afternoons (alone), meditation in the evenings. As innocent as Chartres. And especially in relation to my children. Especially the last child, the little boy. I always had this craziness inside me of wanting to be a woman. I'd been raised that way. I was an only child and my mother wanted/needed a girl...someone to pass on her 'special knowledge' to. But all that shit was so well-defined, specific, shoes, shoe-fetishism, pantyhose-itis, and I'd always been ashamed of it until Chichi came along and liberated it and said it was OK, I didn't have to hide it fulltime but could expand out into my "bunnyness" in the privacy of our shared time. And they knew, Mabel and Myrtle did, that the whole Bunny business was simply fulfilling my mother's careful role-modeling. And then to use that center of my shame, my hidden little sin, and cold-blooded to accuse me of having sucked on my baby's penis, and on top of that, convince my daughters that I'd done it and try to break their bonding with me, fuck up all their primal ties, muddy everything up...keep them out of school, for crissake...destroy your own kids. And why? Because Mabel was possessed by Myrtle's desire to level the world? It was like a shark feeding-frenzy. You know how that goes. You can throw bottles and tin cans, rags, revolvers at frenzied sharks, and they'll eat um like candy..."

He stopped, clenched, clotted, half a degree away from Absolute Zero.

And Larry empathized with the poor fucker, him of all people, to have his own secret "sin," not only pinned on the wall, but totally distorted...misdefined...

"So Kalakofsky answered you from Babbitt Brothers, and then...?"

"Then NOTHING. How's that...then NOTHING...kapu, fini, finished..."

"Yeah, sure...and there's no blue butterflies flying around inside my head!" another Larry inside his head following the butterflies into the forest, toward a mountain filled with ancient caves filled with petroglyphs and bones....

"Blue what?"

"Forget it...."

"Well, I'd better get back to work," Fudge up, moving toward the door, waving to his pal behind the counter, the two writers over in the corner, Fudge one of those guys who likes/needs to be 'known,' part of a neighborhood, group, tribe....then suddenly the butterflies, mountain, jungle wiped clean off the board of Larry's mind and SHE was there again, the acetate pants-suit woman, and he could smell her rancid, sticky Opium-masked sweat, taste her cold, sourdough flesh...

Larry following Fudge outside.

"So what's up...."

Larry disgusted by the stench of the acetate pants-suit woman, her face holographically hanging there in the center of Fudge's psyche, staring out of the fetid swamp of his guilt.

"Doesn't she ever take a bath?" asked Larry.

"What are talking about, for crissake!" Fudge protested. But he knew, he knew, he knew...could feel Larry's eyes, like boney hands reaching inside into the middle of his psyche, "I've gotta get going," running across the street, almost getting smashed by a big wholesale food truck...at that moment the acetate pants-suit woman's name whispered out hoarsely into the crumpling air...

THE LORD SAID UNTO SATAN

UR

As in Sum-ur or Ur-Faust...

What kind of name was that? Ur's fat sour presence expanding and filling all the space between Larry standing in front of the Cafe Espresso and Fudge across the street in front of the Great Lakes Federal Savings...

Ur-Faust in Sumer,
what is your name,
I almost have you,
fast by your mane...

And she knew too. Wherever she was, tuning into the vision too, trying to blur it, block it out...but it didn't work...there she was, five stories high smelling like a lake of moldy milk and bacon-fried beans...

"I'm inside, pal, you can't keep me out!" Larry screamed at Brian across the street, as Brian rat-skittered around the corner of the bank and disappeared.

It was always this way, wasn't it, a moment of piercing agony before the revelation, the Resurrection postulated on Golgotha, Mot must be ground and crushed by Anath before he and Baal (Bel) can re-arise and Spring can begin...

Larry walked down to the corner of Grand River and (looking up at the street sign) Abbott, the sidewalks all filled with Reeboked and T-shirted students, like flocks of Spring birds, all squawking and preening themselves.

He wanted to go back to his car and chill a little, put back the seat and die a short death, but instead crossed the street, walked past the giant brick hulk of the Student Union, on to the quad, past Norwegian pines and oaks and Dawn Redwoods, past the library, the botanical gardens, the rhododendrons and forsythias already out, down by the river again, the scene of his battle with Myrtle's spirit, over by the administration building, finding a grassy knoll next to a stand of old Norwegian pines overlooking the river.

No trace of Myrtle here in this caramel corn bursting world. A black guy walked by, blind, carrying a white cane, knew perfectly where he was going, full-speed; you'd never have guessed he was blind if you didn't look into the hollow sockets where his eyes had been.

At one point he got so enthusiastic, so 'exalted' at just being alive, that he took his cane and twirled it like it was a baton. He was King of Spring, alive, alive, alive...who needed eyes?

Larry lay back and closed his eyes...

Old Father Sun, shining down on me,
Old Father Sun, help me to see...

Only once his eyes were closed, Windy was suddenly there, at the end of a long, bare, white room, rushing toward him as he walked in the door. She was all dressed in a white ballet outside, white wrap-around skirt. Rushed toward him, into his arms...

"Why don't we start all over again?" she begged, kissing him tenderly, exploratory, puppyish..."

"If you get out of your 'relationship' with that miserable faggot you've been hanging around with," said Larry, painfully jealous of anyone else she even talked to.

"Don't start in again," she said, "that's what made it all so ugly in the first place, your insane jealousy..."

"I'm not jealous for nothing, baby..."

"I have a right to friends."

"Very indiscriminately chose."

She pulled away. Hurt. She wanted a puppy and what she'd gotten was a bear.

"I'm not just yours," she said, slipping out of his arms, turning the Turn of Regret, the Turn of Desolation, head angled down, right hand up across her face, "other parts of me have other needs..."

"Not in my script!" he called after her as she started to run away and the room filled with the middle section of Tchaikovsky's Romeo and Juliet Overture.

THE LORD SAID UNTO SATAN

He started to run after her, mirrors on both sides of the room, ballet practice bars on both walls, their images tunneling down into infinity, as...

Suddenly the whole vision shattering and Larry opened his eyes to see a huge crackling, cracking Norwegian pine falling down right on top of him...

"Holy Malolly!"

Rolling over as fast as he could, out of the way of the falling tree, escaping from the trunk itself, but one of the branches lashing down on his leg like a heavy horsewhip. But nothing broken. Just stabbing, burning pain.

As he got up, testing his legs, for a moment in the sunlight, he saw, or thought he saw, a glinting stainless steel wire coming out of a third floor window of the administration building, attached to the top of the tree, the window slightly open, the wire twitching, disappearing, the window closing.

Dismissing the whole thing as illusion. How could anyone have known where he'd be, when he didn't know himself. Nonsense. Nonsense. Had there been anything in the coffee? The guy behind the counter who knew Brian? More dope, more drugs? Didn't the assholes realize that the more dope they pumped into him, the stronger his Powers became...?

The tree real enough -- and the pain.

He limped over at looked at the snapped trunk, rotten inside, all brown and crumbly, like stale chocolate cake. And it was a windy, gusty day, a the-world-is-filled-with-the-grandeur-of-God, gusty Spring day. A bunch of gangly, blonde-beast girls rushing over to him, "Are you alright?," "Anything broken? ""You're lucky you're still alive."

A cool, loose, trim cop came hurriedly out of the administration building.

"You OK?"

Larry pulled out his badge and flashed it.

"I wouldn't refuse a ride over to where my car's parked."

"You've got it," he said, grabbing Larry's arm and helping him over to the left side of the building, where his car was parked. Larry got in.

"So where's your car?"

"Over by Jacobson's."

"OK," he said and off they went, as they rounded the corner by the University Museum, the cop asking Larry, "So what's going on?"

"Futurotech...a woman who used to work there got killed down in Chicago."

"Not Myrtle Bannister...?"

"She touched all bases, didn't she?"

"Well, I was on the Futurotech case. And she was pretty damned abrasive, a personality like a piece of industrial strength sandpaper, but, OK, cast as a monster if you like, but Mascher and Sax, the head honchos in the company...I mean all that crap about stealing the cells she had created..."

"'Created,' huh. Sounds like God..."

"Well, in a way it is like god. Those monoclonals are lab-created. And in her contract it was very clearly stated that whatever cells she 'created,' were legally hers. Yeah, Bannister told me one day, me and Officer Uitveldt, that she could genetically engineer anything. You want a gorgon, Minotaur, an albino Chinese with Black African hair? Masher and Sax claimed they'd never signed the release-form for the cells, but I SAW Bannister's carbon of it. Signed by both of them. That's why their case against her not got past pre-trial..."

"You saw a carbon...a Xerox?" asked Larry.

"Yeah, I don't know, it's been a while..."

"Well, it doesn't take a lot to cut out a few signatures, create a pretty authentic-looking document..."

"Look, I hated Myrtle as much as anyone else, but I still think that all that shit against her was engineered by Mascher in revenge for her calling him a fake."

"Only why call him a fake in the first place? Hubris!!"

166.

"Hu...what?"

"Pride! Lucifer, the Morning Star, with all his aspirations to become the Sun itself...," Larry all booming and theatrical, then a sudden switch

THE LORD SAID UNTO SATAN

back to the everyday, as they turned around the corner by the Student Union, "You can just let me out here."

"You sure you're OK?"

"I thrive on pain," Larry said cynically, as he edged his way out of the car, intrigued by the fact that he'd actually found someone on Myrtle Bannister's side!

Of course he wasn't in the company, never got in her immediate line of fire, had never been on her shit-list.

"I'm gonna have to make out a report," said the other cop, Larry reaching into his wallet and handing him a card. Always handed out cards. Something about a little card that professionalized your whole image.

"Thanks a lot!" said Larry, for the first time looking at the guy's badge number and name, filing it away in his memory banks -- Robert Van der Molen. Robert of the Mill? "Seeya!"

"You're sure you can make it?"

"No problem."

Trying not to limp too dramatically as he walked away from the car.

"Take it easy."

"You too..."

Molen, molina, moulin, moinho...recrossed Grand River, limped back to his car.

He wasn't going to stop now.

Next stop, the big boss, Mr. Hubris himself, Pride against Pride, Morning Star against Evening Star...a trip through a zodiac of lions and hydras and giant crabs...

CHAPTER 13

As he drove down Grand River toward Futurotech everything slowly got more and more surreal for Larry. He was almost totally "out of his body," floating, unsure about the reality of the street itself, the cars and people all around him. At the same time felt invincible, infinitely flexible and adaptable, able to pour in and out of matter like a Frankenstein fog.

Waiting for some car to come at him head on, for someone to throw a grenade in through one of the car's windows. He knew too much already, didn't he...? And they knew that once he was on a spoor, he never let go until the curtains of Total Revelation had opened on the stage of his soul...feeling followed, pursued, persecuted. He looked in the rear-view mirror and saw a giant Tibetan masked lion in the back seat. Blinked, and it was gone.

East versus West. It was such a joke. Reality and Illusion/Dream. They all thought they had it by the tail, but then you walked through the Doors of Perception and a whole other reality turned on... his eyes smoking mirrors, snakes slithering around his arms, stop-lights talking, the whole town scrolling up into serpentine Shang dynasty curls and loops. This was the way it really was, he thought, as he jaguar-shamaned into the heart of real reality, all tusks and claws -- and immense clarity.

Now was the time to snuff him out, wasn't it. He'd already colored in 81.7 % of the picture, and all he needed now was the eyes...and MOUTH...the better to talk to you with, my Dear!

A big Futurotech sign on a building over to his right.

He pulled into the parking lot in back and the sky burst wide open, like the day was painted on a canvas stretched across the vault of heaven and as it split open he could see the infinities of black Mother Night Space behind it all...

"Beautiful!" he said to himself, "my mono-rail into Reality..."

OMMMMMMMMMM, down, re-centering, creating a needle out of thin air and reaching up and grabbing the edges of the sky and re-sewing

THE LORD SAID UNTO SATAN

them together again so that it was just a normal, sprightly spring day again.

Got out of the car. Spirit sounds of giant, echoing "crackings," hybrid images of mastodon-skull-shaped ice-caverns, cracking and splitting open, the cracks roars, as if the skulls were alive....

He took a deep breath, time for a little Turandot on his mind-radio. Vincerá! I will conquer! At the very beginning where it's all so sensuously arabesque veils and spiced coffee.

He walked up to the front of the building and opened the big glass and aluminum door....

Olin Sax was sixtyish, blond and tanned, almost burnt/burnt-out. A Nordic Brahman, at the same time something infinitely namby-pamby weak about the man. Slippery, protozoid, protoplasmic, hidden cities and veiled waterfalls, trap-doors and dead-end slaughter corridors! And all kinds of sizzling bratwurst HATE.

The office was modest. The public face -- not a fang or claw in sight. No big oak desk, but everything steel and plastic, the standard picture of the standard wife and two standard kids on the desk...

"Not that we haven't 'met,'" said Sax with a reptilian, desultory handshake.

"And I always think of myself as so inaudible," smiled Larry, expecting the walls of the room to heat up red hot and start to close in on him, sitting down in the large, old wing-backed oak chair that Sax offered him.

"I trust your stay among us hasn't been too boring," smiled Sax, sitting back down behind his massive desk, "A little coffee?"

"Why not?" answered Larry, waiting for nets and gas, slithering coils and fangs, the Great Lanzón in the middle of the central labyrinth at Chavín, time to open chests and pull out hearts...

Sax pushed a button on the desk. Two shorts and a long. Code for GIVE THE OLD CROCODILLE A KILLER DOSE...?

"You, with all your vast powers, must have come up with something by now!" Sax mocked him.

"Oh, a few hints here and there, but not a lot," lied Larry, the Tibetan lion-head peeking out from behind the drapes now, ready to devour Sax if Larry gave him the high-sign, but instead Larry waved him away, Sax looking at the drapes and only seeing drapes, happy to see that Larry really was even spacier than everyone was saying.

A old pendulum wall clock just above and to the left of Sax's head, Larry fighting against getting drawn into the hypnotic back- and forthness, back-and-forthness of the pendulum.

"Maybe I could offer a little of my own input into the case," said Sax, very Louis Quatorze as an ample woman in acetate pants came in clumsily carrying a huge silver-plated tray with coffee, cups and a plate of croissants on it, the smell of almonds filling the air again, Larry walking through the Schönbrunn Palace in Vienna for a moment, for a moment a deep, rich coloratura "Ewig, Ewig" hovering around him like a humming bird. For a moment Larry thought that the woman with the try could be HER...UR...but no, her face was much too powder-puffy white, refined...none of Ur's vulgar, beer-hall swagger...

A touch of almonds in the coffee too. Arsenic was garlicky, almonds were, not cyanide, but...getting old, the blanks not filling instantly the way they used to...

"Enjoy!" said the secretary and left, Sax pouring out two cups of coffee, adding lots of sugar to each cup, topping it off with a head of whipped cream, very Franz Josephish, just like Larry's cafe mit schlagsahne/coffee with whipped cream, Viennese mother-in-law.

"So," said Sax, yawning, sitting back in his black iron swivel chair with thickly padded (black) back and arms, putting his feet up on the desk, all so weakly mauve and effetge in his shantung silk suit, blue shirt and ecru silk tie, "Myrtle's canonized now and all us po' sinners has got to pay?!?!"

"I know what Myrtle's supposed to have done, but what did she really do, and why did she do it?" said Larry, putting lots of butter on his croissant, playing out his line, waiting, waiting, waiting for a strike...almost adding why did she come to Earth in the first place, what do we have here that they don't have out/down there...?

"She was an angel, we all mourn her loss. I don't know how we're going to make it through without her," said Sax sarcastically, sitting there grinning like an under-nourished jack-o-lantern.

THE LORD SAID UNTO SATAN

"I'll be honest with you," said Larry, deciding to match Sax's sinuousness with dangerously straight-line candor, "I find myself somehow sympathizing with the 'executioners.' Myrtle's real talent seems to have been to take advantage of everyone's particular little weakness, like an opportunistic virus..."

Which worked, Sax's jack-of-lantern grin slowly being replaced by a sensitive, harassed, long-suffering middle-aged face full of hurt, guilt and doubt, the playboy turned Socratic warrior.

He knew the kinds of games that Larry was playing, but all of a sudden he was too old, too affluent, too world-weary to care.

"Can I talk?" asked Sax, "it doesn't have to all be the stalked and the stalkers, does it? I'm sick to death of courts, lawyers, cops..."

"I didn't hear myself reading any rights," said Larry.

"OK..." He sat back, the room filled with edge-of-audible whispers and sighs...little girls crying sitting in the middle of puddles of tears...," I might as well warn you/inform you, that this is all going on tape..." Pointing to a bouquet of fresh lilies on the desk.

"Fine with me," said Larry, sitting back and giving himself up to the moist, sad despair of Sax's soul.

"Myrtle was a kind of master psychologist/game player. She'd burrow into your skin and infallibly get right to your liver and start to lay eggs. She was viral. Always there, always alert, waiting for any kind of break in your immune system...whatever weakness you had, that would be her portal of entrance..."

"And what's yours?" Larry chanced. As long as they were in such a candid, confessional mode...

"Passivity. See no evil, hear no evil. The indifference of a rich man who has inherited and not earned his riches. Allowing myself to be bled. I mean I've always taken pride in a certain distancing I've allowed myself from the normal affairs of men. A little of the Sans Souci Syndrome, walling myself up in my own private Paradise Garden. And then being magnanimous. But every virtue has its built-in vice. Distancing and magnanimity become callousness and amorality...it's like, what's her name, Grump. On one pole was the fanatic mother, on the other the fanatic worker. You attack her fanatic mothering and you undermine the fanatic worker. I mean Myrtle's using Grump's whole breast-feeding ritual as the instrument of cutting her soul out, and using me as the obsidian, ritual knife. I mean most of us want our little space, a soft pillow, acceptance, a face to meet our face, hands to reach out when we reach out to them...we don't consciously, full-time negate our people-pleasures in order to eviscerate others...I didn't make my fortune, most of it came from my parents, a lot comes from my wife...and maybe I felt I needed to prove myself too, financially...and then to be taken for a fucking ride, to have my passivity and generosity turned into instruments of revenge or whatever else Myrtle was all about, and to ride against the Good and the Honest and the True, all under the banner of Capitalism...to be betrayed by my top general...do you see where I'm coming from...?Sax stopped and stared at Larry with obsidian intensity, suddenly transformed into an elaborately feather-head-dressed Aztec priest bringing an obsidian knife down into the chest of a sacrificial victim spread eagle out across the stone surface of the sacrificial altar...the room filled with sacrificial blood...

"The why behind Myrtle's slaughter. Some sort of ritual cleansing..."

"Only when the victim is impure the whole ritual itself becomes defiled...," Sax's voice down to a whisper now, barely able to hold back the tears."The executioners whispering things to tell the gods, into the ears of the victims...only when the victim herself is diabolical...."

"I'm sorry," said Larry, talking into the bouquet of lilies, "I don't know how I ever got into this rotten business...there's laws and then there's Laws...," Larry's head suddenly filled with dark streets, gangs, drive-by shootings, the Law and law, and how much really was dealt with, and how much escaped to come back and kill again and again...

"I was so stupid. Why did I ever give her so much power, for crissake? Why did I ever make it such an Act of Faith? DO WHATEVER YOU HAVE TO DO AS LONG AS YOU BRING HOME THE BACON! And she betrayed me anyhow. The whole time she was here she was applying for jobs elsewhere, never intended to stay here in the first place. And then, when she took the cells..."

"But she had the right!" Larry interrupted impatiently.

THE LORD SAID UNTO SATAN

"To steal the core product of the company? The right to name her particular cells, the right of a creator, OK, but not to use the company as a springboard to start your own fucking company," Sax whispering now, hardly able to talk, Larry afraid he was having some sort of attack, too much emotion, going over the edge, "She made a total asshole out of me. I already suffer from deep problems of self-image...pride...my parents always took great delight in humiliating me...and then this total betrayal of trust...and then to realize that that's what she'd always intended to do...from the very beginning..."

"That's one thing I can't quite fathom. Why didn't she stay inside the company and profit from your profits...even ask for a percentage...?"

"And I would have given it to her. Only she wasn't really out for money, she was out for carnage for the sake of carnage. Evil is its own good. It's only purpose is disorder. It roams the universe looking for victims. I guess things around here were getting just a little too orderly. We really were on the brink of a real breakthrough...." said Sax, wiped out, limp as an old wet string-mop, staring down at the floor.

Larry poured himself another cup of coffee, took this one black, let his eyes stray around the empty room, the secretary gone now, no sound from the adjoining rooms. All this dead, empty space. Shadows and silence. Nacht und Nebel/Night and Fog. He usually loved and trusted Emptiness, welcomed the Angeles of Death and Nothingness with open arms...but the emptiness here filled him with a fuzzy, amorphous, sizzling sense of terror...

"There were still courts, legal recourse," said Larry, marking time now, treadmilling, his voices inside him whispering "Get out, out of here, while there's still time," the emptiness slowly starting to fill up with jaws, hooks, claws...

"They used to burn witches, didn't they?" said Sax, staring at Larry with sharp dagger eyes.

"Well, the old pagan gods had their priestesses, didn't they, the serpent had been the symbol of fertility before...," Larry starting in on a discourse about the introduction of Christianity into pagan Europe...when suddenly the door opened abruptly and his heart spasmed with terror.

But it was only the acetate secretary.

"I'm leaving now, Mr. Sax."

"OK, Julia. See you in the morning..."

And she was gone, Sax's face suddenly very old, relaxed...and very rich...

"Why don't you come over to the house for dinner?"

"Why not?!?" answered Larry.

Sax up on his feet, pulling a camelhair coat that matched his hair off a coat rack on the wall, "It gets pretty creepy around here in the late afternoons. I think your being here changes things a little...alters the balance of 'powers,'" down the stairs, out into the parking lot, as if they'd been doing it this way for a hundred years.

"You follow me, OK?"

Sax got into a caramel-colored new Cadillac and Larry followed him down Grand River, content, pissed at his contentment. The bonding of wealth. And it was a good town to be wealthy in. Minimal crime, no hordes out there at the gates raging to get inside. And to be honest with himself about if, if Myrtle hadn't been "executed," would The Law ever really have stopped her? Asshole judges and gink lawyers, a system that put murderers on parole to murder again and again...and again...remembering this art student from Little Rock who had come up to Chicago to study at the Art Institute, had gotten a job as a waitress, first week, coming home late from work...killed by some asshole on parole for murder....

Down Grand River, as they moved into Lansing everything getting seedier and seedier. It didn't make much sense, did it?

Weird turn, following a sign that pointed to the airport, a little further down, industrial stuff, old factories, a cement works, some old farmhouses that obviously had been there for more than a hundred years when it was really wilderness, then a quick, abrupt turn on Delta River Road and, wow, all of a sudden it was Grimore Park, Beverly Hills, Scarsdale...like they were in the middle of the country, Sax's place on maybe a hundred acres, a Bavarian castle up on top of a hill..a long driveway winding up to the front door...

Larry parked behind Sax in the driveway.

THE LORD SAID UNTO SATAN

"Impressive!" he said, as they walked up the broad stone steps to the massive oak doors with big wrought-iron door-knockers and locks...the doors swinging open as they reached the top...and there was a little grey Fox Terrier of a woman standing there waiting for them. When she saw Larry positively beaming, as if he were the Risen Mot, Osiris, Adonis, Christ...

"Oh, Detective Gugel...do come in...Louis is so terribly slack about letting me know who's coming to dinner."

"If it's inconvenient..."

Larry all set to turn around and go back to Brian's place, give the Kellogg Center a second try.

"Not at all, not at all, my dear man..."

Larry not at all happy with Mrs. Sax's overfriendliness. Like she'd just finished reading his autobiography and knew almost as much about him as he knew about himself.

Counterattacking with "If we were in Grimore Park, we could always go to Prasad's and have a little Thai shrimp," as he walked into the massive front hall, facing the expected bi-lateral long oak-banistered stairway, the massive candelabrum with a hundred little candle-shaped bulbs in it, hanging from the vaulted ceiling.

Sax and his missus exchanging uneasy glances at the mention of Prasad's. Larry could hear their heads talking --Who's the goddamned fuckhead who has been blabbing things all over the place?

Then Mrs. Sax forcing herself back into her Fox Terrier mode, not a care in the world, aren't we all just the silliest, most frivolous things, "How about some beer-fed, hand-massaged -- while the steers were still alive, ha, ha, ha, ha-- Japanese beef?"

"The ultimate trade deficit luxury! Wonderful!" smiled Larry.

"Much better than anything Argentinean," said Sax.

Anchorite Larry had forgotten how the rich still hovered over all this gourmet bullshit.

"We could have a beef contest," helped Mrs. Sax, "we've got both kinds on hand!"

"That's OK, Frieda," said Sax patronizingly, with just a little sprinkling of contempt, "we can just have dinner," walking through a vast sunken living room over to the left, long, stained-glass windows set in grey stone, down another hallway into an oak-paneled room filled with plush brown leather sofas, the expected monster TV...wasn't that a Monet on one wall, Toulouse Lautrec's portrait of Oscar Wilde...it couldn't be the original...could it...?

"This is practically the only room we ever use," explained Sax, sitting down on one of the sofas, with a huge weathered door made into a cocktail table in front of it, Mrs. Sax explaining "The door's from an actual wreck off of Beaver Island. That's where we have our summer cottage, although it's hardly a 'cottage.' You've got to come up there some time," Sax pushing a little buzzer on the table and a maid appearing through a door at the far end of the room, a gothic blonde in an anachronistic beige maid's outfit...nice legs, though, sheathed in black nylon...Larry could just imagine her in action, the ample breasts, totally orgasmic...

"We're having a guest for dinner, Helga. We'll have some Japanese steaks -- and make yourself one too..."

"Aber das ist nicht möglich...sind sie swabisch?/But that's not possible, are you Swabian?" asked Larry, listening to his voices, which never lied...

"Ya, richtig/ Yes, you're right," she said. "but how did you know?"

"Oh, just practice," he said.

"So your reputation for clever guessing is somewhat earned," said Sax as Helga curtsied an anachronistic curtsy and vanished, back into the kitchen.

"I wouldn't call it guessing," objected Larry. And it wasn't just his voices either, but years of physical anthropology, skull measurements, shapes, forms, "like the time I went to a cocktail party in Chicago and I got talking to this guy who looked just like the sculptures from Mohenjo Daro, and turned out to be from Karachi..."

"You're practically a legend in your own times, from what I gather," said Sax, going over to a wooden file cabinet in one corner, pulling out a manila folder filled with what looked like fresh Xeroxes of old newspaper clippings (mainly from Chicago newspapers) about Larry's cases:

THE LORD SAID UNTO SATAN

MYSTERIOUS NORTHSHORE SUICIDE NEITHER
MYSTERIOUS NOR SUICIDE, SAYS DETECTIVE GUGEL...
PUFFER FISH POISON DISCOVERED IN OREGANO LEAVES
BY DETECTIVE GUGEL OF GRIMORE PARK P.D...

"What fun!" said Larry, feeling like a big happy face all over, "I've never collected this stuff. I'd love to...."

"It's done! I'll have a duplicate set sent to you," said Sax magnanimously, laying the file on top of the cabinet, "I just always like to know what/how I'm dealing with."

He took a video tape out of out of the built-in oak shelves next to him and stuck it in the VCR next to his monster TV, pushed a couple of buttons and the screen was filled with images of a long, lanky woman going in circles with a discus cupped in one hand, circling around and around in slow motion...around and around and around, and then she suddenly let it go with a shout of triumph that he could see but not hear, music dubbed in, though, Bruckner's totally inappropriate 7th....

"She was rather impressive on the playing field," said Sax, "took great pride in her body...," adding in a hushed voice, as if he were afraid the air itself would overhear him, "as if she hadn't had it very long, as if it were all very new to her...flesh and blood and glands...it's easy to imagine her a dancer, isn't it, if she hadn't been so tall..."

"Isadora Duncan was tall," said Larry, tall Windy there, dancing inside him for a moment, black lycra legs and swirling lycra skirts, Larry suddenly realizing that Modern Dance was the invention of ballerinas who would have been awkward on points...the image on the screen now of Myrtle throwing javelin, a long, graceful run, stop, then the release, the exultant sense of joy, the beautiful, full, graceful, savage expanse of leg...

"Interesting 'monster,'" said Larry bitterly, thinking yes, once she'd gotten a body, it was a whole different game for her, she must have been torn between simply 'being,' being 'here,' and having to function as Pure Negativity, tearing out the bowels of the Good and the True...

"She didn't know who she was," said Sax, unconsciously echoing Larry's thoughts, as Helga came in with three flagons of beer, the flagons with little hinged, peaked "hats" on top, Mrs. Sax busily explaining "Czech pilsen...there's a certain Old European resonance.."

Sax impatient with her footnotings.

"Myrtle never knew who she was, she could have been a gazelle, a porpoise...watch this..."

STOP, then FAST FOREWARD, STOP again, PLAY, Beryl up on top of an Olympic high diving board, first regular speed, then slow motion, Larry focusing on Myrtle's python-anaconda legs as she leaped off into infinity, her legs starting to wrap around and around his soul and he started to want her the way he wanted Yayé, Teonanacatl mushrooms, immortality, to have been at Tiawanaku in ancient times, on the day of the Winter Solstice when all the tribes of the world took their sacred drug, died and were reborn as immortal jaguar shamans....

"Beautiful!" he allowed himself out loud.

"I think we all felt something like that about her...at least at the beginning," said Sax...then stopped, his face slowly going tragic, limp, melting, his eyes wide, wet, amphibian...

"Louie, are you alright, Louie...?" Mrs. Sax desperately concerned.

Sax ignoring her, totally inselved, interiorized, sitting there staring at Myrtle breast-stroking through the pool, up on the diving board again, sleek in her black lycra swimsuit that barely could contain her huge, pendulous breasts, the rest of her insect slim...the perfect body...a black guy on the screen with Myrtle now, handing her a towel, a look of disdain and contempt on his face, like he'd bitten into a rotten banana...then a sudden switch to Myrtle on a track now, black lycra tights, her muscles rippling and flowing under her black lycra second-skin...

Sax's face as big as the room by now, a mesmerized, spaced-out...then suddenly contracting down into a pinpoint of punishing rage, turning the whole show off...the whole screen blank...that was it, fuck it....

"What wrong? That was a great video," complained Larry, over-reacting, then calming himself down, imagining he was blowing reddish-

THE LORD SAID UNTO SATAN

purple libidinous smoke out of his left nostil, all his runaway desires contained in the smoke itself, filling the whole room with a reddish-purple tinge as his own inner landscape flattened out and cooled down again, Sax, not as savvy as Larry in the gymnastics of the soul, still boiling with rage, grief, loathing, turning to Larry...

"Do you believe in diabolical possession?"

"I believe in everything," answered Larry, "Especially in the fact that the so-called Devil is really Lucifer, the Morning Star, Quetzalcoatl, the Plumed Serpent, Hermes with his caduceus and winged feet, psychopompos traveler between worlds, the serpent in the Garden of Eden House of the Sun who couples with Mother Eve and yearly re-fertilizes the world.....replaced by the Begone-Satan-Christ and his serpent-treading virgin Mother...so if you're possessed, what possesses you, my friend, the Herald of the Dawn...?"

Sax suddenly vicious, mouthing a silent "Asshole!," getting up and going over to a teakwood cabinet against the wall and getting out a big, black cigar.

"I thought you'd gotten rid of all those?!?!" Mrs. Sax said irately.

"Just an emergency stockpile," said Sax, lighting one up, puffing out big dragon-bursts of flame, then re-directing himself back to Larry, "So it's all just astronomy, astrology and myth, huh?"

"Or witch burning? How's that? Exorcism. Only who's the possessed and who's the possessor?" answered Larry with a twisted paper-clip of a smile thinking that the only mythology he was interested in right now was a big unpossessed bed in an empty room.

"Let me go check on the food," said Mrs. Sax, all fluttery and bubbly, disappearing out the door at the far end of the room.

"No real devils in your system, then?" asked Sax, sitting down and drawing on his cigar like his life depended on it.

"I look up at the night sky and all I see are question-marks," said Larry with tragic candor.

"OK! In your terms, then," Sax's face softening, pacified by his cigar, "Do you know how much I lost because of Myrtle? Maybe twelve million! She was on the edge of a momentous technological breakthrough that would have changed the whole trajectory of human history. In fact I think she did break through and withheld the data," his voice all dry bones being ground into a powder in an ancient stone mortar, "was using the capsules herself...the area around her eyes, her breasts, legs....," stopping, standing there in Antarctic, Tristan de Cunha aloneness...

"Who was the black guy in the last few feet of the Myrtle tape?" asked Larry, suddenly cerebral, 'occidental,' on the case again.

Sax following suit, unfreezing, turning on a cassette player on a table behind him, six monster speakers all around the room bathing them in Bartok's *Microcosmos*, turning down the volume so that the music was just a scrolled ripple in the background, sitting down in one of the plush leather sofas opposite Larry, all rational and urbane again.

"Oh, that was Kelley, one of Myrtle's last victims. A black Cherokee from the Carolinas. He was supposed to take care of the liquid nitrogen levels in the tanks. So far, so good. But then Myrtle started doing it herself and he assumed that that would free him to do other things. Which was logical, wasn't it? There were always all kinds of projects going on, and he started getting involved with other things, got scarcer and scarcer and the scarcer he got, the more interested in him Myrtle became. She wanted his head! Maybe she was already stealing cells and he'd stumbled on to her storage-space...," Sax beginning to get agitated again, starting to whisper, trying to keep it down, under control, "I don't know, there were always all these stories about how Myrtle was born 'dead,' strangled by her own umbilical cord, oxygen deprivation. Which -- on a logical, rational level -- could explain the behavior deviations. Born out of wedlock. Her mother didn't have anything to do with her until she was in her teens. Raised by a grandmother who treated her like a chair, a chest of drawers. You know the crazy-monkey experiments, no touch, no sanity. And all the shit in the lab was only a prelude. Look what she did to Fudge and the little boy. Didn't someone, some-THING have to stop her?"

"This horrible illusion that we really ARE..." said Larry, his voice, spirit, dissolving like the smoke from Sax's cigar.

"What the fuck are you talking about?" Sax practically hissing now, no patience for Larry's games.

THE LORD SAID UNTO SATAN

"Aunque sea jade, se rompe, aunque sea pluma de Quetzal, se desgarra, todos vamos al lugar de los descarnados/Even though it be jade, it breaks, even though it be the plume of the Quetzal, it shreds, and we all go to the place of the unfleshed," answered Larry, "A little Aztec poem...and you can't say the Aztecs didn't function in the so-called 'real' world..." Larry said, closing his eyes, coming in and out of being, in and out of nothingness, at every breath staying just a little longer in the real of Non-ness...

"Everything's ready!" Mrs. Sax clickty clacking back into the room, followed by Helga carrying a big bamboo tray loaded with metal plates in molded wood bases, huge steaks, bright lime-green beans, delicate curls of French Fries, "and the Beef was made Flesh," handing Larry a plate, steak knife, fork, "life is too short to get all involved in abstractions..."

Larry dipping one of his fries into the steak sauce, cutting a chunk of steak and carefully getting them together on his fork, sticking them into his mouth.

Perfect.

The meat marinated in some sort of soy-sauced vinegarish garlic sauce, as soft as putty or wet clay, so refined that it had lost the weedy, fibrous pungency of real flesh but had become a chunk of dream-beef, full of chants and incantations, the fry crunchy, primitive, primal...

"The Great God Krazny is pleased!" smiled Larry as he closed his eyes in a moment of perfect nirvanic peace...

"Krazny...?" asked Sax.

"Chief god of the Zakut Indians in Ecuador...well, sometimes they're in Ecuador, sometimes in Peru, Colombia...nomadic...I spent a lot of time with them...they choose their wise man at birth...chosen by other wise men. Feed them on powdered coca from the time they are born, never see the light of the day, are only taken out at night when the moon is out...and when they grow up, these are tribe's shamans/soothsayers/rulers...wisdom is darkness, sanctity is living inside the womb of Mother Night..."

"Interesting, interesting...," said Sax, his mouth filled with a bulky wad of meat, after an intensely pleasurable chewing session, asking Larry, "How's this for the real thing...?"

"Bring your bullocks unto me, saith the Lord, burn them in front of my tabernacle, for that is how you shall do expiation for your sins," said Larry, taking a healthy swig of beer.

"Vill there be anything else, Ma'am?" asked Helga.

"Maybe some mud-pie later," said Mrs. Sax, "but not for a long while...enjoy!"

Helga smiled, Larry lusting after the monumental athletic-ness of her black-nyloned legs as she sinuously walked across the room and disappeared through the kitchen door....

The beer smarted a little, tingled as it pearled down Larry's throat and he welcomed its sweet minor narcotization . A heavy weight of fatigue/sin/guilt weighted him down, Maxine on a flat-bottomed boat inside him, the Angel of Death poling her through the misty Waters of Death to Death Island, every moment her tiny little white face getting fainter and fainter, for a moment the steak and beer and the Saxes themselves and the carefully planned opulence of their house becoming totally unreal, and the only reality becoming Maxine's eyes, wide and fixed, filled with realization that she was only yards away from the black looming cave-riddled rock of Death....

Larry yawned and closed his eyes, trying to see the face of the Death-Angel, hidden in a black cowl....sliding slowly down into blank, zero obliviousness, his whole consciousness inside-outing like a giant black glove, the Bartok irritating, too cerebral, theoretical, Schönbergian, Bergian....

Sax going on, oblivious to Larry's slow sliding into Non-Ness, the nether-side of Death.

"It could have been so good for the two of them. I'd just signed a contract with them. Myrtle at sixty thousand a year for five years, Mabel, because of her more 'amateurish' research-status, twenty thousand a year...eighty thousand together. And I offered them ten percent of my gross annual profit once the pills were on the market. They could have made millions through me. Which even makes less sense for Myrtle to be

THE LORD SAID UNTO SATAN

applying for other jobs the whole time, undermining the whole company here so that without her there would be really anything left. Like it wasn't enough to abandon the ship, she had to sink it too. And then the crucifixion of Bryan Fudge. All that shit about Bunny -- and who had encouraged all that Bunny shit in the first place? Myrtle!"

Larry inside Death now, no (wir haben/we have) afterlife (nur/only), only (einmal/once) bones, skulls (einmal und nichts mehr/once and no more), all the Earth was was a vast cemetery for billions, trillions of people who had hoped that when they died some other Self would rise up like an ignis fatuus swamp-gas butterfly and fly up to a Heaven that never existed except in the realm of (gewesen zu sein/to be) wishful thinking...although...

"Just think about it for a second," Larry said, more to himself than anyone else, "if demons and angels exist..."

"Here, I can't drink anymore," said Señora Sax, pouring almost her whole flagon into Larry's, which was almost empty.

A very sexy little move. She must have been an exquisite piece when she was young. Even now she was still a cute little pug, but subtract forty years, and...Larry thinking of the ugly old lizard ladies with rheumy, running eyes who you can't even imagine young and beautiful, with their rose-petal skin and bright marble eyes...remembering Maxine's all-spice, mincemeat, marzipan flesh when he first met her.

"If demons and angels exist...?" Sax interested.

"Who can fathom how it all began. We create God to explain it because we can't imagine it to have eternally been, so we create an eternal God, who we can't imagine either. And we can't imagine it just 'beginning' by itself either..."

Wanting to just get up and leave, drive back to Chicago while Maxine was still warm and breathing, one last act of homage to all the beatitude they had experienced together...

"That's a little too deep for me!" said Señora Sax with a little blonde snicker.

"Me too," said Sax, "I don't know, I've been sitting here thinking about how Myrtle had corrupted Mabel...like Brian showed me a letter she'd written him when he was first in Brazil. He'd gone on ahead alone to get an apartment, gets things set up, Mabel was with her family in Nebraska, and she wrote Fudge that what they had between them actually 'defined' marriage, that she totally understood the story of Ruth, and leaving father and mother, country, identity, and cleaving to your spouse and the two become one flesh and one spirit...," his voice cracking, but still not stopping, "I was touched by the miracle of a blessed marriage in the Age of Doubt...and the Lesbian...I always felt it was something Myrtle had invented in order to turn Mabel into a willing stooge...and when Chichi testified against Myrtle and Mabel by simply telling the truth about what she regarding the missing cells and they took the little boy and stripped him down naked and started massaging his penis with Cortisone cream and suggesting to him over and over that his father had sucked on his penis. Didn't the skies cry out for justice? But Myrtle and Mabel got this amoral little Pit Bull lawyer who crucified Fudge in the courtroom, and the two monsters went off with the three kids like three cats in a bag...."

"Suppose there is a 'Spirit World, that my shamanic revelations aren't just hallucinations but realities'" said Larry, feeling 'presences' begin to accumulate in the shadows around the four corners of the ceiling, under chairs, under the rugs, "and it's not just all one continuous piece, but it has its own cycles... and..." moving toward a WHY behind Myrtle's incarnation.

"From what I understand, anything I'd say couldn't be used in court against me. You never read me my rights, as they say...I don't know if you're aware of that...you seem to be so...," Sax stopping, his Mrs. getting all piqued and disturbed at him.

"Shut up, will you! We have everything and then you..."

Ringing for Helga, ringing, ringing, ringing...break the flow...

Sax calming her down.

"It's OK...I know what I'm doing..."

"See no evil, hear no evil, speak no evil, that's me," said Larry thinking of molecules as universes, and our universe as the molecules of yet another larger universe, universes contained inside of universes, the body (mummies in the Field Museum/Brooklyn museum) as merely the temporary vehicle for the spirit. He knew they were there, the spirits, didn't he, knew that the physical world was merely the unreal terminal for the ghost/geist/spirit plasma that swirled and eddied around him,...and then slowly all the cases he hadn't solved beginning to run through his mind, all the faces without eyes, or eyes without faces, bloody shot-gunned corpses on bright green Spring grass, or slumped blue-faced, forward on top of a shattered blue Ming plate...

"I'm really tempted," said Sax, his voice getting all mossy, sea-weedish, tea-leafy, limp, "tempted to spill the beans, as they so vulgarly put it...but I really am dying to know just how much you have...how much is pure Gugelian bravado, and how much is, if I may use the word, evidence..."

Mrs. Sax desperately ringing her servant-summoning bell again, Helga finally coming in with more beer, Larry hungry for a little, what was it chocolate mousse, something cloyingly, pathetically sweet. But he compliantly took a beer and refilled his flagon, wondering if they slipped something into his food, coated the lining of his particular flagon, the room beginning to perceptibly slide away from him, everything going hollow and brittle, "framed," letter-box edition, tunnel-vision/-acoustics...

"How much do you HAVE...
HAVE...HAVE....
HAVE...?

Sax's voice all over the place, like a stone bouncing around on the sides of an old primitive flagstone well.

"Oh, I'm there and back a thousand times," answered Larry from the bottom of his own private well, "only you can't sell visions to judges; I've got to be a little careful with what I say about spirit voices..."

Trying to laugh, not quite making it to a whimper.

"You look so tired," said Mrs. Sax, her voice all wrapped in seductive lace and leather, "maybe you'd like to lie down...we've got a guest room just down the hall..."

"No, no, I'm fine," his voice falling off the edge of the Atlantic Trough, tumbling down to its deep, black bottom.

"You must be totally exhausted," Mrs. Sax grabbing him by one arm, Sax himself by the other, pulling him (slow motion) to his feet, like the time he'd almost OD-ed on Jimson Weed, when his gallbladder had ruptured in the middle of the Madre de Dios jungle, when he'd had mastoiditis when he was five, letting himself be pulled, in a way grateful for the peace-that-passeth-understanding, guiltless calm he felt/always longed for, both of them leading him gently into a marvelously pastel guest room with a giant comforter covering a giant bed, squares of muted reds and blues and grees, a muted Madras color landscape of pure hallelujahs...

"A little background music?" asked Mrs. Sax, pushing a button on the stereo over in the corner. Late Delius...luminous shards of visionary stasis...

They pulled off his shoes as he collapsed on the bed. It was almost like cork, no, more like a slightly deflated basketball. His bier. Death of Beowulf, consumatus est, death wishes flooding through him as Delius poured out moistly into the Turneresque fog-light and Mrs. Sax got another comforter out of a simple cherry-wood cabinet against the wall, and carefully spread it over him so that he was sandwiched between soft feathers...

"If you need anything, pull this..."

Yellow cord hanging from the ceiling.

"Just relax, you're in safe, albeit somewhat frustrated hands," said Sax, his wife giving him another shut-up-will-you-you-idiot glance.

"Sor-ry!"

"Sleep! Sleep!" they both intoned over him, like they'd been practicing for years, "Sleep! Sleep!"

Out the door. Once last solicitous look.

And then they were gone and Larry let himself go back, back...

What, thirty years? The picture he had in his study at home, of him lighting up Maxine's cigarette at a tea-time party at her sorority house at Northwestern, the way we were, only when we were that way never aware of our "wereness"...

His eyes closed.

THE LORD SAID UNTO SATAN

Next slide. Changing channels. What now? Letting himself. Letting it crowd in around him...floating along on the edge of a people-circle in the dark, breaking through the circle, Myrtle there, burning, screaming, still trying to get away as everyone kept throwing flaming darts at her, Larry feeling infinite compassion for her, not transcendent, immortal Evil, but very mortal, agonizing CRAZY, the way she'd been raised, crooked bricks and bad mortar, Myrtle trying to roll herself around in the wet leaves in the driveway now, and snuff the flames out. But the gasoline she'd been covered with was very special, sticky, persistent...he could (slow motion) see her mouth opening in the midst of the flames, screaming, at the same time trying to suck in air, but only sucking in the flames themselves, Larry reaching down to her, Come unto me, all ye who suffer..., but she was unreachable, falling into her own private dimension of unutterable pain, Larry looking back at the circle and seeing all the faces, the keystone fat woman in the acetate pants-suit there in the center, everyone else in a way her assistants, all the faces he would have expected to see...reaching out, reaching out to her burning body, still alive, her eyes still able to see him, transferring her pain over to him so that he began to burn too, I AM THE BURNED SHEPHERD, I LAY DOWN IN HELL FOR MY SHEEP...suddenly down on the ground with her, embracing her, engulfed in the same flames that were consuming her, whatever she'd been or done absolved now by his all-consuming messianic, sacrificial pesach lamb redemptive will-act: THOU SHALT COME UNTO ME AND BURN A BULLOCK AND THY SINS SHALL BE FORGIVEN THEE...

Passing through/beyond pain now, all pain receptors burned away, lying down on their backs together like two figures on an old Norman tomb, the flames dying out, the killers blowing away like morning mist off the surface of the ancient sea, dead atop the wet leaves in the driveway, charred beyond recognition...a thousand years passing, cosmic and earthly dust covering them, bones at Çatal Hüyük, Morhenjo Daro...the sun coming up as diggers uncovered them, as anonymous as if they'd never been...

Larry opened his eyes.

Only one light in a mango yellow shade over in the corner. Such a garden salad room, cabbage purple and kiwi fruit green, parsnip ecru, anise greenish-white...

The stereo just a hiss now. He got up and pressed OFF, wandered back into the living room. No one there. A little after three AM and part of him just wanted to go back into the guest room and sleep it off. Obviously that was what was expected of him. Only The Enemy always underestimated his Neanderthal recuperative powers, didn't they?!? Took a piss in a bathroom off the living room. Of course there'd be bathrooms and half-baths sprinkled all over the place, wouldn't there...then was making his way down gothic corridors toward the front door when *something inside him began to hum again, something "clicking" off on the fringes of hearing, something like the clicking of insect mandibles...anthropods...joint-footed exoskeletons...*

Old Grandfather Fire, Huehueteotl, whispering in his mind, "To your left, that door, it's open...then the big oak desk..."

He opened the big oak door at the end of the corridor, just before you got to the outside door.

He was almost afraid it was a bedroom and they'd be in there. But Old Grandfather Fire wouldn't do that to him, would he.

It was an office.

Reached over to the wall next to the door looking for a light, but Old Grandfather Fire whispered to him "You don't need a light, I will direct you." Feeling himself pulled into the room, back to a big squat desk, listening to old wrinkled Grandfather Fire on the edge of solstice waiting to be reborn with the bright shining vigor of the Morning Star, "Into the big desk, bottom left drawer...," his fingers feeling deftly in the dark, coming across a stack of envelopes all lined up lengthwise in a row, "Any one envelope...," lifting one out, turning on the desk light, the place full of computers and diskette storage cabinets, the financial heart of Saxdom?

It was just a simple phone bill and Larry got all sour-apple cynical for a moment, asking Old Grandfather Fire, "Why?," his voice cracking back at him like a bullwhip, "Open it up, you're on your own now," his

THE LORD SAID UNTO SATAN

crackling sun-hum presence chillingly gone, The Sustainer no longer there to sustain.

Larry opened the envelope. There was a whole list of calls from Sax's East Lansing phone to an unidentified number in Skokie -- 312-594-6911, Larry afraid he'd forget the number (the "clicking" in the corridor approaching the door now, closing, closing, closing), taking a little memo pad sheet and pen out of the middle drawer, worried about leaving an impression of the Skokie number on the notebook, taking a square of memo paper and putting it in the palm of his head, writing down the number.

Something "real" this time.

OK, OK. Remembering that evidence clause about THINGS IN PLAIN SIGHT being Kosher...carefully putting the letter back in the drawer and wiping everything clean, slipping the paper-slip with the number on it into his pocket, light out, back to the door, carefully and fearfully opening it...seeing the black shapes half way down the corridors suddenly contract into compact running legs and lunging at his throat, all dream-silent, de-barked silent, killer SHADOWS...

He'd never make it to the front door but at the same time couldn't allow himself to get trapped in the office, so he sat quickly down on the door, hands over his head, and turned himself into a passive victim-ball, the dogs still descending on him, starting to rip at claw at him, his voices within him whispering WHEN THE DEMON, MARA, DESCENDS TO DISMEMBER ME, IF THIS BE DEATH, SO LET MY DEATH BE THE FULFILLMENT OF THE STASIS OF MY LIFE...so saith the Buddha...

Then hearing, what was it, some "throb"/"pulse" in the air and the dogs immediately pulled back, off, melted back into the blackness of the corridor, and Larry got up and stepped out the front door into the starry, new-moon Spring night, frogs somewhere in the distance screaming their piccolo-pitched mating-screams, quickly out to his car, amazed at his own Jack-be-nimble quickness, one last glance back at the house, not quite sure if he saw one drape close as he looked at it, light softly slipping back to black again. It was all dreamlike, and he wouldn't have been at all surprised if he'd opened his eyes and found himself back in the salad room again. But when he stopped at a stoplight and looked down at his hands, he saw them all cut and bleeding, the sleeves of his white coat all shredded...

Abbott and Saginaw, there was an all-night Standard station on the corner. Larry parked over to the side, got out and went to the phone inside. There was a beautiful young girl in a Plexiglas cage, pale white lily face, black eyes and long black ponytail. Mimi, Act III of La Boheme. Fucking crazy to put a beautiful young woman like this alone in a gas station after (3:25) midnight...

"I just wanna use the phone."

"OK..."

She was close to panic, him all so chewed- and bloodied-up.

Went to the phone and, using his calling card number, dialed the Chicago number that had been on the phone bill.

Three rings. Four. Five. And then on the sixth ring, someone answered and Larry's hands suddenly got all sweaty. Like in the old days before he'd even imagined that would could ever be a Maxine, when he was in love with Petra Bolini and he'd stalk the blocks around her house on the Near North Side for hours before he finally gathered up nerve to walk up the broad stone steps of her father's mansion and ring the bell.

"Hello? What the f....?" the voice on the other end of the line all broken glass and twisted barbed wire. The Ur-voice. It was Ur, wasn't it? Her face starting to flesh out around the voice, her whole body (and acetate pajamas) beginning to image-out in his mind.

"How the fuck you doin', Ur?" asked Larry, weisenheimer-mode...the only way he could function without stammering...

"Who is this?"

Her voice suddenly all Crystallnacht-terror, and he was inside her head as she began to image him out around the skeleton of his voice.

"This is the Human Torch come to illuminate your memory a little!" he laughed.

A short quick 'in-breath,' and the line went dead, then back to the dial-tone.

"So what's going on?"

THE LORD SAID UNTO SATAN

The girl in the Plexiglas cage a little worried, but more curious than worried.

"Cops and robbers, and believe it or not, I'm the cop," he said, his huge fat German face oozing old man benignity, as he started out the door, then turned around, the girl in the Plexiglas's hand instinctively going down to the panic button, Larry oozing just a little more benignity, magnanimity, "One more call, my wife's had a stroke and I just want to check in on how she is..."

"No problem."

Dialed home. You never knew.

And Mrs. Barker, after six rings, lifted up the receiver.

"I didn't know whether you'd be there or not."

"I figured it would be better for me/us to stay around here...take a little break from home, at the same time be 'available'...."

"I appreciate it," said Larry, Mrs. Barker, her man, her whatever, always at the center of trust...

"And Maxine?"

"I went down to see her last evening. The doctor says she could last for years...or for hours..."

"Couldn't we all!?!" he answered, mordant, soaked in despair, never more aware of his own slipping, sliding, evaporating mortality.

"Ain't that the truth!"

"So, listen, I'll be back as soon as I can...if I don't manage to get wiped out up here."

"It don't make no sense to me why you're there in the first place. With all your money, why don't you just quit, retire already, look at a wall," Mrs. Barker genuinely concerned, maternal, sisterly...close, oh, so close to Larry...

"I know, I know," said Larry, "maybe I'm running away from the Angel of Death..."

"Or toward him!"

Larry stalled for a moment, remembering his mother and father, all their friends, all his uncles and aunts, grandmothers and grandfathers...a whole world wiped out...the continuous holocaust that never stopped...

"Thanks, pal..."

"I love you, Larry," she said.
"Me too."
And he hung up. The sister he'd never had.
Then one last call, like the calls were life, breath, survival for him. The Grimore Park P.D.
"Hello, Grimore Park Police Department, this is Linda..."
Popsicle-sized blonde, all fluff and feathers, soft toilet seats and lacey white Kleenex box holders.
"Hey, Linda, this is Larry. Still in Michigan. I need an 200.
address from a phone number. Give it to Monaghan, he's never got enough to do..."
"I'm gonna tell him, Larry!"
"So, tell him. The best favor you could ever do me is to make him my enemy. Here's the number...."
And he gave her Ur's number.
"So howya doin', Larry, anyhow?"
"Getting the bad guys restless!" he laughed.
"Larry, get the fuck outa there..."
"The last full measure of devotion and all that," he said, joshing, but scrape the surface and you hit permafrost.
"Just be careful, sweetheart!"
"Be seein' ya, pal!"
Hung up, feeling dead, imagining Linda as his real sweetheart for a moment, the lazy, nyloned legs and the lean anxious body, overloaded breasts, coming home to that every night...a spark of hope and then blackness within blackness within blackness again, and the worst part was that he was falling more and more in love with nothingness, feeling more and more that it was all pointless, los siglos por los siglos, eternity, infinite universes like bacteria in the bowels of God...standing there immobile and lost for long moments...

"I'm going to start charging you rent," said the girl in the Plexiglas cage, Larry looking over at her, the perfect proto-Indo-Mediterranean beauty, wondering up to what caliber and at what range the cage was bulletproof.

THE LORD SAID UNTO SATAN

"I'm sorry," he said, forgetting to be wiseass, "it's me and the hour, we don't mix too well," going over and buying a Payday candy bar, loving being fat, solid, the Rock of Gilbratar, fat was security, solidity, sanity, thin was weakness, chicken-shitedness, defenselessness, wispiness....

"Thanks a lot!"

"You'd better get those hands taken care of!" she said.

"I'll be OK," he said, "but thanks...seeya..."

"Take it easy."

Out the door, smiling, but under the smile fighting with the horrible premonition that within a week she'd be gunned down...Back to his Volvo. Dizzy, crazy, but afraid to sleep. Pulled the suspect list out of the glove compartment where he'd left it. What's his name, Kevin Kelley, knew he'd find him up, three AM his noon...Back inside the gas station again.

"You know where the Cherry Lane apartments are?"

She came out of her cage just as a guy in a black leather motorcycle jacket came in and Larry's hand started automatically edging toward him gun.

"I just wanna buy some cigarettes."

"I'll be with you in a second," she said, and walked over to a map on the wall, pointed out where the Cherry Lane apartments were, "You go down Harrison. There's a big sign CHERRY LANE APARTMENTS. But why don't you let it go until morning. Go down to Sparrow Hospital, emergency...get yourself fixed up..." And she showed him where Sparrow was. "Right down Michigan Avenue...you can't miss it...."

"Thanks," he said and handed her a five dollar bill.

"I can't take that," she said, getting back into her cage, handing it back to him.

Bonding. How come it always happened to easily with him.

"OK, I owe you one," he said, waved and went out, sat in his car until the guy in the motorcycle came out and he drove by and saw her in her cage, A-OK...

Took off for Cherry Lane. Put on a little Fudge:

The whole Mabel-Myrtle relationship is so forced. Mabel one day told me that "My mother better accept us or that's the last time I'll have anything to do with her." Another day they were talking about Abigail, Mabel's sister, and what would happen to her if and when her parents died (she lives with them -- unmarried)...and Myrtle said "If she moves in, I'm moving out." Another day Myrtle told Jeff, Mabel's brother, that she felt 'strangled' by Mabel, that she couldn't take it anymore...

What I'm getting at is the constant presence of the possibility of RUPTURE. Mabel loved/loves being courted by me (The Male). She liked/likes sexy clothes, earrings, The Feminine.

And there's always the implied need/pleasure of Male Adoration of The Female, which she never gets/can't get from Myrtle, whose whole orientation in life is abstract, theoretical, battle-directed.

Mabel feels a profound sense of the lack of bi-polar sexuality, with all its pluses and minuses. After all, we're genetically, cellularly bi-polar...and nobody can tell me what they have is 'normal,' because if it were, the person telling me wouldn't even be there to tell it....

The person telling me wouldn't even be there to tell it? What the hell was that supposed to mean? Larry switched it off. Fudge so awfully doctrinaire and closed. Talk about Myrtle being theoretical and abstract, what about him!!!!

And what about his own weird tendencies? Who was he to play fucking Last Judgment. People in glass houses and all that....

Larry feeling filthy and crazy for a moment as he drove down Harrison past the Kellogg Center, filled with a horrible sense of confused doubt for a moment about the voice on the phone in Chicago. Was he really tuned in to the gods...was his shamanic sixth sense on line, or...it could have been Mabel Fudge on the line in Chicago...Myrtle herself...phone line into Hell...slithering tove voices (presences) hovering around him as he drove past the Kellogg Center, past the Michigan State Police headquarters...and there it was, Cherry Lane Apartments...

He located 14 D. Second floor apartment. Institutional housing. No chispa/spark. Long, dead, grey, grey-beige carpeted corridor. Looking for D, looking back over his shoulder, down to the end of the corridor, feeling on the run now, "things" out there in the shamanplasm, a three-

THE LORD SAID UNTO SATAN

headed, thousand-headed Myrtle humming, buzzing, rasping around him, feeling the almost-incarnation of pincers, fangs, eyes on stalks, scaled tales terminating in hard little scaley rounded-edged triangles. The perfect time to do him in, whatever he knew, had guessed at, surmised, whatever had been given to him by the gods, going to Hell with him, thinking that he should have taken notes, sent postcards in to the Grimore Park P.D., left some record behind, make some permanent squeak...although...would all his scraps, hints, potshards, synodal risings of the moon, add up to anything for anyone but himself...?A baby crying behind a wall someplace, the smell of cabbage, a toilet flushing, a solitary TV news-voice, something about Bulgaria...a tiny, tiny little terrier barking from inside the Pyramid of the Sun...D. Stood listening outside the door to some sort of strangled-string Chow Mein string quartet music. Messien....? Quartet for the End of Time....Ashamed as he knocked. A little peephole in the middle of the door. It opened up. Voice through the door.

"What can I do for you?"

If he was straight he'd stammer, so...

"I know it's c..c..c..crazy, crazy late and everything, b...b...but...I'm Lieutenant Gugel, Grimore Park PD... as long as we're both up..."

The door opened. No hesitation.

"Come on in."

He was coconut husk brown, wearing an immaculately white terrycloth bathrobe and matching slippers, the room big boiler hot. Lots of books. Flat black stereo, TV, computer, Fax. He'd been sitting on the sofa reading and taking notes, the notebook full of fanatically careful diagrams, numbers, graphs, lots of computer-shit carefully taped in with transparent tape.

"I'm investigating the Myrtle Bannister murder," Larry said.

Which got a laugh from Kelley.

"Looks like someone's been trying to murder you? You'd better wash up, get some band-aids...," looking down carefully at Larry's hands, "maybe a few stitches here and there...," surface-worried, 'busy,' at the same time tearing a sheet of paper out of his notebooks and writing with a big purple Crayola marker:

AFTER YOU WASH UP LET'S GO OUTSIDE; WATCH WHAT YOU SAY!!!

"Nah, I'll just pull the edges together," said Larry, "at my age, who worries about scars," going into the washroom, feeling eyes behind the mirror, ears in the showerhead, washing the wounds, ouch, starting to bleed again, nothing deep, though, hydrogen peroxide, mercurochrome and band-aids in the medicine cabinet, quickly drawing all the bloody edges together, pouring the hydrogen peroxide over the slits, then mercurochrome, wrapping his hands in a little gauze, then out into the living room again.

"Hey, hey, hey, that's better," said Kelley, "you wanna go for coffee someplace..."

"Doughnuts," said Larry, "coffee and doughnuts."

"OK, we can manage that," said Kelley, pulling a big bulky cotton coat, elastic-waist pants over his robe, a pair of squishy black boots...

And they were out the door, leaving Messien's end of the world birds twittering on...

Out into the hallway, Larry all set to start gabbing, "Well, I'm glad we're...," Kelley's hands up, shushing him, WAIT UNTIL WE GET OUTSIDE-OUTSIDE, and then, once they were out, relaxing a little, but still looking around, suspicious, tense...

"You never know where they might be. I'm iffy about everything these days, surrounded by...," he makes a little sign in the air for INFINITY, "you really want doughnuts?"

"What do I look like?" laughed Larry, giving his paunch a little pounding.

"OK," over to his car, an old, old beige Ford Falcon, "the original Wundercar!!," still signaling Mum's the Word, the minute they got in, pushing in a cassette, more Messien...

"What's with the Messien...?"

"Bruckner for Winter, Messien for Spring..."

Still no talk, silently driving down to Grand River, right, past campus to a Dunking Doughnuts -- Open 24 Hours.

THE LORD SAID UNTO SATAN

Larry welcoming the rich smells, orange walls, anything to fight back the depression that was settling over him like ashes. An old guy at the counter with a cup of coffee in front of him, keeping out of the cold.

Larry got a couple of chocolate crème-filled killers, Kelley just had coffee, shepherded Larry over to a table way in the back in the corner, next to an enormous plate-glass window.

"It's like being a fish in the Shedd Aquarium!" laughed Larry, munching in to the doughnut, sucking on the chocolate crème filling, Ahhhh, Valhallah...."

"I think we're OK here, although...," Kelley lightly touching Larry's arm, "look!" A car pulling into an empty bank-lot a quarter of a block down, "Sax doesn't know what to do with his money...Sax, and then...if I were you, I'd disappear into the Andes somewhere and forget the whole thing..."

The girl behind the counter could have been the sister of the girl at the gas station. No Plexiglas here.

"Great little college town and adjacent state capital!" said Larry, all set to vanish up the world-tree at the world-center for another death and rebirth, his jaguar-shaman self beginning to wear thin, get all watered-down by some much contact with the petty and profane...

"It was pretty laid back until...," Kelley suddenly getting up, getting a bran muffin to go with his coffee.

"Until...?"

"I came to the point when, the minute I went to sleep, I'm slash and dismember her all night long. She had this 'gift' for getting into the heart of whatever was most sacred to you. Like, OK, I'm part Indian, part Black, Gay...so, you know, the Gay-bit was supposed to be some sort of link to her, the Indian-Black bit meant irresponsible, lazy, makeshift...my Ph.D. from Chapel Hill didn't mean shit. Irresponsible is as irresponsible does. When the real problem was that she was always fucking around under the counter, one scam after another. I was doing my liquid Nitrogen job just fine, then she comes along and starts doing it for me, so I pull out...and why is she monkeying around with the liquid Nitrogen? Because she's starting to steal and store cells...so she really wants me out...no witnesses...and it all gets twisted around to look like I'm not doing my job...cover-up after cover-up..., " movement in the middle-distance, the car half a block down, someone had just gotten out, the interior lights flicking on and then off, Larry feeling sudden supersonic pings of misgiving, black, membranous wings inside himself starting to unfold, the occupant of the car beginning to move toward them through the shadows, "the irony being that I'm still working in the same lab, and she's history...," Kelley picking up Larry's uneasiness, following his eyes out the window, only he doesn't have Larry's owl-eyes, lizard-skin, aura-skin, "What's coming down?"

Larry "feeling" the guy in the car moving toward them, like he was crawling up his own arms, into his ears, shadow demons snuggling along the fringes of bushes and along the sides of old brick buildings, pseudopoding toward them, Kelley just beginning to relax and spill a couple of beans, and now....

"Listen!" Larry said, all wind and spinnings now, "there's someone out there...maybe we ought to just..."

"Listen yourself, ever since Myrtle was killed...it's like it's full-time..."

Larry suddenly cold, hard steel. Landmines and lugers.

"Why don't you really tell me about it, quit the bullshit!" Before the Evil coming toward them totally wrapped around and engulfed them, squeezed the juice out of them, clawed out their eyes, "I'm not here on vacation, pal..."

Kelley moving toward hysteria now, peering out into the unfathomable, dead darkness, "The finger always comes back pointing to me, doesn't it...but it wasn't be, for crissake, all of her victims weren't here, the minute she go to Chicago, she started the same kind of shit she was doing around here...what is Evil anyhow, but disorder...and Buckley and his scattershot habit of..."

The presence of Evil so strong now that Larry could smell it, like unwashed bodies, rotting bodies, old piss in abandoned stairwells...And suddenly it was THERE, not just vibrations any more but a Study in Grey (trench coat, hat) and Black (glasses, moustache, pants, shoes) emerging from the shadows, framed in the window, something in his black-gloved hand.

"Oh, my god, my father's Palestinian!" the girl behind the counter screamed as Larry grabbed for Kelley as he himself hit the deck, Kelly resisting, "I know that guy, he's one of those droids who work for the Hyde Brothers..."

Too late, too late. Larry saw it coming, grabbed for Kelley's legs as the giant figure in the window tossed something through the glass, right at Kelley's chest, the whole restaurant exploding, Larry feeling his left hand and his back erupt into pain, struggling to his feet to see...Kelley painted all over the walls....

The grenade must have gotten him right in the gut and the remains of a rib-cage of sorts was hanging on the chair opposite Larry, his legs were intact, his head was over in the corner in front of the shattered doughnut case, but the rest of him had been blown all over the walls. Larry could see pieces of tomato and green pepper, half-chewed crusty dough -- the pizza that Kelley must have had for dinner. Oddly enough Kelley's head, his face, had been oddly touched...eyes closed, Buddhistic calm...if you didn't know better you'd think he was peacefully asleep...

Larry reaching back to his back, a big piece of plate glass stuck in him. But not too deep, he didn't think. Took a handkerchief out of his pocket and with his right hand, painfully pulled the glass out, threw it on the floor, looked at his left hand, another piece...pieces...of glass...which he carefully picked and pulled out...

Larry talking to Kelley's head.

"I'm sorry, pal, you seemed like such a great...."

Wrapping his handkerchief around his hand and looking out where the window used to be, going into Kelley's pants pockets, finding the keys to the Falcon, leaving the girl behind the counter crying to herself, stretched out on the floor.

"Someone'll call the cops, just stay there...it's a 5.2 on the Richter Scale." Limping outside, every step his back and arms erupting into wild, tingling, slashing pain, like he was being devoured by fire-ants.

He got into Kelley's car, his head all full of agendas, get back to HIS car, back to the Kellogg Center, get his stuff, over to the East Lansing PD, hospital, report, wrap things up, close, no loose ends...but as he started up, the other car half a block down started up too, his ears, shamanic sensors better than ever....

Out of the lot. Praying to the gods of the four quarters, Ekekko-Kubera, leprechaun dwarf-miners to the North, Pacha-Camac-Varuna, He Who Plots and Seasons and the Courses of All Things, to the West, Illimani-Indra-Lightning-Power, to the East...and more than anyone else 210.

Yama/Ah Yamas/Satan-Chavin, He Who Judges, Lord of Hell...to the south, south, south....

"Fuck you!" he screamed at the black car that pulled out after him as he zipped by, gave him the Royal Finger and jammed the accelerator down to the floor....

* * * * *

He didn't have the foggiest notion where he was, and he didn't care. 4:05 on his watch. Side road down to a lake, kept going along the shore untill he found a little cul de sac screened by bushes, backed in, as far as he could go, turned everything off, collapsed inward, exhausted, but at the same time strangely up, high...

He'd thought he'd lost the droid time after time on the freeway, would began to relax, and re-check his rearview mirror and there he'd be. Very patient. Very determined. And no matter how fast Larry had gone, no matter what circus tricks he'd put the old Falcon through, no cops. It was a strange message -- you're on your own, baby, there is no God.

Got off the freeway at Kalamazoo, played the Old Possum Game in a driveway near downtown, quick around a corner, the droid at least a block behind, quick into a driveway, all the way, way, way back, out of sight behind conically trimmed firs, everything off, waiting, waiting, waiting, another car zipping by, then the droid who must have taken the other car for him, kept going, amazed at the droid's stupidity, although he must have been exhausted too...waited one eternity, another half an eternity...then got out and borrowed a car parked in front of the house, very slowly started out of town and drove just as far into Nowhere as he could get...

"Shit!"

THE LORD SAID UNTO SATAN

Got out of the car (an old Buick station wagon, full of tools in the back), took a piss, then climbed into the back, pushed aside some of the tools, cradled his head on his arm, didn't even take his gun out and hold it in his hand, the way he'd first intended to, figuring that he'd probably end up shooting his own brains out...then just let himself go...slide into whatever came...Delevan, Wisconsin, their summer home, him and Maxine alone, the kids off with friends, the upstairs room (with the fireplace), the two of them in bed after sex...reaching out for a crazy moment, almost expecting her to be there...the last thing he was aware of before he moved into white chalk dreamlessness, the corrosive, burning-rubber presence of a skunk in the vicinity, who had sprayed the night with the unmistakable protective I.D. of his stench...

* * * * *

Five hours later Larry woke up cold, cold, cold. A wet, heavily-clouded morning. Murkey. Like being at the bottom of a muddy pond.

Sat up, lotus position, turned on his own (Tibetan) inner heater. Like the time he was in the Himalayas and they had this sheet-drying contest where you had to sit out all night covered with wet sheets and turn up your own body-heat through meditation. The driest sheet winning the contest. And it was him and they couldn't believe it. A gringo yet. Not quite. Bringing with him the jaguar-shaman wisdom out of the Colombian jungles that tapped into earlier, more powerful layers of the same savvy that his fellow sheet-driers were also using. The more primitive, the more powerful...as if there had been some ancient moment when the gods, yes, had descended and shared their tricks.

OMMMMMMMMM, HMMMMMMMMMM, HUMMMMMMMMMM.

Gradually heating up, driving away the sniffles he felt coming on, driving away the stiffness and the tingling, even the chronic bursitis in his left shoulder.

Old Fire Grandfather spreading a sheet of warmth over him.

"My beloved son in whom I am well pleased..."

"Ay-ya!"

Karate-chopping at the empty air, getting out and going into the bushes, performing his necessities, on the lookout for Poison Ivy, wondering if he might be able to immunize himself, or, if once contaminated, bring down the welts with yogic-shamanistic concentration. Something he'd never tried.

Suddenly hungry. Good sign. Drove in toward town, still warily on the lookout for Mr. Grenade, thanking the Lords of the Four Quarters for having let him survive, Old Fire Grandfather who had deflected the shrapnel away from his heart, brain, eyes....

A McDonald's. Shit, man... drive-through, a half dozen little McMuffins and a nice creamy chocolate shake, coffee, as he paid, the girl in the drive-through window looking horrified at his hand as he gave her a twenty-dollar bill, his hand, face, reaching up, feeling his forehead, cheeks, all kinds of little cuts, little pieces of glass that he hadn't even felt.

"Are you OK?" she asked.

Cute girl. 20. Hair a carefully curled shambles. Bright-looking. She was going to be an archaeology professor. It was THERE on her face, even if she herself didn't yet know it.

"I've been better," he smiled and the smile worked, the smile of Abraham, the smile of Father Christmas, Jesus Ascending....

Ate in the car and then got out, found a washroom, looked at himself with horror, all clotted blood and tatters, washed what he could, left what it was better to leave (scabs) alone, then out to a phone, kind of expecting cops to be called, but no one coming, no sense of menace...and he always knew, didn't he....

Dialed home in Chicago.

9:30 in Kalamazoo, 8:30 in Chicago/Grimore Park.

No answer for five rings, and then on the sixth a heavy, tub of lard voice on the other end challenged him.

"Who the fuck is this?"

"Great phone-etiquette, babe."

Sarah, his fucking pig-harpy daughter. What the fuck was she doing there?!?! Filled with sudden forebodings, impenetrable clouds all around on the edges of his mental horizons.

Tempted to just hang up, Kelley's dead face twitching around on the edges of his consciousness like a face painted on a kite in a windstorm.

THE LORD SAID UNTO SATAN

"Is that you, Larry?"

"Dad to you, asshole!" he said, more ashamed of her lard, her stomach that hung down to her knees, than anything else in his life. At the same time dismayed and ashamed at being dismayed and ashamed.

Sarah took a deep breath and he knew what was coming...

"I don't know how you can just let Mom die and take off and disappear on one of your stupid cases. You must care a little, in spite of all your fucking around over the years...although all the years and all the money don't seem to mean piss to you. All you seem to be able to manage to do is..."

He held the phone away from him like he was afraid it was going to explode; cupped his hand over her butcher-knife voice, just waited until she'd gotten it all out of her system, like waiting out a thunder-storm.

Then tried to summon up the most benign father-self possible.

"She doesn't know who anyone is any more. And who says she's dying? She'll outlive us all, yet! That's what the Passavant Oracle says anyhow. I'm out of East Lansing. On the way home. Genug ist genug. A little wounded, bloody, but I look a lot worse than I feel. Or let's reverse that -- I feel a lot worse than I look..."

"Don't give me a lot of bullshit. You sound fine," she answered, still playing rawhide, but less convincing, "I told Mrs. Barker to go home. I'll take care of the dog for a couple of days, and then I'll put him in a kennel. Or maybe just take him down to the pound...."

Wanting to scream back at her You stupid barrel of lard, don't tell MY employees what to do, and don't you dare take my sacred dog anywhere, but instead managed "Whatever you think best, baby, but the dog isn't yours, right...so just take it to the kennel if you want, but...I love you..."

And he did.

All the years with her sweeping through him, her little girl cute pudginess and cleverness and rebelliousness, the gradually increase in her weight, M and M's, endless liters of Mountain Dew, pies, Twinkies, the guys who never married her, the children she never had, her nastiness directly proportionate to her weight...but she still was/would always be his little girl.

Hung up, called home base, got Monaghan on the line.

"It's getting pretty rough here in Michigan. One murder last night, intended for me too, I guess..."

"It's all over the morning news, Larry. That girl in the doughnut shop gave an unmistakable description of you...where are you now, pal?"

"On the way home, I guess..."

"Are you OK?"

"No...but let me ask you...anything new on Mabel Fudge. Did you try her again?"

"She's left town," he answered, "gone back to...let's see, it's a little farm just outside of Lincoln, Nebraska. The family's name is Hochglaube..."

"High belief!!," he answered, flat as an ironing board.

"Wha...?"

"High belief. Hochglaube means 'high belief' in German -- or it could be Flemish.."

"Yeah, yeah, yeah...I've got the name and address on that phone-number you phone in..."

"I'll get it from you when I get back..." answered Larry, surprising himself, his voices inside him wailing Genug ist genug/Enough is enough, one big moaning ache right now. Wounded ache.

"It's the..."

Monaghan had the can-opened poised over the can.

"Seeya!"

And Larry hung up.

Einmal, wir haben nur einmal, einmal und nichts mehr, gewesen zu sein/once, we have only once, once and not more...to be...

He didn't need to be told anything; his voices would tell him all he needed to know...in due time...

The old Vishnu story, the demon comes and says "I cannot be killed by any man, either day or night; so Vishnu turns himself into a man-lion and kills the demon at dusk...

He was in the cracks now, alternative universes breathing in and out of invisible pores. If he'd had it all to do over again, all of it...but, of

THE LORD SAID UNTO SATAN

course, he didn't..."presences" tuning on inside him, pink (vaginal) and alert...

Drove the station wagon into downtown Kalamazoo, found a men's clothing store, exchanged his torn white jacket for a brown-green Harris tweed, new wool pants, perfect for Northern Forests' Spring-Fall, asked the unaskable, to use the bathroom in the clothing store itself, the old wise-man old Jew who had sold him the clothes giving him a careful once-over, "She must be a large woman."

"I wish!" smiled Larry, went in and washed up, all the bleeding stopped, the dog-bites and scratches already half-healed. The wound in his back sore, but nicely closed. He healed fast. Neanderthals always did.

"Many thanks."

"And these?" the old man holding up Larry bloody, shredded rags.

"Exhibit A...watch the evening news...WGN, Chicago..."

And he was out the door, following the ghost-radar that was beeping inside him, down into this little downtown mall area, feeling HIM half a block away before he saw him. And then Larry saw him before he saw Larry, his trench coat off, in an executivish charcoal suit, just regular sunglasses, but the same stupid metallic-look fedora (helmet) on...and sticking out of the bottom of his executive charcoal pants, those incongruously clunky, black shoes with the steel-reinforced toes.

When the guy saw Larry he started to go for his gun, but Larry, head down, rhino-rushed him, totally baffling him, butting the gun out of his hands, grabbing him and spinning him around, putting his arms under the other guy's arms and joining his hands at the back of the guy's head, painfully pushing his head forward, laughing, loving it, this was the life, the Conquista, Jihad, Holy War, this was what made you immortal, divine, Larry bellowing out "Where are the diamonds, asshole, you'd better fess up right now, or I'm going to break your fucking neck..."

"What are you, crazy, you sonofa...."

Larry putting on the pressure, laughing and laughing.

"Where are the fucking di-a-monds?"

Larry Gargantua, King Kong, monumental, imperial. He hadn't had so much fun since the last time he at been at Tiawanaku for the winter solstice, The World Mountain (Illimani) to his right, The Sacred Lake (Titicaca) to his left, nibbling on teonanacatl, the flesh of the gods.

Meester Señor Hit-Man finally kicked Larry in the shins as hard as he could, once, twice, Larry yelping, laughing, letting him go, the guy off like a flash, Larry grinning a big broad grin at the gathering crowd as he pulled a cheapy alligator stamped leather wallet out of the pocket of his new jacket. Voila! The asshole's wallet.

No cops anywhere.

An old grey lady with a blue hat, blue coat, touch of blue veil, standing watching him like he was a TV in a store-window.

"There's gotta be an airport around here somewhere..."

I don't fly," said the Study in Blue and Grey, "what's going on anyhow?"

"You just go south out of town, you can't miss it," said a guy with a black and red check over-shirt and COORS plastic hat.

Larry picking up the gun on the ground, putting it in his pocket, telling the old lady to take it easy, making his way back to his borrowed station wagon, south to the airport, found a flight to Lincoln (via Chicago), called Woods at the East Lansing PD...

"Listen, do me a favor, OK? Go over to the Kellogg Center, have someone pack my bags, pay my bill, get my car and drive it up to the Grimore Park PD. They will be handsomely rewarded!"

"Where the hell are you, anyhow? I don't know how you're still alive. That little girl over at Dunkin Doughnuts is in the wacko ward, man...."

"I've got the goon's wallet," said Larry, "Kelley said something about him working for the Hyde Brothers. "

"The Hyde Brothers practically own this fucking town. Between them and Vest..."

"There's not that much to own, don't get overly impressed," said Larry, Palenque, Teotehuacan, Mohenjo Daro floating through his head.

"Where the hell are you now?" Woods unctuous and oily.

"Off the screen, pal!"

And he hung up. Distrustful. Everything too well organized. Who wasn't owned? East Lansing was a fucking Sicilian hill-town!

THE LORD SAID UNTO SATAN

Called the Kellogg Center himself and settled his bill with his VISA, arranged to have his stuff packed, his car driven back to Grimore Park. That was that. The guy on the desk (Singapore) was going to drive the car back himself that weekend. Fair enough. Wanted to take a train back. "I love trains...I love scenery...seasons...."

Then got the name and address of the owner of the station wagon off the registration form in the car, made another call. "Listen, I don't know if you've noticed that your Buick station wagon is missing..."

"Who is this?"

Must be the wife -- Mrs. Loris Zinder.

"I'm the guy who borrowed it. I just wanted to tell you that it's parked in the Kalamazoo Airport parking lot. Close to the terminal. Letter A. And as soon as I can I'll send you a five hundred dollar bill for your trouble..."

"The thing isn't even worth five hundred!"

"It was worth it to me," Larry said and hung up, went to wait for his plane thinking if you try to use symmetrical methods for dealing with an asymmetrical reality...nothing's really amorphous, it's just *itself*...a *new* form..."

Light snow. About 30. He'd gotten a nice heavy white cotton shirt with a little brown stripe in it, a nice woven brown tie. Could use a sweater now.

Too bad about Kelley. He'd had so much future in him.

Maxine's presence circling around and around him a giant urubu/vulture, darkening everything he did or might do. His voices and energy gone now. Feeling dumped on and abandoned, centimeters away from deep, clinical depression, the universe just a random throw of the dice. Or not even a throw. That implied Designer. Just The Dice from Nowhere.

A bureaucratic, autoclaved female voice announced pre-boarding for his flight: "Anyone with small children or anyone else who needs a little extra time."

That was him.

Got up and made his way to the gate.

And as usual he was the first to board the plane.

CHAPTER 14

The farmhouse was set on top of a hill like a Grant Wood painting. Poplars off to one side, surrounded by wheat and cornfields.

The land behind the house took a romantic dip and there was a creek, the trees already full of leaves, a hill off to the left, fenced-in, three horses inside, all curious about him, The Man Who Fell from the Sky.

It was cloudless, almost hot. He was pleasantly surprised how far things were already into spring here. More like it.

Rang the bell and an old, old lady opened up like she didn't care who it was, she trusted the world. It was all OK out there. Benign reality.

"Yes, sir, what can I do for you?"

Pretty woman still. Must have been in her nineties. White hair. Dark gypsy eyes. Must have been a real beauty when she was younger.

He showed her his badge.

"I'm working on the Myrtle Bannister case. Just checking out a few leads. Really need to talk to your..."

"Mabel's here. Come on in. The kids are in town at their cousin's house and Gordy won't be back until after six, probably bring the kids with her. But Mabel's downstairs."

Whoever Gordy was...the name was fun.

She went over and called over the basement stair railing, "Mabel, visitor!" No response.

"I'll go down and get her. I don't know if she's ever going to get over this one. Whatever was wrong between her and Brian, she could come down here and cool off for a couple weeks and it was good for another six months. But this time...she's been diagnosed for severe clinical depression...but I don't believe in that stuff. Depressed, OK, but what do you expect her to be after they deep-fried her girlfriend..."

"Yeah, it was pretty horrible," sympathized Larry, feeling Myrtle's presence there around them, filling the room like a pea-soup fog, feeling like he and all the rest of them were somehow still just dancing around in her hand.

THE LORD SAID UNTO SATAN

"Totally out of it. Gone!," said the old lady and started down the stairs...as he walked into the living room. White lace curtains, old, handmade pioneer furniture. Museumish. The house must have gone back a hundred years. Looking out the side window he could see a graveyard way on the other side of the vast open expanse that served for a front yard. He'd love to have a chance to go look at the dates and names on the gravestones.

The room was cold. They'd been very successful in shutting out Spring.

There was a stirring on the stairs, the old lady helping Mabel up.

She was unhealthily pudgy, puffy, white; looked like a powdered-sugar-dipped doughnut, a double scoop of cookies-'n-cream ice cream...

They sat down at the dining room table.

"Let me get you all some coffee," said the mother.

"I won't say no."

"No one ever does." Allowing herself a little sadistic laugh, as she shuffled into the kitchen and started running water and clacking crockery, within what seemed moments, the room burgeoning with the pungent smell of fresh coffee.

"Maybe you remember me from Chicago," said Larry t o Mabel, cautious, all webbed-feet and goose-down gloves, treating her like she was a piece of vintage Meissen, "I've investigating the Beryl Grogan murder."No response. Down at the bottom of her personal psychotic well, wandering blindly through endless clinically depressed swamps, almost like Maxine, almost as if she'd had a stroke, as if she'd been meat-cleavered down the center of her walnut brain, "I was just wondering if you mightn't be in the market for a little revenge...unloading...release...cleansing..."

Nothing. No reaction. And it wasn't that she was throwing up screens and barriers; the more he psycho-probed inside her, the deader it got. Dead, blank, zero. Slaughter at the midnight zoo.

He wished the mother wasn't there, nor the house, sun, coffee, the whole twentieth century. Even the spring wind outside. What he wanted was primal desert, the road to Sinai, Eleusis...Chavín...

He began to will DESERT, waste, wasteland, a crackling prehistoric sun...
OLD GRANDFATHER FIRE,
WE
RIA
WIA
WIA,
it's (WE) hovering (RIA), coming (WIA), coming (WIA)
KISHPA --
THE CRY OF THE EAGLE.

Moving into the Godscape where all spirits were spinozaishly ONE, dead and dismembered, ashes, and out of the ashes his jaguar spirit crippling to its feet and moving toward the World Tree at the World Center, crystal, crystal skull, the coffee, room, old lady and even Mabel gone...just pure emerald vision in the middle of the mind of the Sun, at the end of the yellow brick jaguar shaman road, the third, fourth, fifth eyes open, all barriers down between the I and the Thou.....

Not my voice, but Thine:

"They killed your God; what are you going to do about it?

The words pouring across her like gasoline her whole brain suddenly exploding into a thousand scraps of ripped-up photos...

The side of the house in Grimore Park, Myrtle and her getting out of the car, no side-light on, only the light from the car and the street lights out in front, but he could still infra-red them out, sliding down his own private sendero luminoso /shining pathway, the Fire-Bombers of the Lord, The Divine Fire Cleansing Crew...Ur front stage center...

Myrtle screaming, "What the bloody fuck's going on?"

Not that she didn't know, as the circle surrounded her, but still not really believing it was happening after so many millenia of having it just her way...

"I'll call the fucking cops!"

Trying to make her way to the door.

"Get your asses out of here, you fucking goddamned losers!"

Blocked by tiers of them as they shadowily floated out of the back yard and from under the trees, an army of her victims who she knew only

THE LORD SAID UNTO SATAN

too well, Ur with the bucket in her hand, everything flawlessly choreographed.
　"You think I'm afraid of you fucking losers?!?"
　Almost feeling herself bodiless spirit in endless space again as she heard the unmistakable massaged-beef voice of Sax give the final order.
　"NOW!"
　The gooey, viscous napalmish guk running all over her and whooshing up like a giant gas burner, glued to her flesh, slowly sliding down, cooking her alive, her mind still working for a moment, trying to think her way out of the pain, then going on autonomic pilot, screaming her choking, silent death screams, Mabel seeing her whole life raison d'etre charbroiling up into evil smoke, anti-Messiah, Savior from Hell, Larry inside the core of feeling now, feeling her remorse too...only why remorse....? Mabel screaming at the blinding pyre "I really did love you. I'm so sorry. You were always everything to me!!"
　Sorry, sorry, sorry, standing there in frozen horror until the twitching body stopped and the flamed died out and the army of executioners melted back into the shadows and disappeared as quietly as it had come.
　Nothing but the wind left now, blowing through the nimble Spring trees. And Mabel couldn't even cry but sat on the ground staring at the Myrtle's charred, smoldering corpse, total disbelief, expecting until the last moment that some other timeless, unburnable HER would emerge out of her tinsel body and strike them apocalyptically all down.
　Sat there until down when the dog began to scratch at the side door and her oldest daughter woke up and came out and saw her mother and the body and was filled with a (expected?) sense of total relief, brought her mother into the house...and all these numbers began to slide through Mabel's head...more phone bills, phone bills, phone bills...more records of lost voyages across despairing optical cable seas...
　Then blank again and Time re-started.
　"How about some oatmeal cookies?" asked Mabel's mother.
　A moment to step back into Now.
　"Sounds good to me," he said.

"The way I make um, they're a meal in themselves. Skimmed milk, raisins, sesame seed oil, date pieces, chocolate and carob chips...they're like pemmican."

Her voice slowly flattening out in his mind. Pemmican. An unexpected learned touch.

Brought out a big plate of cookies, Mabel still unmoving, brain dead again. She could just as well have been buried.

The mother pout a cookie to her lips and she bit it, started to chew, her mind filling with viscous, globular shapes and a circus pipe-organ played (melting) under water.

"You've gotta feed her like a baby. Of course this isn't the first time she's gone psychotic. With Brian it was all just sick games, but when her first husband got killed crop-dusting, she was gone; for almost a year. But she came back. There's something inside her like a hidden spring that periodically resurfaces...she's like a seventeen year locust...mosquito eggs in the Arctic..."

"Yeah, I guess," said Larry, deeply liking the old lady and all of her spunk and chutzpa/spark.

"Yeah, I guess," he said, Adonis, Melqart, Osiris, Mot, Jesus...time to re-surface again now, reanimate, begin to flow; remembering a river full of iron that would flow like blood every spring in ancient (Phoenician) Lebanon...becoming a symbol of Adonis, the year-god...

The old lady pouring out the coffee now, all clunky, homemade/craft class-made crockery.

"Nice stuff," he said, "Love it!"

"One of my ex-daughters-in-law made it. Her hippy style. I must be a hippy too, 'cause I really like it."

"All hippy was a little experiment in being human, and I think we all wanna be that..."

"That's for sure!"

Starting to feed Mabel again.

Lots of cream in her coffee, then a load of honey. Lifting it to her lips.

When suddenly there was this big blast of a howitzer voice firing out of the back of the house.

THE LORD SAID UNTO SATAN

"**COFFEE!!!**"

Larry instinctively going for his gun.

"Come on, relax!" the old lady laughed at him, "That's only Big Red, my big bull husband. He's invalided, full of patched-up aortic aneurysms, bowel and bladder fistulas. After he retired he made it a point to never MOVE, some kind of rural Kansas Buddha-act. I don't know. So he started to fuse together in some spots, split apart in others. He just smells the coffee and goes ape. That's all he can do. He hasn't lost his voice, though, has he?!?"

And she smiled a wicked smile.

He liked her. Educated. Complicated. The same generation as his Aunt Elsie. M.A. in French from the University of Chicago...the same generation as Margaret Mead....

She got up and dosed up another cup of coffee with cream and honey and shakily made her way into the back of the house, Larry making a tremendous refocusing effort, deep diving to the center of Mabel's stone-cold mind....where, under layers and layers of rock and water there was something still going on...*a turned-down radio in a rubber bag inside a load of fresh cement...a velvet swamp inside a squishy uterine cavern at the bottom of the world, filled with froggy voices croaking out "You can't copyright a natural law," "We'll build a castle in the Marquesas someplace...mean annual temperature of 22 degrees Centigrade, you can't beat that, a couple degrees above or below...," "I love your breasts...," "You have so much hair down...," and then all kinds of slobbering, slurping sucking sounds. Myrtle's voice, the Master Conspirator...Seductora...*Seductress...

And then the telephone bill numbers began to run through Mabel's mind again, accompanied by fragments of all the faces he knew, plus some he didn't know...

At first sitting there mindlessly mind-fused with her, watching the muddy black stream of her lowest, back-burner consciousness as if it were all perfectly normal and expected, THEN SLOWLY REALIZING THAT NONE OF THIS SHOULD HAVE BEEN THERE, ROSE TO HIS FEET LIKE THE SPHINX STANDING UP AND STARTING TO ROAR, "BUT YOU'RE NOT SUPPOSED TO KNOW ANYTHING ABOUT ALL

THE CALLS AND SHIT. I thought if there was one person in the world who you could have LOVED...
 Her mind suddenly going totally blank again. All levels, even the lowest. And He began to deeply distrust the globality of her catatonia, suddenly suspecting that perhaps he was in the presence of another jaguar shaman mind, at least his equal, perhaps his Master...
 "Well, he's quieted down a little now," the mother rattled on as she came back into the kitchen, "And, of course, he's as curious as a hound dog about you! That's all he's got left now, is a nose. And you can imagine how many visitors we have out here..."
 Larry took a deep breath and dove...
 "Your daughter and Myrtle Bannister, were they....?"
 No hesitation. As guileless as a sun flower, a field of ripe corn.
 "Well, they were what they were. Nothing's so weird these days...you can't tell a man from a woman in downtown Lincoln any more. And it's all pre-schools and nursing homes, no center any more, it's all 'out there,' institutionalized...and can you believe the size of our prison population?" Sitting down and pouring herself a cup of coffee, started to gleefully munch on one of her own cookies, "Not that it solves anything. Big debate about suicide. You'd think we were in Japan. And that whole business of accusing Bryan of child-molestation. Although Mabel was more The Led than The Leader, still she went along with things. What she should have done was to kick Chichi the hell out of the house way back when, when she first started trying to edge her out of the threesome. Reclaim Bryan, fight...and not just run away and change her stripes, start doing all kinds of weird things she'd never done before." Stopping, lowering her voice, as if the air had ears. "Of course Myrtle was a POWER, you picked that up, didn't you. She could make a gargoyle fly down off an old church tower and dance an Irish jig! "Laughing to herself, as shrill as shattering glass...ending up in a dry, painful fit of coughing. "Damned allergies. That's why I like winter, everything's dead, not a mould spore in sight...but let me tell you...Mabel was just too damned passive. Like me. I've always been a passive fool. And all that crooked stuff. Did it make any sense if you just look at it in people-terms. They were both loaded. Doing great. What was the point

THE LORD SAID UNTO SATAN

of starting their own company. Mabel and all her special 'gifts.' The Holy Spirit in her like in no one else! That's what our Reverend used to say. Myrtle never knew when to stop. She was Evil for the sake of Evil. When she was around out here, I'd feel like...like a whole other 'something' was closing in on me, the sky wasn't empty, but just on the other side was...I don't know...and Mabel began to feel it too...something all scaley and snake-ish...drove into the driveway that last night," voice to the smallest whisper now, and didn't Larry feel an intrusion into their space from other dimensions? "...that last night...she drove into the driveway knowing full well that judge, jury and executioners were waiting for Myrtle!"

"You knew they were there, didn't you? You were in on the phone games, weren't you" Larry asked Mabel.

The quiet ground inside Mabel beginning to shift and wrinkle as she got up and started for the basement stairs, her face still a Kabuki death mask but inside everything quaking and rumbling, breaking through even her reinforced concrete WILL.

Things she couldn't (really didn't want to) hold back.

One message coming through -- she was not alone in her powers. It was shared, equaled, if not excelled by... he couldn't get through...tried to reach into the thick minestrone soup of her mind and get out a couple chunks of carrots and a few noodles...but all of a sudden the glass was up again and it started opaquing, thickening into concrete...

"Why not just let me in, let me see it whole?" he suddenly mind-screamed at her, his voice flaking, chipping off a little of the concrete that she was secreting against his intrusion.

She stopped at the top of the stairs and stared back at him, face of an idiot, mind of a god, her mind talking back at him like a snake-charmer's flute.

"If you really wanted to become one of US..."

"What US?"

And suddenly the wall was up between them. Ten layers thick. Perfectly fitted, gargantuan Inca stone.

"What is going on between you two?" asked Grandma, "there's always been something weird about that girl. She had a friend back in grammar school and they'd sit and talk without talking...too smart for her own damned good....nothing but trouble...be a simple soul like me...I've had a relatively long, simple-soul life, the inevitable aches and pains, but...."

Mabel turned scornfully and walked down the basement stairs with her dark gitana eyes and mashed potatoes white skin, trim off a little pudge and she'd be classic Flamenco...like his lost Maxine...Larry feeling everything inside himself dissolving, lost, like all he was was a vast swirling annihilating sewer...

"What's going on now? The two of you. You knew each other before, didn't you. Something extra-curricular...," the old lady with her own rudimentary, undeveloped but still present 'powers.'

"Maybe we should have!" answered Larry, creaking to his feet, a bunch of little stabs rippling up his spinal column, muscles all stiff, ankles aching, bursitis in his left shoulder, "I don't know why we just didn't move down to Bocaciego Bay in Tampa and just sit and get salty, watch the dolphins and smell the sea. I've got the mazoola!"

"But you're not the type," said Mabel's mother gypsyishly, "and besides, with your wife...."

She stopped.

"With my wife...what about her?"

She'd seen into him, hadn't she, one stroboscopic unasked for, unwanted stab of illumination.

The old lady catching herself, pulling back from further insights, getting all country fiddle folksy again.

"You're just not the Florida type. And besides, retirement's for the birds. I sweat that's what is killing off Mabel's father!"

"Sometimes I envy the dead," he said, staring at where Mabel had stood before descending the stairs, her face still there etched on the antique air. Then mindlessly moved toward the front door, "I thank you for your hospitality," feeling an overwhelming sense of home here, belonging, stability, the sailor home from the sea, the hunter home from the hill, painfully aware of the old gold sense of HOME that Bryan and Mabel must had had before Chichi had moved in and started her little demolitions. Mabel had been no match for Chichi. Mabel was all

THE LORD SAID UNTO SATAN

shadows and watercress, Chichi a boulder from the sky. When it came to the tactics of invasion, no matter what shamanic powers Mabel may have had, she was no match for Chichi's super-ego tactical clarity...it was Night versus Day, fur versus steel plate, tea leaves versus sledgehammers...

"Be well!" said the mother as he went out the door.

"Thanks for everything!" he waved, "Be seein' ya," knowing he'd never again see the wunderbar old lady again, not in a thousand lives on a thousand re-incarnated worlds.

Down to his Avis (very neon Neon) car, tears in his stupid eyes, very much inside all of their tragedies now, Mabel's and Bryan's, the whole crop of careers that had been scythed to the ground by Mabel.

Got in the car and waited a moment until his eyes cleared. Patches of sun and cloud moving across the rolling landscape. A metaphor for the human (his) condition.

Uncertain Spring. Started up, back to the main highway that went to Lincoln...and the airport.

CHAPTER 15

"Hello, Monaghan, this is Larry..."

"Larry, where the fuck are you? Everyone's worried crazy about you. And Ackermann's furious. What's going on? Are you OK? You've got a job here, pal, as in JOB..."

"JOB as in The Book of Job. I'm wrestling with the demons, pal. I've gotta be The Invisible Man for a while, pal. I almost got a grenade in the gut in East Lansing, the Powers out there are still there. A few more days, a few more links -- and then comes the juridical harvest..."

"This is Chicago, Larry. Stacker of wheat and all that, Larry. Screw all that hocus pocus stuff of yours. I don't care what your record is, there's limits. Lemme switch you over to Ackermann. Talk to the man. Be real."

"Switch your ass for your brain, Monny, I'm not interested in being the Lamb of God in order to satisfy Ackermann's sense of bureaucratic tidiness. And look over your own shoulder, pal. And trust me! When Jesus casts out demons, what do you think he's casting out? Do you think the Age of Miracles is really over?"

"It's not me, Larry. I went to Lourdes once..."

"Look, pal...," Larry allowing his voice to get deep bass, oracular, Orson Wells, The War of the Worlds, "were there every rebel angels, was Lucifer the Morning Star? 'Be gone Satan, for I am the Lord thy God!' Yama, the Lord of Hell...and there isn't any Hell?"

"Larry, you need medication!"

"Les jeux son fait!/ The dice are cast!" said Larry, softly hanging up, got up, put on his new coat. He'd have to buy some more clothes. Which he always needed anyhow. With Maxine always on the edge of the edge for years, he'd hardly given a shit if he walked around in rags.

If he got back into his usual grooves, it would be like writing SHOOT ME all over his forehead, but this way, down at the Palmer House in the Chicago Loop, he'd stay invisible. Loved the old chandeliers and plaster busywork all over the walls, the Baroque ornamental dream, spacious, opulent, the spirit of Versailles lifted up and set down in the midst of hog-butcher-of-the-world Chicago.

Down to the lobby, over a block to the Art Institute. Member's Lounge. Another invisible spot in an invisible world. Or at least visible only to those he wanted to be visible to.

"Back with us again, Mr. Gugel!"

Francis (Francees), the Maitre d'.

"Ça va?/How's it going?"

"Tres bien, et vous? /Great, and you?"

"Jamais meilleur! /Never better."

A table by the window, facing the glorious inland sea, Lake Michigan.

Lisa (from San Miguel de Allende) his waitress again today. She "knew," didn't know she knew, but "knew" -- the jaguar's children come together to die and be reborn at the bellybutton of the world.

Sniffed the air without looking at the menu...

"Que bueno verte./ How good to see you," she said. Put a red dot on her forehead and she was a high caste Hindu.

"Igualmente./Me too. Son tiempos dificiles./Difficult times."

"Confie en los viejos dioses...y en el pato asado./Trust in the old gods...and in the roast duck."

"Exactamente lo que estaba pensando./Just what I was thinking."

And that was that. He handed her back the menu.

She brought him his usual little carafe of wine. And he toasted her.

"El sangre de Xipe Totec, el dios de la primavera./The blood of Xipe Totec, the god of spring...."

She smiled. Wished that she could sit down and join him, abolish all hierarchies and social categories...but, OK, it was OK the way it was...in other lives...other times.

He sat back and dreamed the Dream of Chicago, where the sack of Lake Michigan drips the drop that became the city, the Exposition of 1893, the Dream of the Museum of Science and Industry, the Dream of Rockefeller's gothic University of Chicago, Potter Palmer, as in Palmer House, Marshall Field as in Field Museum, Louis Sullivan's seed germ ironwork dream of industrial Gothicism bringing the forest back into the forum (the facade of Carson, Pirie, Scott), the munchkin gothicism of the Near North Side, all that heavy, castle stone...Lincoln and Jackson parks, all the forced opulence of the Drake, Water Tower Place...Loyola still striving, Spanish post-Reformation reform, and the best Italian sausage sandwiches in the world, not another city in the world with so much input and so little...the worst minds of my generation...triumph of the (West of the lake) ID...violence....

Wine, a side dish of dumplings and sauerkraut. The duck-skin a crispy, salty, greasy brown, just the way his grandmother had made it. He could forget the meat and just eat the skin; remembering his grandmother going into the bottom of the pan and scooping out the grease and spreading it on rye bread, salting it, taking a gallbladder pill and THEN downing the whole schmeer with gluttonous glee...

The dumplings just so-so. Wheat. What he loved were big, greasy cannonballs of potato dumplings. But these were too bland; they could have browned both the dumplings and sauerkraut in the duck-grease...more garlic, onions, caraway seeds...

Larry wallowed in the food, finished the carafe of wine. And all of a sudden got boneless, weightless sleepy. Paid, tipped with Romanovian generosity.

Could hardly bear the beauty of the wide, wide-open sky. Two months more to solstice...and then the slow bleeding death of yet another year.

Struggled to his feet. An abrazo for the Maitre d'.

"A bientot!"

"A bientot!"

Then fighting fatigue, going up into the galleries, a little Renoir, an afternoon on the river, an evening at the ("La Loge") opera, a moment on Monet's Calais Beach, inside the gold-violet shimmer of the fascade of the cathedral at Rouen, the whole time Ravel's Mother Goose Suit playing inside his head, then Debussy's Images...engulfed cathedrals, footsteps in the snow...what the West Wind knew....

He felt like he was made out of sand...or feather quilts...cloud....

It was so much effort to walk back to the Palmer House, but he still stopped in Trader Vic's for a little rum and coke and only then went back

THE LORD SAID UNTO SATAN

up to his room for a glorious Crabtree and Evelyn sandalwood bubble-bath, sank slowly into the at first too hot, then just perfect water...

It was his world, these older hotels built in The Age of Leviathans and Tycoons, as if The Builders, when they had built, had anticipated his coming.

All this White Nile gluttony and reptilian laziness had a purpose, though. He was simply waiting for dark, waiting for Place to speak to him, getting sensitized and fine-tuned, sinking into the selfless emptied-out receptivity of The Great Vision...

He closed his eyes and sank into oblivion within oblivion...and then, in the midst of absolute oblivion, the immortal past, like microscopic traces of bright paint on bone-white Greek statues, could arise again, the inner life of Things in the eternal memory of God/the gods....

CHAPTER 16

Late, late afternoon and Larry left the Palmer House in his rented Cavalier, took the long way up North, for him the whole lake front a layer-cake of memory after memory.

Before Windy, the Oak Street Beach and Petra Bolini, his first girlfriend. Even before Maxine. Petra and her father's big brownstone mansion on Dearborn Parkway. That wasn't even brown, really, but more purple-chocolate.

Shipping, coal fortune. The House that Commerce built.

He thought Petra and the air was filled with cut glass glasses filled with narcotically sweet chartreuses or curaçaos, Bach in the background, white lace shawls, teak paneled walls... a night at the opera, a drink at the Drake...no such thing as weather, anything five yards beyond themselves...

She was a widow now, living alone. No children. But he never called her. Never would. As long as Maxine still breathed....

Up to the North Shore, where the Edgewater Beach Hotel used to be. Where his life used to be.

Past Loyola, Rogers Park, Evanston, up to Grimore Park, over to Mabel and Myrtle's place, The Invisible Man moving through soft, veiled layers of invisibility, the day fuzzing over now and moving into moth-wing soft darkness, long licorice shadows, wolf-whimper soft wind, amazed at how much the trees had come out in the last week, weeds in wheels, so long and lovely and lush...

As he drove through the opulent, almost Gothic streets of Grimore Park, he started to get existentially "cold"...he was driving through Nagual Time now, into Alternative Universes where The Truth spoke full-time...where the real "gods"/"spirits" were that Whitey usually never saw, and when he did see it called it dementia...

Drove into the driveway of their place, a For Rent sign out in front. Everything cold and dead, the rest of the neighborhood already behind its oh-so-proper walls. No one outside to bother him. No dogs, kids.

Just him and the scene of the murder.

THE LORD SAID UNTO SATAN

Putting on a fuzz-lined raincoat he'd bought at Carson, Pirie and Scott the day before. Still chizzy when the sun went down.

Went into the driveway and sat Buddhistically down amidst the still-un-raked leaves, allowing himself to expand/fly out of himself into Dimension E...Enlightenment...V...Vision...all his vast past soul-flight apprenticeship-years spreading their wings now. For the Great Shaman, the Blue Deer came even if there was no five-pointed star. Floating out of himself into All time, giving himself up to the voices and the gods in an act of unbodying black crystal release...

His dead grandmother (scooping out the burnt grease at the bottom of the pan when she roasted a duck, eating it on the rye-est of bread) dipping into his mind for a moment, Petra there one instant playing Debussy's "Arabesque...then elevatoring further down into past-less Blackness...beyond Time now...the squirrels coming sniffing around him, only he was stone now, mossy with age, a lichened Budda in the stone-god garden, birds in his hair, tree tassels and seeds, day dead, night-vision starting to swell, dead, withered, desiccated, millennial bone piles moldering into dust, cupped and scattered by the winds, forgetting he ever was, who...a bat flitting across the bilious vestiges of day, as he sank amnesiacally into the memory banks of night...worms burrowing, beetles stretching their night-legs, trees, yawning out into the spirit wind...emptied of emptiness, wiped clean and transparent and then the wiping wore through the surface and the emptiness became a huge hole through which the "other' Reality poured in...not I but the gods speak through me, voice of the five-pointed Evening/Abend Star/Stern, Morganstern/Morning Star, the Babylonian Nabo-Nabu Morning Star of Peyote Blue-Deer Enlightenment....

Totally black now, the streetlights going on in the distance and black advancing toward him like the Angel of Death, out of the World Noise into the (ultimate) Quiet Place...paye, justicero, vigilante in his vigils...taking the bracelet that he'd found in the driveway earlier and had been very consciously transferring around from pocket to pocket for just this moment...put it on his own wrist, Gugel, the Great Spirit-Magnet...

He blew out his Self now, purple Self-smoke out of his left nostril, green Self-smoke out of his right nostril, feeling his ego (Hubris) slowly diminish...his soul's litmus-paper slowly sensitizing...spirit-radio...ghost Geiger-counter...

He became the leaves and the driveway, inside-outted his precariously membranous inner Self, became the night-hawk, the night-hawk's croaks and caws, became the trembling hair of the trees, the still un-ravished bride of slow time...as he moved into Time's divine Other-(Over-) Soul...

The moon slowly rising, moon-voices coca-snuff swirling around him, breathing it in, his eyes widening into giant turquoise disks...

Oh, Grandfather Fire, come, Nabu, Naba, Naga snake-dragon roar...
**TI
TIRAWA
FIRE-SUN-TIN-TITAN
NOOOOOOOOW!**

And he began to hear voices seeping out of The Past That Is Always Present, shapes beginning to appear, at first like oily light-show globs, then slowly focusing and taking on detail, Mabel standing there, Myrtle just turning the car lights off, getting out of the car, when this too-familiar voice came screaming out of the dark.

"I was gonna be your 'man' forever, huh? Bull-SHIT! If you'll pardon my Czech. You got the technology that you wanted from me and now I'm nuddings. You and all your African bullshit!," pulling the bracelet off her wrist , the earring (that still must be there, hidden under the leaves) out of her ear, bouncing them off of Myrtle's incongruously ample tits. Myrtle murderously superior, ironic, mocking, taunting, the kind of ridicule that begs for revenge. The crime itself already in the air like coming rain, snow...

"You be my MAN? You almost qualify, don't you, you poor wimp of a blob!!!"

And then the others emerged, sudden ghost-fish floating out of the shadows.

"You're all assholes!" Myrtle screamed at them, "Get the bloody fuck outta here before I call the cops. Asshole wimp losers!"

Ur turned, lifted up the bucket and splashed the gasoline that wasn-t just gasoline all over Myrtle, and it bonded with her skin, slowly and

THE LORD SAID UNTO SATAN

clinglingly oozing down her body like caramel syrup as Ur reached forward, barbecue gas-lighter in hand, everyone else threw their napalmish darts at her, and Ur clicked on the lighter, and WHOOSH, SHE WAS ALL LIVING WHIURLING DERVISH DEATHDANCE SCREAMING FLAME...

Larry wanting to stop, but couldn't, the film obsessively playing on and on, the screaming continuing and Myrtle, in scathing demonic mockery fell down on one knee, whispering "Christ falls the first time," then, out of control, falling backward and the autonomic burning frog twitching began as Larry's own skin began to burn and he was engulfed in a terrible envelope of pain, the flames worming their way around on the roof of his mouth, down into his throat, cracking and sizzling, burning, burning, burning...

Desperately wanting OUT now, struggling to his feet, half in, half out of visioning, desperately breaking out of the burning Plater of Paris dream-cast of Big Time, grasping desperately for the asylum of any small, ordinary, petty NOW.

"OOOOOOOOOOOOOOUT!"

And suddenly it was all gone, the soft, fresh, cold night winds blowing across him again, blessed Lake Michigan in the distance, hosanna, hosanna, hosanna, qadosh, qadosh, qadosh, holy, holy, holy...and he was just standing there amidst the leaves, drenched in sweat. And he'd managed to sit in some dog-shit. Goddamit! Taking a bunch of leaves in hand and starting to wipe if off when he looks up and there in the moving shadow lights of trees and streetlights there was a little man with a clipboard in hand. Larry barely able to make out a black/blue blazer and a stripped (Harvard?) tie.

Where the fuck did he come from?

"So what's happening?" asked the little man, shining a heavy-duty flashlight on Larry.

A fakey not-quite-there Yaley accent; like Larry trying to make his flat-ass Santa Catarina Portuguese into something juicily Carioca....

"May I ask the same of you?" Larry countered with his own version of East Coast-Old-Boy-Talk, "pulling out his badge, "Gugel, Grimore

Park PD, what the fuck are you doing poking around here at this time of night?"

"It's almost dawn, my friend," said the little man, Larry hardly able to believe that the whole night had been consumed by what had been for him a few quick stroboscopic dice throws of revelation, "I'm Thompson James. I work for Spryszoki...I do his footwork for him. Sinuses. Couldn't sleep. Spring. All the moulds and sproutings...."

All defenses down, sounding like the Chicago streets.

"I never trust anyone with a reversed name," said Larry, tossing down the leaves in his hand. That's all the dog-shit he was going to be able to get off anyhow. All that was left was a little brown stain and a touch of vivid, hovering stench. "Now....if I could just get into the house for a second...," new voices inside Larry whispering inside, inside, inside...

And just to complicate things, the image of Maxine beginning to rise from the bottom of the lake of his worst nightmares. A long visit the day before, as soon as he got settled down in the hotel. Over at Passavant, like visiting a funeral parlor, lying there, attached to a million tubes, hardly breathing, Dr. Zukowski ridiculously optimistic, "You never know about these cases...she just might open her eyes and..."

Open her eyes and close them again permanently?

Wanting to gently pull out all the tubes and then see what the gods decide. But instead leaving wordlessly, filled with the vision of all his dead -- his parents, aunts, uncles, parents' friends, his own friends, colleagues....hardly able to believe that all those faces, voices, "energies" had just been totally cancelled out.....erased....

Maxine there for a moment again in front of him.

"Basta!" he said under his breath, and the vision of Maxine disappeared.

"What?" said Thompson James.

"Just a little exorcism," said Larry as Thompson James opened the front door.

"Why worry about search warrants and such things, why not just...."

"I'll keep exorcising," said Larry, not sure whether he was kidding or not.

THE LORD SAID UNTO SATAN

"Wellllllll," Thompson not quite sure what accent/persona to assume, very unsure about what he/they might find inside. The whole house/case had already begun to assume mythic proportions in his mind, the collective Grimore Park mind, the annals of Chicago crime.

A little trouble with the front door lock, as if the house didn't want to be violated, resisted penetration, Thompson's light melting tunnels into the blackness, the whole place filled with the bat squeak Doppler Effect screechings...

"What in the world's that? This is my first visit. Spryszoki has this Old World sense of, what would you call it, 'respect' for the dead...for the murdered...."

"**THE SEVENTH DAY AFTER DEATH, FROM THE CENTER OF THE WORLD MANDALA, THE LOTUS LORD OF DANCE, THE SUPREME KNOWLEDGE-HOLDER, WILLCOME CARRYING A CRESCENT KNIFE AND A CHALICE-SKULL FILLED WITH BLOOD,**" chanted Larry, feeling the whole world here tilt to the edge of the fifth, final Sun.

"Come on, OK!!" Thompson starting to back out the door again, "let it go for another week."

All the furniture still there.

"Did you rent it unfurnished?"

"As a matter of fact, yeah...but, what's her name, Mrs. Fudge, must have left everything behind. "

"I'm afraid she's one step away from leaving Life behind too!" said Larry, seeing Mabel as just a few notches away from becoming Maxine...or worse...body bags and crematoriums...ashes scattered on the ancient Kansas winds....

"I'll send someone over here this afternoon," said Thompson, in the doorway, knowing better, but still trying to switch on the lights, some slight pickled-herring-colored light from the outside beginning to embalm and entomb every object and surface in every room.

"Wait, wait, wait," Larry's voice whittling down to a whisper, "I only want to go to one place...the basement..."

"This afternoon!" Thompson firm.

Larry not even answering but grabbing Thompson's flashlight and walking toward the back of the house. Not that he needed any more light than his own shaman-vision to steer by. Old Maestro Rastrero, Master Spoor-Follower, that's what they used to call him in the Madre de Dios jungle in Peru. "Tu tienes la nariz de un perro!/You have the nose of a dog!"

The nose of a Neanderthal.

"Myrtle's still very much HERE," Larry whispered, Thompson following along, as if attached to Larry by an invisible rope, walking down the long central hallway to the back of the house.

"What do you mean?" asked Thompson in a lilliputian whimper.

"You don't want to know!" Larry answered, just waiting for her through break through the spirit-wall and go for his throat...

Back to the basement door, the flashing cutting into huge basalt blocks of shadow, one bedroom window open, the new leaves cellophaning in the wind outside, the basement door over in the corner by the stove.

"Maybe we ought to...." Thompson started to object.

Larry blanketing him shut with a heavily quilted SHHHHHHHHHHH...opening the door, going down the stairs, another door that led out to the side of the house, then the stairway continuing on down to the basement, Thompson making for the outside door, "I'll...I'll be in my car..."

Larry descending alone, Yama is as Yama does, Larry horned and mutiple-armed now, his hard, heavy tail whipping against the walls, his eyes red and bulging, full of fire...a corrosive, daggerish urine stench in the air, stabbing into Larry's sinuses, The Scream getting more and more desperate now, as if this were her temple and shrine, the center of her soul, and all alarms were being sounded...and under The Scream the sound of multiple chirrupings and squeakings.

Down to the bottom stair, past the washer-drier into the basement proper, shafts of growing light from street-level windows falling on a long lab table filled with racks of tubes, pipettes, two centrifuges, a Rolls Royce of a microscope....stacks of rat cages over in one corner, the rats seeing him and going crazy. Food over in one corner next to a little sink...

The air drenched in the sharp, sick-earth smell of rotting flesh, most of the rats dead, chewed on, eyes chewed out, little red-black carcasses of protruding bones.

He opened all the cages and emptied the bag of food pellets out on the floor, filled a big plastic bowl up with water and put it on the floor, the survivors tumbling out after the food and water as he started pulling the drawers in the lab table...eye-droppers, a catalogue of scientific equipment...one locked bottom drawer...

"Fuck this shit!"

Gugle Little Universal Lock-Opened, one, two, HEAVE, and that was that, el viejo impotente still with a little bit of Beowulf left in him...

On top, inside the drawer, was a financial record book. Licensed business, State of Illinois -- JUVENTUD. Vials of pills over to one side of the drawer, nice shiney metallic-paper labels, people background, yellow J-U-V-E-N-T-U-D letters. It looked cheesey. Like kitty vitamins, not the pellets of Eternal Youth. How much do you learn about marketing dans l'enfer/in Hell?

Took one of the pills and swallowed it, whispering to the churning, thrashing, threatening Dark, **"Myrtle, you asshole, you yourself put the bucket in Ur's hands!"**

A sudden bull-roaring tear cycling around him, a spurt of angry, clawed flame, Kyrie Eleison, Chrisi Eleison, and he could feel the call rip across his throat as he lurched back away from it, still gouging a streak out of him, reaching up to access the damage, his hand coming away filled with blood, as the pain kicked in.

"You shit!" he screamed and raked his own claw-daggered hands through the black air. Only there was nothing to touch. Only the hovering, floating, menacing sound, like a floating world of totora reeds anchored to the floor of Lake Titicaca.

Tempted to unflesh himself and follow her into her own killing ground, but instead running up the stairs, out the side door into the street, Thompson locked in his car, getting out when he saw Larry, with a bloodied handkerchief up to his throat.

"What happened?"

Obviously very relieved that he'd vamoosed when he had.

"I told you she was still there...," said Larry figuring that she hadn't severed anything too big or he still wouldn't be there bullshitting around, "the basement's full of cannibal rats and their cannibalized peers, ratshit and piss...and I didn't close the basement door so they'll be all over the house as soon as they've eaten the feast I prepared for them..."

"What the fuck...Gugel...."

"I am the Simon Bolivar of the rats," said Larry, "Compassion...is that OK with you...mercy...," suddenly very much The Buddha, his old Buddha-self floating up to the surface of his internal sea.

"Yeah, OK...I'm outta here, man. I don't believe in any of this supernatural shit and all that, but..."Back to his car, locking the doors after he was in. One window open a crack. "Spryszoki's gonna love this!"

Larry folding his hands together, bowing, sinking into annihilation, no more incarnations, tuning down his life-force, crawling under a rock at the bottom of the sea, wanting to just vanish, esfumarse, vaporize....only little fingers inside him started typing out so Ur was engaged to Myrtle, Myrtle had used her to get some classified in for for the pill-project, fake liaison, the woman scorned...

More diabolical sprinklings.

Myrtle, blessedly, hardly "there" any more:

$$EVIL = K \frac{1}{Light}$$

"You got what you deserved," he said to the house, driveway, evaporating Presence of The Demon. Knew now, didn't he, where to find Myrtle's last, sad dupe, no need for any phone records now, standing there for a moment feeling as triumphant as the sun beginning to dust its light across the whole vast cloudless vault of the sky...as Thompson disappeared with a silent, barely tolerant wave.

THE LORD SAID UNTO SATAN

Larry sailing now, all wind and optimism, thinking "Clot, stop!," and feeling the bleeding stop, getting smaller, smaller, smaller, until he was one small dot on a sky-wide piece of whitest paper.

A paper boy came by on a bike, curious, but not stopping to satisfy his curiosity.

Larry got into his car, daubed at his neck with his handkerchief, only it was all clotted, dry. What he needed was a some Arby's chicken fingers with mustard-honey sauce, a nice restroom where he could wash off the acrid stench of the shit, fresh up a little, and then....over to Babbit Brothers to put the final pieces of the sick puzzle together.

A deep desire to go see Maxine again, more vigil, talking to her and her arteries, talking to her cancer cells, "Go, go, go away, never come back in any way...."

Into the Cavalier, down toward Skokie. And ahhhhh! An Arby's! Washed up. A little blood on his shirt and coat that he turned into dull candied orange peel stain. Not bad. Nothing shocking. Lots of band-aids. Looked like he'd taken the wrong turn in a dart-factory, came out all wet but almost radiant. Everyone else in line looking at him like he'd just emerged from a paleolithic ice-block in Siberia, naked and slobbering. But he met every furtive glance with a broad-axe smile. It wasn't by accident that the TEO in **TEO**NANACATL/FLESH OF THE GODS and **TEO**TEHUACAN was God in both Greek and Aztec.

Found a corner, mind-erected an antique Japanese screen around him, filled with mountains and clouds and bamboo. Ahh, the honey mustard and the little curley grease-trap fries, everything into the honey-mustard. A giant coke to wash it all down. What they needed in the Middle East was more Arbys, Wendys, MacDonalds, malls, Sears, Penny's, a return engagement of God bursting out of parting clouds and proclaiming "Enjoy! Thou who art in Time, enjoy the time you have!"

CHAPTER 17

Security was in the basement at Babbit Brothers. Fancy, massive, the whole building a steel-glass Bauhaus palace.

"Hi! Can I help you?"

Blonde at the reception desk, all crisp and fresh in a blue shirt and tie, obviously intended to masculinize her, but doing exactly the opposite.

"I'm Gugel from the Grimore Park PD," he said, flashing his badge, "I'd like to talk to..."

"You look like you ought to talk to the Emergency Ward," she smiled. Massive breast implants. Very effective. And he could see right through her clothes, black nylon legs, silky black body suit, one of those secret lingerie fetishists.

"I don't know...security...," the name suddenly beginning to be sung to him by black angels inside his head, "Kala...."

"Kalakovsky. OK," got Kalakovsky on the phone, "OK, go right in...he's kind of expecting you, he said. Right down at the end of the hall."

The hall itself as sleek as an atomic sub. They could have been ten thousand fathoms down; you got the feeling of great depth...wealth...nothing like the old chipped brick, chipped beach Grimore PD. Public versus private money.

The door to Kalakovsky's office was open. Very young, thin, mustached, wavy dark brown hair, brown suit and pants, a discreet gold earring in his left ear, when he saw Larry getting up, shaking hands.

"Come on in! Sit down! I'm been kind of expecting you. You've been all over the papers. Kind of a missing person, from what I gather. I suppose I ought to call what's-his-name over at the Grimore Park P.D...Acker...???"

"Ackermann. Let's not and say we did. I'm afraid I'm on the wrong guys' Most Wanted list..."

THE LORD SAID UNTO SATAN

"Well, you're OK here," said Kalakovsky, closing the door, Larry sitting down and expanding out into a fan-backed chair in front of Kalakovsky's desk, "Jesus, they really chewed you up, didn't they?"

"I'm OK," said Larry, "just a few little cuts."

"That band-aid on your neck, it's a little loose," Kalakovsky taking a little tin box of band-aids out of the side drawer of his desk, ripping the band-aid off of Larry's neck, where Myrtle had clawed at him out of Spiritland, Kalakovsky inspecting the wound as he unwrapped a fresh band-aid, "Nasty wire-cut, you must have run into a wire clothesline..."

"I was clawed," said Larry with absolute finality.

"Nah...you can see the wire-marks on either side of the cut," insisted Kalakovsky, "in fact it was probably two pieces of wire twisted together and you caught a loose end of the twist. Let me put a little fresh band-aid on it for you...no big deal, but close to the Carotid...," carefully stretching a band-aid across the wound.

"Thanks," said Larry, disturbed, Myrtle changing wound-shapes on him in order to shake his grasp of The Real and push him over the edge into total self-doubt, "As you undoubtedly already know, I'm investigating the death of Myrtle Bannister..."

"OK," said Kalakovsky, "yeah, I'm already aware of that...you're famous, Gugel...like I said, I've been on the lookout for you," reaching into the center drawer of his desk and pulling out two big black Cuban cigars wrapped in clear, crinkly cellophane, "how about one of these?"

"Great!" said Larry as Kalakovsky pulled out an old-fashioned silver lighter and lit him up in great clouds of smoke and flame. Larry would have preferred a little Jimson Weed, something a little more mind-opening, but regular foo tsoldier tobacco was sacred in its own way, like the Quiches in Ecuador boiling down huge quantitites of tobacco to a thick, concentrated slime and then start drinking it, vomit a little, sit around in the security of tribal oneness and wait for the epiphany of the Great Snake. Or what about Macumba? Big black cigar enlightenment? Hungry for the spirits. Feeling so utterly "secular" right now, drawing in on the cigar as if it were part of some private, sacred ritual.

"So how's the investigation coming?" asked Kalakovsky.

"It's a real spiral helix," said Larry, dragging in over and over again on the cigar, the smoke starting to speak to him, do you really believe that Thompson James was there at the house at Spryszoki's behest? Are you Simple Simon or what? Check it out, asshole, check it out, out, out...., "Wow," said Larry looking at the primitive, powerful way the cigar was wrapped, the real article, "listen....could I use your phone for a moment? The smoke's talking to me..."

Kalakovsky not quite sure. You could see he was about an intuitive as a loaf of Wonder Bread.

"OK, go ahead."

Larry getting the number for Shore Realty, dialing Spryszoki.

"Whoever it is, it's too early," he answered, "I vas just in the middle of a dream about roast goose and dumplings...sauerkraut..."

"Save some for me!" laughed Larry.

"Ah, so it's you, my friend. Vat's up?"

"I was over at Myrtle Bannister's house last night/this morning, and there was a guy there named Thompson James who said he worked for you..."

"Vat do you tink, Larry? I handle it all myself! Maybe get someone in to clean up, but I'm there, Larry, vat do you tink?"

"I think that as soon as I get this case a little more wrapped up, I'll be back with more doughnuts. Maybe a roast goose..."

"And lots of grease on the sauerkraut and dumplings! You only die once, my friend! Sei gesundt!/Be well!"

"You too, pal."

Hanging up. Of course, Thompson James, or whatever his name really was, was a Hyde Brothers import. Larry wondering just how close he'd come to getting HIT!

"OK," he said to Kalakovsky, sitting back in his chair, "so the guy over at Myrtle Bannister's last night/this morning has nothing to do with the real estate company he claimed he was working for..."

"It was a wire-splice," Kalakovsky, pointing to Larry's neck again, "what do you want it to be, a were-wolf? Man, you oughta chill out, rest up....Are you really sure there was a Thompson James over at Myrtle Bannister's house last night/this morning? The mind, the mind has mountains, my friend...," then when Larry didn't react, but merely sat there sucking on the cigar, softening a little again, "I suppose you'll want to talk to Dr. Irma first, huh?"

Larry suddenly filled with PRESENCES again, beeping, on target, spirit-radar, the twisted Levantine voice of Tatawari inside him whispering, **"Ur/Ir of the Chaldees..."**

She was there, just a few floors above him, and just as Larry became aware of her, she was suddenly alerted to his presence...

HE KNEW THAT SHE KNEW AND IF SHE KNEW THAN EVERYONE ELSE KNEW TOO...

"Sure," said Larry, "whatever you say..."

Trying to stay even keeled, calm, summoning up his own army of dragon spirits, just as she must be summoning up hers.

"I should have gotten an MBA instead of a SNM and I'd be running this company by now, instead of being run ragged," said Kalakovsky as he got up and straightened his tie, carefully squished out his cigar, Larry following suit...as alien, enemy coils began to materialize and curlicue around the corners of the room, across the ceiling.

"SNM?" asked Larry.

"SHOW NO MERCY!" answered Kalakovsky, yakking it up as they both edged out of the office and into the corridor and Kalakovsky carefully shut the door of his office, "You'd think everything would be shipshape and tight, right, you wouldn't have to worry about shit inside the building, right? Well...it ain't necessary so, like the man says, it's ain't necessarily so..."

Larry filled with giant Phoenician ships of emotion, eyes on the prows, choppy seas, Irma's eyes, Dr. Irma Ur-Rat trapped in the giant glass and steel cage of the building being stalked by Larry Kingpin CAT...Larry kind of enjoying her discomfort and panic....

"I'll take you up there. This place is fucking honeycombed with security check-points. I wouldn't want you to go around setting off any alarms and waking up any vice-presidents or anything."

Larry staring at the bright fluorescent lights that lined the corridor like they were giant luminous snakes, Naga, Naba, Nabaroa...., wondering, did he qualify as one of the snake-people himself now after all his years of apprenticeships and initiations?

"You OK, Larry?" Kalakovsky asked as they passed by the receptionist again, Larry somehow "seeing" the little crescent scars under her nipples where the implants had been put in.

She glowed as they walked by.

"Hi, guys!"

Larry filled with a sudden shot of heldenleben vigor, whispering to Kalakovsky as they moved out of earshot, "Nice looking piece, man! I like um obsessed with themselves...."

"She's OK, a little more oiled than usual. Just for you, Larry. With me she's cold butter, pal, cold fries...."

Down one corridor, past a checkpoint, Kalakovsky pulling a little plastic card out of his pocket and inserting it into a little slot, a little turnstile opening.

Another corridor, the fluorescent lights beginning to writhe, descend, curl around Larry's neck, as Kalakovsky chattered on.

"You know, I don't hardly get to know anybody here much, stuck down in the basement and all, but Myrtle and Mabel, M and M's, they melt in your brain but not in your mouth. What nightmare chicks, Jesus! Brian Fudge, Mabel's ex, wrote to me, not exactly me but Security, all about the two of them being accused of Grand Larceny in East Lansing and we should watch out for them here. Wanting to get what they could out of our Long Prolongation Division. All about them being dykes. And then I am the Worm, man, it was getting to be Dyke Heaven around here, babe. Not that I give a shit about anyone's sexual preference, but all of a sudden everything private was getting very pubic...."

Yakking a corn-husker's laugh as he pushed the elevator button and it was there in a moment, a little whoosh, pressed FOUR. Couldn't feel them moving. Inertia-less.

"And you?"

"Nothing, man, I'm a capon...but when it came to M and M...you know, I faxed his letter up to Vice President McCormick, he's like in charge of Internal Affairs...and that damned letter got passed all over the Board of Directors...."

THE LORD SAID UNTO SATAN

Four, the doors silently opening, down another corridor, another check-point.

"Yeah, they were doing pretty well for themselves...," said Larry, pulling the JUVENTUD vial out of his pocket.

"What's that?"

"The product. M & M's youth pills; I took one and..."

An initial UP, only now it was all being submerged into a Chekovian Three Sisters Russian winter wave of clutching paranoid apprehension, enclosing him in its frozen formalin foam. Irma there everywhere around him in the white snow corridor. SHE WHO KNOWS ALL. One of "us." It wasn't going to be an interview, but a shaman-duel. Larry beaming out to her: **You'll find out who the Master is, shithead.** Maxine's favorite word, "Shithead." Everyone was a shithead, shithead-this, shithead-that....she'd never open her mouth again, would she...was it fair, her with all her millions, if living was a thing that money could buy, the rich would live and the poor would...

Moving down a cool blue corridor now past glassed-in walls behind which white-coated, masked, hooded figures worked in quiet medieval monkish rituals, Irma voice bellowing back at him **Live it up, babe, you don't have long now...**

"Lemme try one of them pills," said Kalakovsky, and Larry opened the vial and handed him one, "let's see what they do for you know what..."

"You never know," said Larry, "what Myrtle's real purpose was..."

A part of Larry's spirit suddenly eagle-breaking free, eerie, aerie, eagle eyes peering into Irma's hidden soul, her panicking as she became aware of the intrusion, her mind filling with little escape-holes, fire-escapes, slices of distant, white, anonymous escape-streets, little towns in the coca-dust Ecuadorian highlands....

Then back in charge, all Will, a giant hairy spider in the middle of a steel-cable web, still talking to her, **So you teamed up with the Sax-gang through Bryan...there was that sexual betrayal, and**....

Larry's mind suddenly filled with images of Tibetan temple guardians rearing up and snorting flames, tusked fire-dragons swooping down on him, Larry ducking...

"What's wrong, man?" Kalakovsky curious.

"A little muscle spasm in my back," Larry lied, punching the air a little, a little boxing workout routine.

"I don't feel a goddamned thing," said Kalakovsky, "not younger, older, zero, zilch..."

"Maybe you're too young, huh..."

"I wish, man...," Kalakovsky getting philosophical for a moment, "Do you believe in an afterlife?"

"Lives!" said Larry, always having wanted to be agnostic, but then with all this spirit-reality flying around him, all these voices and presences, sometimes it was as if the spirit-world were more real for him than chicken fingers and a bad back.

Closer and closer to Irma.

She'd picked up his thoughts about placing them altogether at Prasad's and plumes of fire began to billow out of her nostrils into the thin Himalayan-Andean air of her raging TERROR.

"OK, here we are," Kalakovsky opening the door into Dr. Irma's special area, a very unmade-up chunk of a blue denim secretary.

"Hi, Kal!" she said.

"I thought you never got to know anyone," smiled Larry.

"Well...."

Like she didn't need makeup, face or body. Just perfect. Unblemished. And she and Kal-baby...all this hushhhhhhing coming out of them, like a leak in a steam-pipe.

"We're here to see Dr. Irma."

"Don't worry, she's very well aware that we're already here," said Larry, "in fact why don't you just let me handle it on my own from here on in. Things could get a little..."

Irma there inside him, backed against the wall, rearing up, trying to claw/hoof into him, her own identity shifting back and forth between tiger and raging (Tibetan Yama) bull...

"I don't know, we've got all these protocols around here," said Kalakovsky, going into his breast pocket, pulling out a little green book: Procedures -- Security...

THE LORD SAID UNTO SATAN

Larry reaching over and taking it out of his hand, putting it back in his pocket.

"It's fine...fine...."

"I don't know. It's hard to put all your trust in anyone so filled with band-aids as you!" Kalakovsky smiled, "You gonna be OK? Maybe I'm a little worried about you..."

"Unbreakable," said Larry, "not unpuncturable, but unbreakable..."

"OK," said Kalakovsky and he was gone, the secretary starting to get up, "Let me take you..."

"I already know..." he said, gently pushing her back into her chair and starting down another arctic-white corridor, homing in like a heat-homing missile right up into the jet-ass of Ms. Superbomber, the corridor itself lurching with giant-lunged moans and sighs, **HOW DO YOU DARE VIOLATE MY SANCTUARY, WE SHALL NOT LET YOU SURVIVE...WHATEVER YOU KNOW OR WILL COME TO KNOW, WILL DIE WITH YOU,** Larry answering her back **MY POWER SURPASSES YOURS, I CAN MOVE AS MANY WORDS AS YOU**...as he put his hand on the doorknob of her lab/office, her answering back **WE ARE THE FINAL STEP OF UNIVERSAL EVOLUTION, IN US SPIRIT AND FLESH BECOME ONE AND ALL DUALISMS ARE FOREVER RESOLVED...EITHER YOU ARE ONE OF US OR YOU ARE NOTHING...**

"I guess I'm nothing, then," he said out loud to her as he opened the door, "if you can manage it...."

She was sitting at her desk at the far end of a room filled with stone-topped lab-counters, microscopes, centrifuges, cages of rats, computers and fax machines, rows of test-tubes, shelves of chemicals. It was a real show.

And Irma herself older and even bigger than he'd expected, wrinkled, sagging, downbeat, sad, crucified on the melting Buddha-wheel of Time.

Approaching her desk with fat-man calm, unrushed assurance, putting

260.

his hand on the desk and pulling up up sleeve, flashing Myrtle's Zimbabwian engagement bracelet, still tight around his wrist.

Whatever he'd let her see in the landscape of his mind, he hadn't let her see that.

"So that's why Myrtle was your Messiah too, she promised you the apples of immortality!"

"I'm afraid you're got that a bit half-ass backwards, my retarded friend, I'm the one who had the golden apples -- dehydroepiandrosterone, to be specific."

"And all her input from the Royal Jelly Project?" he asked.

"Wishful thinking, mainly...with all their faking figures and fooling around...and the last thing I was ever interested in was immortality, myself. Kevorkian is more my style. Clinical depression. Castrati years at Berkeley, MIT and then all of a sudden the Great Heart Hunger was upon me, demanding satisfaction..."

She stopped, sat back and closed her eyes and let the Liebestod images flow through her, and he sat back and flowed with her, *their minds merging as two women in a bed appeared, silhouetted against a pulled-down shade, spread-legs, licking, panting, oohing, aahing...then massaging...sleep...breakfast in a giant hot tub (Irma's basement?), Irma's dolphinesque body all sudsy and sleek, twining around Myrtle's long, lean full-breasted boney-ness, shifting down to what looked like the Lincoln Park boat harbor, the Lincoln Park zoo, coffee at some sidewalk cafe...beach (Oak Street?)...lying back on the sand, sunning, all inside a sense of immense, cosmic calm that was its own kind of immortality...then moving into the labs past rows of white-hooded techno-monks, Myrtle's eyes peering out of her germfree outfit, into The Big Vault, Myrtle doffing her helmet and kissing Irma, "the more DHEA you've got, the longer and healthier you live..." Myrtle dropping off her sterile-suit and standing there in a long-sleeved shining black spandex bodysuit, her hand moving down to Irma's groin with practiced, calibrated, surgical precision. The Technician of the Prone. Larry suddenly feeling a squirt of Irma's wry bitterness...what she had been/believed, what she was/what she she been...the image moving into an old-fashioned needle-point chaired and couched living room as*

THE LORD SAID UNTO SATAN

Myrtle got all rosily sentimental and book a bracelet and earring out of the pocket of her purple sports-jacket, "In my country, the natives had a custom, when the couple got married, the bride would give her husband a bracelet and a single earring as tokens of eternal fidelity...and I'd like to 'reactivate' that custom between us...," slipping the bracelet on to Irma's arm, trying to stick the earring into her ear, as Irma squealed "I don't have pierced ears, silly!," both of them laughing, falling into each other's arms...then a mall somewhere, ear-piercing, a sudden ping of pain and they're both laughing. "It's only taken me fifty years," says Irma, a post in her ear now; and she asks the woman who's just done the piercing to take the post out and put Myrtle's earring in instead, totally believing that this is true love, IT...per omnia saecula saeculorum...Larry's eyes starting to tear up a little as he is engulfed by Irma's deep, ingenuous, sacral sense of bonding...which plays on and on for a long time, Larry and Irma standing there, eyes closed, facing each other, sharing the vision as the image moves into downtown Grimore Park now, Le Coq D'or II, wonderful smells of sauces and wines, things getting braised and souffled, Irma walking in just by chance, attracted by the golden cock on the sign, the promise of "class," and finding Myrtle in a passionate tete a tet with Mabel, suddenly the whole thing as clear as chemically pure water, nothing else in it....THIS IS THE REAL BONDING IN MYRTLE'S LIFE, ANYTHING ELSE IN PURE POLITICS...

"You've used me; you got what you wanted out of me and what am I now, ready for the garbage?" Irma screamed at her, the whole restaurant turning their way, the one thing Myrtle never wanting was being focused in on, noticed.....

"Shut up, will you; get out of here, go crawl in a hole some place and die already," Myrtle answering back as flat as cold French Fries, "It's not a question of one shipment, it's a question of production techniques...all your little arcane secrets...everything's so double-wrapped with you...you think you've got the cake out, and all you really have is another box..."

Irma standing there crying, simply crying, passive, limp, destroyed, a waitress coming up and mindlessly asking "Will this be a single, or will you be sitting with this ladies?"

"It won't be anything!" she said and started to simply walk out, thinking about the passivity of the Jews going into their final (gas) "showers," wondering (back in The Now) "Why didn't I just throw her bracelet and stupid earring at her then, why did I wait?" Larry suddenly breaking in on her, filling in the blank -- UNTIL THE NIGHT OF HER EXECUTION!!!"

Irma's mind suddenly switching off, cold showering back into The Now, Irma's eyes full of real time tears, "I don't know why, even for a moment, I ever thought/hoped that you might understand..."

"I do understand," said Larry softly, an ancient, fragile, ancestral, guardian figure rising up inside him, giving him his words, "I do understand, only I just keep wondering what would have happened to Myrtle if you hadn't done anything and just left her to her own private machinations, in the private Hell that she carried around inside her..."

Only he wasn't getting through. She was all great stone walls now, lead boxes inside lead boxes. Myrtle had been right about that, hadn't she...the idea of boxes within boxes...

And Irma knew what would have happened to Myrtle if she hadn't been incinerated, that much still filtering through, a family history of colon cancer, father, mother, aunts, uncles, cousins....Larry surprised that she even had a family/family history, as if the demon world had been planning this incarnation into Human Time for generations now, not "possession," but "passing over" into human reality...only why...why move from timelessness into sad, melting, cancerous Time....?

"I'll have to ask you to leave now," she said with obsidian sharpness, right into the sacrificial center of his big fat pumpkin gut.

Her hand hovering over the phone on her desk. Call out the harpies, spider brigade, Kalakovsky...a killer-dwarf inside him pulling his own obsidian dagger out of its sheaf... Windy suddenly there again, all naked in furs, her hair plastered back off her face and around her ears after a particularly hot love-section, whispering to him (MM deliciously tipsy at JFK's birthday party) "It's all confirmed, you got what you

THE LORD SAID UNTO SATAN

wanted...come on, baby, let's just blow," snickering on the word "blow." Spirit-whispering to her "OK, let's get the hell out of here," Irma very much privy to his thoughts...

"Disgusting!"

Larry dwelling on Windy's flesh now, her aristocratic collarbones and the pouting puffiness of her lips, "The way I love you, there's no such thing as age," just añejo, like old wine, paintings, vases...Irma whip-thinking back at him "What about Maxine?," him mind involuntarily moving down humped corridors of pinched, wrinkled, torn-apart, disintegrating mummies hanging from the dead brown walls...

Horrifying Irma who somehow saw herself in the hollow eyes and hanging jaws and moleskin flesh....

Larry turning and walking out, back through the glass-wall tech-monk section again, check-point ahead, crawling over the turnstile with elephantine gracelessness, no alarms here, but downstairs, one way to get Kalakofsky on the move again, Larry feeling like he was already dead, just a few years left, separated from Maxine by a hair's breadth of Time, his parents dead for twenty years now, all his uncles and aunts, piles of his friends, AIDS, cancer, strokes, car accidents, muggings...never before feeling so mortal, but feeling he didn't need an Afterlife, whatever he'd had, he'd had...

Down at the end of the hall by the elevators a giant in a dark blue suit, ostensibly waiting for the elevator, but really waiting for Larry...turning as Larry ambled along. No one Larry had seen before, but he obviously recognized Larry, broad Assyrian bull face and wrap-around sunglasses, they were all over town, weren't they, but wasting their time, what the fuck kind of "case" did he have anyhow, what are visions, insights, intuitions, worth in a fucking court....?

The guy turning like a mountain, Stromboli about to blow, filling up the whole corridor...

Emergency door/stairwell over to Larry's left, a big DO NOT EXIT EXCEPOT IN CASE OF EMERGENCY sign on it, Larry suddenly going into automatic pilot, banging through the door and breaking the seal, an alarm wail filling the air, Larry banging the door behind him, down the stairs as fast as he could go, amazed at his own grace/speed, strong impulses to just stop with Buddhistic fatalism, turn the cobra into an umbrella, but then at the first turning of the stair he stopped and turned back and as the man-mountain/-volcano burst through the door, Larry pulled out his gun and fired right into the goon's chest (one), then one right between the eyes...or not quite...right in the middle of his forehead...becoming the bullet, digging into the goon's lungs and heart, brain...taking all the goon's agony upon his own broad, sagging shoulders, Not My Will, but Thine be done...the man-mountain suddenly collapsed, splattered, punctured flesh, Larry beginning to cry, hearing the Dalai Lama talking about passive resistance to the invading Chinese "Evil is intrinsically week and self-destructs..."

Kalakovsky at the top of the stairs.

"Jesus, Larry...."

White, yellow, red fibers and goo spattered all over the wall. Kalakovsky starting to gag, then re-controlling himself...

"He's not alone...there's others...I better get the fuck out of here," said Larry.

"You can't just...."

Still wanting/needing a picture of Irma. Someone had to buy the can of gasoline, and someone had to Aristotelianly track things down chip by chip, getting hostesses and waitresses to remember, putting together phone records of lists and lists of calls between people who weren't even supposed to know each other, an inexorable syllogistic-circumstantial case against the Forces of Evil...

"They're tracking me down, babe...," feeling Evil oozing toward him again, not quite there yet, but..."Listen, get me a picture of Irma, OK? Send it over to the Grimore Park PD..."

"Larry, you're not going anywhere!"

"You wanna stop me?" asked Larry, taking it all in, the dead hulk, gore-splattered walls, gun still in his hand, walking downstairs sideways, Kalakovsky's mind like a spinning slot-machine, not knowing where to stop, Larry down to the bottom of the stairs now, out through another emergency exit, Apocalypse Now, the opening of the Seventh Seal, Nacht und Nebel, Night and Fog....just as he was driving out of the driveway a huge clunker of a vintage black Cad driving in, Larry

THE LORD SAID UNTO SATAN

slouching down in his seat like the car was driving itself, for crissake, gunning it, maybe he'd made it through the minefields after all...

Up to the Grimore Park PD, the gods still speaking to him, "knew" that his Volvo would be there in the parking lot with a manila envelope hanging from the steering wheel on a rubber band, with a note inside that he hardly had to read...

Larry --
You think you're the only one with intuitions. Think again! Maybe the chief and I are crazy for going along with this shit of yours, but if you find this, first off, I'm glad you're still alive, do what you've gotta do to stay there...the phone number you asked me to check belongs to a Dr. Irma....

Larry starting to tear up again. He never cried but always was coming to the edge, the air filled with groans and presences; they were everywhere, weren't they...infinitely sorry about the murder...he'd betrayed Viracocha-Grandfather Fire, hadn't he...

THOU SHALT NOT...

Raising his eyes to the blazing sun.

"Grandfather Fire...forgive me...," and in response a great flesh-of-the-gods Peace blanketed down over him...still the beloved son in whom the gods were well-pleased...

Tape recorder still on the seat next to him. Turned it on. First a visit home, then down to Passavant. The Bryan Fudge Hour. How that man droned on:

Of course why should I be totally exempt from the ancient needs of simple revenge? Clytemnestra kills Agamemnon and Elecktra kills Clyemnestra in a state of HIGH ECSTASY. Revenge in the Greek world wasn't luxury but necessity. Even more, a right, a need to re-establish cosmic order. And for me, everything I ever was taken into court and ridiculed, my "me-ness," my honor. If they hadn't faked the tape trying to get my baby boy to say that I'd sucked on his penis, if they hadn't done THAT...but that requires such forethought and planning... and forethought and planning demand counter-forethought and counter-planning. **Quid pro quo**. The gods weep until vengeance has been accomplished...

"Why not just sign a confession, asshole?" Larry asked the cassette player as Bryan droned on.

...but there's some sort of deep existential paralysis and despair in me that seems to always disenable me from ever doing anything. I am 'unreal' to myself and my life is rounded not merely in a sleep, but in amnesia...

"You sound like me, asshole!" Thinking of the Koan -- IF YOU MEET THE BUDDHA ON THE ROAD, KILL HIM. Kill the Buddha? Why? Bryan on tape answering:

...if even the Buddha becomes a 'system,' then escape from him, because only beyond systems can you ever become 'human.'

"But if you want to become superhuman?" asked Larry. And again the tape recorder answered:

...thinking about how I thought about the future twenty or thirty years ago, the Perfect Crystal Catholic Life. I was going to marry the Perfect Wife and have the Perfect Children in the Perfect House, shit perfectly regularly, one life, one wife...and then everything began to go sour on the honeymoon night of my first marriage -- when Maria del Carmen was menstruating. And it was downhill from then on. The sad part was that I thought that Mabel and I had the perfect marriage. In fact I have a letter from her to me in Brazil before she came down and Chichi entered out lives that says just that: "I love you more than even my own family, what we have defines and illuminates the nature of marriage." Do I think she's really homosexual, has to be homosexual and nothing more than homo-sexual? No, I think that that female homosexuality is practically normal, easy, unstrained, beauty intertwining with beauty, no beasts

around at all...but to take sexual tastes and turn them into a political platform, banner, creed, übermensch WAY OF LIFE and break up a marriage because of that...I constantly feel the injection of the diabolical into our oh, too human lives...

When you see the Buddha on the road, kill him!

THE LORD SAID UNTO SATAN

CHAPTER 18

He was three blocks away from the house when he already sense their presence, saw them vaguely in his mind...as through a glass darkly...

Classic trench-coats and fedoras. Right out of an old Bogart-Edward G. Robinson movie. Unamused, though, at their faces, weaponry, intentions...

Parked the Volvo by the Grimore Park Promenade, one of his favorite little lake front spots. It had been there for a century. Big poplars, maples, chestnuts, sycamores, all fronting on the ancient lake, full of memories of his kids when they were still kids, and Maxine was still the constant nymph in short Indian print dresses and tennis skirts and shorts, sexy thigh-high boots and short black suede boots in winter. A woman for all seasons. And after the cancer had begun, after the first, second, third surgeries, when all that was left of her was wide, staring eyes in a paralyzed body, he used to come here with Windy. Survival techniques of his own. Something to hang on to. Before she finally "cut" with him...

He walked across the winding path toward the lake, surprised as how big the Spring leaves had gotten, Windy suddenly there, hanging on his arm, all lanky and angoraish, always eminently touchable in fuzzy stoles and soft skirts, with all her hair and perfect long legs and long arms, lovely, long hands. The only thing she was short on was patience.

"You have no right to either limit my activities in any way or brutally and cruelly

criticize my friends!"

All these sick-head little masturbatory faggots she'd hang around with down at

the Art Institute, with all their little thickly encrusted "neo-garde" (their term) canvases and weird-ball "constructions" --when he wanted (demanded!) absolute fidelity to him...

"I've finally made a decision about us. And it's final. No more guilt. I'm the

Blue Bird of Happiness, uninterested in cages, no matter how gilt they are.

See, that's it, guiltless and giltless -- maybe they go together. I'm not for sale..."

And that was it. The last time he'd seen her. Living in Lincoln Park West now, working to the State of Illinois Tourist Bureau on Michigan Avenue.

But she might just as well have been living in the middle of the Andromeda Nebula.

"Shit!" he coughed out, crying real tears as he reached the beach, his head a haunted house with all sorts of old ghosts knocking around in it. "Hi, Mom!," his mother there for a moment, putting a dish of her horrible baked (not fried) Chop Suey on the dinner table. Kind of a veal stew drowned in soy sauce. And his father sitting there being very much his old fat-faced, solemn, male-role-model father. "Hi, Dad!" The infinity of death. There, and then totally wiped empty again, back in the empty wind.

Although he loved the cold wind off the primeval lake, for him still full of ice-ages and before that Loch Ness monster dinosaurs. And he needed lots of wind to blow away the ghosts. Started walking along the beach toward his house. Goddamned seawall at the end of the park area. No choice, really, but to walk out into the fucking killer cold water and go around it.

Cold stabs up his whole spine. Like he was being hacked to death with ice-axes. Shivering. Around he'd shake a filling loose, unmoor/snap an artery. Getting too old for any of this shit any more. All he wanted was a nice soft chair somewhere in the sun, where he could fine-tune himself into God's own NOW....

Around the wall, then more beach.

The cold knifing into the top of his head now, his whole body going through rattling, retching spasms of grand mal spasms. Afraid he'd pass out, go under.

"Not the old Gugel-monster, man!" he growled. Pure Will! Thinking FIRE now, Guayaquil on a hot, muggy Neolithic day, starting to warm up, steam, Old Fire Grandfather, Old Father Sun, past half a dozen more

THE LORD SAID UNTO SATAN

walls, feeling like a polar bear now, seal, dolphin, whale...getting to his place and clunking up the rusty iron ladder onto his pier. Already knew who was in the house, felt more than ready now for a confrontation with any-one/-thing...

There was a big glass door/wall that fronted on the lake. "The Sunrise Catcher!," the kids used to call it. A key under the overhang, just for a case like this. Opened it with a click and put the key back' slid the door open with a tiny hush, hush, little babies, don't you cry, your mama's in a coma and your papa's gonna die...

Slipped inside with sloshing, three-toed slothful shadowyness. Not that he'd wake them up, the lazy toads.

In fact, why try to be quiet? Clomped, slopped, squished u p the stairs into his and Maxine's bedroom, stripped and went into the bathroom and took a nice long, luxurious steamy shower, lavender, patchouli, sandalwood, a real smorgasbord of soaps, gels, ointments, sprays, feeling them off in the shadow-areas of his Nagual-soul, beginning to stir and come alive, into their minds, Lissie wondering IS THAT SARAH, Sarah wondering IS THAT LISSIE, both of them slowly beginning to realize that the shower-noise wasn't coming from either of their rooms...

Turned off the shower and stepped out into a massive grey terrycloth robe, drying himself off with another towel, going into the middle drawer of the medicine cabinet and taking out a massive pair of scissors that Maxine had always kept there, toweled the steam off the mirror and grabbed his hair up into a nice succinct bunch, one slow, scrunching cut, Adios, compañeros de mis vida/so long, companions of my life, Gardel's voice there for a moment, tangoing around through his head...a few more snips, even it out a little. Then butchered the beard, shaved both head and face. A total transformation. Ballface. Señor Pelota....

The two girls in Lissie's bedroom now, like two poaching eggs, crackling and snapping about what to do.

"Don't do anything!" he bellowed through the wall, "It's only me. I just re-materialized....," and Mrs. Five by Five (Sarah) opened the door, screamed.

"My God, Lissie, it's Frankenstein!"

"Frankincense...myrrh...mor, who is this approaching up from the desert, in columns of smoke, fragrant with myrrh and frankincense?," * he said softly, smiling, going over and giving her a hug and kiss, getting a glimpse of the two of them together in the mirror. Genetic predestination.

"What's going on?" Sarah trying to be nasty and cutting, but all she was, really, was Larry's little pumpkin, "and what's all this shit with the hair and beard. I like you to look like Santa Klaus...."

Beautiful, mad Ophelia Lissie pushing her way past Sarah now, looking like Dietrich in The Blue Angel.

"You're such a psychotic! Jesus! Look at you!"

He looked at himself in the mirror. He really did look like a whale now. A granite hill. A sadly obese goblin king.

"I love you both too!" he said, shooing them both out of the bathroom, going next door into his (and Maxine's) bedroom, the place still full of little tatters and shards of their shared past, great in bed twenty, thirty years back, the tiny tummy he loved to bite, breasts that looked like silicone implants but were just her...and the leisurely, goddess-on-a-cloud-couch way she had of making love, as if they had already slipped into divine eternity...

"I love [almost said/thought 'loved'] you!" he said to the air and pulled on a grey sweatshirt-sweatpants jogging suit, sat on the bed and pulled on a snazzy pair of jogging shoes. Stuff he'd bought, worn a couple of times, but never could get into anything to do with exercise...lived totally inside a sense of genetic-dietary doom....

Three quick calls on the bedroom phone:

Maverick Rentals (Adams, downtown)

"Listen, this is Larry Gugel. Maroon Cavalier. You'll find it in the parking lot of the Grimore Park PD, the keys embedded in a piece of gum stuck inside the exhaust pipe. Bill me at the police station for whatever extra charges that will be incurred by the pickup..."

Monaghan at the Grimore Park PD:

"It's all starting to fit together like a brontosaurus skeleton, pal..." Monaghan hot and anxious.

THE LORD SAID UNTO SATAN

"Talk to Ackermann, man, I don't wanna be no one's middle man, for crissake. I'm the one who ends up getting it in the ass. And what the fuck happened over at Babbitt Brothers? It looks bad, man. We all know you're some kind of fucking genius holy man and all that, you solve the unsolvable, you're legendary, immortal, an icon, for crissake...but what the fuck is going on? Get visible already!"

"Remember the Case of the Nez Pierced, how I was off the map for six fucking months? Listen, I'm home at my place right now, two hit men out in front waiting for me to make a cameo appearance. I had to get in the house off the lake and I'm gonna leave by land, or else...OK? Stay on the side of the angels, pal!"

Hung up. The phone immediately began to ring. Let it ring for two minutes, and when it stopped he dialed Kalakovsky over at Babbitt Brothers.

"Listen, sorry about all the untidiness and shit, but I'm on the run. Get that picture of Irma. I'll be over in half an hour, say..."

"Larry, listen..."

Hung up, turned, walked out of the bedroom to face Fatso and Nut-Cake, Sarah immediately starting in as soon as she saw him, anger asthmatically punctuated by wheezes and gulps of air.

"I don't know how you can just let Mom die...without even being there. I don't know why you just don't get a leave or retire, quit, for God's sake...you certainly have enough money, thanks to her...."

"OK, OK, that's enough..."

Getting pissed. Not really "afraid" of getting pissed any more, the way he used to be...always on the edge of going ape-shit violent. Mr. High Plateau Buddha-calm now, that was a blessing. But more permeable, easily hurt now...woundable...thinking maybe it was better to be violent than vulnerable, that violence really was a defense against vulnerability....

Lissie's turn now, skinny, mad viper time. They'd always worked in tandem, since they were kids, like wild dogs...

"Everything you/we have comes from her, and the minute she starts to slide off into Death, where the fuck are you? Out playing gang busters....."

Very effective sulfuric acid voice. The Haldol was working a little too well. Next thing you know and she'll go into law school, remembering her growing up, her voices and visions, one particularly persistent little green voice that kept gnawing at her : "Kill yourself, bitch, the bottle of Doze Off in the medicine cabinet, they're your door into happy-happy land...go, do it...."

And she almost had, once....six months inside the padded white walls after that...and ever since then...he guessed he'd never see a grandchild....no one to pass it on to...the money and...The Wisdom...

Wanting to scream out **I AM HE FOR WHOM THE AGES HAVE WAITED!**

Instead just played it journalistically.

"Listen, there's two goons outside waiting for me to come home. I don't think they know I'm here, although, who knows, maybe the phone's bugged. Monaghan'll have a SWAT team over here fast. Just sit tight, they're not interested in you...all they wanna do is turn this archive [pointing to his head] into brain-meal mush..."

"That's disgusting!" said Sarah.

"I'm going down to Passavant to see your mother. I've got my own rhythms. Just go down to the basement and sit it out...see ya..."

"The least you could do is..."

"Seeya..."

Out on to the deck, this need to get away from them, all the Goddamned best schools, Briarmoor Prep, then Swathmore...always a little "moor"/"more." Proceeded by all the years of concerts at Orchestra Hall, operas, classes at the Art Institute. He really hated them, didn't he....

Wanted "daughters" more than anything in the world, but not these daughters, two Florence Nightingales, Mother Teresas, white swans on the looking glass river of his nightmare life.

"Seeya...."

Down to the beach, over one house, starting to jog toward the street. If someone jogged out of MacIntyre's back yard, he must be MacIntyre, right? The goons looking his way for a moment, waiting for Mr. Hirsute, not the Bowling Ball Wonder. Jogging heavily down the street away from the house, tuning in on his daughters, down in the basement now. "He's such an [wheeze, gasp, wheeze gasp] asshole!" (Sarah) "Well, he's under a lot of stress..." (Lissie) "And we're not? He treats us like strangers." (Sarah) "Well, in a way we are...we've made ourselves strangers..." (Lissie)

Wanting to scream out to them, "I love you both!," wanting to play it all back, all the years. He never should have eaten his first mushroom or sniffed his first snuff, drunk his first drink...opened one door into the alternative world of psychedelia/The Demonic. Never should have gone into detecting, but just played the Leisure Gentleman and lived off Maxine's millions...

Sudden immense black wings above him in the spirit-world.

The curse of Maxine's cancer. What was the difference what he'd done; the beating knife wings would have descended anyhow. And if they hadn't, that would have made all the difference. As it was they were all victims of The Curse.

Trying to understand the Mind of God as he jogged down the street away from the house, back to his car, the Promenade one block away, feeling suddenly that a great revelation was about to descend on him, that there was a "plan" in it all, even if (up to now) he hadn't seen it:

HA! (Behold!)
TIRA (This)
TARASAKA (sun)
RIKI (standing).
HA! (Behold!)

Stopped at his car and looked up at the pale communion wafer of the sun obscured behind heavy wool tunic clouds.

Responding to the "directions" he was receiving from the sky, going into the trunk of his car and getting out Fudge's bag of tapes....all of them dated...all...except one...no date...and that was the one, wasn't it....

A strange unexpected drawing on a label on the tape: a hangman's noose, knowing, somehow, that this was the one.....starting to get in the car, then stopping, seeing his monster-daughters as little girls again, they'd been such sugar-plums, they'd been such a perfect, affluent, richenbucks family, with their fancy house on the lake and all doors open for them, whatever they wanted/needed, from La Boheme to Wozzeck...he loved them so much, really...as they loved him...their whole world caught in the centrifuge of Maxine's terrible cancer...

Then worrying about Monaghan and the SWAT team... Monaghan and his pals for decades. Wanting to bring down jaguars from the sky, an army of spirits against....

What the connection between Sax and Chicago? Were Sax and the Hyde Brothers the Michigan "connection"? The whole elaborate international drug-scene and all its high tech delivery systems...

As if it were all invisible and undetectable....

A woman coming down the street with an old-fashioned baby carriage with an old-fashioned real baby in it. Like an old movie.

Black hair and coat and nice ankles.

Getting into his car. She smiled at him.

"Hi."

"Hi."

As if the world made sense, as if someone could actually walk down a street somewhere unafraid and normal and have a few moments of real LIFE, for god's sake, the sake of the gods....

Into the car, heading over to the Eden Expressway, shoving the tape with the drawing of the noose on it into the cassette-player. The voices small and distorted. As if it were the recording of a phone-tap.

Ahhhh...not as if...that's what it was...

First voice (female) --Well, I think that whatever she gets, she deserves...

Second voice (male) -- I guess we can both agree on that.

First voice -- So the whole gang'll be down here for the convention?

Second voice -- You got it!

First voice -- I don't need them, but I think I can control them. And the idea of control appeals to me.

Second -- Which is very sicky-sicky. But I must be sicky-sicky too because it appeals to me too.

First -- With "life" in our hands. It's the dream of ultimate-control...

THE LORD SAID UNTO SATAN

Second -- Couldn't care less. All I'm after is simple, necessary revenge....get my world back on its proper course again...

Fudge and Dr. Irma. A break, buzz, and then...

Fudge -- No, you don't have to do a fucking thing. She wants to do it. She just wants "witnesses." A kind of public execution. Blessed Oliver Plunkett. They cut out his bowels and held them up in front of his face while he was still conscious...

Second voice (Sax this time? It was Sax, wasn't it!?!) -- What are you talking about now. You're such a maniac. If Myrtle ever starts manufacturing and marketing Eternal Life down in Chicago, we'll be fucked forever. She's simply gotta be stopped for economic reasons. Forgot all that bloodbath crap. You sound absolutely medieval. We'll do it quietly. Things happen. People disappear...

Fudge -- She doesn't know shit about marketing. She's a great old tech and all that, but that's where it stops...

Sax -- But she can always learn...or hook up with some smart entrepreneur down there. I don't know why the fuck she didn't just stay in it with me. I was going to give her a generous percentage, why does she need, the whole cake? And this Dr. Irma's a slimeball....

Fudge -- She's coming up next week to visit. Let's see how you feel after you meet her. She claims she's got some kind of big psychic control power...

Sax -- I've got some psychic powers myself -- Greenbacks (laughing abrasively, then mellowing out again)...well, I'm curious to meet her. She actually let Myrtle get into the DHEA-supply at Babbitt Brothers? I don't know, I'd rather see Myrtle in jail than dead..

Fudge -- If she was "jailable." But you know how white collar crime goes, always more and more appeals, everything gets so subjective and contradictory....

Sax -- I know. If they don't get you with the smoking gun glued to your hand...(Sax taking a deep breath)...well, I'm dozing off here, my friend. Getting old, tired, 'transparent,' 'unreal,' even to myself...But I'll see you tomorrow for lunch, OK? The Club at noon...

Fudge -- OK, pal. Take it easy...

Sax -- Do I have a choice...?

Another irritating stretch of buzzing, and then a click. Another voice that Larry recognized. What was her name, the blonde downtown, Priscilla....

Priscilla -- I really do feel muddled ever since I met Dr. Irma. I was all against involved with all this ugliness. Although, you know, for years I used to rock myself to sleep at night with the delicious image of Myrtle's face getting smashed by a big rock, a maul, a sledgehammer...but now I keep saying to myself 'What's the difference if I just watch, it'll just be like a film...if I don't do anything. Irma's this real powerhouse of a person. I feel guilty if I don't salute and shout HEIL IRMA!

Larry switched off the cassette-player. This was his favorite component -- the arabesques of motivation. Will against Will. The psychological snake-pit where Irma was Queen Cobra.

And that whore, Fudge, man, anything for a buck, keep the old bank account on cruise control....The Powers of Dusk(moving into Dark) against the Powers of at least honest Dark...always feeling just beyond the periphery of The Known...the mystery of the other Presence...how could the universe always have been, or how could God/the gods always have been, or if they began, where did It/they come from...no way to ever understand any of it....

Turned off at Skokie, over to Babbitt Brothers, feeling "presences" again...someone inside the visitor's parking lot, waiting like a giant Trapdoor Spider. Larry secreting a circular lead wall around his psyche. He wasn't THERE any more, just a black hole in the radar-screen, a scar from a scooped-out mole, absence, non-ness, an appendix scar...

Parked a block down and got out of the car and started joffing again, *I'd better watch out, man, or I'm gonna start losing fucking WEIGHT*...over to the service entrance. DELIVERIES ONLY,

A little guy made out of grey plastic-clay in a glassed in "cage" over to the right, a little turnstile block the way.

"Can I help you?"

Clay-textured voice. You could bake this guy, man, use him for a candle holder.

THE LORD SAID UNTO SATAN

"This is just deliveries, you'll have to go around to the front door..."

"Deliver this!" said Larry, gave him the finger and vaulted over the fucking turnstile, amazing himself. Amazing grace...get rid of all the hair, and...

Big times alarms. And two corridors into the building, Kalakovsky coming toward him, gun drawn.

"OK, hold it there, ugly!"

"You don't know me, Mom?"

"Jesus...I can't believe me...what next!?!?"

"Ain't I a beauty. What a skull, huh!"

"You're liable to get fucking shot!" he yelled over the clanging, took a little electronic control panel off his belt, pressed a button and all the alarms stopped, "I mean, I ought to take you in right now. What's going on?"

"Someone's lying in wait for me in the parking lot!" said Larry funereally, suddenly very tired, old, wanting nothing more than to find a plush chair in the shade somewhere close to the beach, enjoy the wind on his face, passively celebrate the coming of Spring....

Kalakovsky impressed, shaking his head, pulling a little I.D. photo out of the left front pocket of his shirt.

"This is what you wanted, right?"

Moon-face, bland, innocent, but a good likeness.

"Thanks. Let me...," reaching under his shirt and pulling out a little shell amulet he had on a cotton cord around his neck, on one side and on the other

Larry put it around Kalakovsky's neck with ancient priestly solemnity, thinking to himself *I am the Way and the Life, the Alpha and the Omega, the Thought and the Act, Creation and Destruction*....chanting while he put the amulet in place, Mataling...Matelingling...Mata Hari...Day's Eye...Daisy...Nabu, Morning Star, Naku, Center, we all die and descend into the Underworld, but return in glory on the third day...

Kalakovsky getting overcome with emotion, starting to cry.

"I don't know what's going on, Larry, but...."

"Believe, that's all. Believe in Quetzalcoatl, the Morning Star," Larry tracing a stairway with his thumb on Kalakovsky's forehead:
Then putting a daleth-delta-doorway into the stairway's base:
And adding a lamed curlicue of rebirth to the top:
The whole time whispering, almost unintelligibly, "We ascend the Stairway of Faith and enter the Door of the Horizon to be reborn, **Gadol, Geddell**.... may you find the ancient Mountain at the Center, take of the immortal fruit, and live forever like/among the gods..."

"Thanks, Lar, hey...."

"You're a good man," said Larry, "wish me luck..."

"Why don't you let me...you shouldn't try all this crap on your own, why don't you let me..."

Walking back toward the deliveries entrance.

"Nah, I'm OK,": said Larry, when they got to the turnstile, Larry trying to leap back over, only not making it this time, falling down hard on the smooth linoleum floor.

"Hey, Larry...," Kalakovsky over to him, like he was his father, brother, a duplicate of himself. He'd never gotten so close to anyone else in his life in so short a time, "Are you OK, Larry...?"

"Old shamans never die," said Larry, getting up, an encyclopedia of pain, "they just tiger away...," limping toward the door.

"I'll get the bastard in the parking lot!" said Kalakovsky/

"Let him alone. He's just a foot soldier!" answered Larry with a sad wave, thinking that it was too bad he hadn't had a son like Kalakovsky, had so monumentally screwed up with his daughters, something inside him now wanting to just lie down next to Maxine, a quiet white room somewhere, into a coma slowly getting thicker and thicker, heavier and heavier...into his car thinking that maybe something was broken. Right wrist. Line fracture? Let it be, let it be! Grasped the pain to him and embraced him like the best of old lovers. Even hurt to turn the key in the ignition. Fuckit! Laboriously drove out into the street, back to the Eden Expressway, down to the Altar of the Dead/Almost Dead -- Passavant Hospital and Maxine.

THE LORD SAID UNTO SATAN
CHAPTER 19

All sorts of flutterings and whisperings among the nurses as Larry identified himself at the nurse's station on the tenth floor.

He's the guy who...you know...he killed someone over at...he's been missing for weeks, everyone thought he was....maybe we ought to call the...but he is the police...but cops aren't exempt from...

Like the butterfly flutterings of violins at the beginning of The Firebird. Stepped outside of himself and look back at himself hard and unflinchingly. Was he The Hulk, the Bulk, St. Francis Borgia, Buddha, or just dog food...? Et Cum Spiritu con carne... and a side-order of refried beans...

One sun-baked, bleached blonde nurse escorting him down to Maxine's room and opening the door for him, the room almost dark except for some weak blue light seeping in between the cracks in the blinds.

The room was cold.

It was a taboo zone, a sacred grove full of bandersnatches and borogroves hovering around in the shadows. It was a holy of holies chapel, with her bed as the altar, her tiny shrunken body, dwarfed in the immensity of white, the sacrificial offering to the cannibal gods.

She was nightmarishly stuck with tubes and attached to all sorts of sci fi monitors, his pale, drowned Ophelia, Juliet in her aseptic tomb, Eurydice in her cobalt underworld, and he a dumb, songless Orpheus unable to snatch her out of death's dream kingdom and bring her back to the world of the living, wanting to stay forever with her, if the Earth never came to life again, so be it...

Strange how totally unwrinkled she was now, like an embryo waiting to be born, a seeding waiting to sprout...no such thing as death, only renewal...passage on to the next existence...no matter how much you wanted to crawl under a rock at the bottom of the ocean and cease to be...

He sat down next to the bed and allowed his soul to drift slowly into hers. Smoke invading smoke. Her mind slowly beginning to be invaded by children and she was up in Wisconsin at their farm, on the porch of their neo-classical hundred and two year old white wooden house in the middle of a classic field of wildflowers, Chris, Sarah and Lissie there in front of them gathering wild flowers...late summer...the sound of the cicadas already getting heavy and irritatingly insistent....

He'd have to call Chris. Kept forgetting him, as if being in Seattle were somehow being in some other life/dimension.

And Sarah and Lissie...he'd better call them...

Getting up, reluctantly pulling his psyche out of the late summer scene when it had been as close to the romantic-transcendental ideal as you can get in this sad, machine-gun-stuttering world....but pull out he did...suddenly it was all gone and he was totally in the cold, white world of the hospital...

Out into the hallway, down by the elevators. Used his calling card to call home. Never carried change in his pockets. Hated the jingle and weight.

Sarah answered.

"So what happened?" he asked.

"It's all over. It was horrible. We could have been killed..."

"Crater Lake."

"What?"

"Who says as asteroid or meteor couldn't hit old Mother Earth in the kisser right now? You think the age of asteroid-showers is over? Worlds in collision. Read Velikovsky..."

"Oh, shut up!" said Sarah.

"What a witch you are!"

She was about to hang up, but didn't. Suddenly became the little girl in the wildflower field again.

"So how's Mom?"

"Happy. Stabilized. But mainly she's happy....dreaming the right kinds of dreams...she's up on the farm in Wisconsin. Late August. Remember how you call always tell it was the end of summer just by the sounds of the cicadas and crickets....?"

"I remember," said Sarah, a few tears, defenseless, vulnerable, permeable.. ..

THE LORD SAID UNTO SATAN

"So I'm sorry about all the confusion. This is probably Gugel's Last Case!"

"Why don't you get out right now, while you're still alive...."

"It's tempting," he said, one last "I love you...."

And he hung up just as she was knee-jerk reacting back with a return "I love you too..."

Walking back into Maxine's room again, back into the rubbery soap bubble of her dreaming. This time not on the farm but in their place on Boca Ciega Bay, Christmas, she'd just gone out and picked a basketful of ripe papayas and seen a dolphin swimming by in the canal. Christmas dinner. A huge ham. On purpose. Just to push her orthodox Jewish past still further into the past. High church Episcopalian now. Just half a step away from Latin. More "Catholic" now than even the Catholics. But still a menorah on the table with all the candles lit, the words passing through her mind as she looked at it -- *Lest we forget.....*

The girls in white party dresses, Chris with a white shirt and tie, Maxine's mother at the head of the table, older than old, kind of puffy, dark-eyed. If she pulled out a gypsy violin and started to play Bartok you couldn't have been surprised....

Larry overwhelmed with love for Maxine, getting into bed with her. Just for a moment. A moment. His face against hers, his arms around her frail body. Like a dried bird's skeleton, really. Like white saltine crackers. Holding her as if he were afraid she'd break. Closed his eyes. Could feel Sleep coming like a tidal wave toward him. Her mind filled with sleep now too. Their years of entire nights spent wrapped around each other, as if they were one body with four arms and four legs...letting the wave come and wash over them....both inside the same dream now...the years hadn't passed...their bodies hadn't aged....the Young God and the Great Mother...coming together into a classic, giant splice...Jesus...feeling it come...all wet...embarassed...if anyone came in right now...pulling out a handkerchief and wiping himself dry, wanting to get up but her dreaming of his hand Down There, so he obliged and she came both in dream and reality, as if they were one and the same thing...really were for her...

Their dreaming twisting together into abstractions now, like twisted tubes of grey, white, black paint, a linear, smooth expressionistic flow, white rivers flowing into black rivers, the Underworld of the Vishnu Purana, the Black River flowing out from Mount Kunlun into the Underworld...Yama, the Green Dragon of Spring....flowing through endless solar cycles of death and rebirth...the happiest he had been for years...to have her, just have her in his arms again...

Giant ice floes of Time drifted by. He slept. Oh, how he slept. Like he hadn't slept in years. Even nurses coming in and checking tubes barely entering into the Kubla Khan pleasure dome underground rivers of his deepest sleep...

Waking up, what was it, 3 AM.

Quietly getting out of the bed. She/they were on the beach now, big storm in the Gulf. But she loved it. Always loved high winds and high water, him always warning her, "What if one of the big ones comes in?," her always answering, shouting over the wind, "No bigger than me...."

Little Czech-Jewish waif-face and tiny, scrawny body.

Getting up out of the bubble of their shared dream, suddenly extracting himself out of it with a big POP!

"I'll be back!" he whispered in her ear. But it didn't get through. She was on the beach with the palms whipping above her head and the wind howling and he was there with her, his arm around her back. No matter where he went in Real time, he would always be there with her in Dream-/Coma-Time....

Out into the hallway. A lizard skin Goldilocks at the nurse's station. Reading a book about Françoise Sagan. Looking up, startled.

"Gugel. Larry Gugel."

"I didn't recognize you, Mr. Gugel. All your hair...beard....," wanting to say you look like a real piece of shit, man, but instead being diplomatic, "Interesting change..."

"Disguise. Really. They're out to get the hairy guy with all the beard...not me...thanks for letting me sleep...it was nice to be with her..."

Nice? Was that the word? Nice? More like overwhelming...letting his psychoplasmic probe snake its way back into Maxine's mind for a moment...they were on the back deck of their Boca Ciega Bay place

THE LORD SAID UNTO SATAN

now...a boat coming down the canal, him smoking a big black Macumba cigar, her smoking a clove cigarette and drinking a glass of Canada Dry ginger ale...

"No problem, Mr. Gugel," said the nurse, allowing herself the luxury of a little last minute honesty "You look better hairier!"

"I know, I know...thanks..."

And he was in the elevator, zooming down, filled with a special "clarity" now, feeling he was twenty again, in sync with the god-voices chirruping and squeaking inside him. He was theirs and they were his, the night a Xipe Totec offering to Spring, sternum cut open, heart calling out "Cut me, cut me out, lift me to the blood-thirsty Moon!"

His old Volvo didn't want to start.

"Behave yourself, man. Or the Crusher's gonna getcha!"

Banged on the dashboard, the starter again.

And it started.

Over to Skokie. Dr. Irma's address in the pocket of his jogging pants. Headed West...goofy Chicago, the Dream of Opulence on the lakefront, and then you went west and the dream slowly rusted down to the Nightmare of the Class Struggle (to the death)...

Feeling totally on track. On a homing beacon into Truth. His internal voices/presences all furry and warm tonight. This was his time. 3 AM.

He was on a Huichol peyote hunt in Chihuahua tonight, hunting for the Blue Deer, the Five-Pointed Star of Enlightenment. Finding it. Chewing it (a little box of wafers that he always carried with him), dying a little, the car filling with the mangling claws of the Great Jaguar Spirit for a moment, but letting himself die and be reborn, passing through the vaginal-Scorpio Gates of Rebirth into the Land of Viracuta, everything in its clearest, rightest, most perfect place...totally inside the certitude of divine Peyote rightness...

Stopped at a Shell station and filled up with their best super-duper extra, asked directions. OK. He was doing fine. Voices on track, *follow the fella who follows his dream...beam...*

Following the moon and stars, turn right at Leo/Flint, past Scorpio (the clashing claws), toward Sepens, the snake-dragon at the center of the world...

Moon, stars and his own peyotero internal, inertial guidance system. Out by Cermack. Saw the name and the whole Haymarket Riot came flooding in through him, Chicago/Chicago-history soaked in his soul, only "different" now as the Blue Deer Peyote sat waiting to be tracked down, speared and turned into a communion wafer of divine vision (one more wafer out of the little box in his pants)...

Metzger Street. A Total gas-station on the corner. Her house couldn't be half a block away. Hearing the voices now. Debussy's Sirens...

Put a little air in one of his back tires, went insider and bought a Butterfinger -- his mainstay candy bar when he was a kid. He'd go downtown and have a couple of Butterfingers, sneak into the Medina Club screw around, play a little pool, go through the gutted, burned-out ruins of the Copacabana, at least until they redid it, screw around on State Street, see a film...then later it was the Blue Note for jazz, Orchestra Hall for the serious stuff, the Art Institute for a little immersion in the French Impressionists and ancient Hindus....

But right now the Blue Note stuck there in the air, a big, bloated sax elephanting through his mind, Charlie Bird Parker, Rolsand at Ronscevalles blowing his oliphant/elephant horn, and The All-Evil fell down and went BOOM....

OH MYRTLE, MYRTLE, MYRTLE, WHAT DIMENSION ART THOU IN NOW, WAITING TO WRESTLE THIS OLD MAN BACK TO THE GROUND...?

Pulled the picture of Dr. Irma out of his pocket. Freckled, red-headed guy in a Plexiglas cage. Looked just like Huckleberry Finn.

Pulled out his badge and flashed it, then showed the guy the picture of Irma.

"You wouldn't happen to have ever seen this woman before, would you?"

"Yeah, sure," he answered guilelessly, "she lives right down the street. She's got one of our credit cards. Some kind of doctor or something..."

"You wouldn't happen to remember her getting a can of gasoline recently, would you?"

THE LORD SAID UNTO SATAN

"Yeah, sure...I don't know, a week or so ago. One of those over here..." Pointing to a stack of red gas-cans over in the corner next to the pop, "and a can of Pennzoil...I remember cause I said something about bringing her car in if she was having oil problems, there's this old Spanish saying about Shoemaker to your Shoes, something like that...leave the doctoring to her, the mechanicing to us..."

"Zapatero a sus zapatos!, " said Larry.

"Hey, man, that's it, that's the one."

"Let me get your name, OK...?"

"Right here," holding up his name-tag, "Buck Thomas...what's going on?"

As innocent as a carp, a poppy-seed roll, a glass of tomato juice....and then the kid's mind was filled with the image of a front page headline, WOMAN NAPALMED IN HER GRIMORE PARK DRIVEWAY, and then the image of a barbecued woman lying charcoaled on the ground....

So he'd figured it out, had he?

"So you think Irma's behind the Grimore Park barbecue?" said Larry, a little cat and mouse sadism....

Images of Irma floating through the kid's head, Napoleonic death-masks, heavy, menacing, ominous....

"I don't know nothing about nothing, man," he answered. That was it. The doors of his mind closed, sign up -- OUT TO LUNCH...

Permanently.

"OK, pal...," said Larry, paying for the Butterfinger, out the door. He'd be back. Next came Prasad's restaurant. A thousand little pieces of The Big Puzzle. Shouldn't there be a Nobel Prize for detecting...?

Tossing the Butterfinger wrapper in the trash case outside the station, crunching down into the bar itself. Pure health. All the good things. Almost shattering his melancholy and depression for a moment.

More and more of a problem every year, every year feeling increasingly hollow, porous, "not there" at all...hanging on to whatever he could to keep him in his body, functioning...

And if/when he did retire, what then? Images of Prague tumbling into his mind. Beer and sausages....Bohemia's meadows and forests.....

Back into his car, across Red Bridge Road down Metzger, clairvoyantly sailing into whorls of dark, shadowy trees. New neighborhood. Old forest. Irma's house as totally predictable as possible. Standard grey brick three-bedroom, one and a half bath deal...

Car in the driveway.

Only she wasn't there. Quick house-scan. Something alive in the living room, but it wasn't human. A bird, snake.....

Where the fuck could she be at 3:30 AM? Totally illegal, what he was about to do, but...but...but...but...there are laws and then there are Laws...

Around to the back to the side door which she always left open. OK.

Slipped shadowily inside expecting, what? Some giant anaconda? An Irma-sized spider? Even thinking beyond thought...that she herself might assume different "forms," might even be one of the Legion of the Beyond-People....whatever was out there that wrestled with Jacob and talked to Eve, whatever lived in the Ark and demanded blood in the Temple....whatever face Moses couldn't see...but only was allowed to see the backside...

Only what was there in the corner? A little movement. A slight whine. A dog with smashed back legs in a wheeled "bucket" that somehow Larry knew Irma had designed herself. A drop of compassion in a sea of hate....

Larry slid down to his knees and passively let the dog smell him and lick his hands, all guards down. Too many he hadn't bought another Butterfinger. But he did find the stub-end of a Tootsie roll, two little soft brown, malleable chunks left. Which the dog gobbled up, one two three.

"You're supposed to suck on them...chew um...let the flavor soak in!" laughed Larry.

What would the World of Man do without the World of Dogs?

The dog following Larry as he following his voices into a little side office-room off the living room. Light on. The voice of Tatawari whispering to him "**Now the desk**...," maple desk in front of him, next to a TV opposite a tweedy, quilted sofa full of gingham pillows, Larry mind suddenly filled with an image from...yes...Iowa...Ames, Iowa...the house

THE LORD SAID UNTO SATAN

Irma had been brought up in...replicating, always replicating our childhoods...

The desk suddenly becoming his whole universe, glowing there like a giant crystal skull. He could see through the wood, the front middle drawer, envelopes inside, his mind becoming psychoplasmic fingers rummaging through folds of white paper...

Pulling out the drawer, scads of old letters fluttering in his hands like white doves.

Opened one with a special glow about it.

July 15, 1990
Dear Dr. Lawder:
By indirect means I have come to the knowledge that you are the direct supervisor of Myrtle Bannister and my wife (soon to be ex-wife), Mabel Fudge.
Before you (and Babbitt Brothers) fall prey to Myrtle and Mabel's schemes, I feel you should know a little about who they are and what they do/have done....

Buckley! My god, what a monumentally pedantic un-rolling stone!

My wife and I were living for almost ten years in a ménage-a-tois relationship with the woman I am still living with and who I'll undoubtedly eventually marry. Mabel and this "other woman" (whom we shared) somehow didn't hit it off together once we got back to Michigan from Brazil -- where we had originally all met and first gotten together. Maybe it's a lot easier to be "unusual" in Brazil than in East Lansing, Michigan. Maybe it was money problems. Mabel's job was put on hold after we got back. Maybe Mabel wanted too much from the other woman. Her name is Chichi. I might as well just reveal it here. In fact there was one point when she tried to get Chichi to go off with her alone and leave me. Only Chichi had (has!) her loyalties to me too. And then Mabel decided she was definitely a Lesbian and didn't want a man (me) at all, but wanted/needed/couldn't live without a WOMAN!

The woman she found was Myrtle, who I've always seen as a particularly mysterious, enigmatic monster, who, I always felt, didn't appear on the scene by accident, but very intentionally. Apart from all sorts of substructures in her that I see as raw, obvious EVIL, I've always wondered why she was so particularly interested in life-prolongation research, as if her only fear in life was old age and death.

It was almost as if some sort of major change had taken place in worlds beyond our normal ken, and that Myrtle was the advance guard in some cosmic drama that we could only vaguely guess at.....

Not bad!

What were the wheels within wheels described in Ezechiel? What did all the Inca legends mean about the Sun descending on to the Island of the Sun in the middle of Lake Titicaca and out of the sun stepped the first Incas...? The demons in Sumerian myth...? All invention or....?

Basta!

Put the letter down on the desk.

OK, it established a link between Buckley and Dr. Irma. It was a conspiratorial start.

Only there were so many more letters. Larry reaching down, one of them practically sticking to his fingers.

> *September 5, 1992*
> *Dear Irma,*
> *I hope you're destroying these letters as you get them.Tear them up. Into the toilet. Let them soak for half an hour, and then FLUSH.*
> *We all enjoyed your visit up here. It's amazing how many people Myrtle totally alienated. People who never saw themselves as capable of destroying anything more than a mosquito, suddenly turning into warriors in a Holy War.*
> *I keep thinking about Jimmy Hoffa. Or the fact that they discovered arsenic in Napoleon's hair, indicating that he was poisoned. Only who?*
> *I guess the Powers that Were already had a why!! As do we! It comes to a point, doesn't it, when Evil must be battled with and destroyed. If we allow Evil to flourish, then we become collaborators in Evil too. Sometimes I feel that by destroying*

THE LORD SAID UNTO SATAN

Myrtle, the advance-guard, we close the door to the hordes that need her to establish a foothold in Real-Space and Real-Time... I can't tell you how much I am impressed by the power of your personality. Without your "will" and sense of purpose, the enterprise on which we are about to embark would never have taken on form and purpose in Real-time, but would have remained forever merely a series of internalized, private hates....

Well, how much more did he need? And why hadn't Irma shredded these letters, flushed them down the toilet? Bryan was such an innocente...or was it cretino, ignorante, bruto/idiot, ignorant asshole...

Other envelopes in the back of the drawer still calling him.

Only...she was coming back...out "walking"/"jogging"? Fucking maniac....still far enough away for a quick escape, but his whole being starting to fill with a high-pitched white scream...searchlights, prison-yards, Gestapo voices...high speed trains screeching around tight curves....

One quick glance, though.

Phone bills. She was a real pack-rat, wasn't she!

Whole lists of calls to Michigan. Didn't know/remember the numbers, but his voices told him these were the ones...that linked everyone in Michigan together in a bond of inexorably damming electronic inevitability.

And then at the very back of the drawer, tiny little answering-machine cassettes. She wasn't another Buckley, was she? Ms. Incrimination. What was the point of keeping an electronic diary of your crimes?

Everything back in the drawer.

Beginning to feel all prickly and twitchy now, his heart skipping a beat now and then, his skin beginning to crawl, assume a life of its own.

Speed of light; speed of darkness.

All lights out and back to the side door, the crippled dog dragging himself along behind him.

"So long, pal...you're OK, you know that, huh?"

Impressed by at least this one sign of compassion in Irma. Or (second thoughts) was she the one who had crippled him in the first place, a tiny splinter of a dramatic fragment playing through Larry's mind, *the dog peeing on the kitchen floor one night after Irma came home extra late from one of her romantic encounters with Myrtle the Beast, taking a rolling pin out of one of the kitchen drawers and....ah...Jesus....*

Out the back door now, the screams of steel wheels on sharp steel curves intensifying now....smoke alarms, carbon monoxide alarms, air raid sirens, London, the Blitz...she was half way down the block already and he couldn't get out to his car. Quickly moved into the immense nineteenth-centuryish garden in the back of the house, carefully tended grass, trellises laced with climbing roses. An old park bench over next to the trellises. Must have been very nice at dusk in the middle of summer...

She was in front of the house now, into the driveway, noticing his car on the other side of the street.

There weren't unusually any cars out on the street at night , everything usually tucked and folded carefully and quietly stashed away in garages. Like Grimore Park. The dream/mystique of the perfect street on another perfect

300.

night, away, away, away from the world's noise and confusion.

Automatic garage door opener. Driving into the garage now, getting out, walking back to the front of the house, still curious. Larry quietly moving to the other side of the garden, away from the garage, standing behind some just-sprouting bushes, the moon bathing the entire garden in a dull aluminum-oxide glow, so far successfully surrounding himself with a thick brick wall of psychic neutrality, through which nothing could penetrate....

He thought!

But then he felt these psychoplasmic tentacles /pseudopodia exploring around the walls of his invulnerability, finding tiny little microscopic cracks....

THE LORD SAID UNTO SATAN

AND SUDDENLY SHE WAS AWARE THAT HE WAS THERE, AND HER MIND LOCKED IN ON HIS, LIKE AN INFRA-RED-TRIGGERED MISSLE-LOCK SYSTEM...

And she knew it was him, her mind suddenly a helter-skelter of exploding letters, phone bills, cassette tapes. Knew he was there (in psycho-space), then switching into a real-space mode, zeroing in on him.

Wanting to make a break for it, try to get to his car. But his voices calming him down, "You have nothing to fear, we are with you...make your statement/stand..."

She "oozed" around the side of the house into the garden now, as he stepped further back, behind the gigantic trunk of an ancient oak.

"Well, did you find what you were looking for?" her voice a little woozy, lopsided, beer-logged.

He didn't answer, kept telling his mind he wasn't there, no, he wasn't there....

"But you are," she answered his thoughts and started walking across the cold, wet grass directly toward him.

Something in her hand. A gun?

Drew his own, as she marched directly toward his oak tree, stopped in front of it.

"You stupid, inferior fool. I really believed that you understood that we were/are the Forces of Light against the Forces of Darkness...they are coming back...can't you see that? They want to become immortal versions of US......"

"I don't know what you're talking about!"

"The gods talked, right? The demons cohabitated with the daughters of Man and produced races of giants, right? Always then, back then...as if there were some invulnerable brick wall between Then and Now...about as invulnerable as your own psychic wall..."

Suddenly feeling a hand beginning to twist around his will, like someone grabbing the steering wheel of his car. Resisting with all his might.

"Not ME!" he snarled, pulling his mind back under his own control, and (hubris) deciding that if anyone was going to be dominated, it wouldn't be him, but her, projecting out two huge, fat, chunky psychic arms and grabbing on to her soul, twisted.

"Sobre tus rodillas, puta! En el nombre de Dios y Santiago, el gemino de Jesús, Abendstern und Morganstern/ On your knees, whore! In the name of God and Santiago/Saint James, the twin of Jesus, Evening and Morning Stars..."

"Puto, tu!/Whore, you!" she screamed back at him, as he put his gun back in its holster and focused all his power on wresting her gun out of her hand, flinging it to the ground.

Wind rising, thunder breaking over them, gargoyle voices beginning to howl through the trees. She was powerful, yes. Nature, raw power, just a modicum of training, but he'd spent the center of his life in the Lamasary of the Tibetan-Amazonian-Chihuahuain school. And she began to stagger, her gun took on a life of its own. One shot, the garage door opened. And it thudded to the ground.

Walking past her now as he mind reached out and started trying to squeeze around his rib-cage, envelope and pound his heart, tug at his bowels and jump up and down on his bladder. At least tried. But slowly the protective nimbus of Old Grandfather Fire circled around him like a stream of frozen quicksilver, and she couldn't through. Walking right past her, thinking DOWN ON YOUR KNEES, BITCH, AND THE PROUD SHALL BE HUMBLED AND KNEEL BEFORE THE PURE OF HEART. Irma resisting. But it wouldn't work, breaking out in sweat all over her body, shivering in the night chill under the nimbused moon, Larry enjoying grinding her down into the ground, HUND!/DOG! AND THE CROWS SHALL BECOME EAGLES, AND THE FEATHERS OF THE QUETZAL SHALL NO LONGER BE STAINED WITH MUD.

"I'm not ready for the land of the descarnados/unfleshed! Not quite yet!" And he stood in front of her triumphant and holy, the chosen one of the (grand) father. "Down!"

"Never!" she squealed, but down she went down anyhow.

"Ate logo/Until later!" he said, and kept walking, paused a moment, "Ten points for that thing you made for your dog!"

"I didn't make it. Myrtle did! I crippled him... the same way I'll cripple you..."

THE LORD SAID UNTO SATAN

"Sure! Let me tell you something! The gods never left!!! And neither did the demons!! They're all right here in ME...in ALL OF US...QUIEN LO SABE/WHOEVER KNOWS..." The Lone Ranger never alone for the last forty years ever since he took that first tentative sip of Ayahuasca in the Madre de Dios jungle in Peru from an old Indian woman who was a re-, re-, re-, re-incarnation of the goddess Kore...the whole sky becoming a vast echo-amphitheater, "unfleshed among the unfleshed, but then the sky dips up against, Nabu, the Morning Star, becomes the reborn Naga-Naku snake, sheds a skin and becomes immortal....."

Trying to spit at him, her spittle running down all over the front of her beige acetate blouse/suit.

Across the street into his car, when he was half a block away released all her bonds, surprised that she didn't get immediately up and come after him. But she didn't/couldn't/didn't want to...the first time in her life that she had met a shaman-master stronger than herself.

Back down toward Passavant, feeling comfortable when he got down to the plush, old elegance of the Gold Coast, the dark Spring promise of the Lake Michigan inland sea to his left, the Drake up ahead, sheer cliffs of stone, bangles and points of light, the Dream of Earthly Paradise made flesh, all thrusting up into hallelujahing hosannas of prophetic futurity...drums and bugles and chanting inside him, the Psalm of Chicago --

I shall life my towers to the Eloheinu
high sky, arrows away from the dying
earth to the migratory paths of hope
to other planets, other stars...

"Christ, I love this city!" he whispered to himself.

Suddenly the car was filled with a giant bat-face swish of hate leaping out of the back seat toward him...in the rear view mirror fiery Myrtle eyes and Myrtle fangs...

Ducking, swerving, the Myrtle-bat banging against the front window. Almost hit the curb, a fragile old lady in a beige knit suit and once elegant mink stole, out walking an arthritic poodle...but didn't...pulled around a corner, stopped and made the Sign of the Sun to the Myrtle-Presence hovering there in front of him, readying for another attack:

MATALINGA -- EYE OF FIRE, MATAAHO -- EYE OF DAY

Feeling the night suddenly cleansed, washed as with a sudden flashflood, rain, not a sign of evil in sight, pulled away from the curb and cautiously U-turned, and proceeded on his way to Passavant hospital like Good Friday on wheels.

THE LORD SAID UNTO SATAN

CHAPTER 20

Larry's first stop in the hospital was security. He flashed his badge, solemnly announced "I'm Gugel from Grimore Park PD, my wife's a patient here and I wanna go up on the roof."

"What's coming down, man?"

"Nothing right now. I just need a little meditation break..."

The security officer a young guy with the ski jump Bob Hope nose, hair slicked back like a sea otter.

"I can dig that, man!," getting up and pushing a button on a control panel in front of him. Roof. "OK. The door's deactivated. You know, one of those USE ONLY IN THE CASE OF EMERGENCY doors. Lots of crazies around here looking for a high place to jump off of. The last one who did it impaled himself...you don't wanna hear it..."

"Impaled himself...?"

"In the groin. I was there when they un-shish-kabobbed him, man...it was horrible...you want I should come with you?"

"Nah, I'm fine...."

"It's a little chilly!"

"I carry my own built-in overcoat around with me!" answered Larry, squeezing the roll of fat around his middle.

"Seeya! Good luck!" he said and Larry waved goodbye, a little smile. Not a bad guy. One of the reasons why the world itself was allowed to survive. Out into the hall, elevators. No one around. No sign of Myrtle-Bat/ -Presence...the whole way up in the elevator, for no reason at all remembering Hal Guthrie over at the Grimore Park PD. Such a severe case of curvature of the spine that he had to walk practically doubled over. Then prostate cancer, surgery, but it had already spread out beyond the bladder into his bones, so he became brittle and if he just walked, his bones would shatter, so he got a wheel chair, started living on liquid morphine, Ackermann letting him stay on until his mind began to wander fulltime through snowfields of vanilla amnesia...always maintaining his Buddhacalm through it all.

Cling!

Top floor.

Suddenly The Book of Job starting to flow through his mind:

Again here was a day when the Sons of God came to present themselves before the Lord, and Satan came also among them to present himself before the Lord. And the Lord said unto Satan From whence comest thou? And Satan answered, From going to and fro in the earth, and from walking up and down in it.

And the Lord said unto Satan, Hast thou considered my servant Job, that there is none like him in the earth, a perfect and upright man....

And Satan answered the Lord and said, Skin for skin, yes, all that a man hath will he give for his life....

Larry's eyes filling with tears as he walked down the sepulchrally empty corridor and pushed the emergency handle on the roof door and he went outside...

Clear cool almost-dawn Spring night, the sky still strewn with the seeds of the stars. But still only a weak echo of the brilliance of the night sky up in the sacred Chilean Andes, the Atacama Desert, San Pedro de Atacama, where the stars were twisted across the sky in brilliant jewelled strands, woven like shining strands of pearls across the dark absorbing velvet of deepest space...

He sat down. Lotus position. Facing northeast in a direct line to East Lansing. Took off his left shoe and swiveled open the heel, took out a fresh little tin of candied Peyote wafers, broke the seal, opened the can and took out one wafer...like chewing sugared Kleenex.....

HIRI IRI -- They who are far away

RA -- Moving this way

WA -- Darting through the air...

His mind took off into deep trance, like scuba-launching off into the deepest of the deep sea, the outer world numbing, collapsing, then disintegrating around him, rising out of The Deep and breaking back into the air above the waters, like a giant condor, giant condor bat, up into the night sky that was also the sky of hiks mind, moving across the ancient black waters of the sacred lake, dream-timing toward the world-tree of Buckley's mind wherein he would settle and vision...across the Jurassic

THE LORD SAID UNTO SATAN

dunes, through the ancient pine forests, zodiacing past the Lion and the Deer, the Sign of the Knife, Flint-Monster, past the Seven-Headed Serpent, through the gates of the clashing clouds/scissors/Scopio-claws of spiritual rebirth, opening and closing, poised for the perfect moment, and then through them into Buckley's quaint Victorian house, into his mind and dreams...

It was late Fall in Buckley's dream, the house all lit up at dusk, standing proudly illuminated on top of its tree-surrounded hill, the highest point in East Lansing, all the trees like red and yellow flames..

Dinnertime, and they were all there, Mabel, when she was still his wife, Chichi, while she was still the guest in the house, the little boy, what, five...? Hamburgers and fries and apple cider, Buckley out on the front porch now with the little boy and his scruffy little terrier named Toto. Named after the Toto in the Wizard of Oz. Toto on his back, the little boy feeding him fries, Buckley tousling the boy's hair, the wind weak and variable, as if the dusk itself were slowly falling asleep. Crispy dry, the leaves rustling, a leaf falling down now and then, the maple in front of the house as red as blood. The sun was going down over the trees and houses across the street, the whole scene suffused with an expansive, cushioned sense of perfect joy...joie...earthly, paradisal beatitude...holy, holy, holy....

Larry starting to cry.

Thaw.

It made no sense that this perfect reality should ever have gone awry.

If only he could have painted it all, The Essence of Our Town, capture it...Pas dans le niege...Monet at Giverney...that last picture of Van Gogh's...add just a few more crows....

The old white porticoed house. American neo-classical. White columns that gave it that classic touch, green steps and green-floored porch, father, son, dog, setting sun, wanting to hold back the fading light, not allow it to end but eternalize and expand it out into all time and all space...Mabel appearing at the door....Bryan looking up...that was it...no changes, additions, subtractions....

How could anything have ever been allowed to come in and snap the neck of this most perfect bliss?

AND THE LORD SAID UNTO SATAN, "HAST THOU CONSIDERED MY SERVANT JOB?"

The dream suddenly ending.

Buckley waking up, Larry afraid that he may have felt his spectator-presence in the dream itself.

Larry painfully back in the now of the chill Spring wind, on top of a roof, facing Lake Michigan, a touch of light now in the night sky, traffic quickening in the streets down below.

He felt cheated as he got up with great difficulty, and made his way back to the door. Cheated, cheated, cheated. Wanting to slip back into the paradisal moment of Buckley's dream, wrap the dream around himself forever and ever, that dream, that dream and nothing else but that dream...wondering how Buckley himself must feel, awake now in the midst of the too-real ruins of his life.....

Down to Maxine's floor, checked in with the night-nurse. Emma Goldstein.

"Mr. Gugel! You look terrible! You wanna wash up? There's a rest room right down at the end of the hall. And let your hair grow back in. Soften the lines a little. You know what I mean?"

"I know, yeah..."

Going down to the rest room, looking in the mirror, almost scaring himself. The Phantom of Passavant Hospital. Aging grey hippo.

Washed. Wished there had been a shower.

And he'd have to buy some new clothes. Go it blue denim. And sneakers. Or a shroud. How was that...a shroud and a scythe....

Back down the hall past Goldstein.

"How's that, better?"

Goldstein looking, thinking it over. Not too sure, but...

"Better."

Went into Maxine's room.

On the surface nothing was changed, but in essence everything, everything, everything was tragically changed. He'd known, hadn't he, even before he'd gotten to the hospital...?

He went over to the bed, his eyes filling with tears, Kristallnacht, Tränennacht, Crystal Night, Night of Tears...

THE LORD SAID UNTO SATAN

The hum inside her had vanished, the images that would flit from her mind to his mind, be shared by their common mind, were gone. Maybe she'd/they'd share the memory of a plate of knackwurst and sauerkraut, or an image of a hallway in the Schönbrunn Palace, her favorite eighteenth century settee that had been chewed into splinters by Señor Idiot Dog.....

Now it was just a blank screen, like waking up in the old days after you've fallen asleep watching a movie on TV to find out that the station has signed off and all that's left is a blank, end-of-the-universe fizzle.

All the truisms in the world had just come true -- the worst part was the loneliness. Even with her comatose and almost dead, as long as there had been something that bounced back when he bounced an idea off of her mind, there was hope. Now -- THE REST WAS SILENCE....

For without cause have they hidden for me their net in a pit which they have dug for my soul without cause...

Give it a second!
Sat down on the chair next to the bed.
He was full of remorse. He should have been here when she "went," really should have gone, should now still, still go WITH HER!!!
He sat there for eternities of emptiness, wishing himself empty/dead, but to no avail. Wanting to be with her, even in Dimension Blank.....only his heart beat on, he breathed, his stomach gurgled, he was still disgustingly THERE.
And then slowly the room began to fill with strange, unexpected, unwelcome energies...
Presences...
The beasts of Revelation slowly began to materialize across the wall. And the Great Dragon slowly began to lift himself off the wall like a fresh wad of bubble gum, and plop-stepped down into the room...
Larry stood up and lifted his hands as its fiery breath whirled around him in a roaring fire whirlpool and then sat down in the middle of the whirling fire-storm, sat and began to breathe slow, deep breaths as he moved into the haven of emptiness, became a small spot, dot, speck,

erased himself out entirely, until he was non-ness, a negative hole in the anti-world of Total Emptiness, breathing back and forth between non-ness and being, non-ness and being until the walls flattened out to their wallness again and the leopard and the bear and dragon became flat empty vinyl ecru paint, the roars and the hisses stopped, and the cool, blue light of early morning came flooding into the room...

When Larry's daughters were just little girls, he used to take them to cemeteries to teach them about death, figuring that if they could really see it whole, see it how it really was when they were just kids, they'd live their whole lives differently. And wandering amidst gravestones and mausoleums he'd spell it out for them: "Everyone dies, I'll die, you'll die, hopefully a long time after me..." And Lissie had asked him "But you'll come back again, won't you. Won't be all come back again?" and Larry had stepped back into the paleolithic solar/soul rebirth religion of the caves, and answered "Sure, we'll all come back, why not, the sun comes back every year, doesn't it?"

And who could say, confronting beginning ess gods and/or universes (that self generated out of nothingness) what was possible...?

What was John of Patmos on when the angels came down from heaven and the beasts arose from the sea and he walked into the twelve-gated city and bathed in the river of the waters of life? Let him that hath understanding count the number of the beast, for it is the number of a man, and his number is (why?) six hundred threescore and six...

And why, if there was any God any where at any time, would he point the Raging Beast of Evil toward any innocent, paradisiacal house on any green hill bathed in the breezes of late Summer -- **Hast thou considered my servant, Job, there is none like him on the earth, a perfect and upright man......**

THE LORD SAID UNTO SATAN

About Hugh Fox

Hugh Fox is a Professor Emeritus, archeologist, editor, writer, and iconic writer of international fame. His style ranges from super academic to Dadaistic to surrealistic to avant garde to post-Bukowski realism. For decades, whatever his creative style at the time, fans have celebrated the earthy and erudite experience that is Hugh Fox. His works tell a personal, intimate epiphanal unfolding of an exceptional man's life. He allows readers to feel the textures, taste the bitter and sweet, see the ghosts of his past. Between these covers lie dramas, great and small: cosmic rumbles; erotic romps; thermonuclear apocalyptic visions; ecological nightmares; cultures and rituals seen through a wormhole into primeval times. Readers share the Hugh Fox reality.

Made in the USA
Charleston, SC
20 May 2011